Ramses' Ric

Text copyright 2018 Fi

All Rights Reserved

This is a work of fiction.
Names, characters, places and incidents
either are the product of the author's imagination
or are used fictitiously.

Chapter 1

Early 2017

'Once we get to Abu Simbel I should think our chances of finding a stash of buried treasure – let alone anything related to Helen of Troy – are non existent,' I said flatly. 'Let's face it; the entire temple complex was broken apart and re-sited further up the cliff by UNESCO back in the 1960s to escape the rising floodwaters of Lake Nasser. I've heard the expression *"leave no stone unturned".* In this case, it's nothing more or less than a statement of literal fact!'

Adam made no attempt to argue. 'True enough. The re-siting of the temples was a feat of modern engineering to rival that of the ancient workmen who carved them. I'm eager to see them for their own sake. But, like you, I don't hold out much hope of new discoveries.'

We were talking, of course, about the Great Temple of Ramses II, that vainglorious pharaoh who granted himself godlike status; and the smaller temple he built for his Great Royal Wife and favourite consort, Queen Nefertari. Originally located on the banks of the Nile in ancient Nubia, once the southernmost border of Egypt's ancient empire, they now overlooked Lake Nasser, one of the largest artificial reservoirs on the planet, just north of modern Sudan.

I'd hoped Adam might make at least some token effort to contradict me. Sadly, his readiness to agree with my pessimistic pronouncement underlined just what a hopeless cause we were pursuing.

'It doesn't help that Georgina's being so secretive,' I complained. 'I've lost count of the number of times I've attempted to pump her about this supposed stash of treasure she mentioned. Each time she simply looks at me with a maddening gleam in her eye and promises all will be revealed when we get there. Honestly! How I've stopped myself slapping the smug expression off her face is beyond me! I must be going soft!'

'Georgina Savage is a law unto herself,' Adam agreed. 'But she's not stupid. She knows those temples have been broken apart and rebuilt as well as we do. And she knows her ancient history well enough. Maybe we should just play along. She's the one who'll end up with egg on her face when we get to Abu Simbel and find there's no treasure. After all, she's dangled it as the carrot to make us invite her along as we journey south. I imagine she must have a notion of finding *something*. Or else she has another ulterior motive I can't begin to guess at. It's not as if she doesn't have a track record for stringing us along. I haven't forgotten how long it took her to come clean about her real reasons for muscling onboard back in Cairo!'

He was right of course. Our ballsy and go-getting houseguest (by which I mean self-invited hitchhiker aboard our dahabeeyah) had taken an age to confess her direct descendency from a certain Henry Salt, British Consul General to Egypt in the early 1800s. Perhaps this was because Adam and I were engaged on a mission in the Nile Valley to follow in the footsteps of Salt's bitter enemy Giovanni Belzoni. The two men had an acrimonious falling out over antiquities secured for the British Museum.

Georgina had spotted an opportunity in our retracing of Belzoni's journey along the Nile two hundred years after he unearthed so many of Egypt's ancient treasures, and had been quick to grab it. She'd been on a quest to track down a set of granite stele referenced in papers inherited from her ancestor. As it happened, so had we. Although in our case we'd learned of them from a journal kept by Belzoni's wife, Sarah. It had been she who'd originally discovered them in Nefertari's temple while her husband was digging through the mountain of sand blocking the entrance to the Great Temple of Ramses.

Our shared adventure bringing the stone tablets to light was perhaps the reason we'd forged a bond, such as it was, with Georgina. While I still wasn't sure I wholly trusted her, I found it impossible not to like her. She was such a forthright steamroller of a woman. And so we'd become friends of a sort.

'The wonder to me is that she still seems intent on coming with us,' Adam went on. 'She surely has no need of yet another treasure hunt. I'd have thought all the hullaballoo over Nefertari's narrative enough to keep her in gin and tonics for life! It's not as if she isn't already enjoying her moment in the sun!'

He was right again. There'd been no hope of keeping our discovery of the granite tablets secret. We'd known all along we'd have to hand over anything we found to the authorities. In our case these authorities came in the form of Director Feisal Ismail from the Ministry of State for Antiquities.

Adam and I have never courted attention. If anything the reverse is true. We were perfectly content to wait respectfully to see what Director Ismail would do with this latest discovery.

Left to his own devices I have no doubt that, like us, he'd have preferred secrecy and silence to media exposure and worldwide headlines. Sadly he didn't have the luxury of choice. Others were party to this newfound knowledge, and demanded action. These included Georgina, of course – our resident *"fully independent"* – journalist. But she wasn't the only one. Also in the know were Habiba Garai, a Ministry Inspector, who reported to the Director; and Saleh el-Sayed, a Marketing Manager who reported to Zahed Mansour of the Egyptian Tourism Authority. Zahed Mansour, I feel compelled to confess, was my employer too.

If Director Ismail had been inclined to hush things up, Zahed Mansour was having none of it. Disappointed at the absence of the hoped-for hidden chambers behind Tutankhamun's tomb last year, he saw Nefertari's narrative as his best chance of re-booting Egypt's ailing tourism industry.

I tell no lie when I say the closing months of 2016 became something of a media circus. Georgina, looking for a way to re-launch her journalistic career, and proud of her questionable ancestry, was more than willing to hog the limelight. The story of how she'd read about the stele in papers inherited from her forbear Henry Salt, gone in search and discovered the granite tablets grabbed headlines everywhere.

I was pleased she had at least allowed Ahmed, our bodyguard and erstwhile police pal, some small crumbs of recognition. The Abd el-Rassul family was instrumental in making the find after all. Ahmed, as you might imagine, enjoyed his moment in the spotlight too. Whether or not the matter of Nefertari's descendency from the Amarnan royal house could rival the fabled mummy cache found by his ancestors was a matter for conjecture. But Ahmed took the media coverage as no more than his due, basking in his newfound fame, while lamenting the fact there was very little in the way of fortune to go with it.

Adam and I preferred to keep a low profile. But of course it was important for the British Museum and its senior Egyptologist Rashid Soliman to get a mention. After all, they were sponsoring this trip. It was thanks to the British Museum's Belzoni exhibition that we were here in Egypt at all. So we'd been forced to take our share of the limelight since the discovery had been made as part of our Belzoni-inspired trip. It's fair to say the number of followers of my online blog-cum-travelogue exploded. It was all immensely gratifying, if a bit overwhelming.

The international press coverage was no doubt helped by the fact the stele didn't just shed light on the origins of Nefertari, that hitherto mysterious ancient queen. The tablets also provided mind-blowing revelations about her husband, the mighty pharaoh Ramses the Great. He was in actual fact her cousin. Both were descended from the youngest daughters of Akhenaten and Nefertiti. It meant they had the royal blood of the glorious 18th Dynasty kings flowing in their veins. This was sensation enough. But it paled into insignificance alongside the explosive news that they had Hebrew lineage too.

And so the story had to come out. And what a story it was! Ramses the Great, far from being the commoner pharaoh everyone believed – descended from a line of military generals elevated to Pharaonic status by that great usurper Horemheb – was in fact descended from the once-glorious 18th Dynasty! That this was via the youngest daughter of Akhenaten and Nefertiti, the princess Setepenre, was revelation enough. That his father was High Priest of the Aten in Akhenaten's Great Temple in ancient Akhet-Aten was beyond all imagining.

The stele hinted at links to the Exodus story.

The global Media went nuts.

Images of the granite tablets appeared everywhere. Director Ismail, perhaps realising he had no choice, stoked the flames. The letters we'd found hidden inside wine jars in a cellar in Amarna – once ancient Akhet-Aten – now became media fodder.

(The Director was able to explain away the lengthy delay in their publication by the need to carefully preserve the fragile documents before putting them on display.)

Thankfully as these were unearthed during a genuine archaeological dig in Amarna, there was no need to mention our names. The role Adam and I played in bringing them to light remained unknown. I was pretty relieved about this since they revealed the identity of the Atenist High Priest and told his story. There's only so much publicity a girl can cope with, and I was keen to return to my anonymous little life and carry on with my Egyptian adventures unhindered by all the Press intrusion.

The High Priest of the Aten was Meryre, half-brother to Akhenaten.

Meryre was also Biblical Moses.

Ramses II, often posited as the Pharaoh of the Exodus, was originally born Gershomre, son of Moses.

It was a moviemaker's dream. I had no doubt Hollywood would soon beat a path to Director Ismail's door.

Whether or not this proved to be the case, it provided a hefty dose of much-needed hype in the run up to the opening of the Grand Egyptian Museum in Cairo, tabled for 2018. If it was enough to entice holidaymakers back to the land of the Pharaohs remained to be seen.

The difficulty was there were other weighty considerations for tourists. Egypt was still considered a politically unstable nation – unfairly in my view. Syria and Iraq, sitting so close to its borders on the map, remained war zones. And Islamic State continued to operate alarmingly on Egypt's doorstep. It was only a little more than a year since terrorists downed the Russian Metrojet over the Sinai peninsular, killing everyone on board.

It's possible these factors alone were enough to keep people wary. I'm not sure whether matters were helped or hindered when in November 2016 Abdel Fattah el-Sisi's government decided to devalue Egypt's currency. Central Bank floated the pound in an attempt to stabilize the economy. The advantage for travellers to Egypt was the significantly improved exchange rate. It more than doubled overnight. The downside was the difficulty in actually laying hands on this extra cash as so many mainstream bureau des change stopped stocking Egyptian currency.

Perhaps this explained why visitor numbers through the latter months of 2016 remained a trickle rather than a flood. Even so, the newly re-opened tombs of Seti I and Nefertari proved popular. Local tour guides were quick to add the story of the discovery of the stele to their patter. But the trouble was, there was nothing physical they could include in their itineraries and actually *show* people. Egyptophiles the world over could read all about Nefertari's tablets and the Amarnan wine-jar-letters online, in newspapers, and in specialist publications. The History Channel and National Geographic were rushing to make television documentaries. This was all well and good as it kept Director Ismail fully occupied, and less inclined to keep a close eye on us. But it did not necessarily betoken a resurging tourist industry.

I'd worried a consequence of all the publicity might be for Zahed Mansour and Feisal Ismail to call time on our current enterprise. I wasn't sure there remained any great need to bring Giovanni Belzoni's travels to life for a modern audience by following in his footsteps. I was concerned too that Rashid Soliman might end Adam's sabbatical early and call him back to work at the British Museum. Much as I preferred to stay out of the media scrum, I had no particular desire to go home just yet. Our re-tracing of Belzoni's adventures in Egypt was barely out of the starting blocks and I very much wanted to see it through. To be fair, this was as much for its own sake as in the hope of making any further discoveries.

Thankfully my fears proved unfounded. Like us, Zahed Mansour of the Egyptian Tourism Authority realised the ability to read news stories – no matter how sensational – about ancient Egypt on the worldwide web wasn't necessarily enough to encourage people to make holiday bookings. He still wanted to evoke the romance of sailing the Nile, the splendour of Egyptian sunsets, the fabulous winter climate, as well as the glories of the ancient civilisation within such easy reach on both banks. For this, he needed someone in Egypt who could write first hand about the marvels along the Nile.

And there was a subliminal message I'm sure he hoped to convey too. The very fact of my being here – a westerner – writing my blog-cum-travelogue helped reassure people Egypt was no more or less safe than anywhere else in the world. If I were here happily waxing lyrical about the tombs and temples of the land of the Pharaohs then maybe other would-be travellers might be encouraged to follow suit. So he was more than happy to maintain my employment on the same terms and conditions as before. Halleluiah said I, heartily relieved.

Adam and I had returned home to England for Christmas. Now we were back. It was the start of a new year. The media storm waned as other News grabbed the headlines. Phew! It meant we could carry on pretty much as before, and pick up our journey where we left off.

We'd been moored up in Luxor since the story of the stele broke. Now it was time to unfurl the great sails on their long diagonal poles at either end of the *Queen Ahmes* in readiness to start sailing south.

'Treasure hunt or no treasure hunt,' I said, snapping back into the present and picking up the threads of my conversation with Adam. 'I'll be glad to get back to what passes for normal around here. Georgina may enjoy all the media attention. As a journalist it's part of her stock in trade, so it's alright for her. But if this last couple of months has taught me anything, it's that I prefer to live my life flying under the radar. Truth to tell, I'm rather hoping we *don't* find buried treasure when we get to Abu Simbel!'

Adam's blue eyes grew round and twinkled at me, 'Meredith Pink!' he exclaimed. 'I didn't think I'd ever live to hear the day you'd say *that*!

'Tennyson-Pink,' I corrected. 'We're married, remember?'

'Oh yes!' he gleamed. 'But surely hunting for buried treasure is the definition of what passes for normal around here!'

I made a face at him. 'I suppose we should be grateful all the hoo ha over the tablets and Amarnan letters have distracted attention away from the tomb,' I remarked. 'Nobody's asking awkward questions about that whole debacle with Eshan Abadi and Ibrahim Mohassib last year. It seems to me we've dodged a bullet where all that's concerned.'

'Poor choice of words, Merry,' he observed wryly.

I caught his drift immediately and grimaced. 'Hmm, yes, sorry. Of course dodging a bullet was the one thing Eshan Abadi was unable to do.'

Perhaps I should explain ...

To cut a very long story short, Adam and I hold the dubious honour of having stumbled across an undiscovered royal tomb. Feisal Ismail of the Ministry of State for Antiquities had long since relieved us of responsibility for it. He'd also decided to keep it secret. But he'd left a couple of loose threads hanging. These came in the form of Eshan Abadi, a philologist who'd helped translate papyrus that revealed the hidden location. And also Ibrahim Mohassib, curator of the Luxor Museum, who'd looked after the fateful scrolls. They each knew just enough to pose a risk. But as it turned out, this was to each other. Director Ismail's attempts to buy their silence had proved somewhat misplaced. I was still unsure whether the two men had teamed up or whether one had attempted to steal a march on the other. Whatever; Ibrahim Mohassib had shot the philologist dead. Director Ismail had been quick to limit the damage. Our tomb remained a closely guarded secret.

'Feisal Ismail seems inclined to keep a lid on it, and that's just fine by me.' I finished.

'He bought off Ibrahim Mohassib with that fantastic promotion in Cairo,' Adam nodded. 'The wayward curator is hardly likely to rattle the cage now the Director's put him in charge of getting everything ready for the opening of the new museum next year. It must surely beat running the Luxor Museum with so few visitors.'

'The good thing is, Ibrahim Mohassib is in Cairo where the Director can keep a close eye on him,' I said with satisfaction. 'I remain strongly of the view that Egypt needs a good few settled years before Director Ismail should even begin to *think* about announcing the discovery of that tomb.'

'Amen to that!' Adam approved. 'The longer it remains secret the happier I'll be. I think the contents of Nefertari's tablets have just treated us to a glimpse of what it's like to be at the eye of a media storm. Like you, it's not an experience

I'm in any hurry to repeat. But it does rather leave me wondering what we should do about Helen of Troy.'

He had no need to explain this rather opaque announcement. I was fully aware what he was referring to.

'We can't really be sure it's Helen of Troy,' I said doubtfully.

He looked at me as if I'd gone mad. 'Merry, we found a solid gold statuette, Grecian in design, its base inscribed with the words "Helénē", and "Lakedaímōn" in ancient Greek. In antiquity that was the city within Sparta. I'm struggling to see what other conclusion we're supposed to draw.'

Forced to concede this, I nevertheless frowned. 'But that doesn't explain how it came to be here in Egypt! We know only that Abdullah Soliman found it at Abu Simbel when he went in search of Nefertari's tablets and then hid it in a secret compartment inside the casket he used to bring the stele home to Luxor.' Abdullah Soliman had been the Belzonis' *Reis* (a kind of foreman and guide) during their years in Egypt. Out of loyalty to them, he'd made it his mission to rescue the tablets once he learned of them.

'Exactly my point!' Adam exclaimed. 'While the casket itself may be only a couple of hundred, rather than over three thousand, years old like the tablets, by my reckoning the statuette dates from a similar time, some thirty three centuries ago. I'm merely pointing out we need to decide what to do with it.'

'We were crazy to let Ahmed keep it,' I declared.

'Probably,' he nodded. 'We got carried away by all the excitement over finding the stele. This other discovery coming on top was too much to take in. I think we took momentary leave of our senses!'

It was no excuse really; for all that we'd made our pact in the heat of the moment. I may also have been swayed from my better judgement, I think, by wanting to make to up to Ahmed for the various mishaps that had befallen him on the initial leg of our trip. Now thankfully fully recovered from the gunshot wound to his shoulder and badly bruised toe, he had, at the time, been shrouded in bandages, and limping.

Anyway, whatever the cause, rightly or wrongly, Ahmed, Georgina, Adam and I had agreed to keep our discovery of the golden statuette a closely guarded secret. But now, of course, a number of months had passed and there was no way easily to disclose how we'd come by it. Not without calling down a whole heap of trouble on our heads.

'Well, he'll have to hand it over sooner or later,' I stated. 'Dodgy ancestry notwithstanding, Ahmed knows he can't hang onto it forever. It's a priceless antiquity, for heaven's sake!'

'You'll get no arguments from me,' Adam said. And then his eyes lifted to meet my gaze. 'But still, wouldn't you love to know what it was doing in the Great Temple of Ramses at Abu Simbel, where Abdullah Soliman found it?'

'It's more interesting to me to know how everyone else missed it,' I said tartly. 'Early explorers beat a path to Abu Simbel in droves after Giovanni Belzoni first cleared sand from the entrance! It must have been well hidden, is all I can imagine.'

'Granted,' he acknowledged. 'But, admit it Merry; aren't you just a teensy bit intrigued to see if we can find out how and why a statue of Helen of Troy came to be at Ramses II's temple in Nubia before we decide how to go about handing it over?'

He had me, and he knew it. I recognised that look in Adam's eyes. It meant he was fired up at the possibility of unlocking more secrets from the distant past. I knew my husband well enough to know that he wasn't swayed by treasure or gold. But, like me, he loved an ancient mystery. The chance to discover new knowledge and shed light on a story from antiquity shrouded in more myth and legend than historical fact was simply too tempting to pass up.

This perhaps, while still not an excuse, provided further explanation for why we'd kept hold of the statuette. I reminded myself also that Ahmed hadn't wanted Helen of Troy (whom he'd never heard of) to steal the spotlight from Nefertari, his beloved country's ancient queen. My own knowledge of Helen of Troy – admittedly not quite non-existent – was decidedly patchy. But I too had been more than willing for Nefertari to take centre stage since hers was the story we'd been seeking to unveil all along. And now I could feel myself hooked by the puzzle of whatever the link might be between the Trojan War and ancient Egypt.

'Ok,' I said. 'I'm willing to allow Ahmed to hang onto Helen's statue until we reach Abu Simbel. As I said earlier, I should think our chances of finding anything to shed light on how it came to be there are nil. We've already talked about how both temples were taken to bits and put back together again in the sixties. Still, since we're going there anyway, I can see no harm in having a look to see if there's anything scholars, historians and Egyptologists the world over have missed.'

'No chance,' he said, grinning at my tone.

'Good! So we're both agreed we hold out no hope whatsoever of finding anything. That being the case, I would think our best option, once we've visited and we're on the way back, is to find a way to hide the statuette somewhere else in Egypt, preferably a dig site. That way some bone fide archaeologist can legitimately discover it. It's the only way I can think of to keep ourselves out of jail!'

Adam smiled at me. 'And let's not forget Georgina's mysterious stash of treasure! Yet another great incentive to go to Abu Simbel and find nothing at all! You know, I really can't wait to get going!'

Chapter 2

On their journey southwards two hundred years ago, the Nile took the Belzonis to Abu Simbel via the temple ruins at Esna, Edfu, and Kom Ombo, and onto the town of Aswan, where they moored for a few days.

The sites along the stretch of the river between Luxor and Aswan have long been popular on modern Nile cruise itineraries. Adam and I had visited them before but it was some time ago and I was eager to refresh my memory.

Sarah and Giovanni Belzoni sailed south with a Copt interpreter and a janissary – that is, a member of the Turkish infantry that formed part of the Sultan's guard. The Belzonis' servant, the young James Curtin had gone back to Cairo, unable to cope with the climate.

My own little party comprised Adam and myself, Georgina Savage, still paying us handsomely for her board and lodging; and Ahmed in his capacity as security guard. I might add this was a role he took immensely seriously and with a puffed-up pride I found quite endearing. Also accompanying us were Habiba Garai, still employed as a Ministry Inspector reporting directly to Director Ismail; and also Mehmet Abdelsalam, the gangly and likeable photographer Zahed Mansour had appointed to capture a stunning photographic record of our trip to accompany my travelogue.

I could only hope Habiba wasn't conflicted in her role, since she was now engaged and shortly would be married to our erstwhile police pal. I had no idea whether or not Ahmed had told her about the golden statuette we'd found. I hadn't asked, and he hadn't said. I decided this was probably for the best since it required no dissimulation on either of our parts.

We also travelled with Khaled, our skipper, and his wife Rabiah, who'd taken up duties as our housekeeper, chambermaid and cook.

My joy once underway, sailing the mighty Nile and watching the dusty scenery drift by on both banks, knew no bounds. I was once more following in the Belzonis' footsteps (if such a thing is possible on a boat), eager to share their experiences of the ancient sights along the riverbanks.

Giovanni Belzoni actually went to Abu Simbel twice. The first time, in 1816, his wife went with him. It was the trip on which she discovered Nefertari's granite tablets. Giovanni returned the following year, this time without Sarah. He wanted to have a proper go at digging through the mountain of sand blocking the entrance to the Great Temple of Ramses. He'd been unable to achieve it the first time around, lacking the manpower and ultimately running out of time. He'd needed to get back to Luxor to oversee the transportation of the bust he'd heaved from the Ramesseum. On Giovanni's second trip to Abu Simbel Sarah stayed behind. She camped on the roof of the island temple of Philae with just her young servant for company. Presumably young James Curtin had by that time acclimatised.

Our journey south would take us past all the places the Belzonis visited two hundred years ago. Now I knew so much about their story I was longing to see for myself all the places they had spent time.

For reasons best known to herself, Georgina Savage turned self-styled tour-guide at each of our stops. As Adam had pointed out, her historical knowledge was sound. Egypt had been her holiday destination of choice ever since her ancestor Henry Salt whetted her appetite with the marvels along the Nile in the papers passed down through their family. For all that Salt was her forbear; Georgina admitted she'd always had a bit of a "crush" on Giovanni Belzoni. As a youngster she'd devoured books about his exploits in Egypt, at a time most people had never heard of him. And she'd certainly made liberal use of our small library of Egyptological picture and reference books in the time since she'd come on board the *Queen Ahmes*. It was fair to say she knew her stuff so I was inclined to indulge her. That it might also furnish me with some useful titbits for my blog was also a small point in her favour.

Our first stop was the temple in Esna, approximately fifty kilometres south of Luxor. The temple ruins now stand in the middle of the modern town at a level of about nine metres below that of the surrounding urban sprawl. We made our excursion to see it while Khaled steered our dahabeeyah safely through Esna lock.

Egypt this early in the year was pleasantly warm rather than furiously hot. Even so, the sunlight was blinding in a clear blue sky. Georgina positioned herself in the shade of the well-preserved hypostyle hall to begin her lecture. Adam, Ahmed, Habiba, Mehmet and I crowded around in the dim portico and removed our sunglasses.

'This temple, once sacred to the ram-headed god Khnum, dates from the Graeco-Roman period,' Georgina began. 'It is a Ptolemaic building with Roman additions, nowhere near so old as the temples of Karnak and Luxor. This perhaps accounts for the generally good state of preservation; although I should add there are further remains of the temple buried beneath the surrounding buildings of the modern town.'

I gazed at the wall carvings, the raised reliefs showing several Roman emperors styled as Pharaohs making offerings to the gods. This was not the period of Egyptian history that grabbed me the most. With the possible exception of Cleopatra, I'd have to admit to losing interest once Alexander the Great stuck the Ptolemies on the throne.

Georgina called back my attention as she went on, 'When the Belzonis visited, the portico was choked with sand and rubbish almost to the top of the columns. The rest of the temple was quite inaccessible.'

I craned my neck back, looking up at the stone roof, still intact, supported by four rows of six tall columns. I'd guess each at twelve metres high; they were topped with composite floral capitals of varying design, many retaining some original painted colour. Thanks to modern excavation it was hard to imagine the place filled almost to the brim with the detritus of centuries. Georgina enlightened us further with her next insight. 'The ceiling and top of the walls were blackened by the manufacture of gunpowder the locals made out of the urine-soaked filth.'

These blackened surfaces were still very much in evidence. 'Ugh,' I said, wrinkling my nose.

Adam smiled. 'Belzoni recorded in his *Narrative* that he thought it "*a great pity such edifices should be inhabited by dirty Arabs and their cattle*",' he remarked, quoting from memory and putting speech marks with his fingers around the explorer's words.

Georgina opened her mouth to respond. But we were never to learn what pithy comment she was about to make. Instead she gave a small gasp. The expression froze on her face. I darted a glance over my shoulder to see what it was behind me to cause this reaction. There was nothing there. As was normal in these travel-stricken times, we had the temple pretty much to ourselves. The sun shone brightly into an empty space beyond the portico.

'What is it?' I said quickly. 'Georgina, what's the matter?'

She continued to stare round-eyed into the sunshine behind me. Then she shook her head, visibly pulling herself together. She looked at me and shrugged. 'It's nothing,' she said. But I could see on her face and hear in her voice that she was rattled. 'I thought for a moment I saw someone I recognised; that's all. I see now I was mistaken. There's no one there.'

Ahmed, in his capacity as bodyguard, turned, frowning heavily. 'You are sure? I can check…?' He slipped his gun off his shoulder.

'No, no; I was imagining things,' she protested, shaking her head again. She added briskly, 'Now, let us get on with our tour, shall we?' And she turned and marched off through the columns.

Adam and I exchanged a glance as we trailed her through the small temple complex. Ahmed kept his gun unslung and looked this way and that. But it was quite clear we were the only visitors.

It was strange to see Georgina jumping at shadows, even if only for a second. Her habitual demeanour was a brazen gung-ho confidence that left others breathless and gaping at her energetic and forthright bravado.

A large woman in her mid-late forties at a guess, even her style of dress suggested a force to be reckoned with. She tended to drape herself in big shapeless tent-like dresses that swathed her from neck to ankle. Typically she scraped her hair back into a clip. The sad truth of this was it made her look like a wigwam, although I'd never be so bold as to tell her so. Her only concession to femininity was her colourfully painted toenails. Today they were bright purple.

The incident was quickly forgotten as we toured the temple and things got back to normal. When we'd seen all there was to see we made our way back to the dahabeeyah. Rabiah was waiting to welcome us with cool flannels and chilled lemonade. She made this from a recipe I'd provided, originally given to me by staff at the wonderful Jolie Ville Hotel in Luxor.

I dashed off a quick blog post before dinner, Khaled unfurled the mighty sails, and we were on our way again, making good use of the seasonal winds to sail further south against the strong Nile current.

Our port of call the following morning was the rather grand temple of Horus at Edfu. It was another cool sunny day with a pastel blue sky and a stiff breeze blowing. We moored up and travelled from the riverbank to the temple perimeter in a couple of hastily hired caleche – horse drawn carriages to you and me.

Having Ahmed, Habiba and Mehmet in our party was helpful as it avoided the need for the whole bartering rigmarole. This is a way of life in Egypt and, though I'd acclimatised and consider myself perfectly capable of playing the game and settling on a fair price, it could be a protracted and ear-splitting negotiation. It was a relief to be saved the bother.

Adam and I rode in one carriage, making up a cosy threesome with Georgina, while Ahmed and Habiba shared the other with Mehmet, just behind us. This was easily decided. It really would have been a bit much to expect a poor horse to pull the combined weight of two such large people as Ahmed and Georgina.

We clip-clopped in a small procession through the dusty streets of Edfu, observing the noise and bustle of the modern town going about its business. Egypt is a place where the old and the new co-exist in a scruffy sort of harmony, neither one jarring with the other. But it's possible to ignore the modern vehicles, neon signs above the bazaars and poster boards; and see the streets much as the Belzonis must have known them, crowded with laden-down donkeys, stray cats, mangy dogs, a camel or two; women shrouded in black robes and men in floor length galabeyas with turbans wrapped around their heads.

Once through the security check at the temple with our tickets in hand, Georgina yet again led the way in her self-styled role as tour guide, glancing at her travel book before stuffing it in her bag.

'Here we have the best preserved of all the Egyptian temples,' she instructed, leading us across the forecourt in front of the gigantic pylon carved with immense figures of the gods. 'It possibly gives the best impression of what these structures must have looked like when first built as it still has its roof fully intact. Once again, what we see here dates from the Graeco-Roman period, built not long before the time of Christ, which makes it over a thousand years younger than the temples of Luxor and Karnak. Apparently it took almost one hundred and seventy years to build.'

I'd heard this particular fact before, the first time Adam and I had visited a few years ago. Back then we were on a Nile-cruise to check out the competition for our fledgling business. Hearing it again, I stared in awe at the massive edifice. It always boggled my brain to think of a building project being initiated, seen through and ultimately completed over a period of time representing several lifetimes. I tried to imagine anybody committing to such a mammoth enterprise nowadays; and failed. Ours is a transient; one might almost say throwaway society. Very little is built to last.

Mehmet wandered away, set up his tripod and immediately started taking photographs. It has to be said, it was a particularly impressive temple façade.

Adam shaded his eyes with his hand and looked at the enclosure walls. Unlike at Esna, here the modern town had been pushed back beyond the perimeter boundary. 'When the Belzonis visited, the temple lay smothered under an Arab village,' he said. 'The huts of the fellahin plastered the roof like wasps' nests.'

'Oh yes,' Georgina re-joined, not to be outdone. 'Belzoni said the excretions of man and beast seeped down to the sanctuary.'

'How disgusting,' I remarked, frowning at the evident relish with which she recounted this rather unpleasant morsel of local colour. She seemed quite taken with the toileting habits of those who'd lived here over the centuries. I wondered whether maybe my readers might also appreciate this extra insight, even if I did not.

'Not really,' she countered. 'It's probably to be expected after centuries of human inhabitation and without the sanitation we take for granted these...'

I'm sure she was about to add the word "days". But she broke off with an exclamation, shock freezing her expression almost as if in an action replay of yesterday.

'Georgina?' I questioned, once again craning over my shoulder to see what she was staring at.

This time I thought I caught a movement. It might have been someone ducking behind one of the enclosure walls near the quaintly named birth house close to the entrance. But it was fleeting, gone in the time it took me to blink.

Different again from our visit to Esna yesterday, today we weren't the only visitors. When we'd arrived I'd noticed small knots of tourists traipsing along behind a guide waving a red flag atop a long pole. Edfu was a popular cruise stop whereas Esna, being so close to the lock, was often missed off the tour itineraries.

I waited to see if I'd catch another glimpse of the person emerging on the other side of the stone structure. Several seconds elapsed and there was no further movement. Frowning, I turned back to look at our hefty houseguest.

She was still staring transfixed at the spot with no discernable change of expression.

This time Ahmed didn't wait to ask her permission, but strode off with his gun on his shoulder to take a look. We watched him disappear into the shade of the small outer chapel. He returned almost immediately, frowning.

'There is no person there,' he said flatly. 'No person and no animal, not even a stray cat or dog. I saw only pigeons.'

'I must have imagined it,' Georgina said with a nervous little laugh. Once again, this was so at odds with her usual robust persona, I raised an eyebrow.

'Georgina, is there something we should know?' I ventured. 'Are you worried about something... or someone?'

'No, no,' she said airily, recovering herself. 'I thought I glimpsed someone I used to know, that is all. Nothing to be in the least bit concerned about, just a surprise, that's all.'

'The same someone you thought you saw yesterday?' I quizzed, unwilling to let her off the hook.

She looked at me crossly. 'There was nobody other than us in the temple yesterday,' she snapped. 'And there is patently nobody over there in that chapel today,' – nodding towards the out-building. 'Just pigeons! My eyes are quite clearly playing tricks on me! Let's just leave it there, shall we?' And she turned and stomped off across the forecourt, disappearing through the huge pylon into the inner court beyond.

The rest of us exchanged confused glances, and then followed. But it seemed Georgina's appetite for playing tour-guide had waned. We trailed through the roofed hypostyle hall and inner sanctuary without saying much. There's no doubt the temple was impressive. We toured the outer wall, remarking on the carvings of the mythical battle between the god Horus and his evil uncle Set. But after an hour or so it became clear Georgina wanted to go. She remained nervy and watchful, completely unlike herself. The trouble with having such a big personality was it tended to rub off on everyone else. In the end it cast such a pall, I think we were all relieved to head for the taxi rank and direct our driver to take us back to the riverbank.

Once on board the *Queen Ahmes*, Georgina was once again her normal self. She informed us of her intention to dash off a few emails, and then retreated to the upper deck with a gin and tonic and her laptop.

Adam and I shrugged at each other and let her go.

Over lunch – a rather tasty Nile perch served in herb butter by Rabiah – Georgina regaled us with the news that her younger sister had given birth to yet another sprog – her word! – And also that she'd had an article accepted for publication in a national newspaper about Egypt's longed-for economic growth.

I decided if she'd seen something to momentarily unsettle her, it had not been worrisome enough to throw her off her stride for long. In all honesty I didn't give it another thought.

I spent the afternoon penning another blog about the dubious delights the nineteenth century explorers had to contend with: clearing urine-soaked filth and both human and animal excrement together with sand, bat poo and other detritus from the temples along the Nile. I hoped this angle might enliven my usual tales of Giovanni Belzoni's great discoveries.

That evening after dinner we banked at Kom Ombo. The temple was a short moonlit stroll from our mooring at the riverside. Georgina declined to come with us, saying she was all "templed-out" for the day and preferred to relax onboard with a good book and her ubiquitous gin and tonic.

Mehmet walked along the causeway with us then wandered off with his tripod and camera to get the best shots of the temple with the crescent moon rising above it.

So it was just Adam, Ahmed, Habiba and myself enjoying the romantic delights of an ancient Egyptian temple by moonlight. The temple was not bereft of visitors, although I'd hardly call it crowded. Once again, this was a popular cruise stop, famed for its mummified crocodiles.

Adam took my hand as we climbed the wide shallow stone steps to the forecourt. 'In the Belzonis' day the Nile around Kom Ombo teemed with crocodiles; enormous and ferocious creatures, which lay in wait along the riverbank to snap up any unwary animal or human in their jaws.'

'I'd rather not talk about crocodiles, if you don't mind,' I shuddered, reminded of the time Adam had a too-close-for-comfort encounter with one. He still wore a crocodile tooth on a bootlace around his neck as a kind of lucky charm.

He grinned. 'Here at Kom Ombo you have no choice but to talk about crocodiles. One half of the temple is dedicated to Sobek, the crocodile god! But as far as I know Giovanni Belzoni never had any close calls; none that he mentioned anyway.'

Together with Ahmed and Habiba, also walking hand-in-hand, we toured the temple ruins. Another Graeco-Roman edifice, the raised wall reliefs were well preserved but, in my view, lacked the finesse of those of earlier dynasties.

Kom Ombo is unusual for being a twin-temple, dedicated to two gods, Sobek being one and Horus-the-elder the other. Designed in two halves, each is a mirror image of the other. We wandered through the twin pillared courts and sanctuaries, enjoying the novelty of being simple tourists out to see the sights.

But before long I felt a prickle across the nape of my neck. I turned quickly, expecting to find someone standing close behind me. There was no one there. But the prickly sensation of being watched wouldn't go away.

I was unable to stop myself from constantly glancing back over my shoulder. Each time it was to find empty space behind me, or to observe other tourists taking holiday snaps, chatting or exclaiming over the wall reliefs. There was nothing at all to account for my ridiculous nervy jumpiness.

I glanced at my companions. All seemed blithely unaware of anything beyond simple enjoyment of visiting the temple at night. I was just deciding I must be going mad when Mehmet leapt out from behind one of the columns.

I gave a small involuntary shriek of alarm.

'You didn't spot me, did you?' he grinned gap-toothed, joining us. 'I've managed to get some great shots with all of you in them!'

I could cheerfully have throttled him. But my relief at this explanation for why I, like Georgina, appeared to be jumping at shadows conquered my instinctive inclination towards violence.

'You could have said,' I muttered. 'I'm not a great one for candid camera! I much prefer to look down the lens and say "cheese".'

He smiled, unapologetic. 'You'll change your mind when you see the pictures!'

And so it proved. We all gathered up on deck under the stars for a nightcap before bed. Mehmet brought his laptop onto which he'd loaded the images from his camera's SD card. We crowded round to take a look.

'Seems I missed out,' Georgina huffed, looking over his shoulder. 'It all looks very atmospheric in the moonlight.'

33

Mehmet was a skilled photographer. Many of the shots captured the crescent moon dangling in the sky casting a silvery light across the temple ruins. But it was the photographs containing the four of us that really dazzled. Shot in a monochrome that was more silver and grey than black and white, our features were obscured while preserving the sense of two couples strolling hand-in-hand through the temple enclosures.

Georgina was right. The photographs were atmospheric. They were also romantic. And each gave a sense of perspective, showing the temple with its columns and porticoes with our four figures providing a sense of scale. The wall reliefs were cleverly captured in light and shadow. They seemed almost to have more definition in Mehmet's images than when we'd been studying them with the naked eye. They were altogether an extremely accomplished set of pictures.

'You could sell these as postcards,' I observed approvingly.

'You certainly have a great eye for composition,' Adam agreed. 'And for capturing a mood.'

'Yes, I see now I'd have been gate-crashing had I decided to join you,' Georgina remarked waspishly.

The romantic angle of the Belzonis' adventures along the Nile wasn't one I'd played up before now. This was an omission, I realised. Of course they were travelling as man and wife. That said; it was certainly true they weren't together for the entire duration of their time in Egypt. Indeed their relationship seemed to be characterised by lengthy absences followed by joyful reunions. During one such, Sarah had an adventure of her own, taking herself off with just the young James Curtin for company on an independent trip to the Holy Land. There she dressed as a male Mamluk to gain admission to a temple forbidden to females, and even bathed in the Dead Sea. Nevertheless, from everything I'd read and learned I had a sense of a couple very much in tune with each other; which is as good a definition of love as I've ever heard.

I decided I should rectify the oversight. Mehmet's photographs would provide the feeling I was looking for. I felt sure I could evoke the romance of sailing the Nile through this antique land with the love of one's life. It was after all an experience I shared. Spurred by this sudden muse, I headed for the cabin I'd converted into my office and spent a happy hour or so with my fingers dancing over my computer keyboard before, feeling suitably amorous, I joined Adam in bed. I'm pleased to say his response didn't disappoint.

The following morning we docked early in the southern city of Aswan. The temperature was warm and balmy so we took breakfast up on the sundeck to enjoy the view as Khaled secured the ropes at the quayside.

Aswan is a thriving metropolis today. I imagine there's little the Belzonis would recognise in the city itself. Although I daresay the picturesque ruins on Elephantine Island in the middle of the Nile, and the Swiss-cheese-like tombs peppering the west bank where the Sahara desert sweeps down to meet the mighty river might appear familiar.

'Sarah Belzoni had an interesting time of it here,' Adam remarked, sipping the hot coffee Rabiah poured him, and nodding his thanks.

'Oh?' Georgina queried.

'As we know, she was the first European woman to travel this far up the Nile,' he said. 'It seems she became something of a curiosity to the local ladies.'

I took up the tale since I'd read the memoir Sarah published as an appendix to her husband's *Narrative.* Her own account, entitled *"Mrs Belzoni's Trifling Account"* was anything but. 'Yes, she paid courtesy visits on the two wives of the local Agha,' I said, putting down my spoon alongside my cereal bowl. 'One of the ladies was apparently old and very fat, but for that reason considered a great beauty.' I cringed as these words left my mouth, remembering to whom I was talking. Thankfully Georgina is a woman who appears to rejoice in her size and has the hide of a rhinoceros. Relieved at not having caused offence, I continued. 'The other was young and, by western standards, very pretty.

'Sarah tells us how she drank coffee and smoked a water pipe – two luxuries denied the wives. She'd brought gifts for the women of some beads and a hand-mirror. Apparently it was the largest looking-glass the wives had ever seen and they fought over it like children!'

Adam put down his coffee. 'My favourite part is Sarah's description of how the two ladies marvelled at her strange European clothing. She goes into great detail about how they coveted her black silk neckerchief, and how they believed her coat buttons must have money hidden inside. The only way she could persuade them otherwise was to open one. She says that, had the Agha not come home at this point, she believed the women would have become quite troublesome!'

'It taught her to put on what she calls "a greater deal of consequence" with other women she met,' I expanded. 'She realised that in being so free and easy with the ladies, on account of her ignorance of their character, she risked them taking advantage of her.'

'She really was a steely character,' Georgina said admiringly, stirring a third spoonful of sugar into her tea, and sitting back to enjoy it. 'So, what's the plan for today?'

'Today,' I said with a thrill of eager anticipation, 'we are visiting the island temple of Philae. I'm keen to see it for two reasons. Firstly, it was the first of the major rescue projects undertaken by UNESCO, so it should give us a flavour of what to expect when we reach Abu Simbel. In this case, it was flooding caused by the building of the Aswan Low Dam in the early 1900s that threatened the temple. Philae spent literally months partially submerged in water every year until 1960, when UNESCO started the project to take it apart and rebuild it on another island.'

Georgina sipped her tea without comment so I went on, 'But, most of all, I'm looking forward to seeing it because we know that steely character you just referred to –Sarah Belzoni – spent weeks camping out on the roof in 1817 while Giovanni travelled back to Abu Simbel. Saleh el-Sayed will meet us there, and I understand he's been granted a special dispensation to allow us to climb up onto the roof to see it for ourselves!'

I wonder now if perhaps I jinxed us with those words. The sad truth is, I may not have looked forward to our visit with anything like as much excitement had I only known what would happen when we got there.

Chapter 3

I was quite looking forward to seeing Saleh el-Sayed. An old nemesis, there'd been a time I'd have to own up to distinctly disliking the young man; and him me. Thankfully we seemed to have got past all that. He no longer resented me for stealing this job out from under him. And I was willing to overlook the part he'd played early-on in trying to sabotage our mission to retrace the Belzonis' travels.

Employed as Marketing Manager with the Egyptian Tourism Authority, he was sent to greet us at each of the most significant stops on our trip. His instructions were to grant us access all areas.

When we'd first arrived back in Egypt this had included permission to climb the Great Pyramid, an activity forbidden for years. I still count it as one of the highlights of my life. Today our privileged status meant we were allowed onto the roof of the temple so I could see for myself the place where Sarah camped out under the stars. Saleh had said he would meet us at the landing platform on the island.

We travelled across Aswan in the hired minibus Saleh arranged for us. This was large enough to take Mehmet's photographic equipment and also the six of us. Once deposited at the shore-side jetty, we managed to avoid the market traders prowling outside their souvenir kiosks ready to pounce on the unwary, and also the youngsters who thrust their concertina postcard packs under our noses, welcoming us loudly in every European language they could think of. With Ahmed taking the lead, dressed in his crisp security uniform, we headed straight for the ticket office. With the tickets Saleh had left for us in hand, we boarded the small, motorised water taxi that would take us across to the island.

I should have known we wouldn't get away that easily. The local hawkers and pedlars of touristy knick-knacks are masters of their art. A couple of enterprising young traders leapt on board our little boat just as the boatman started up the engine, and began badgering Georgina and me to inspect their wares. They took carved scarab beetles, various plastic gods and goddesses and an assortment of handmade jewellery from a large wicker basket and lined them up on the bulkhead, jabbering incessantly. Ahmed leaned forward to intercede, barking a few words in Arabic. But I took pity on the young bullies. It wasn't their fault there were so few victims for them to accost and hassle into purchasing their dubious trinkets. I bought a bead necklace, willingly paying over the odds, just to get them to leave us alone. I didn't want to miss out on my first proper view of the temple complex as we crossed the water. Georgina followed suit, purchasing a woven bracelet. It did the trick. The young rascals retreated to the back of the boat and left us in peace.

Philae is an enchanting temple; I should rather say complex of temples. It sprawls across the lush green island of

Agilika, one of the many islands in the first cataract above the High Dam. Its golden-toned sandstone structures are set picturesquely among clumps of feathery palms and other foliage. I'd say it has a distinctly feminine vibe; possibly unsurprising since it's dedicated to the goddess Isis.

I knew Sarah and Giovanni Belzoni had stopped for a picnic here on their first visit before travelling on to Abu Simbel. Much later, Giovanni returned and was instrumental in shifting a gigantic obelisk for the gentleman traveller William John Bankes. It stands proudly in the Bankes' family seat at Kingston Lacy in Dorset to this day. But that was on another trip. On their first excursion to see the island temple complex they would have seen it very much as I was seeing it today – albeit on a different island.

'It really beggars belief, don't you think?' Adam murmured at my side, picking up on my thoughts in that uncanny way of his as we chugged across the glistening water and gazed up at the monuments. 'To think every one of the temple structures was taken apart stone by stone, transported here and then rebuilt! Astonishing, really!'

'Just goes to show what the international community can do when it pulls together,' Georgina remarked sagely. 'Shame human beings can't do more of this sort of thing and stop fighting each other!'

Mehmet was already lost to us, peering through the viewfinder of his DSLR camera, to which he'd attached a huge wide-angle lens.

Ahmed kept a watchful eye out in his capacity as our security guard, whilst still managing surreptitiously to hold Habiba's hand.

As promised, Saleh el-Sayed was there to meet us as our little water taxi deposited us at the island jetty. He came quickly along the wooden boardwalk as soon as he spotted us, already calling out a greeting. A smart, sartorial chap in a crisp linen suit with a pale blue shirt open at the throat, and sporting designer sunglasses; he was every inch the handsome young professional. Now he'd dropped his air of excessively polite yet insolent disinterest, he was a likeable one too. It was a shame it had taken a strike from a deadly cobra to break the ice between us. But there you have it. I guess stranger things have happened.

'Welcome... Welcome...!' he cried out, reaching forward so he could help me along the little gangplank the boatman hastily lowered, and up onto the jetty.

'Saleh!' I said warmly as Adam helped Georgina off the boat. The gangplank creaked ominously under her weight. The others followed. 'It's good to see you.'

'Now, I must tell you,' he said eagerly as soon as greetings were over and we were all gathered around. 'Latest statistics show holiday bookings for this year already up by almost forty percent on the same time last year!'

'That's wonderful!' I exclaimed.

'It is still a long way short of normal, considering how badly the bottom fell out of our tourist market. But it is a start.'

'Saleh, it's fantastic news!' Adam grinned, slapping him on the back. 'Fingers crossed it's a sign of better things to come.'

'I think maybe we have you to thank,' Saleh smiled, with no hint of his former sly subtext. 'Publicity over those tablets has revived international interest in Egypt as an archaeological hotspot!'

Georgina smiled benignly. 'I told you all along I could get you into the mainstream Press. Lucky you had me along!'

I let this flagrant egoism go since she had indeed borne the brunt of the intense media mania – a role she relished – and therefore enabled Adam and me to take a back seat.

'Your blog continues to reach a wide audience,' Saleh said to me, perhaps feeling the need to massage my ego too in the face of Georgina's brazen braggadocio. 'Zahed Mansour is pleased with the ever-increasing number of followers. You seem to think of a fresh angle in every post.'

'It's what he pays me for,' I said modestly.

'And I'm sure Mehmet's photographs are also helping to do the trick,' Adam added warmly. 'Reminding people of the endless blue skies and wall-to-wall sunshine is no bad thing. Who wants to be in cold, grey England at this time of year, when they could be here?'

Thus settled into a warm camaraderie, we turned to begin our inspection of the temple ruins.

'Of course, you are more expert in your ancient Egyptian history than I,' Saleh conceded as we strolled through the temple's gigantic first pylon into the main outer courtyard. 'You will know this sacred site was dedicated to the cult of Isis and venerated from the Pharaonic era up to the Greek, Roman and Byzantine periods. Each ruler added their stamp onto the stones here.'

'You've been boning up,' I grinned at him. The ancient history of his homeland had never really been Saleh's strong point. He'd been far more comfortable marketing his nation as a holiday destination for those seeking suntans, souks and shisha.

'I can read a guide book as easily as the next person,' he smiled back, not in the least offended. 'When we are inside the vestibule, remind me to point out the Coptic crosses carved into the walls that show how the temple was transformed into a Christian place of worship during the early Byzantine age.'

I glanced at Georgina, wondering if she minded having her thunder stolen. It was all the invitation she needed.

'The temples of Philae have dazzled travellers for centuries,' she said airily, as if she were a leading world authority. 'I think it's safe to say this place charms all who visit. You can see why, don't you think?' She gestured around us as if to demonstrate the temple's beauty spoke for itself.

Colonnades of tall stone pillars fronted either side of the forecourt buildings, leading to a second huge pylon, deeply carved with immense figures of the gods. With a magnificent doorway set in the centre, it was a fittingly regal entry to the inner sanctum of the temple of Isis.

'It's lovely,' I concurred. 'Thank goodness UNESCO was able to save them from a watery grave. You'd never know it, would you? These monuments look as if they've been standing here for millennia.'

'There's an evening sound and light show, you know,' she added. 'It tells the whole story. Perhaps we should come back later to see it.'

'Yes, maybe,' I said non-commitally, reminding myself I was here to work, not just for pleasure. 'Now, Saleh; I'm happy to have a scout around the outer precincts. But most of all I want to know how do we get up onto the roof?'

Standing just behind me, I heard Habiba clear her throat.

'All in good time,' Saleh smiled. 'As you can see, we are not the only visitors. While it is wonderful to see tourists returning to the sights, Habiba here has reminded me of the instruction issued by Director Ismail at the Ministry – that we may climb onto the roof only after the majority of tour parties have returned to their cruise boats.' He glanced at his watch. 'You'll see, the place will empty out in an hour or so. This is usually the first sightseeing trip of the day in Aswan, followed by the unfinished obelisk and then a visit to the High Dam. The lucky ones are then treated to lunch at the Old Cataract Hotel.'

It was a timely reminder that the Director was still pulling Habiba's strings.

'I'm sorry,' she murmured, stepping forward. 'It's a safety thing. Director Ismail doesn't want any accidents, or awkward questions from other visitors denied the privilege of a photo opportunity on the roof.'

'Fair enough,' I shrugged. I understood well enough that Habiba had to walk a fine line between her personal and professional lives. She was here to work too, and would carry out a detailed inspection of the temple complex for filing back to her bosses.

So we spent a happy hour traipsing around the island, admiring the various edifices and monuments while Mehmet took photographs and Georgina kept up a running commentary.

'This is one of the most popular photo spots,' she informed us as we approached the strangely named Kiosk of Trajan 'It's known colloquially as Pharaoh's bed,' she lectured. 'You can see why, don't you think?'

I looked up at the huge stone structure, which did indeed resemble a four-poster bed, although with twelve posts, columns in fact, rather than four.

'It was a favourite subject for famous English artists during the age of the great Victorian explorers,' she added.

All in all, it wasn't hard to see why visitors were dazzled by Philae. On its island setting, surrounded by sparkling blue water, dense with lush green vegetation, and dotted with picturesque ruins glowing gold in the sunlight, it charmed with its light and airy feel. But even to one as passionately obsessed with Egyptian history as I, there's only so much information one can take in. I was itching to get inside the sanctuary and up onto the roof.

Saleh saw me glance at my watch. 'Ok,' he said with a small laugh. 'There are not so many tour parties here now. I think we may make our way inside the main temple for our private visit.'

He led us through the immense pylon and into the columned vestibule, where he did indeed point out the Coptic crosses carved by early Christians. From there we passed through a number of antechambers flanked by dimly lit side chambers and came to the inner sanctuary. This would once have housed the sacred barque bearing the image of Isis. It was dark, lit only by ground level artificial tube lighting casting a yellow glow up at the walls. Saleh checked we were following, and turned to the west.

'That doorway leads back outside to the Gateway of Hadrian,' he said, nodding at it. 'But we will ascend here.' Another door was set into the inner wall. I'd have walked straight past without noticing it if he hadn't pointed it out.

Georgina took one look at the narrow passageway and baulked. 'I don't think so!' she said emphatically. It was apparent there was no way she would be able to squeeze her bulk through such a confined space. The thought of her attempting it and getting stuck was almost too horrific to contemplate.

Ahmed also made a noise deep in his throat. It sounded very much like, 'Hrrumph.' For our erstwhile police pal it wasn't so much his girth as the breadth of his shoulders and his height posing the problem. He'd trimmed down considerably in the last couple of years. Looking upwards into the narrow stone stairwell it reinforced just what a small race of people the ancient Egyptians must have been.

'Ahmed, why don't you accompany Georgina back outside?' Saleh suggested politely. 'I remember well from our climb to the top of the Great Pyramid that you do not enjoy heights.'

This was true. But Ahmed turned at once to me and started to protest. 'Where you go so must I...!'

'Actually, it might serve a better purpose for you to remain below,' Saleh added. 'You can ensure no casual tourists take it into their heads to follow us up onto the roof. There are still a few tour parties remaining, I observe. As Habiba mentioned earlier, I would not wish to invite unwelcome attention from those who may request admission too, and be disgruntled at having it denied them.'

I nodded at Ahmed to confirm my acquiescence to this plan, even while I wondered who had taught Saleh English. But then Arabic is quite a formal language, so perhaps he was performing a literal translation. Whatever, I couldn't fault his vocabulary.

So it was just Saleh, Adam, Mehmet and I who climbed the stone steps, each worn into a hollow at the centre from centuries' worth of footfall.

I tried to imagine Sarah treading this same steep staircase two hundred years ago and felt a ripple of timelessness across the nape of my neck, as if I might close my eyes and open them to find her brushing past me.

Not that there was the room to do other than ascend in single file. Georgina was right to stay behind. I'd swear the stone staircase got narrower the higher we climbed. And it was dark, lit only by the torch Saleh had brought with him.

Finally we stepped out into blinding sunshine once more. I could see at once why Director Ismail didn't want tourists up here. The roof of the temple was exactly that, with no nice safe perimeter wall around it, just piles of loose stones strewn here and there. In many places it was a sheer drop to the ground. But it has to be said the view of the surrounding temple complex was spectacular. With the doorway at the top of the staircase closed and barred, I imagine Sarah must perhaps have felt this a safer bet than asking to be put up in one of the grubby hovels the locals lived in back then.

'You know, I never understood why Sarah didn't go back with Giovanni on his second trip to Abu Simbel,' I said to Adam as Mehmet set up his tripod and Saleh wandered off to admire the view. 'Why did she have to stay behind and camp out up here?'

'Giovanni said there was no room in the boat,' Adam supplied with a shrug, looking around as if trying to visualise her campsite. 'Interestingly enough, the couple actually rendezvoused here before he sailed away; Belzoni from a further spot of antiquities collecting in Thebes, and Sarah from a period staying with a family in Cairo. By the time Sarah arrived, with young James Curtin in tow, Belzoni had already made arrangements for his second journey south; this time determined to dig his way through the sand to find the entrance to the Great Temple of Ramses. As you know, Merry, he was unable to do so on their first trip – which was when Sarah spotted the tablets in Nefertari's Smaller Temple – because he needed to get back to Thebes to oversee transportation of the bust he'd hauled from the Ramesseum. Henry Salt was waiting for it in Alexandria.'

I walked slowly across the temple roof, watching my step, and trying to imagine what it might be like to call this place home. 'Do you think it was true that the boat couldn't accommodate her and James Curtin too?' I frowned; thinking I'd take a decidedly dim view of it should Adam ever take it into his head to go off adventuring without me.

Adam shrugged, following me. 'Yes, possibly; or else he thought it more dangerous to take her along than to leave her here. You may recall, Merry; Sarah had to use Belzoni's pistol to fend off an attack onboard their dahabeeyah while moored at Abu Simbel the first time. Anyway, the fact is, Belzoni sailed south as one of a party of eleven men. He travelled with two adventuresome navy officers, named Irby and Mangles; a chap called Beechey, who was Henry Salt's secretary; a janissary called Finati, and an interpreter named Yanni. There was also a crew of five local men. So his boat was pretty crowded.'

'Even so …' I looked around me, trying to imagine Sarah camped out under the stars on these unforgiving stones.

Adam took my hand as we crossed the temple roof. 'By her own account, she made herself comfortable enough,' he reminded me. 'Giovanni left her sitting on a large quantity of luggage and surrounded by a mud brick wall. He trusted her safety to James Curtin and her own inimitable character.'

I knew this well enough from what I'd read in Sarah's published memoirs and in her two diaries. If she was nothing else, Sarah Belzoni was a stalwart of her age; brave, intrepid and independent.

Just in case I didn't remember the finer details, Adam supplied them. He'd become something of an authority on the Belzonis for the British Museum exhibition, after all; as well as devouring the contents of both her journals. 'Sarah made what she cheerfully calls "two comfortable rooms" of mud brick,' he said, looking around as if to picture them as we walked across the stone roof. Of course there was no sign of them now, so I too used my imagination. 'While James Curtin cleaned Mr Beechey's silverware under the goggling eyes of the Arabs – you have to remember, Merry, nineteenth century gentlemen travelled with most of their worldly goods – Sarah would casually handle a pair of loaded pistols. Every day the women came across from both sides of the Nile to see this wonder. They brought her eggs and onions and little '*antikas*' in return for beads and small hand mirrors. I don't think she was overly troubled by Giovanni's absence. When Belzoni and his team returned to Philae two months later, it was to find Sarah serene and unruffled here on top of the temple of Isis.'

'What a woman!' I breathed admiringly.

I was about to add more, but a sudden movement in the corner of my eye distracted me. A sudden movement – followed by a holler and a deafening scream from below.

After a second frozen rigid with shock, I spun to face the movement. Saleh came running forward from his position close to the edge of the roof. Mehmet dropped his camera while the scream still resonated through the air. Rather than come to join us he edged closer to the precipice.

'What was that?' I gasped. Unaccountably, it was neither Saleh nor Mehmet I'd expected to see when I turned. Neither was on exactly the same spot where I thought I'd glimpsed movement, close to the doorway on one edge of the roof at the top of the stone staircase. I couldn't see what had caught my eye. There was nothing there.

For reasons of his own, Adam ran across to the doorway; stopped and listened.

'What's going on?' I repeated desperately, rooted to the spot. 'Is anyone hurt?'

Mehmet, steadying his balance, peered over the edge. 'It is Ahmed!' he exclaimed. 'He appears to have been struck by falling masonry! He is lying sprawled on the ground!"

I couldn't get back across the roof and down that stairwell quickly enough. Adam was ahead of me, and Saleh brought up the rear. It was only when we got to the bottom I realised Mehmet had not descended with us.

We burst through the side entrance to the temple, almost falling over each other in our haste to get outside.

Georgina and Habiba were kneeling in the dust, leaning over Ahmed's inert form. I could see a large stone block on the ground alongside him with a splash of bright red blood on one corner. It was the approximate size of a breezeblock. I could only begin to imagine its weight.

'Did it hit him?' I cried in panic.

'Just glanced off his shoulder,' Georgina grunted, hoisting herself up from the floor, clearly dazed and shaken. 'He's bleeding. But I think he just saved my life!'

Behind her Ahmed groaned and Habiba ripped off her headscarf, using it to stem the blood oozing through Ahmed's white shirt.

I took this in at a glance. Then stared back at Georgina trying to make sense of what she'd just said. I was starting to discern that a block of stone of that size was unlikely to have come loose and fallen of its own volition. 'What on earth do you mean?' I asked in strangled tones. 'What happened?'

Georgina took a single shaky step into the shade of the temple. There she collapsed heavily onto the low wall of carved blocks, fanning herself with one hand while drawing a few steadying lungfuls of air.

'We were sitting here in the shade,' she began, sounding nothing like herself. Her breathing was shallow as if she were drawing it from her chest not her stomach. She gulped a couple of times and went on, 'Habiba was standing over there, looking up and shading her eyes to see if she could spot you on the roof. She must have spied something. She called out a warning. The next thing I knew Ahmed leapt up hauling me with him. He shoved me to the ground. But he wasn't quick enough to get out of the way. That rock struck his shoulder, and sent him spinning. He crashed to the floor where you see him now.'

I stared, speechless, at the bloodied chunk of stone, trying to take it in. Even in my shocked and dim-witted state, I was starting to discern that it was probably of a size and weight just about possible to lift.

'If Ahmed hadn't moved when he did,' Georgina said in wobbly tones, 'that building block would have landed square on top of me!'

'You?' I said stupidly, trying to get my befuddled brain to keep up. I was so used to Ahmed being the intended victim of the various mishaps that had dogged our first leg of this trip, I didn't seem capable of assimilating anything else. I even darted a suspicious glance at poor Saleh el-Sayed, wondering if perhaps he'd gone all turncoat on us and was still trying to sabotage things.

Then I remembered that inexplicable movement I'd imagined up on the temple roof. Saleh had not been standing on the same spot but had run towards us from further away, beyond the doorway.

As I re-registered this, Mehmet joined us, bursting from the temple, leaving the door swinging on its hinges behind him. 'I stayed behind on the roof to keep a watch on the exits,' he gulped, catching his breath. 'Nobody emerged from either of the doorways I could see from up there. But I did catch sight of a person running across the forecourt as if he had left by the main entrance into the temple.'

'I thought I heard a noise on the stairway,' Adam said grimly. 'Dammit! I should have given chase straight away. That split second of hesitation, trying to figure out what had happened, probably gave him time to get away!'

I gaped at this, slowly slotting the pieces together and realising there had been someone else up on the roof with us. Adam and Mehmet had both grasped this essential point too, and much more quickly.

'Was it definitely a *him*?' I asked Mehmet searchingly.

'I wouldn't swear to it – the person was too far away, and running. But yes, I think so. He must have followed us up onto the roof.'

I stared back at Georgina. She was slumped on the wall, leaning forward with her head in her hands. 'I should have known it meant trouble when I thought I spotted him at Esna and Edfu,' she wailed.

Chapter 4

There was no time to get Georgina to explain this cryptic remark.

Habiba jumped up from the ground where she was tending to Ahmed. 'He needs medical attention!' she demanded urgently. 'The stone block struck him on the same shoulder as the bullet! It's opened up the old wound! I'm struggling to stem the bleeding!

I'd only seen Habiba once before without her headscarf. And that on the occasion of said gunshot wound, when she'd also used it to stem Ahmed's blood. Her hairstyle came as a shock now as it had then. I'd always imagined her to have long hair beneath the hijab she wound carefully around her face. The short pixie cut was a surprise, even seeing it for a second time. But it has to be said it suited her. Even in this moment of *extremis*, so to speak, I couldn't help but register how beautiful she was. Habiba always manages to look as if she's stepped from the cover of a glossy magazine modelling the latest in desert chic. Whether it's tailored trousers, leather boots and a fitted white linen shirt, belted in at the waist, as now; or one of her many knee-length silk tunics worn over nipped-in-at-the ankle oriental pants and soft slippers; she's a sultry, dusky Egyptian beauty.

But a moment to register it was all I had. Saleh el-Sayed was already calling out in Arabic to one of the island's security guards, eliciting a look of panic in response as the guard took in the scene. Adam was asking if they had such a thing as a stretcher so we could get Ahmed onto a boat. Mehmet pulled his mobile phone from his pocket and was calling for an ambulance to meet us on the shore.

It was all pandemonium after that. Ahmed was conscious but clearly in pain and bleeding copiously. Worse, it was clear he'd dislocated his shoulder. Whether this was a result of being struck by the stone block, or his resulting fall was impossible to say. Grunting loudly, he managed to stumble to his feet. With support from Adam, Saleh and Mehmet, and in the company of three security guards, we were able to get him back to the landing platform and onto a water taxi without the need for a stretcher.

A few stray tourists stood open-mouthed and curious. They made way as we commandeered the first boat. I looked at them all suspiciously, searching for guilty, shifty expressions, or generally anything amiss. I noticed Georgina similarly scanning the faces of everyone we passed. She looked shell-shocked and nervy, and was walking stiffly. I daresay she was bruised from crashing to the ground after Ahmed unceremoniously hauled her out of harm's way.

Everyone watching us help Ahmed onto the boat seemed exactly what I'm sure they were: ordinary sightseers visiting the island temples. If someone had indeed followed us up onto the temple roof with the objective of dropping a stone block on Georgina, he had seized his moment and scarpered – probably onto another water taxi that had already returned him to the shore.

Unimaginably, this was apparently what had happened. Opportunistic was putting it mildly! But there was no other explanation I could think of since I was sure Saleh and Mehmet were innocent of any nefarious intent. And Georgina evidently feared the worst. It made sense of her bizarre behaviour over the last couple of days. But it was beyond me to imagine what she had done to invite such violent attention.

It wasn't until we returned to the dahabeeyah much later that we were able to quiz her and get a sense of what was going on.

We'd spent most of the rest of the day at the hospital, not a place conducive to conducting the interrogation I had planned. Saleh el-Sayed left us there after seeing Ahmed safely into the care of the medical team. Saleh had arrangements to make for the next part of our trip. He promised to come to the *Queen Ahmes* in the morning to check on the patient.

Once back on board, Mehmet also left us to head straight to his cabin and start uploading his photographs. So it was just Ahmed, Habiba, Adam and me up on the sundeck waiting for Georgina to join us for the council of war I was intent on having.

Ahmed's dislocated shoulder had been re-set. He'd been patched up with surgical tape and stuffed full of painkillers. Now, understandably grey-featured and grim-faced, sporting bandages and wearing a sling, he was lying on one of the steamer chairs in the shade as the sun started to sink towards the tomb-riddled hills of Aswan's west bank. Rabiah fussed around with hot, sweet peppermint tea.

'Thanks Rabiah,' Adam said. 'But, speaking for myself, I feel in need of something stronger. There's a bottle of Jack Daniels on the bar, if I could prevail on you to bring it up?'

Perhaps alcohol was a good idea for the shock. I don't think it escaped any of us just how much worse today's incident could have been had Habiba not happened to be looking upwards at the crucial moment.

Habiba herself was much calmer now the medical staff had put Ahmed back to rights and discharged him. She hadn't replaced her headscarf since coming back on board. Perhaps now we'd all spent such a large part of the day with her without one, she thought it unnecessary. I don't claim to know the Muslim rules for headscarf wearing among one's friends. But I'll admit to the little buzz of shock I felt every time I looked at her. I figured I'd get used to it in the end, but I wasn't accustomed to the sight of her without it, or the cute pixie cut, just yet.

Rabiah brought the Jack Daniels and a gin and tonic for Georgina (she knew better than to bother offering Georgina tea). Georgina followed her slowly up the spiral staircase.

This was no mean feat, given her size. She slumped heavily into one of the padded chairs under the wide canvas awning and accepted her drink. Personally I stuck with the tea. I wanted a clear head for the conversation we were about to embark on.

As soon as Rabiah departed to finish making dinner and was out of earshot at the bottom of the spiral staircase all gazes turned inevitably to our hefty houseguest.

'Ok Georgina,' I started. 'Who is it you spotted at Esna and Edfu? You said you should have known it meant trouble. I don't imagine it's escaped any of our attention that he tried to kill you today.'

'And could have killed Ahmed,' Habiba interjected hotly before I could finish.

'I daresay we'll have some questions to answer assuming the guards have to report the fact there was an incident at Philae today,' I continued.

'If they don't, I will report it,' Habiba interrupted again, stony-faced. I allowed her this since I fully understood her distress.

'So I think you need to tell us what this is all about.' I finished. 'Who is this man? Why is he following you? And why did he make an attempt on your life?'

Georgina gave a hearty sigh. 'I can only presume he wishes to stop me getting to Abu Simbel.'

I stared at her. A glimmer of comprehension started to dawn. 'So, this has to do with the treasure you say is stashed there.'

I heard Habiba gasp. She hadn't been in the room when Georgina first mentioned the treasure.

Adam put his tumbler down on the deck at his feet and leaned forward. 'Georgina, there can't possibly be a stash of Pharaonic treasure hidden at Abu Simbel. It would have been discovered long since. The whole place was broken apart and rebuilt stone by stone in the sixties.'

'Who said anything about Pharaonic treasure?' she challenged.

'Er, *you* did!' I said with a frown. 'If I remember rightly, you said you had it on pretty good authority that there's a stash of treasure hidden away in the walls of the Great Temple of Ramses II.'

'Yes,' she said. 'But not royal treasure. And not dating back to ancient Egypt. Actually it was put there in the sixties. The re-siting of the temple provided a great opportunity to hide it away from prying eyes. And, if I'm honest, to call it treasure is stretching it a bit. I daresay I was being dramatic. It is in fact a stash of money. But worth a king's ransom nonetheless.'

I stared at her again. 'Georgina, you're not making any sense.'

She sat back in her chair, sipped her gin and tonic and regarded me over the rim of the glass. If the events of the day hadn't been so bone-chilling I'd say she was starting to enjoy herself; maddening woman. 'Tell me,' she invited. 'What was one of the biggest news stories to hit the headlines in the early 1960s? It had to do with a huge haul of money.'

'News stories?' I said blankly, not following.

'Yes,' she nodded. 'A daring heist that created headlines everywhere. Think of one of the largest sums of stolen cash you can.'

Adam choked. 'You're talking about The Great Train Robbery!'

'Yes!' she said with satisfaction. 'The gang got away with £2.6 million. That's about £50 million in today's money. Much of the stolen loot was recovered in the months after the robbery. But not all.'

'And you're saying some of it was walled up in the Great Temple of Ramses at Abu Simbel during the project to re-site it in the sixties?' I gaped.

'Yes!' she said. 'And it's still there!'

Ahmed shifted his weight on the steamer and cleared his throat. 'What is this Great Train Robbery?'

Adam picked up his tumbler and leaned back. 'Yes, Georgina; I too am distinctly hazy on the details. Why don't you start at the beginning and tell us the whole story, up to and including why someone is trying to kill you, since I presume the two are linked.'

Georgina put her gin and tonic on the little table at her side and looked around at us. We sat staring expectantly back at her in the glow of the sinking sun. Ahmed sat up straighter and adjusted his sling. Nobody loves a story quite so much as Ahmed. Particularly one in which he has a starring role, even if only a minor one.

'Ok,' Georgina said. 'It was the summer of 1963. England was embarking on the swinging sixties. It was a colourful decade but newspaper and television reports were still in black and white.'

'Is that relevant?' I asked.

'Probably not,' she admitted. 'Only to say I always picture The Great Train Robbery in black and white since that's how everything I've ever watched or read about it has been reported or published. My apologies, I was simply setting the scene. It's a great story: characterised by daring deeds, silly mistakes, a national police hunt, prison breakouts and the pursuit of fugitives who fled abroad.'

'So what happened?' Ahmed said eagerly.

Georgina made herself comfortable and got on with it. 'In the early hours of the morning on 8 August 1963, a fifteen-man gang of robbers attacked a royal mail train travelling from Glasgow in Scotland to London's Euston station. They'd had a tip off to say the train would be transporting almost £3 million in banknotes through the night.'

She went on, 'The gang, drawn from south London's criminal underworld, tampered with railway line signals on a bridge near Leighton Buzzard in Buckinghamshire. They covered the green signal light with a glove and powered up the red so it would stay lit. They also cut all communication cables. Then they stormed the train, badly injuring the driver, and tying up the postal workers on board. It took them half an hour to remove one-hundred-and-twenty sacks of money, forming a human chain to transfer them to a truck waiting at the roadside.'

I found myself hooked on the story almost in spite of myself, much as what I really wanted to know was how all of this related to Ahmed's brush with death today.

'They made their getaway and holed up at a remote farmhouse,' Georgina said. 'There, they divided the money into equal shares, each of approximately £150,000. That would be around £2.65 million in today's money.'

I saw Ahmed's eyes round like saucers, no doubt trying to work out how many tens of millions that would be in Egyptian currency.

'Believe it or not, they whiled away their time in hiding playing a game of Monopoly, using real money! The gang's plan was to stay holed up at the farmhouse for as long as it took for the initial fuss to die down. They knew the postal workers would raise the alarm immediately. They'd brought supplies to see them through several days.

'But from listening to their police-tuned radio they learned the police had calculated they'd gone to ground within a thirty-mile radius of the crime scene rather than dispersing with their haul. They realised police were using a dragnet tactic, and would probably discover them much sooner than they'd anticipated. As a result, they had to bring forward the plan for leaving the farm. One of the gang was supposed to go back and torch the farmhouse to remove all trace of their stay. But it seems he got spooked and did a runner. His failure to burn down the farmhouse became the gang's downfall.'

Ahmed was listening bug-eyed and agog. It had all happened before any of us was born. Even so, as Georgina recounted the tale I found I was familiar with some of it. I guess this was because it was such an audacious heist it had somehow entered the British national consciousness. Georgina hadn't identified any of the robbers but I had the names Buster Edwards and Ronnie Biggs floating around in my head. I seemed to remember seeing a film as a kid with Phil Collins playing the lead role as one of the gang members who got away.

'So what happened? Did they get catched?' Ahmed asked in his usual execrable English. Nobody corrected him.

'When the police found the hideaway, they were able to lift a number of fingerprints,' Georgina said. 'A manhunt followed. Police arrested eight of the robbers and several associates over the following months, although some of the ringleaders managed to flee abroad. Police were also able to recover much of the money. The trial of the eight men began in January 1964'

'That was the year the UNESCO project to re-site the temples of Abu Simbel started,' Adam interjected. 'The project ran from 1964 to 1968.'

'That's correct,' Georgina nodded. 'And I will come to how that fits in in a moment. The story is about to get interesting.'

I realised my tea had gone cold so took a small sip of Adam's Jack Daniels. Georgina also paused for a glug of her gin and tonic.

Putting down her glass, she swallowed and resumed the tale. 'One of the robbers was an Irishman called John Daly. He was brother-in-law to one of the main masterminds behind the heist, a chap called Bruce Reynolds. Reynolds had gone on the run. Police finally caught up with him four years later in 1968 and he served ten years. You'll see why the family relationship was relevant in a sec.'

She folded her hands in her lap and looked around at our faces, ensuring she had our full attention. I guessed we were coming to the crux of things.

'In February 1964 there was a sensation at the trial,' Georgina announced. 'John Daly was found to have no case to answer! But of course he was as guilty as sin. He was the man who stopped the train and was also the getaway driver!'

Ahmed leaned forward and grunted as the sudden movement jolted his shoulder. 'He was set free?' he gaped.

'He was,' Georgina confirmed. 'It's called being acquitted. And you'll never guess why...?'

She had us all now, listening intently with eyes fixed on her face.

'Tell me,' Ahmed pleaded.

'It's all down to the game of Monopoly the robbers played while they were hiding out at the farmhouse.'

'Game of Monopoly?' Ahmed parroted with popping eyes. I'm not sure if he was familiar with it, or whether there's an Egyptian version.

'It's a board game,' I supplied.

'Yes,' Georgina nodded. 'And John Daly's fingerprints were found on the pieces. But this is where his counsel played a masterstroke at the trial. He said the only evidence against Daly was those fingerprints and the fact that he'd gone to ground after the robbery. The QC claimed Daly had played the Monopoly game with his brother-in-law Bruce Reynolds earlier in 1963, which accounted for the fingerprints, and that he had gone underground only because he was associated with people publicly sought by the police. He pointed out that this was not proof of involvement in a conspiracy. The judge agreed, and the jury was directed to acquit him.'

'Blimey,' I said, not very articulately, and with raised eyebrows.

'It was a lucky escape,' Georgina said. 'The other seven men were each sentenced to thirty years in prison. This was before the parole system came in. The severity of the sentences handed down caused a media storm. It was more than many murderers or armed robbers were given at the time. There was a public outcry. You see, to many the Great Train Robbers were seen as modern-day highwaymen. They achieved something like celebrity status. Although I have to say, in my view, they deserved to be charged with attempted murder, not just robbery. While they may not have boarded the train intending to hurt anyone, they hit the poor driver over the head with a metal bar, causing brain damage. Then, because the robbers had no idea how to move the train, the poor driver was dragged back to his post in the cab, with blood pouring from his head wound, and forced to carry out their instructions. He never fully recovered from his injuries and died prematurely – although the Coroner said his injuries played no part in his death.'

'So where does Abu Simbel fit in?' Adam asked, bringing us back to the point.

'To understand that, you need to know the story of John Daly's arrest and what happened after he was released,' Georgina said. Then she paused. 'Do you think Rabiah might be prevailed on to pour me another G&T?'

'I'll get it,' I offered, and went below deck. I mixed one for myself at the same time.

The sun was quite low in the sky by the time I returned. I'd been so caught up in Georgina's story I hadn't noticed the lengthening shadows. It was cool too this early in the year. 'Why don't we de-camp to the lounge bar?' I suggested. So we all trooped down the spiral staircase, Habiba helping Ahmed hoist himself up from the steamer.

Once settled inside and with refreshed drinks – Habiba and Ahmed chose cola – Georgina, seated regally on the divan, smoothed out her skirt and took up her tale once again. 'I'll start by letting you know that John Daly was an antiques dealer. He had a shop in Notting Hill's Portobello Road. He also had a string of convictions for petty theft. He associated with people who traded in antiquities.'

'Egyptian antiquities?' Adam queried.

'I believe so,' she nodded. 'Now, as we know, John Daly was guilty of The Great Train Robbery. He was a core member of the gang. He knew the police were closing in after they discovered the farmhouse, and went on the run. Two business associates helped him go to ground. They arranged for him to hide out in a flat in London's Belgravia. Once there, he went on a crash diet and apparently lost three stone in weight. He also shaved off his beard to change his appearance. But the two men he trusted to shield him in actual fact betrayed him to the police. They knew where Daly's share of the cash was and wanted to get their own hands on it. Apparently they'd helped him bury it in the garden of a house in Cornwall, if you can believe it!'

'That's a county in the west of England, a long way from London,' I said for Ahmed and Habiba's benefit.

Georgina sipped her gin and tonic and went on, 'Anyway, these so-called friends informed on Daly to the police, even revealing the secret bell rings – two short and one long – they used on the front doorbell to let Daly know it was safe to open up. When the police went to the flat all they had to do was ring and then pile in through the door when Daly opened it.'

'No honour among thieves,' Adam murmured.

'His "friends" clearly had a vested interest in seeing him put away for as long as possible,' I said.

'I think it's fair to say a number of the robbers had money stolen by people they trusted to look after it for them while they were on trial,' Georgina added.

'So what happened when this Daly man was found not guilty and released?' Ahmed asked impatiently.

'The first thing he did after his acquittal was have a massive party,' Georgina said with a grim smile. 'The second, as you might imagine, was to drive with all possible speed to the house in Cornwall to retrieve his stash from the garden. But his joy turned to despair when he realised the men who'd turned him in had already dug it up. He went looking for them but apparently, hearing of his release, they'd gone into hiding.'

Ahmed grunted with outrage. It was easy to see whose side he was on. And him a police officer!

'Fact being stranger than fiction,' Georgina went on, 'John Daly turned over a new leaf! He gave up his life of crime and went straight. Maybe he realised his freedom was riches enough when he saw his comrades go down for thirty years apiece. Freedom, and a chance to have his life back must have seemed pretty damned good, even without the money, when the alternative was thirty years in prison without parole. He moved to Cornwall with his family and became a dustman and road sweeper. He died in 2013 having stayed on the straight and narrow for the rest of his life.'

'What happened to the two men and the money they robbed?' Ahmed asked.

'That's where the story becomes even stranger,' Georgina said. 'Both men died of natural causes within six months. Perhaps that was divine retribution, or justice, or whatever you wish to call it. Whatever, they didn't get to enjoy the profits of their subterfuge and theft for long. Their names were Bill Goodwin and Michael Black. Police never discovered what Black did with his share of the money. But after Goodwin died detectives found what remained of his share of the loot bricked into his kitchen wall.'

Adam sipped his Jack Daniels and swirled it around in his glass. 'I imagine you're about to tell us how Michael Black's share came to be bricked up into another wall entirely,' he said. 'I'm guessing that's where all of this is leading up to? He somehow arranged for it to be hidden in the Temple of Ramses II at Abu Simbel?'

'Black knew the police were closing in,' Georgina nodded. 'As a trader in antiquities he had contacts who could put him in touch with people being signed up for UNESCO's project to save the temples of Abu Simbel from the rising floodwaters of Lake Nasser. I can only presume he didn't know his life expectancy was so short. He just needed a safe place to stow the cash; somewhere the police would never think of looking. I imagine he planned to come to Egypt and retrieve it at some later date. Anyway, he stuffed a large suitcase full of the money and travelled to Abu Simbel.'

'He blagged his own way onto the project?' Adam gaped with bulging eyes.

'No; that would have been a bit much to expect,' Georgina admitted. 'But he struck a deal with one of the Arab labourers assigned to the team. Black transferred the money into a metal security box – one of those ones with a combination lock. He was the only one who knew the code. He paid the labourer handsomely to hide the box away as the temple was rebuilt, somewhere he would be able easily to retrieve it from later. My information is that there is a false wall in the inner sanctuary of the temple.'

'That's where the four rock cut sculptures of Ramses seated among the gods Amun-Ra, Ptah and Ra-Harakhty are!' Adam exclaimed wide-eyed.

'Yes, neat to have the gods watching over the haul, don't you think?' Georgina said. 'Anyway, the essential point is that it's still there. The Arab labourer was killed in an accident; crushed when one of the huge blocks slipped from the crane that was shifting it. And, as we know, Black died not long after leaving Egypt. He'd sent word to the labourer that his son would come back for the cash.'

'How do you know all this?' I asked suspiciously.

Georgina regarded me steadily and jutted out her chin. 'As we have already established,' she said somewhat defensively, 'I was involved in the phone hacking scandal that rocked the British Press a couple of years ago. I lost my job as a result.'

'You said you were fired for writing a politically sensitive piece your bosses didn't like,' I reminded her.

She continued to meet my gaze. 'Yes, well, that may not have been strictly true,' she confessed.

'They sacked you for phone hacking,' I said.

'Yes,' she admitted. 'But don't for one minute think I was the only one guilty of it.'

I raised an eyebrow, but decided to let this go. 'So you learned about the Abu Simbel cash through hacking someone's phone?'

'Every time one of the great train robbers dies, the Press re-hashes the story,' she said, still in the same defensive tone. 'A new book came out to mark the fiftieth anniversary of the heist, and a documentary was made not long afterwards. Since not all the money has been recovered, there is naturally public interest in what may have happened to it.'

'Granted,' I said. 'So where does the phone hacking fit in?'

'I was researching the story quite legitimately and stumbled across the fact that Goodwin and Black stole John Daly's share of the haul. Since one half of the trail went cold when Black died I decided to do some investigating of my own. It turned out, not only was Black an antiquities trader, he was also a petty criminal, part of the network of crooks John

Daly was mixed up in before the Great Train Robbery. His son, Mickey Black followed very much in the family tradition. He was unable to come to Abu Simbel to retrieve the strong box because only a couple of months after his father's death he was locked up for fifteen years for a bungled bank robbery in which a bank clerk was seriously injured. The poor chap later died in hospital.'

Ahmed's face was a picture. 'These men, they were not very good at robbery, were they?' he remarked. Ahmed would know, of course. He's descended from a villainous family of thieves with a rather more successful track record.

Georgina continued as if he hadn't interrupted. 'When Mickey Black was released in the early eighties, he did indeed travel to Egypt, only to be killed in a road traffic accident when the bus he was travelling on from Aswan crashed into a truck. It was reading about his death in Egypt that put me onto the trail. Why, I asked myself, would a man just released from prison make it his mission to travel to Abu Simbel; literally as the first thing he did, and on his own? I decided to hack into the Black family phones. I don't mind admitting it was the work of more than two years of my journalistic career. But over the course of those two years, I pieced the story together. Suffice it to say, the Black family has made a number of attempts over the years to get to Abu Simbel to retrieve the money. They have always failed. And now, of course, they realise that a stash of 1960s cash is worthless to them. The bulk of the banknotes of the Great Train Robbery were 1960s £1 and £5 notes. As I'm sure you know, Merry and Adam, the £1 note went out of circulation as legal British currency in 1985. The haul of £5 notes from the train robbery was a mixture of both the older white note and the newer blue note, which was half its size. There were also ten-shilling notes and Irish and Scottish money. These have all ceased to be legal tender over recent years. I think it's fair to say the Black family – very reluctantly – has given up on the loot.'

'You're telling us it wasn't a descendent of Michael Black attempting to clunk you on the head with a chunk of stone at Philae today?' Adam enquired.

Finally we were getting to the nub of things. 'No,' Georgina admitted. 'That strong box full of cash from The Great Train Robbery may be worthless to the criminal fraternity but it's worth its weight in gold...'

'...To a journalist!' I finished for her.

Chapter 5

Before Georgina was able to respond to my deduction, Mehmet interrupted us. He burst into the lounge bar waving a sheaf of printed photographs. 'I think I may have a picture of the man on the temple roof!' he announced excitedly.

We all looked up in surprise. He'd been holed up in his cabin since we got back, and hadn't heard any of Georgina's revelations. Instead it seemed he'd been doing some investigation work of his own.

'I scanned the faces of all of the people in the shots I took at Edfu, Kom Ombo and at Philae,' he said. 'I like to have people in my pictures. It helps with scale and perspective. And, look! This same man appears in several shots.' He went across to the table, not yet set for dinner, and spread out his photographs.

We all jumped up and crowded around.

'As you can see, he is turning away in most of them, almost as if he has spotted me with the camera and does not wish to be photographed. He appears to be on his own, which is what drew my attention to him. Everyone else is in couples or else in groups. And look! I have managed to capture this one shot of him where he has not noticed me.' Mehmet pointed at a picture taken at Philae earlier. It showed the Kiosk of Trajan, that strange four-poster-bed-like structure. At the far end of it, climbing the steps into the monument was a man. I'd have to say he was pretty nondescript. Wearing a tourist's garb of pale cotton trousers and a checked shirt with trainers on his feet, I'd have walked past him and not noticed him. In fact I'm quite sure I had probably done just that.

Mehmet pointed to another of his pictures. This time it was taken at Edfu, a nicely composed photograph of a stone carving of the falcon god Horus. I remembered seeing the statue in the temple courtyard, one of a pair flanking the doorway into the vestibule.

This time the man was in the distance and in profile. But it was undoubtedly the same chap.

'And here he is again, look,' Mehmet invited pointing to one of his images from Kom Ombo.

This was not one of his black and white atmospheric shots. It was a wide-angle picture of the entire twin temple complex. It showed Adam and me standing at the foot of one of the tall stone gateways. Habiba and Ahmed were slightly off to one side looking up at the wall reliefs. I didn't immediately spot our mystery man. In fact, it looked as if avoiding being spotted was his objective. He was peering around one of the stone columns. And the person he was peering at so intently appeared to be me.

'I had a feeling we were being watched.' I breathed on a note of discovery. 'When you jumped out on us, Mehmet, I decided it must have been *you* secretly taking your photographs. But, looking at this picture, it seems I was right to feel jumpy. It certainly appears he was spying on us, don't you think? Perhaps he's been looking for an opportunity to strike all along.'

Georgina let out a low groan. 'His name is Philip Sinnerman,' she said dully. 'And yes, Meredith, he is indeed a journalist.'

* * *

'She said she trusted him before he threw her to the wolves at work,' I reminded Adam as we were getting ready for bed in the privacy of our cabin later that evening.

'If there's no honour among thieves, it appears it's even worse among journalists!' he remarked. 'They positively stab each other in the back!'

'Or, worse, go around with murderous intent, dropping chunks of stone from temple tops onto unsuspecting ex-colleagues down below!' I sat down on the little stool in front of my dressing table and stared at him across the bed.

'Thank God for Habiba and Ahmed!' Adam said, pulling his shirt over his head. 'Between them they averted an incident that could have put paid to this entire trip.'

I turned to my own reflection in the mirror and smoothed moisturiser onto my skin. 'You know, just once, it would be really nice if we could get on with our lives here in Egypt without some troublemaker on our tail jeopardising things.'

He came to stand behind me and squeezed my shoulders, dropping a kiss on top of my head. 'I'll second that,' he murmured. 'But, for once, it's not you and me he's after; it's Georgina. It seems shopping her for phone hacking to their newspaper bosses and getting her sacked wasn't enough for him. Now he wants to steal a march on the scoop.'

'It sounds to me like he dobbed her in to save his own skin,' I remarked acidly. 'From what Georgina said, he was just as guilty as she of phone hacking. It seems they were all at it. Trinity Mirror had to fork out damages totalling nearly one-and-a-quarter million quid after the High Court ruling a couple of years ago. A whole load of journalists were involved. Georgina Savage was quite clearly one. And so was this Philip Sinnerman. He only escaped dismissal because he cut himself a deal informing on the others.'

'Exactly my point about being a bunch of backstabbing crooks! And, my God, they're aptly named, aren't they? Savage and Sinnerman! Honestly! You couldn't make it up!'

I met his gaze in the mirror. 'I wonder why he didn't head straight to Abu Simbel when Georgina was fired.'

'According to Georgina, he didn't know the full story of what she was working on. She'd hinted she was on the trail of some of the missing money from The Great Train Robbery, and that there was a link to Egypt, but she hadn't told him the finer details. It seems it was only when he saw all the Media coverage of Nefertari's tablets at the back end of last year, in which Georgina's name featured so prominently, he put two and two together and realised she may be here hunting for the stash.'

'Well, I fail to see how he hopes to find it first by killing her!' I remarked. 'You'd think his best bet would be to lay low, follow her, and then swipe the money out from under her nose at the last minute.'

'Perhaps he knows more than she thinks he does,' Adam speculated. 'It's possible he was able to hack into her files after she lost her job. Although, that being the case, you'd think he might have high tailed it straight to Abu Simbel as you suggested, rather than dogging her footsteps.' He shrugged. 'I'm at a loss. Maybe he was just trying to scare her today. Or perhaps buy himself some time. If any one of our party were killed or badly injured it would stop us in our tracks.'

'I still think we should report it to the police,' I said. 'I mean, Georgina has told us his name. So it's not as if we don't have a suspect.'

He met my troubled gaze in the mirror. 'You're probably right,' he acknowledged. 'But as she also pointed out, there were four of us up on the temple roof and not one of us actually saw him. Mehmet's photographs don't necessarily prove his guilt. Georgina seems pretty keen to avoid police involvement. She doesn't want to rake up the whole phone hacking saga again. And it will massively slow things up if we have to hang around to be interviewed. We're here to do a job. I don't dare imagine what Director Ismail will have to say if he hears we're up to our necks in it within a few scant days of leaving Luxor. In all honesty, Merry, while I'm sure going to the police is probably the right thing to do; I'd prefer to stay in control of our own destiny insofar as such a thing is actually possible. We're alerted to the chap's presence. We know what he looks like thanks to Mehmet's photographs. And from now on we'll be on our guard.'

'Forgive me for not being convinced,' I parried, and turned around on the stool to look up at him. 'Do you think we're doing the right thing allowing Georgina to come with us to Abu Simbel?' I asked with soft seriousness. 'As you rightly said, it's her he's after, not us. So having her along is drawing us into danger. And, you're right; we're here to do a job. Ahmed was injured today. I don't want it to be one of us next.'

Adam crouched down in front of me and took my hand. 'I really don't see that we have much choice. Georgina has taken us into her confidence now.'

'We could suggest she flies down to Abu Simbel, or takes the bus; and we could meet her there in a few days?' I suggested.

'But what if Sinnerman gets to her and hurts her?' Adam frowned. 'I'd never forgive myself. At least all the time we're together as a group she has a measure of protection.'

I looked into his eyes. Adam is a total sucker for a damsel in distress – even one as un-damsel-like as Georgina Savage. He stared back at me, darkly lashed eyes blue and beguiling. Unexpectedly I felt a slow spreading smile steal across my face. 'You want to go searching for the money, don't you?' I accused.

I watched his face split into a grin. 'For my sins, I do!' he confessed, completely changing the tone of our discussion. 'That was quite some story Georgina came out with this evening. I'll admit she's got me hooked! Surely even Director Ismail can't fling us out of Egypt if we happen to find a stash relating back to a thoroughly British heist…?'

'Even if it means searching for a false wall in the inner sanctuary of the Great Temple of Ramses…?' I challenged back.

'Look at it this way, Merry,' he invited. 'Saleh el-Sayed has been told to grant us access all areas. He's so far managed to arrange for us to climb to the top of the Great Pyramid, and go up onto the roof of the Temple of Isis at Philae. Both are unauthorised to tourists, and have been for years. I'll bet he can pull a few strings to get us into the Temple of Ramses II after hours so we can have a little scout around in private. There are advantages to having friends in high places in the Tourism Authority. Not to mention travelling with an Inspector for the Ministry of State for Antiquities. They're both trump cards Georgina's old nemesis Philip Sinnerman doesn't hold.'

I scarcely dared dignify this with a response. 'Director Ismail will have no need to fling us out of Egypt if we're dead,' I pointed out with a touch of acerbity. 'That was a pretty big gauntlet Philip Sinnerman threw down today.'

'No, Merry, it was a rock,' he said. 'And we're onto him now. Like you, I'm sick to death of people setting out to sabotage us. But he's played his hand and, frankly, I think we stand a better chance of putting a stop to him than the police here in Egypt do.'

We stared at each other for a long moment. I could feel my instincts going to war with my better judgement. Despite – or perhaps because of – everything that had happened, his eyes were alight. And I could feel the urge to giggle bubbling up in my throat. He had me and he knew it. I love it when Adam is all buoyed up with the spirit of Boy's Own adventure. It's part of the reason I fell in love with him in the first place. It occurred to me it perhaps ought to be the British police we should contact. But that would assuredly put an end to our current venture.

Adam could see me wavering. He leaned forward and touched his lips to mine. 'Willing to take the risk, hope for the reward and live with the consequences?' he asked. 'After all, Ahmed's the one who got hurt, and he's game.'

'Ahmed has the blood of his dodgy ancestors flowing in his veins,' I muttered. 'Of course he's game. He's got pound signs lighting up in his eyes!'

But we were grinning at each other now, both caught up in the thrill of adventure. It's a characteristic we share, part of what makes us soulmates. Although I'm sure many would say we lead each other astray. That there may be consequences,

I had no doubt. But I was starting to think it was a bridge we could cross as and when we came to it.

'I think all that talk of The Great Train Robbery may have gone to my head!' Adam admitted.

'Either that or the Jack Daniels,' I remarked.

'I'm not interested in the money,' he said, lest I should think he'd finally gone over to the dark side never to return.

'I should think not. Georgina has already pointed out it's worthless.'

'It's the thrill of it,' he admitted, and then chuckled. 'You know, we set out on this trip to Abu Simbel with absolutely no hope of finding anything. I'm perfectly willing to accept that Helen of Troy is a lost cause. But knowing for sure there's a stash of cash hidden there has set my brain on fire. Put it this way, I feel very motivated to find it before Philip Sinnerman does.' His gaze locked with mine. 'Let's not forget we've dealt with worse villains than some sleezy British journalist,' he reminded me. 'I say we give this Philip Sinnerman a run for his money. Literally. What do you reckon, Merry?'

I gazed back and felt a slow smile tug at the corners of my mouth 'I reckon Georgina needs our support,' I murmured. 'A chance to find some of the money stolen in The Great Train Robbery sounds to me like a damn fine reason to go to Abu Simbel. I'm sure Giovanni Belzoni won't mind our ulterior motive!'

* * *

Habiba put up some token resistance of course. This was only natural and to be expected. She was in a conflicted position, torn between her employer and us. And it was her fiancé who'd been injured after all. I could fully understand her protests about the recklessness of our plan to proceed as if nothing had happened.

In the end it was Ahmed who swung things. He pointed out she could perhaps turn a blank eye – by which he meant blind of course – to our search for the stash of loot at Abu Simbel since it wasn't Pharaonic treasure. Habiba knew us well enough to know we would in no way damage the temple. But, he said, it might serve all of our interests to put the security team at Abu Simbel on red alert and ensure no one was left alone inside the Great Temple at any time. As a Member of staff for the Ministry of Antiquities, Habiba was uniquely placed to say she'd had a tip off about looters in the area. In these straitened times, and with all the News coverage of the discovery of Nefertari's tablets, interest in the twin temples of Abu Simbel was at an all time high. There were international dealers who would pay handsomely for a chunk of the wall reliefs chipped from the temple ruins.

Thus assured Philip Sinnerman would have no chance of making a search for the money should he beat us there, even assuming he knew where to look, we could get underway again. Nobody would be any the wiser about the mishap that had befallen us at Philae.

Good old Ahmed. He might have a tomb robber's instincts but he also had a police officer's nous. I feel quite certain he also had his own ways of persuading Habiba around to his way of thinking in the privacy of his cabin away from our prying eyes.

So it was decided. We were to continue our trip to Abu Simbel and throw in our lot with Georgina Savage. But we knew we'd have to make a report of some sort, even if only to satisfy the curiosity of the guards who'd helped us get Ahmed to the boat at Philae.

We decided our best bet was to take responsibility ourselves. I felt sure we could talk Saleh and Mehmet around to our way of thinking, since they too in their roles as Marketing Manager and Official Photographer had such a big stake in the success of our trip.

I made the report jointly to Director Ismail and Zahed Mansour myself. My email said simply that while on the temple roof I had inadvertently leaned on one of the loose stones, which had come free and fallen. I admitted to Ahmed's injury but played it down. I finished by thanking them for the opportunity to see where Sarah Belzoni had camped out, but added it was a good thing visitors were not allowed on the roof. It was a health and safety hazard too far. I had my fingers crossed behind my back the whole time – not easy when typing. Luckily I mastered the art of one-handed typing when I broke my wrist a few years ago.

Inspired afresh to make a success of this mission, and perhaps to assuage my guilt, I penned an evocative blog post. It described Sarah, a woman before her time, camping out on the roof of the Temple of Isis at Philae with quantities of silver and two loaded pistols. I hit the "publish" button very much hoping my readers would thrill to learn of her serene stoicism as I did. From here onwards, the story of digging Abu Simbel from the sand would be very much her husband's. And it was just possible even he was about to have his thunder stolen should we prove successful in finding the train robbers' haul.

'Now we just need to wait and see if Saleh el-Sayed has been successful in arranging things for us to sail across Lake Nasser on the *Queen Ahmes*,' I said to myself, and went to find the others.

Even allowing for the construction of the Aswan dams in the twentieth century, it would have been impossible for us to sail on past Aswan in the dahabeeyah. Even in the Belzonis' day and further back into antiquity, the Nile was impassable at this point thanks to the First Cataract. This was a shallow length of white water rapids full of small boulders and stones breaking the surface, ready to rip the bottom out of any boat attempting the crossing.

Belzoni commissioned a new boat to take him into Nubia. It looked distressingly as if Adam and I may have to do the same – or else accept a booking on one of the cruisers offering the Lake Nasser crossing to tourists.

But Saleh el-Sayed once again worked his magic. I couldn't help but think what a good thing it was that we'd made friends with the Marketing Manager at last. Perhaps saving him from a deadly cobra strike had been a lucky omen after all – the goddess Wadjet looking out for us.

Whatever; while Ahmed and Habiba took a trip back to the hospital to get his wound re-dressed, and while Georgina, Mehmet, Adam and I visited the Unfinished Obelisk and the High Dam, lunching at the Old Cateract Hotel; Saleh oversaw the repositioning of the *Queen Ahmes* from the Nile to a mooring platform on Lake Nasser. This was achieved by virtue of a huge crane, which hoisted her onto the back of an enormous wide-load-bearing truck for the short drive to her new location. There, she was once more lifted into the water.

The beauty of being able to sail across Lake Nasser onboard the *Queen Ahmes* was we could set our own course and pace. Had we been forced to join one of the cruise boats it would have meant slowing down to take part in their touring itineraries. These took in the numerous monuments UNESCO and the world community saved from the flooding of Lake Nasser back in the sixties.

I fully planned to visit them on our journey back from Abu Simbel, some 280 kilometres to the south. I hadn't seen them before and didn't want to miss out. But since it was imperative to get to Abu Simbel as quickly as possible we instructed Khaled to set our course full steam ahead and agreed not to break the journey for sightseeing.

I could only hope Philip Sinnerman had opted for a cruise; perhaps believing it's what we would do. If so, we would beat him to Abu Simbel and also foil any further attempts on Georgina he may be planning. I didn't suppose he could imagine we'd have enough string-pulling power to get the *Queen Ahmes* relocated to Lake Nasser.

Still, seeing as we had at least a full day's sailing ahead of us, I decided my next blog should tell the story of the international rescue mission to save Nubia's monuments, even though I wasn't seeing them for myself just yet. I hoped it may encourage tourists to take the tour and visit some of these wonders of modern as well as ancient engineering, rather than just do the day trip to Abu Simbel offered on the standard Nile cruise packages.

Zahed Mansour at the Egyptian Tourism Authority would approve, I felt sure. In fact, he needn't know we were hell bent on getting to Abu Simbel with all possible speed. I could see no harm in allowing him to imagine we were taking a nice leisurely time over our trip. So long as I kept posting blogs to my online travelogue I considered I was upholding my part of the bargain. He'd be none the wiser, and it seemed a reasonable way of ensuring we both got what we wanted. I call that a win-win.

So I sat at my computer as we sailed across this, one of the largest manmade reservoirs in the world. It was strange to look up from the screen and see a huge expanse of water from the window rather than the dusty palm-lined riverbank I was more used to. With little in the view to distract me I lost myself in telling the story of "UNESCO's monumental project".

I was quite pleased with this title for my piece. I considered it a rather nice play on words. UNESCO – the United Nations Educational, Scientific and Cultural Organisation – brought together missions from around the world to save Nubia's monuments. They moved many to higher ground, the best known being the two temples of Abu Simbel. They relocated a number of others to Khartoum in the Sudan. And dismantled many more, which they gave to donor countries such as Spain, Italy, Germany, and the United States. In the end the international effort rescued upwards of twenty temples and ancient complexes. Even so, hundreds of archaeological sites, including some temples, were inundated. These remain lost forever under the waters of Lake Nasser. Not forgetting the many thousands of people who had to be resettled.

I hoped it was worth it. I knew the Aswan High Dam, which created Lake Nasser, was built to protect Egypt from floods and drought. We'd had quite an instructive visit while the dahabeeyah was being relocated. The dam also enabled increases in agriculture, employment and electricity. Not to mention the benefits to tourism. Nile cruises became increasingly popular after the War. The annual flooding of the Nile, so critical to Egypt's ancient civilisation, made the mighty river difficult to navigate at certain times of year. Summer floods weren't conducive to sightseeing. And during the winter the natural flow of the Nile was too low for cruise ships. So all in all I had to conclude that yes, it had been a worthwhile enterprise.

And, let's face it; the re-siting of Abu Simbel, the largest and most audacious of the rescue missions, had provided a unique opportunity to hide away money stolen in The Great Train Robbery. Fired up by the prospect of finding it, I closed down my computer and went to see what the others were doing.

I found Adam, Georgina and Mehmet up on the sundeck under the wide canvas awning. Ahmed was in his cabin resting, and Habiba was with him.

I raised an eyebrow when Adam told me this, looking up at me with a smile before returning to the book he was reading. I suspected "resting" was a euphemistic term. Still, I had good reason to know of the recuperative qualities of such rest. I'd been of the view for a long time that it was just the sort of remedy Ahmed and Habiba needed to cement things between them after the misunderstanding that had for so long stood in the way of their engagement. So I grinned my approval and said no more.

The sun was once more starting to set. Unusually the sky overhead wasn't clear blue, but filled with drifting white clouds. It looked very much as if some godly hand had pulled apart huge balls of cotton wool and strewn them across the horizon. As the fiery sun sank westwards it tinted the clouds orange, yellow and purple and sent a deep crimson glow across the water. It was beautiful.

Mehmet was busy with his camera, capturing the glory. I noticed he'd attached a filter to his lens, no doubt intensifying the pastel shades to more of a hothouse palette in the sky.

'I posted another blog,' I said conversationally, pouring myself a glass of chilled lemon juice from the jug Rabiah left in the shade. I sank onto one of the loungers alongside Georgina, sipping her habitual gin and tonic. 'I think I managed to tell the story of the rescue project without giving all the facts and figures about every re-sited temple. I'll upload some of Mehmet's sunset photos later. Hopefully it will encourage potential holidaymakers to consider adding a Lake Nasser cruise to their bucket lists.'

Georgina picked up the sheaf of printed photographs from the steamer chair next to her where Mehmet had been sitting, and started to flick through them. 'Yes, we've rather overdone the temples in the last few days, haven't we?' she agreed. 'What with Esna, Edfu, Kom Ombo and Philae. Probably good to have a break for a bit. Still, I'm sorry to be missing out on some of the sites as we sail south. I hear Kalabasha, Dakka and Derr are all well worth a visit. I don't remember which of them it was, but I read somewhere one of the smaller temples was chipped away from the bedrock fully intact before being raised to higher ground! That's some feat of modern engineering. I was looking forward to seeing it.

Damn Philip Sinnerman, coming along to stick a bloody great spanner in the works.'

I wasn't looking at her as she spoke. Instead I was gazing at the sunset, enjoying the bitter/sweet taste of my freshly squeezed lemonade, and starting to drift into a lazy torpor of idle conversation. Even so, I was aware of the sudden stillness that settled over her as she broke off with a gasp.

I turned my head on the lounger and came fully alert as I caught sight of the expression on her face. 'Georgina, what is it?' I sat upright and stared at her. It was a question I felt I'd asked rather too many times over the last few days.

Adam also looked up from his book and frowned.

Hot colour swept into Georgina's cheeks. Her eyes bulged. I could see her throat working as if she were trying to speak. But no words emerged. Only a strangled sort of choke escaped her lips.

'Georgina?' Adam put down his book and got up.

'Dear Lord,' she said, one hand going to her throat, while she stared fixedly at one of Mehmet's photographs on her lap.

I got up too, and went to look over her shoulder.

The photograph was one of the ones taken at the Temple of Horus at Edfu. It was a different image to the one showing Philip Sinnerman in profile beyond the statue. I frowned at it, trying to see what Georgina was so alarmed about. As far as I could see, Philip Sinnerman didn't feature in this shot.

Slowly, with a shaking hand, Georgina reached out and extended one finger, pointing at a rather blurry figure captured standing in the distance of the picture.

I narrowed my eyes on the person. It was clearly a man. But definitely not Philip Sinnerman. This one was bigger, wearing jeans and a polo shirt.

'Someone else you know?' Adam deduced. 'I have to say it's not a very clear image.'

Georgina gulped and swallowed audibly. 'It ... it's – er – it's my ex-husband,' she stuttered. 'I'd know him anywhere!'

'Your ex-husband?' I parroted in surprise, meeting Adam's eyes over her shoulder.

'Max Savage,' she provided.

Adam made a face at me, rolling his eyes heavenwards. He didn't need to comment. I knew exactly what he was thinking.

'We didn't part on good terms,' she said shakily. 'It was an acrimonious divorce.'

Adam put it into words anyway. 'So, you're telling us there are in fact *two* men here in Egypt who might be motivated to drop a stone block on you from a great height!'

Georgina made a visible attempt to gather together her shredded composure. 'Quite possibly,' she said.

Chapter 6

We moored up overnight so we could get an early start in the morning. Khaled said it would only take another couple of hours or so of sailing to reach Abu Simbel. But we wanted to arrive in daylight. And Khaled needed to rest.

Georgina clammed up about the circumstances of her divorce after making her pronouncement. This was unlike Georgina. She was rather more prone to direct uninhibited personal sharing. To see her sitting through dinner picking at her food and wearing a hunted expression was completely unlike her.

Beyond admitting that she may have let slip about the money hidden at Abu Simbel – determined to make it clear to him that she would be just fine without him – she refused to be drawn. I could only think her ex-husband must be a man she wished to avoid at all costs.

'I'm rather glad we didn't go to the police after all,' Adam said. We were in bed discussing the unexpected turn of events. 'We'd look bloody foolish if we'd had Philip Sinnerman arrested only to find Max Savage was the one guilty of attempted murder. I can only assume they must both be here in Egypt hoping for a pop at finding the train robbers' haul themselves.'

'Poor Georgina,' I empathised. 'She's not had much luck with the men in her life, has she? I wonder what she's done to inspire such antipathy.'

'Men generally don't warm to female bulldozers,' he murmured.

I smiled. 'She didn't seem quite such a bulldozer tonight. More like a galleon with the wind sucked out of her sails.'

'Hmm, she's thoroughly rattled, isn't she? I'm glad Ahmed offered to keep watch while we're moored. We really don't want any unexpected visits from disgruntled exes – be they husbands or colleagues. Honestly! Two men out to get her! It beggars belief!'

'She told me once that Max Savage was her second failed marriage,' I said. 'They divorced last year, not long before she foisted herself on us in Cairo.'

'Did she say why?'

I wrinkled my brow, thinking back and trying to recall. 'Something about him being fixated on his mother if I remember rightly.'

He raised an eyebrow. 'Seems like a damned strange reason. I mean, I've heard about breaking up over another woman. But his *mother*?'

I shrugged. 'I don't remember the details.'

'Yes, well, I'm rather thinking you were right all along, Merry. We should have booted her off in Aswan and let her make her own way to Abu Simbel. I really don't want to get caught up in someone else's relationship problems.'

I turned my head on the pillow and stared at him. 'What happened to my Prince Charming husband, always out to rescue the damsel in distress?'

He grinned at me. 'You're right,' he said. 'That wasn't very chivalrous of me. Poor old Georgina; she's obviously a lady who inspires male passion. Even if it's the wrong sort.'

'Speaking of which...' I murmured, and turned into his arms.

* * *

We were up before dawn, eager for our first glimpse of Abu Simbel. We breakfasted up on deck as Khaled unfurled the sails and started up the engine. The first fingers of light stole across the sky as we got underway. Ahmed, who'd kept watch all night, returned to his cabin to sleep. Rabiah took Georgina breakfast in her cabin. Habiba and Mehmet joined Adam and me up on deck. The breaking dawn was almost as colourful as sunset: a golden glow starting at the horizon, sending yellow streaks across a vast velvety sky turning from navy to cobalt to sapphire, finally lightening to a cornflower blue softened at the edges by a pink haze as the temperature started to rise. Today there were no clouds. The sky was clear and empty overhead, a vaulting expanse with no beginning or end.

Mehmet got busy cleaning his camera lenses with chemical wipes, and then went to stand at the handrail at the prow of the dahabeeyah. I fetched my laptop and sat with it on my knees so I could record my impressions of arriving at Abu Simbel over water for the blog I would write later. I was ridiculously excited. Even without all of our ulterior motives, Georgina's menacing men, and despite all the time I'd spent in Egypt, this was my first visit. I felt quite breathless with anticipation to see Ramses' famous temples.

'Giovanni Belzoni didn't know it was a lost temple of Ramses II he was digging out of the sand,' Adam said, reading my mind as he always does. 'But he noted the similarity between the colossi of Abu Simbel and the bust of the Younger Memnon he'd hauled from the Ramesseum. He guessed they might be the same man. It shows he was far from stupid. To a lot of people the statues of the pharaohs all look the same. Belzoni determined there and then he'd make his name as the man to free the temple of choking sand.'

'It seems to me Giovanni Belzoni and Ramses II had one characteristic in common,' I said. 'They were both great showmen. But sadly Belzoni's story has been largely lost, whereas surely everyone in the civilised world has heard of Ramses the Great.'

'It's over three millennia since he was pharaoh, and his name has never been forgotten,' he nodded. 'It's quite some legacy. Of course, it helps that he got a mention in the Bible – at least his new capital city did. And many of his successors chose the name "Ramses" in the futile hope it might endow their reigns with the same glory. "Ramses" is the name synonymous with Pharaonic rule in Egypt.'

'He had one great advantage over the pharaohs who came before and after him,' Habiba said, joining in the conversation. She poured herself a coffee from the silver pot Rabiah had left on the table. 'He ruled for upwards of sixty years. Plenty of time to complete monumental building projects in all corners of Egypt.'

'And he was a man with an ego, a master of self-promotion,' Adam nodded. 'When he came to the throne he sent out a gang of workmen armed with plaster, mallets and chisels to superimpose his cartouche over the names of previous kings. He knew with one hammer blow he could re-write history. By the end of his reign there was scarcely a monument in the Nile Valley without his name stamped on it.'

'Just like Giovanni Belzoni,' I said to reinforce my point. 'He also carved his name everywhere he went.'

'And I suspect Ramses, like Belzoni, felt he had something to prove,' Adam agreed. 'Belzoni wanted to be taken seriously as an explorer and leave his circus strongman days behind. Ramses wanted to be Egypt's greatest pharaoh. That in itself wasn't unusual. Almost every Egyptian king wanted to be a brave warrior, a mighty builder, an educated scribe and an effective priest. But Ramses went one step further. Even in his own lifetime he established the cult of Ramses the living god. All pharaohs were thought to be semi-divine. But Ramses went the whole hog. Until now, scholars have believed it was because he was the third of a line of commoner pharaohs, which made his urge towards self-justification even stronger. But we now know, thanks to those stone tablets and the wine-jar letters we found at Armana, he was in fact descended from the once-glorious 18th Dynasty. He couldn't admit it without linking himself to the hated heresy of Akhenaten.'

'I wonder whether that's why he had his stonemasons target so many of Amenhotep III's temples,' Habiba mused. 'Almost forty peaceful years on the throne allowed Amenhotep to build on some of the most prominent sites in Egypt. Ramses enlarged, rebuilt and stamped his own cartouche all over Amenhotep's Theban monuments. Maybe it was his way of associating himself with his illustrious forbear without owning up to the relationship.'

'They do say imitation is the sincerest form of flattery,' I murmured. 'Whether the same can be said about usurpation is another matter.'

I'm not sure how long we'd have gone on in similar vein. Once we get started, Adam and I can talk ancient Egyptian history for hours on end. And of course Habiba was knowledgeable and educated about her country's antiquities. But a shout from Mehmet, standing at the dahabeeyah's prow as she cut through the waters of Lake Nasser brought our heads snapping up.

'Over there, look!' he pointed at the horizon. 'It's Abu Simbel!'

We leapt up and joined him at the handrail, peering eagerly into the distance. The sun was fully up now. There, across the great expanse of water a rocky headland rose up from the shoreline of Lake Nasser. I squinted against the sunshine for my first view of the temples. Two huge sandstone cliffs were angled against each other in the harsh desert terrain at the lakeside. As we sailed closer I started to see each had a rock-cut temple hewn out of the cliffs facing the water. On the right was the smaller temple built for Nefertari and dedicated to Hathor. It was an impressive façade in its own right. I could just about make out the six colossal figures standing in tall niches carved into the cliff face. But it couldn't hold my eye for long. Set at an angle to its left, the Great Temple of Ramses dwarfed it and captured my gaze. I found it impossible to look away.

I could see at once why UNESCO and the international community had set out to rescue these temples. There was nothing to compare in all of ancient Egyptian architecture. The Great Temple was surely the most magnificent monument not only of the Ramesside age but also perhaps of the entire Pharaonic era. Seeing the truly enormous seated statues of Ramses wearing the double crown of Upper and Lower Egypt, staring out impassively towards us as we sailed closer, I felt goose-bumps rise on my skin. Originally there had been four of them. Now, only three remained undamaged. The colossus sitting immediately on the left of the central entrance to the temple was missing its head and torso, broken off in an earthquake in the distant past. Even so, it was an impressive sight. I was quite sure anyone approaching Egypt from the south in antiquity and sailing along the Nile past those imposing statues was left in no doubt at all he was entering a kingdom of gods and giants. Imposing was hardly the word for it. It was a sight to strike awe, fear and respect into the stoutest of hearts. For sheer majesty, it was without equal. The pyramids of Giza and the hypostyle hall at Karnak didn't come close. Scale, yes; might and power, no.

Georgina came up the spiral staircase and forward across the deck. 'Magnificent,' she murmured, joining us at the handrail and shading her eyes with her raised hand.

'It's hard to imagine it almost entirely engulfed in drifting sand, isn't it?' Adam remarked. 'When Belzoni first came here a river of sand flowed down from the clifftop towards the Nile. Only the head and shoulders of the seated colossus on the far left were visible. The one alongside it had its head broken off in antiquity thanks to an earthquake. The jagged edge of stone at the break was almost entirely obscured by the sand. And of the remaining two, on the right side of the entrance, all that was visible was the tops of their crowns.'

I'd seen paintings by early nineteenth century travellers. Even so it was almost impossible to imagine the sheer daunting scale of the task Belzoni took on in freeing the temple entrance from the sand.

'Nefertari's temple, being set at an angle, was protected and still fully accessible.' Adam added.

'Which explains how Sarah was able to get inside to make her discovery of the stone tablets on their first visit,' I nodded.

'Belzoni – not unnaturally – was always impressed by size,' Adam went on. 'A giant of a man himself, he felt sure that, buried under its mountain of sand, lay a temple to rival the best on the plains of Thebes. Who knew what treasures it might contain?'

'I'm more interested in the treasures it still contains,' Georgina muttered. 'Can't Khaled sail this dratted dahabeeyah any faster?' Now the monuments were within sight it seemed her patience had given out.

I frowned at her. 'We're nearly there. And I'd like to think it won't be necessary for us to go to quite the same effort Giovanni Belzoni did to find it. The size of his task was enough to daunt even him.'

'Belzoni reckoned the entrance to the temple was thirty-five feet or more below the surface,' Adam said, almost as if Georgina hadn't interrupted.

I knew what it meant to him to be here. He'd dedicated more than a year of his life to putting on the Belzoni exhibition at the British Museum, its most successful ever. If I was excited, Adam was aglow with Egyptological fervour. As he spoke, I felt sure he was picturing the scene as Belzoni had experienced it. I tore my gaze away from the mighty temple to watch my husband with a soft indulgent smile as he went on.

'Ignoring the smaller temple altogether, Belzoni stumbled up the steep sandy slope to where the hawk-headed figure of the god Re-Harakhte marked the centre of the larger façade. At every step his foot sank deeper into the soft sand. As he lifted it clear the fine grains poured back into the shapeless print. He must have realised that digging here would be like trying to make a hole in water!'

I stared back at the temple, realising quite what a gargantuan project the Italian strongman had taken on. He'd had no modern machinery to help with the clearance. Just brute strength, determination, and, on his second trip, a party of men armed with spades, picks and shovels.

As we sailed closer to the shoreline the immensity of both temples became clear. The first tour parties of the day had arrived. The small knots of people looked little more than colourful specks dotting the rugged arid terrain of the temple forecourts.

'It leaves you wondering who were the greatest engineers,' I said, awed. 'The ancient Egyptians who carved the temples into the cliffs in the first place, Giovanni Belzoni for digging through the mountain of sand to find the entrance to the Great Temple, or the modern rescue team who took the entire complex apart so they could rebuild it on higher land set into manmade domes.' I gazed at the rocky headland as I said this. Quite frankly, there was no way of guessing the terrain was anything other than it looked: a barren set of shoreline cliffs surviving from the distant past.

'They're all thoroughly deserving of their place in the annals of engineering history,' Adam replied, eyes still fixed on the temple as we drew ever closer. 'As far as the ancient workmen are concerned, these temples are unique. Rather than build them from the ground up, Ramses conceived the idea of hewing them from the cliffs. The façades are carved sandstone, but beyond their entrances both temples burrow back into the living rock. Only the tombs in the Valleys of the Kings and Queens were similarly rock-cut. And of course the ancient architects famously aligned the axis of The Great Temple to the solar system. On two days each year, allegedly the dates of the king's birthday and coronation, the sun penetrated the sanctuary to illuminate the sculptures of the back wall – all except for Ptah, a god of the underworld, who always remained in the dark.'

'You might think that remarkable enough,' Habiba commented at our side. 'But the engineers who re-sited the temple in the sixties preserved the solar alignment. So on the same two dates in February and October every year the sun still penetrates to the heart of the temple. People come from around the world to witness it.'

'…Not knowing that behind the walls in the sanctuary a haul of money from The Great Train Robbery is hidden away,' Georgina added, since to her this was the essential point of our visit.

Habiba frowned at her. I'm not sure our friend from the Ministry of State for Antiquities had yet reconciled herself to our coming here to search for buried treasure. She was once more wearing her hijab wound around her face to cover her hair. With it, she'd re-assumed her air of calm and collected authority. 'The relocation of the temples to these artificial cliffs represents one of the greatest challenges of archaeological engineering history,' she said severely. 'It was so much more than simply a chance for some opportunistic British thief to commit the ultimate sacrilege of stashing his haul here!'

I nearly cheered. Habiba doesn't lack a sense of adventure. And I've seen her bubbling over with excitement. But at the same time she takes the preservation of the ancient history of her country incredibly seriously. It gave me pause for a second to wonder how she and Ahmed ultimately would square the differences between them: he with his villainous antecedence and tomb-robber's instincts despite the police badge, she with her university degree and strict professional scruples.

But Adam was smiling. 'Belzoni would have loved our search for the money,' he said. 'Part of the reason he kept on digging when it must have seemed an impossible task, was because he hoped the great temple, obscured by sand since antiquity, might be full of treasure, or at the very least valuable antiquities he could take away.'

Georgina returned his smile, perhaps sensing an ally. 'Belzoni realised the only way to dig through the sand was to make it wet,' she said, deciding to join in the conversation properly at last. Perhaps she realised no amount of impatience would get us there any faster. 'He hired villagers to bring buckets of water from the Nile. Even so, he and his team took almost a month of solid digging from dawn to dusk to clear enough sand to be able to squeeze through the hole they'd made at the top of the entrance and slide down the slope of sand into the temple. Imagine his disappointment when there was no treasure inside, just a few fragments of statuary.'

I almost blurted out to ask how on earth they'd missed the solid gold statuette of Helen of Troy. But with Mehmet and Habiba looking on, I clamped my jaws shut so as not to let it slip. I still didn't know whether Ahmed had taken his fiancée into his confidence about our beautiful but mystifying discovery. She wouldn't learn of it from me. I had no wish to undermine things between them.

Adam similarly managed to stay schtum. Instead he responded at face value. 'But still, Belzoni could sail away with the satisfaction of knowing he'd opened the largest and finest rock-cut temple in Nubia, indeed the whole of Egypt,' he said.

Perhaps because, for now at least, we'd exhausted the topic of Belzoni as well as the engineering skill of the ancient and modern architectural crews; or perhaps because Khaled was bringing the *Queen Ahmes* ever closer to the shoreline; we fell silent. For the last few minutes of sailing we all simply gawped and let the grandeur of the sight sink in.

* * *

Ahmed was rested, showered and dressed in another of his crisp security uniforms by the time we were ready to lower the gangplank. The sling he wore across his left shoulder remained a slight impediment to his return to full duties. But as he picked up his gun I could see he was determined to not let it hold him back.

Being reminded of the more sinister side of our visit brought me back down to earth with a bump. It was all very well going in search of a haul of hidden loot, but the very real risk to life and limb implicit in Georgina having not one nemesis, but two, on her trail was a bit of a dampener on proceedings.

Still, we'd made good time sailing from Aswan. I could only hope if Philip Sinnerman or Max Savage were dogging Georgina's footsteps with nefarious intent, either or both of them might still be far behind us on one of the Lake Nasser cruise boats. Certainly anyone reading my blog would have no hint of the fact we'd come straight here. I'd been careful to post about the sites along the reservoir as if writing from experience.

Then I remembered the many bus trips taken daily by touring parties coming by road from Aswan, setting off long before first light. And of course Abu Simbel was also equipped with its own small airport for those who could afford the fastest way to travel south to see the monuments, and fly in.

Saleh el-Sayed had told us he'd hire a car to drive down from Aswan. If Saleh could do it, so might anyone. I could only hope Ahmed's idea of alerting the guards to possible criminal activity in the area meant that, should either or both of Georgina's rivals have happened to get here ahead of us, they'd been prevented from stealing a march on us.

It's fair to say, I left the safety of the *Queen Ahmes* with a hefty dose of trepidation in among all the excitement and nervous anticipation. Georgina similarly seemed watchful and tense. I noticed she stayed close to Ahmed, holding her bag in front of her almost like a shield as she scanned the faces of everyone in sight.

It was good to see so many touring parties. Saleh was right. Early signs of a resurging tourist trade were promising. I hoped the number of visitors might also afford a measure of protection should we need it. I failed to see how anyone would take the risk of another attack with so many potential witnesses milling about. But we couldn't afford to be complacent.

Saleh met us, as agreed, at the ticket office. 'You have made excellent time, I see,' he greeted us, coming forward with a smile. Smartly attired as ever, he sported a nice pair of designer shades and filled the air around him with the heady aroma of expensive aftershave. 'I left Aswan to drive south very early this morning and have only just arrived. Now, I can certainly grant you a private viewing of each temple but it won't be until this evening after the tourist parties have left, and before the nightly sound and light show. Until then, I'm afraid we will have to be simple tourists. Zahed Mansour was concerned to hear about the accident at Philae, even though he only knows the half of it. We must be careful. I will arrange for extra guards at the entrance tonight to ensure your safety.'

Saleh didn't know about our search for the hidden money from The Great Train Robbery, nor that Georgina's ex-husband may be here intent on causing harm. We'd told him only that we suspected Georgina might know the man who'd dropped the stone block from the temple roof at Philae, and, that being the case, had good reason for not wishing any police involvement. I felt a bit guilty keeping him out of the loop. Especially when he was going out of his way to be helpful. But it felt like a risk too far to take him fully into our confidence. His first loyalty must surely be to his bosses. And I couldn't help but think the best way to protect Saleh and his continued employment was to keep him in the dark. Should anything untoward happen, he could say, with perfect truth he knew nothing of our ulterior motive.

Habiba was different. She was one of us, and had been there when Georgina told the story of The Great Train Robbery. Even so, I reminded myself to watch what I said. Saleh and Mehmet were both unaware of the full story. We'd agreed to keep it that way, assuring ourselves what they didn't know couldn't hurt them or put them in a conflicted position.

My first impression of the Abu Simbel temple complex as we came down the slope from the ticket office to approach the Great Temple was not of immensity. Nor yet was it of the hawkers and vendors of tacky trinkets who pursued us all the way. It was actually of sparrows. The scrubby trees near the lakeside, there to provide some measure of shade while the tour guides regaled visitors with history, were teeming with them. The air was full of their chirruping.

After half-an-hour or so scanning all the faces in sight, I dared to relax and start enjoying myself. Coming here was a dream Adam and I had harboured for a long time. I persuaded myself there was safety in numbers. Ahmed could be relied upon not to let his guard drop. And, seeing as Mehmet had provided us with photographs of each of the men Georgina was so keen to stay one step ahead of, we knew exactly whom we were looking out for. None of the visitors I'd cast my searching gaze over in any way resembled Philip Sinnerman. True, Mehmet's shot of Max Savage wasn't so clear as to make him instantly recognisable to those of us who'd never met him. But I knew Georgina would spot her ex-husband at a glance should he be prove to be lurking anywhere in the temple precinct.

'I'd really like to visit the Smaller Temple first,' I said eagerly. 'I want to see the place where Sarah Belzoni first spied Nefertari's tablets.'

The others were happy enough to acquiesce. So we trooped to the far side of the temple complex with the vast waters of Lake Nasser stretching alongside us. It was hot and dusty this far south, even this early in the year.

The façade of the temple that Ramses dedicated to his favourite queen was impressive by any standards. Six colossal figures of equal height – two of Nefertari flanked on both sides by four of her husband – stood in niches formed by the enormous buttresses of the rock-hewn frontage. The tall doorway was carved in the centre.

Inside, the air seemed choked with antiquity. Like Nefertari's tomb in the Valley of the Queens, the temple had a distinctly feminine vibe. Reliefs showing the ancient queen playing a sistrum and making offerings to Hathor the sacred cow goddess, and Tawaret the hippopotamus goddess of childbirth, adorned the inner walls. But unlike inside Nefertari's tomb, here I truly felt I was stepping back across more than thirty centuries. The inner sanctum felt at once intimate and resonant with history. Of course Nefertari's tomb had undergone a multi-million dollar restoration and preservation project quite recently. Here, despite knowing I was inside a modern domed structure manufactured within the last sixty years to resemble the ancient cliffs, I had that strange feeling of time standing still. The colours of the wall friezes were faded to be sure, not the pristine olives, ochres and russets of the ancient queen's newly touched-up burial place. Yet somehow they conveyed a greater sense of the true age of this remarkable monument, dedicated by Ramses the Great for his favourite consort.

There was though one important sense in which Nefertari's temple and her tomb were exactly the same. That being my reaction. I walked around with a lump the size of a golf ball in my throat, gazing up at the reliefs and letting the atmosphere settle into my soul.

'Ramses loved her,' Adam murmured at my side. 'Of that there can be no doubt.'

I nodded, blinked the tears back and slowly recovered myself. 'It was over here that Sarah Belzoni found the granite tablets,' I said softly, leading the way to the vestibule. I wanted to share this moment with Adam alone, without our companions looking on.

Here the graceful and poetic bas-reliefs depicted Nefertari and Ramses presenting papyrus to Hathor. Sarah recorded into her journal how she spent time here while her husband was surveying the mountain of sand obscuring the Great Temple. She wrote about how as she walked forward she realised she was crunching a black powdery substance underfoot. She realised this was decayed wood from the chest in which the stele had been stored in antiquity. She added that the few remaining intact fragments mouldered to dust at her first touch.

'Just think,' Adam said, taking my hand. 'If Sarah had taken those tablets away with her rather than just copying fragments of their hieroglyphs into her journal, everything might have turned out differently.'

I pondered this a moment. It was learning of Sarah's desperate bid to mount an expedition of her own to recover them after her husband's tragic death, that first got me interested in her; a woman I'd scarcely heard of until I stumbled across her letter to the British Museum Trustees in the archives. I realised the last couple of years of my life had been leading towards this moment, where I could stand in the same spot and picture her two hundred years ago, making the discovery.

'Or indeed if they'd still been here when she managed to get herself assigned to the Robert Hay expedition in 1825 masquerading as a young male epigrapher,' I added. As ever I felt an unbearable sadness sweep over me. Sarah's had not been a happy story after she lost her beloved husband.

'Thank God, the Belzonis' *Reis* Abdullah Soliman was able to get back here to lay claim to them before Henry Salt did,' Adam went on in a low murmur. 'If he hadn't taken them back to Luxor and hidden them away in that cave behind Seti's tomb, we'd never have found them.'

'No,' I whispered in agreement. 'Nor the golden statuette.'

Even though I'd kept my voice down, Ahmed somehow heard me. I was starting to think he had some sixth sense where that solid gold statue was concerned. He'd found it, hidden away inside a secret compartment in the Ottoman casket in which the Belzonis' *Reis* stored the tablets. His sense of personal pride in the discovery knew no bounds. If Adam and I had come here believing we had no chance whatever of finding anything further relating to Helen of Troy; Ahmed, I felt sure, had not abandoned hope.

Ensuring he cornered Adam and me with his big body, and glancing back over his shoulder to ensure the others were out of earshot, Ahmed's bright snapping eyes locked with mine. 'You speak of Abdullah Soliman,' he said. 'I have made a study of the notebook your old friend the museum curator in Luxor found in his storage rooms. I believe it contains a clue about the location where Abdullah found the solid gold statuette. I think our search may not be so lacking in ripe fruit as you first thought.'

Chapter 7

I'd almost forgotten about Abdullah Soliman's notebook. Our old comrade Ibrahim Mohassib – curator at the Luxor Museum before Director Ismail hauled him off to Cairo to gag him with a dazzling promotion – found it in his museum strong rooms. He'd given it to Adam and me when we asked him for anything he could confidently date to the early 1820s. Lest you should think this strange, I should point out Adam is a fellow Egyptologist, and British Museum employee, and we had the blessing of Dr Walid Massri of the Egyptian Antiquities Museum in Cairo. We were playing detective, trying to track down what happened to Nefertari's tablets in the time between Sarah Belzoni first spotting them in 1816, and returning (disguised as a young man) in 1825 to find them gone.

Abdullah Soliman was the Belzonis' *Reis* during their years in Egypt and Nubia. He was there for all Belzoni's major triumphs. A skilled artist, he befriended Sarah and illustrated her journal. When Henry Salt, British Consul General and Giovanni Belzoni's bitter enemy, stole Sarah's diary and returned to Egypt with it intent on claiming the tablets for himself, Abdullah suspected foul play. Employed as Salt's *ghaffir* after the Belzonis' return to England, Abdullah promptly stole the diary back. When Salt succumbed to ill health, returning to Alexandria, Abdullah Soliman was the one to make the journey to Abu Simbel to reclaim the tablets. What he would have done with them had he lived is anyone's guess. Sadly one of the Abd el-Rassul brothers murdered him – possibly on Salt's instructions, or perhaps because he'd caught wind that Abdullah was in possession of valuable antiquities. The Abd el-Rassul family had an uncanny instinct for hidden treasure and for thievery. Ahmed knew all about this. He is, after all, descended from them. Hakim Abd el-Rassul died in prison, convicted of murder. And there the trail went cold.

But locked away in the vaults of the Luxor Museum, dating to 1824, Abdullah's notebook and a drawing he'd made on a page torn from Sarah Belzoni's diary survived. With them was a strange stone carving. It spelled out the word "Atiyah" meaning "gift" in Arabic. That Abdullah himself carved it was in no doubt.

Now came the twist of fate. Abdullah's sweetheart had been a young woman called Atiyah. She was Hakim Abd el-Rassul's sister. Ahmed also has a sister named Atiyah. And this lady was in possession of a secret, passed down through generations of the female line of the family in the belief that to reveal it would unlock a deadly curse.

Receipt of Abdullah's "gift" from the Luxor Museum storage rooms broke the curse. Even without knowing what was hidden there, Atiyah was able to tell Ahmed the secret location it protected. And so we were able to bring the tablets back to light.

But the granite tablets weren't the only things locked inside. The Ottoman-styled casket also contained the solid golden statuette of Helen of Troy. Ahmed found it inside a hidden compartment, wrapped in another sheet torn from Sarah's journal. On this Abdullah had sketched The Great Temple of Ramses, showing the statuette emerging from the entrance. There was only one way of interpreting this. The statuette had come from inside.

It was a mystery to me how Abdullah had found it there when Belzoni himself had missed it. So too the numerous parties of early nineteenth century explorers and adventurers who beat a path to Abu Simbel after Belzoni cleared the entrance of choking sand. On this, the drawing gave no clue. But I'd forgotten about Abdullah's notebook.

Abdullah Soliman was a rarity among early nineteenth century Egyptians. He could write. But of course this was in Arabic. The small notebook was filled with a small rather faded squiggly handwriting full of loops and dots, quite impossible for Adam and me to read. To be fair, two-hundred-year-old English handwriting is hard enough to decipher. I'd discovered that poring over Sarah Belzoni's journals. We stood no chance whatsoever with two-hundred-year-old Arabic, written in Abdullah's own hand.

We hadn't actually needed the notebook to discover the tablets hidden away in a cave behind Seti's tomb in the Theban hills. Ahmed and Habiba had flicked through it and confirmed it did indeed reveal Abdullah's pilgrimage to

Nefertari's temple in Nubia to reclaim the tablets. That was all we'd really needed to know, confirmation of the supposition we'd already made. Then, in all the excitement and the subsequent Media scrum, I'd failed to check what had become of the notebook. I should have known Ahmed wouldn't be so remiss. I could well imagine that he'd spirited it away. He'd no doubt been poring over it in quiet moments ever since.

'A clue?' I said.

Ahmed's dark eyes sparked with excitement. 'Yes. Abdullah does not say anything directly. But he describes…'

He was unable to complete his sentence. Georgina came marching forward. 'Seen enough?' she demanded. 'Can we go and do a recce of The Great Temple of Ramses now?'

I watched Ahmed's expression close up at the interruption. It occurred to me that perhaps Georgina's impatience might be a blessing in disguise. I really didn't want to have to explain all over again that the entire temple complex had been broken apart and re-sited. Whatever it was Abdullah described in his notebook from almost two hundred years ago was almost certain not to be there now.

I cast a last long wistful look around Nefertari's inner sanctuary and followed the others back out into the sunshine.

'You can tell me later,' I murmured to Ahmed, catching him up. 'For now just keep a watchful eye out for any unwelcome visitors.'

'I have eyes in the front, back and sides of my head,' he assured me solemnly.

We strolled across the forecourt towards The Great Temple, set against the artificial cliff. This time I allowed its full majesty to impress itself on me. The façade was clearly designed to display the king in all his glory. In truth it did just that.

'Each of those four seated colossus is over sixty-five feet high,' Adam said in an awed tone. 'Well, the three undamaged ones are, at any rate.'

As Mehmet set up his camera on its tripod, the rest of us walked up the central causeway towards the entrance, flanked on each side by two of the immense statues. They dwarfed us. Ramses' Great Temple was an egotistical masterpiece.

'If his intention was to impress on all comers their insignificance alongside his kingly majesty, I'd say he made a damn fine job of it,' Georgina muttered, craning her neck back. 'Look! We reach barely up to his ankle!'

Adam paused to inspect the carved sandstone figures standing, one on each side and one in front of the lower half of the seated colossus' legs. Dwarfed by Ramses though they were, they still towered above us; way bigger than life size. 'Ramses revived the Armanan tradition of honouring the royal women,' Adam said. 'These figures are his principal wives and the dowager queen, his mother; as well as a number of his daughters. Only two men, the eldest sons of Nefertari and his secondary wife respectively are included. So, in some ways, we're looking at a royal family portrait.'

I wondered if this was another oblique hint by Ramses at his true ancestry. He couldn't link himself explicitly to Akhenaten's heresy without calling into question the legitimacy of his father and grandfather's rule. But he could emulate Akhenaten's tendency to give his royal women equal billing.

'Shame about the earthquake that toppled one of these seated colossi from its throne,' I said, wandering over to inspect the two broken sections of the massive fallen crown close to the entranceway on the south side of the façade. The UNESCO project had faithfully repositioned them in front of the badly damaged statue in the same spot they'd originally fallen. This colossus had lost its entire upper body in the quake.

'Hmm,' Georgina commented. 'It rather makes me wonder if there were gods among Egypt's pantheon that didn't much appreciate Ramses elevating himself to full divinity, and decided to knock him down a peg or two. This wasn't the only one of his gigantic statues toppled in an earthquake. Those at the Ramesseum were similarly destroyed, if you recall.'

'Shall we go inside?' Saleh invited.

We trooped from the bright sunshine through the tall doorway and into the dim interior of the vast rock-cut temple. As soon as my eyes adjusted I caught my breath, unprepared for the sight that greeted my eyes. We'd entered a lofty pillared hall. It was hard to find words to describe it. Totally unlike the hypostyle halls in the other temples we'd visited, even the roofed ones, it seemed to me we'd stepped into a ceremonial hall designed to welcome visitors to the afterlife. I shivered, and couldn't shake that sinister impression. This was more tomblike than any of the ancient sepulchres I'd visited in the Valley of the Kings. As in Nefertari's temple, the sense of antiquity was overwhelming. This temple felt every one of its more than three thousand years old. Standing here, the 13th Century BC seemed a very long time ago indeed.

Adam, struck similarly silent and awed alongside me, sucked in a breath. 'Can you imagine what this must have looked like to Belzoni and his crew, lit only with a thin shaft of sunlight from the hole they'd dug in the sand? It was its first epiphany in perhaps a thousand years. It must have been frankly terrifying to look up and see those statues...'

He gestured at the eight immense standing figures of the king fronting the line of square pillars stretching along a wide central aisle in front of us. Carved in Osirid form to represent the god of the dead and the underworld, each held a crook and flail, arms folded across the chest. They faced each other in two rows of four staring with mute impassive faces like death masks. They gave me the chills. I half expected the jackal-headed Anubis to appear to weigh my heart against the feather of truth and see if I were deemed worthy to enter the afterlife. 'This place creeps me out,' I whispered back.

Georgina did not appear to feel the same way. It seemed she'd recovered her confidence, given there was no sign of either of the men we'd feared to see. She stepped in front of Saleh determined she should be the one to provide the lecture on the temple's interior. Saleh stood back respectfully to let her get on with it. I saw Ahmed and Habiba exchange an amused glance. Mehmet had stayed outside. He would only be allowed to take photographs on our private viewing later. Photography inside the temple was strictly forbidden to the general public. He'd been granted special permission by the Ministry of Antiquities to set up his camera only once the tour parties departed. So Georgina was free to get on with her history lesson.

'I feel sure Belzoni must have realised the walls here in the main hall were decorated with scenes he recognised,' she started. 'After all, he'd surely seen them before, plastered all over the Ramesseum and in the temples of Luxor and Karnak. Here, once again, Ramses boringly re-enacts his famous charge at the battle of Kadesh.' She pointed up at the scenes on the vast southern wall. 'What Ramses had to be so proud of is a moot point. At best, the pharaoh's war exploits ended in a stalemate. At worst, the battle of Kadesh was an ignominious defeat.'

'Is this true?' Ahmed looked pop-eyed at Adam for confirmation. Ahmed is no Egyptologist. I felt quite sure he'd grown up believing Ramses to be Egypt's greatest pharaoh. Like Belzoni, he'd no doubt seen all the temple wall carvings of Ramses ploughing his chariot into the enemy army, crushing Asiatics, negros and Nubians alike, and believed Ramses the great warrior he appeared.

'I'm afraid so,' Adam nodded. 'Ramses was not the war hero he portrayed himself as – simply a master of propaganda.'

'What happened?' Ahmed asked, clearly interested in spite of himself.

Georgina was only too keen to enlighten him. 'Ramses led his army straight into a trap,' she said with evident relish. 'It started when Egyptian guards discovered two Bedouin skulking in the trees near to where Ramses' army was camped close to the Orontes river. These Bedouin claimed to be deserters from the Hittite army, and swore loyalty to Ramses. They said the Hittites were cowering many miles to the north of Kadesh, too frightened to proceed southwards to meet the pharaoh's elite troops. Ramses was stupid enough to believe them.'

'The Bedouin were actually Hittite spies spinning a yarn that would appeal to Ramses' vanity,' Adam interjected wryly. 'On the strength of this dubious information, and making no effort to check the story, Ramses decided to head straight for Kadesh to capture the city.'

'Yes, thank you, Adam,' Georgina muttered, before once again taking up the tale. 'The Egyptian army was split into four divisions, named for the gods. Ramses, riding at the head of Amun division, forded the river and marched across the plain towards Kadesh. Re division followed at some distance; leaving Ptah and Seth to bring up the rear.'

I had to hand it to her; she knew her history. But so did Adam. He nodded and went on,

'It meant the Egyptian army was strung out over several miles. Of course this wouldn't have mattered if the Bedouin had been telling the truth. Instead, Ramses marched his troops straight into an ambush. The Hittites were already at Kadesh poised to strike, and launched a fierce chariot attack. Taken completely by surprise, Ramses' army panicked.'

Georgina frowned at him and wrested back control, staring up at the wall reliefs as she spoke. 'And now we see Ramses doing what he does best: re-writing history. His temple walls the length and breadth of the land, just like this one, are plastered with images of how he alone, fired up with the godly spirit of Amun, turned his chariot to face the enemy while his army scattered. He shows no qualms over sacrificing the reputation of his troops and commanders to enhance his own valour, fighting, as he claims, single-handed to victory.'

'The truth is, Ptah and Seth divisions arrived just in time to avoid the total annihilation of the Egyptian forces,' Adam added. 'Had that not been the case I think it's possible Ramses would have suffered the humiliation of becoming the first New Kingdom monarch to be captured by the enemy. As it was, Ptah and Seth saved the day, pushing back the Hittite troops. Ramses tells us the Hittite king sued for peace. I suspect the truth is that once both armies got the full measure of each other, they realised they were in fact quite evenly matched. Whatever, they agreed a truce and both armies withdrew.'

'But that didn't stop Ramses returning home victorious to tell and re-tell the story of his great personal triumph on any expanse of temple wall he could find,' Georgina finished. 'Years later, as we know, Ramses and the Hittites signed the first peace treaty in history. It's recorded on the walls at Karnak.'

'How do you know this story of the trap to be true?' Ahmed asked with a frown, perhaps disappointed at having the heroic exploits of his nation's most famous king shown up for what they really were, the actions of a naïve, vain and inexperienced king.

It was Habiba who answered. 'Remarkably, the Hittite records of the Battle of Kadesh still survive,' she said. 'And of course they tell a different story from the one Ramses carved into temple walls the length of the Nile.'

We stared up at the temple wall reliefs, looking at the vivid battle scenes with fresh eyes.

'Right!' Georgina said abruptly. 'Enough of the history lesson! I want to see the inner sanctuary.'

I rolled my eyes at Adam. She'd been the one intent on the historical lecture. But of course we knew very well why she wanted to move on. Still alert and watchful, as we were by no means the only visitors, we explored the rest of the temple.

Beyond the hall we entered a smaller chamber with four square pillars with reliefs showing the king being embraced by the gods. Then we passed through a narrow antechamber towards the sanctuary itself.

A small tour party was there as we arrived. The space was too confined to allow us to enter. I quickly scanned the faces; reassuring myself the two men from Mehmet's photographs were not among them. Relieved to see no one I recognised, we held back while the Egyptian tour guide reeled off his patter. He was pointing out the four slim figures carved from stone seated in a row against the temple's back wall, facing towards the entrance.

'Here on the left we have mummified Ptah with his sceptre of life, power and stability,' the young tour guide pointed. 'Sadly the head has broken off at some point in the temple's long history. Now, what's remarkable about this particular figure of the four you see seated here is this: on the two dates of the annual solar alignment he stays in shadows. The sun's rays only illuminate the other three figures. Next to him here we see Amun-Ra wearing his high plumed headdress. And here is Ramses himself, admitted to the company of the gods,'

'Hmph,' Georgina muttered disparagingly at my side.

'And finally the hawk-headed Harakhte, god of the rising sun.'

I felt a shiver go through me looking at the four statues as the tour party trooped out of the sanctuary and we were left alone, able to move into the narrow space. There was something about imagining those slim figures sitting here in the pitch dark for centuries while choking sand blocked the entrance preventing the sunlight illuminating them on those two special dates each year. It gave me the chills. For all that they were four inanimate statues carved from stone, there was something strangely lifelike about them. To see them sitting patient and impassive for all eternity was unsettling.

'I can quite honestly say this temple gives me the jitters,' I said. 'There's something unaccountably creepy about it. I'm not wholly sure I want a private viewing later.'

Georgina looked at me as if I'd gone mad. 'Of course we need a private viewing,' she hissed, ensuring she was out of Saleh's earshot. 'Just remember what we've come here looking for. There's no way we can search with all these damned people about!' She was already scanning the reliefs, looking for any sign of an uneven stone that might betray the false wall.

'And remember Mehmet and his photographs,' Adam said. 'But I know what you mean. It somehow has a more animate feeling than the other temples we've visited, doesn't it?'

'I think it's because they're mostly golden sandstone from which the colours have largely faded away,' I said, trying to explain to myself why this place spooked me so. 'I suppose because this one was buried under a mountain of sand for so many centuries, the reliefs are better preserved. Honestly, it feels more like a tomb to me than a temple. The inner sanctuaries at Edfu and Philae didn't feel like this.'

'Possibly because this is more than a thousand years older than they are,' Adam reminded me. 'Or maybe it's because this is the work of one man. I daresay that's what's putting you in mind of a tomb. Most of the temples we've visited are the work of successive pharaohs, each trying to out-do the last. But here it's all about Ramses.'

'I almost feel I can sense him here,' I admitted. 'For all that he stamped his cartouche all over Egypt, this is where I think I can feel his ghost. Only, it's not a ghost exactly. It's something of the personality of the king himself. It's knowing he was once here; that he approved the carvings, commissioned the wall reliefs and made this place his own.'

'I wonder if you'd feel the atmosphere in quite the same way if you could see the modern steel dome the temple was reconstructed inside,' Habiba said.

She was quite right of course. 'I keep forgetting we're in the re-sited temple, not the original.' I admitted.

'Oh, it's the original temple alright,' Adam said. 'Just dismantled, lifted and reassembled here in its new location set further back from the water's edge and on higher ground. Almost every block here has had a saw taken to it and then been glued back together. I'd say the fact we'd never know it justifies every cent of what it cost. In today's money, that's something in the region of $300 million. You have to admit, UNESCO did a damn fine job.'

'I can probably arrange for you to see the modern part of the construction – go behind the scenes – if you would like?' Saleh asked.

'Really?' I looked at him in surprise. 'Is that possible?'

'I believe there is not much to see,' he shrugged. 'We are inside a concrete dome supported by steel girders.'

'Maybe concrete and steel is exactly what I need to see to cut through the scary sense of death-laden antiquity,' I smiled.

'For now, I suggest you return to your dahabeeyah for lunch,' Saleh said. 'I will make all the necessary arrangements so you can come back later before the sound and light show.' He turned to Ahmed and added something in Arabic.

'He has asked me to go with him to meet the security team here,' Ahmed translated. 'That way Saleh can return to Cairo on a flight this afternoon and I will have the necessary authorities.' He looked ridiculously pleased to be given so much responsibility.

'Ok, great,' I said. 'We'll see you back at the boat.'

We trooped back through the temple and outside. I don't mind admitting I was heartily relieved to be back in the sunshine. I was also mildly surprised nothing untoward had happened during the entire duration of our visit. Saleh had invited us to be simple tourists and, for once, that was exactly what we'd been.

We thanked Saleh for our tickets and for sorting out our private viewing for later, then waved goodbye as he strode off with Ahmed. I suspected we might not see him again until we returned to Luxor. He'd made it clear this would be a flying visit. Zahed Mansour was expecting him back to re-launch the overseas marketing campaign for the Grand Egyptian Museum opening next year.

'He really is a changed man, isn't he?' I said taking Adam's hand as we strolled back towards the *Queen Ahmes*, moored at the lakeside.

'A vast improvement on his former self,' Adam smiled back. 'Well, Merry, that's something else ticked off the old bucket list! We've visited the temples of Abu Simbel. I have to say they didn't disappoint, not for grandeur nor for atmosphere.'

'I'll start drafting an article this afternoon,' I said. 'Although I have no idea how I'm going to put it all into words. I'm not sure I've taken it all in, if I'm honest. The Great Temple of Ramses is a bit overwhelming, don't you think?'

'The trouble with seeing somewhere like that is that certain words start to lose their meaning,' he nodded. 'We can throw around superlatives like gigantic, immense, monumental and colossal. But when you see Abu Simbel they take on a whole new definition.'

You see; that's why I love Adam so much. He always catches my drift and manages to put into words exactly what I'm struggling to articulate. And I call myself the writer! 'It's really been quite an intangible experience,' I confessed. 'You have to "*feel*" the sense of antiquity. No one can really describe it.'

'I'm sure you'll do a great job of evoking the aura,' he smiled. 'And no doubt Mehmet's photographs will help fill in any gaps. I look forward to reading it.' He let go of my hand so I could precede him up the gangplank. Habiba was behind us walking with Georgina and Mehmet.

I was warm and dusty from our visit, eager for the cold flannel and glass of chilled homemade lemonade Rabiah always greeted us with when we stepped back onboard.

Except today, she wasn't there. Our small wood panelled reception area was empty.

'That's strange,' I remarked as Adam joined me.

He shrugged. 'She didn't know what time to expect us.'

'True, but she usually stands on deck watching out for us so she can be here to welcome us.'

'Perhaps she's in the kitchen making lunch. Khaled is probably taking a nap. He's been sailing the dahabeeyah pretty solidly for the last few days.'

As Habiba, Georgina and Mehmet joined us, we turned along the narrow corridor with our cabins set along it on either side. The lounge bar door was firmly closed ahead of us.

This was unusual. We tended to leave it open to allow the air conditioning to circulate through the public areas.

A sudden deep sense of foreboding swept over me. 'Georgina, Habiba, Mehmet, please lock yourselves in your cabins and don't come out until I give you the all clear,' I said in an urgent undertone.

Adam caught my hand and pulled me back in alarm. 'Merry, what is it?' he demanded,

'Something's wrong,' I said.

He knew to trust my sixth sense. So too did Habiba. And maybe Mehmet sensed that it was best to keep his head down and do as instructed. Georgina of course was a law unto herself. She was having none of it. She thrust me physically aside, barged past and flung open the lounge bar door. I daresay she regretted it. Following close on her heels, I gasped in shock, even though I think I half suspected what we might find on the other side of that closed door.

Georgina stopped dead in her tracks. 'What the...!' she exclaimed, but didn't finish the sentence.

Rabiah's eyes were round and terrified as her gaze came to meet mine. I stared in horror, taking in the scene at a glance.

Rabiah and Khaled were tied back to back to two of our dining room chairs. They each had gags tied around their mouths, presumably to prevent them calling out a warning.

As Georgina burst through the door with Adam and I close on her heels, not one but two men rose to their feet to greet us.

I recognised Philip Sinnerman from Mehmet's photographs. A tall, thin, nondescript individual in his middle years, with sandy hair and a matching closely cropped beard. He was wearing the same outfit of pale cotton trousers and checked cotton shirt as in the pictures I'd seen. My gaze darted to his companion – bigger, darker, with a swarthy complexion and broad chest straining at the fabric of his polo shirt. Max Savage, Georgina's ex-husband, came forward.

'You didn't tell us they knew each other!' Adam said tightly.

Chapter 8

'What the devil do you think you're playing at?' Georgina burst out. 'Release these people at once!'

'Aren't you going to say hello and introduce us to your friends?' Philip Sinnerman said, ignoring her demand and picking up a long-bladed knife as he too came forward.

'Certainly not!' Georgina refused. 'How dare you break in here and take two innocent people hostage?'

'Oh, we dare alright,' Philip Sinnerman sneered. 'Of course, it would have proved unnecessary had I been more successful in slowing you down at Philae.'

'Slowing her down!' I cried in outrage, unable to stop myself. 'You tried to kill her!'

'Yes, well, that would have been unfortunate. But it wasn't really my intention. I was merely trying to buy us a little time. It wouldn't really have mattered who got hurt. Sadly it seems I missed.'

'Our security guard was injured; thankfully not badly.' Adam said. His voice held a leashed-in quality, as if in a supreme effort to contain his anger.

'Ah yes, that explains the sling. Where is he by the way? And your other companions? It has to be said, there are rather a lot of you.'

'The security man will be back shortly,' Georgina said with satisfaction. 'I should warn you; he has a gun. And, believe me, he knows how to use it!'

Her ex-husband spoke for the first time. 'I don't think we need worry overmuch about the security guard.' Max Savage spoke in a deep gravelly voice; the type I've heard described as dark brown. Had it not been for what he was saying, I might have thought it attractive. 'I believe we've managed to persuade that el-Sayed fellow to find a way of parting him from the firearm.'

I gaped in shock. 'Saleh el-Sayed is in on this!' I exclaimed with a slow dawning horror.

'He has been most helpful,' Philip interjected. 'He informed me of your intention to go up onto the roof at Philae and agreed to arrange for some of the party to remain below. I felt sure Georgina would baulk at climbing that narrow staircase. And he was kind enough to give Max and me a lift here to Abu Simbel from Aswan this morning.'

I stared. It was too much to take in. 'But why would he betray us like that?' I looked at Adam in distress, not wanting to believe it. 'I thought we were friends!'

Adam's face was a reflection of my own stunned disbelief. 'We should have let the cobra bite him,' he muttered. 'Obviously he hasn't forgiven us for what happened to his cousin.'

'But that wasn't our fault!' I protested hotly.

Adam's expression warned me not to say more so I clamped my jaws shut. It was certainly true that neither Adam nor I had pulled the trigger shooting Saleh's cousin dead. That had been Ibrahim Mohassib, curator of the Luxor Museum. In defence of the killing, I reminded myself Eshan Abadi had been dressed as a terrorist at the time; wearing a – fake as it turned out – suicide vest. But the reality was, Eshan Abadi and Ibrahim Mohassib would even now be carrying on their nice normal little lives had they not been caught up on the periphery of one of our previous Egyptian adventures. It afforded them just enough information to be curious, and dangerous. So it was hard to shake the conviction that Adam and I were at least partly to blame.

And, truth to tell, that hadn't been Saleh's only reason for disliking us. Even without the drama of his cousin's death, he'd been resentful enough already. His behaviour towards us when we'd first arrived in Egypt was an insolent civility that stopped just short of open hostility. As Marketing Manager with the Egyptian Tourism Authority he believed himself better placed than me to entice holidaymakers back to this antique land. He'd been bitterly indignant at being passed over in favour of our employment on this Belzoni opus.

I really thought we'd got past all that. But it was fast becoming apparent the sense of grievance ran way deeper than I'd imagined.

'The snake!' Georgina spat. She was referring to Saleh, not the cobra.

'So he's been stringing us along all this time,' Adam frowned. 'But what does he hope to achieve?'

'I imagine he harbours some hope of stealing Georgina's scoop,' Max Savage rumbled. 'Reward and recognition are powerful incentives for a man who considers he's been passed over in favour of others.'

'If you're talking about The Great Train Robbery money; he doesn't even know about it!' Georgina objected.

'Not from you, maybe,' he conceded. 'But we were able to enlighten him about your ulterior motive for wanting to tag along on this part of the trip.'

'But why would you use it as a lure to persuade him to betray us?' she demanded.

Philip Sinnerman sat down again and tested the blade of his knife with his fingertips. 'It wasn't hard to get him talking,' he said, taking control of the conversation. 'He'd hoped for a promotion when the story broke about those granite tablets you found. He was there on the spot when you discovered them, I understand.'

'Yes, and so was the cobra,' Georgina muttered. 'Not to mention the scorpion that stung him. We saved his life.'

Philip shrugged. 'That's as may be; but Saleh el-Sayed found himself overlooked in all the attention that ensued. He felt sure his boss would reward him for insisting the find was immediately publicised. There was some suggestion the Ministry of Antiquities might prefer to keep it under wraps, I believe? Saleh knew it might revive international interest in

Egypt as a holiday destination. We learned of his disappointment and thought we might be able to use it to our mutual advantage.'

'You phone hacked him!' Georgina accused.

'Yes, well; let's not pretend we don't both have form for that!' he acknowledged grimly.

'And let's also not pretend we don't both know the individual here intent on stealing my scoop is *you*!' she shot back. 'You phone-hacked him and then either blackmailed him or reeled him in with an offer of cutting him in on the deal to uncover the hidden money.'

'He was surprisingly easy to persuade.'

'But Saleh el-Sayed is in no position to go searching behind the walls of the sanctuary in the Great Temple of Ramses,' she argued.

'Perhaps not. But he can get your two companions here inside for a private viewing,' Philip Sinnerman pointed out.

She stared at him in open disgust for a full minute. I could almost see the cogs of her brain whirring. In truth, mine were too. The despicable plan was becoming all too clear. Poor Rabiah and Khaled were strapped to their chairs, eyes wide with fear, and no doubt discerning the part they were due to play in its execution. I shuddered as this thought skittered through my brain. It was a poor choice of words. But the threat implicit in that knife was all too real.

Georgina found her voice at last. 'So, let me get this straight. You thought you could drop a huge stone on me at

Philae. With me conveniently dead or very badly injured, you could somehow use Saleh to sidle your way into these people's confidence,' – indicating Adam and me with a gesture – '…and…and…what? Get the scoop for yourself and somehow credit Saleh for making it possible?' She was looking at him aghast.

'Well, your companions here wouldn't have known about the stash from The Great Train Robbery,' he pointed out as if speaking to a dim-witted child. 'Although, I feel sure you will have apprised them of the story by now.'

'You didn't leave me much choice,' she muttered sarcastically. 'They not unreasonably wanted to know who might have a motive for dropping a stone block on me from a temple rooftop. It seems destroying my career wasn't enough for you.'

'You should have struck a deal with me when I gave you the chance back in London,' Philip Sinnerman said. 'That way we might both have hung onto our jobs.'

'But I thought – '

'No, the bosses at Trinity Mirror played me along for a while. But as soon as I stopped being useful to them they cut the ripcord. I was given my marching orders just before Christmas.'

'Which explains the timing and why you're here now,' Georgina said thinly. 'You want my scoop so you can launch your own career as an independent journalist.'

He shrugged.

Adam turned to confront Max Savage. 'None of which explains your role in all of this,' he challenged.

Max Savage lifted one dark eyebrow, directing his gaze to his ex-wife in a manner suggesting she knew the answer and should be the one to provide it.

When she remained obstinately tight-lipped, staring unflinchingly back with her chin jutting forward, he let out a low rumble of laughter.

'Ok, have it your own way,' he said. Then he looked at Adam. 'Let's just say independent journalism isn't necessarily all it's cracked up to be. It can have some pretty nasty side effects. Especially if one happens to find oneself the subject – however indirectly – of an exposé.'

'If journalism as a profession ranks so far beneath your contempt,' I started. 'Then how come you're here hooked up with another one?'

'Max and Philip are old sparring partners,' Georgina provided. 'They met when Max was starting out on his political career. I think they scratched each other's backs for a while, professionally speaking. It's fair to say Max fed Philip breaking news and Philip gave Max some of his early Press coverage. This led to his first appointment in the Commons.'

'You're a Member of Parliament?' I exclaimed.

'I was,' he qualified. 'Past tense. My career came crashing down around my ears when –' he broke off, with a hard stare at Georgina. 'Well, it doesn't matter now. But it put paid to a good couple of decades' worth of toil and ambition.'

I darted a confused glance at Georgina. 'But I thought you said it was because you had to play second fiddle to his mo – ' I broke off as she glared at me furiously.

'Enough said,' Max Savage said with an air of finality.

I looked from one to the other and back, trying to imagine the sense of grievance that cut so deep it meant the man Georgina had once been married to could hook up quite happily with someone out to steal her scoop and quite possibly kill her into the bargain. I'd heard it said that love and hate were sides of the same coin. But I'm not sure I'd ever really believed it until now.

'I have Philip to thank for introducing me to Max in the first place,' Georgina said wryly. 'We met at a party. He seemed to think we'd hit it off.'

'More like hit and run,' I muttered, just about managing to keep it under my breath. It struck me that individually and independent of each other these men were a threat. Teamed up and working together to sabotage Georgina's mission – and our trip by association – they were quite possibly a lethal combination.

'And your purpose in tying up our crew at knifepoint is what exactly?' Adam demanded, an uncompromising note of steel in his voice.

'We will wait for your security man to join us,' Philip Sinnerman said pleasantly. 'He is a big man, but I think without his gun and with his arm in a sling, he can pose us no real risk, especially since we have the element of surprise.

Then we will ask your other companions to stop cowering in their cabins. We will keep the beautiful young Muslim woman with us as an added precaution. The security guard is soft on her, I believe?'

He looked from Adam to me with a sneer, or he may have meant it as a smile. Either way, he continued in that same pleasant but softly sinister tone. 'When we have everything here to our liking, the pair of you, your security guard and the photographer fellow will go back to the temple with Georgina. Saleh has arranged things with the tourist police here so that they will expect you at sunset before the sound and light show tonight. We want everything to appear to be progressing as planned. Of course, Saleh has returned to Cairo. We wanted him far away at the critical moment. Saleh knows which side his bread is buttered. He won't fail us. While your photographer is busy with his camera in the temple, you will have the opportunity to search the sanctuary for the false wall, and retrieve the strong box containing the money.'

'There's no way we're searching for it just to hand it over to you!' I burst out.

'Oh yes, you will,' he said. 'Because we will be here with a knife at these good people's throats,' – indicating Rabiah and Khaled with a nod – 'to ensure you do. I imagine your security guard will not want his fiancée's beautiful face mutilated...?'

I stared at him in horror. 'You wouldn't!'

'You don't think?' Slowly, almost lazily, he got up from his chair and approached Rabiah. She watched him approach with terrified, unblinking eyes. I saw Khaled strain at the ropes holding him securely to his chair.

With a studied, purposeful air, Philip Sinnerman held the knife towards Rabiah's cheek.

This was too much for Adam. With a strangled oath, he flung himself bodily across the room. 'Bastard!'

Philip Sinnerman was ready for him. He swung round with the knife outstretched. It caught Adam just below the collarbone, ripping through his shirt and drawing a line of bright red blood.

'Adam!' I screamed.

Georgina lunged forward as if physically to haul her old colleague away from my husband.

'Enough of all this.' In a voice like a whiplash, Max Savage took control. 'There will be no violence. At least, not right now. You've seen what my friend here is capable of. He has a sadistic streak I was unaware of before now. Suffice it to say I shan't hold myself responsible if you try to take matters into your own hands and he decides to practise his knife skills on these good people or the young lady friend of your security man. Philip,' he turned to his partner in crime. 'For now, please control yourself. Everything is proceeding as planned. There is no need to raise the stakes.'

Philip Sinnerman subsided with a last evil look at Adam, tense and watchful in front of him, with blood slowly soaking into his shirt. I saw Rabiah and Khaled sag with relief – so far as such a thing was possible trussed up as they were.

I darted forward, grabbing a cloth from the bar to press against Adam's bleeding chest. 'Are you alright?' I demanded urgently, searching his eyes.

'I think I'll live,' he said grimly. 'The same cannot be said for these two if they touch so much as a hair on either Rabiah or Habiba's heads.'

Georgina was breathing heavily. 'You won't get away with this, you know,' she threatened, glaring at her ex-husband. 'Saleh el-Sayed might be a double-crossing, double-dealing, double-dyed villain, but there are others here in Egypt with the power to stop you in your tracks!'

'You refer to the Ministry Director I imagine?' Max enquired mildly. 'But he and the senior chap at the Tourism Authority are both under the mistaken impression that you are still sailing across Lake Nasser visiting all the sites along the way. You're not officially due to reach Abu Simbel until tomorrow. This young lady's blog,' – he nodded respectfully at me – 'has been very skilfully written so as not to give away that you made a beeline straight here.'

I saw that we were in the clutches of a pair of criminals rather too devious and clever for my liking. That we'd played straight into their hands was distressingly apparent. But then, we'd had no way of knowing they'd paired up. Frantically I searched my brain for a way of warning Ahmed before he walked into their trap as unsuspectingly as we had. Mehmet and Habiba seemed our only chance. There must surely be a way to alert them to the danger. Then we could only hope it might be possible to turn the tables.

But of course I'd told them to stay locked in their cabins. Even as this thought skidded through my brain, Max Savage, watching me closely, smiled. 'I see you have realised we have the upper hand. Now, why don't you ask your companions to join us? It will be far easier to have everyone in one place I think, where we can keep an eye on you all until your security man returns.'

I decided either he could read minds, or else perhaps my expression was as transparent as tracing paper. Either way, he'd cornered me neatly. I saw my hopes for warning Ahmed wither before my eyes.

I'm not sure any of us expected the loud splash from outside. It sent water spraying up at the windows.

'What the…?' Max Savage exclaimed.

Philip Sinnerman crossed quickly to the window, yanked aside the muslin drapes and peered out. 'It's the woman!' he cried. 'She's jumped from her cabin window!'

Hope resurged in my chest. Adam's gaze locked with mine. I could see he too was looking for any opportunity to wrest back some advantage. The trouble was, Habiba's cabin was on the wrong side of the dahabeeyah. Rather than being closest to the shore, her cabin faced the stretching waters of Lake Nasser. It meant she would have to swim around the

Queen Ahmes to reach the bank and then pull herself ashore at the stone jetty where we were moored.

Still, I had to admire her. Habiba wasn't stupid. She knew the story of The Great Train Robbery. And she knew Georgina was the target of one or more individuals with sinister intentions and old scores to settle. She didn't need to have followed us into the lounge bar to figure out what was going on. She'd simply put two and two together and decided to act. Brave girl. But of course she didn't know about the slippery Saleh el-Sayed and his subterfuge in somehow parting our police pal from his gun. Even so, I had to hand it to her. She'd seen her chance of getting to Ahmed, and taken it.

Max was already striding towards the door. 'I see we have a feisty female to deal with,' he muttered darkly. 'But it's a futile attempt. I will be there waiting to scoop her up as she tries to climb from the water.'

With Max gone from the room, Philip knew he was more vulnerable. There were three of us after all looking for any opportunity to overwhelm him. But Philip Sinnerman still had the knife. Quick as a flash he leapt back across the room and held it underneath Rabiah's chin. I'm sure it would have been her throat had she not been swathed in her habitual black burka, with only her face showing. Even so, I could see the sharp blade pressing into the soft skin below her jaw. 'Try anything stupid and I won't hesitate to use this!' he warned.

Adam's shoulders sagged as he saw he'd lost his chance. Any false move at all risked sending the blade plunging into Rabiah's neck. Gagged as she was, it didn't stop her making a small, frightened whimper at the back of her throat. Khaled too let out a low growl. He was tied with his back to his wife, so unable to see exactly what was happening. But it took no great leap of imagination to work it out.

'Hurt her and all bets are off,' Adam bit out. 'I couldn't care less about your bloody train robbery money, or your need for a damned scoop.'

'She is perfectly safe all the time the three of you keep your distance,' Philip Sinnerman replied casually. 'Now, I suggest you sit down and shut up until Max returns with your friend.'

Georgina, unusually, did as she was bid, sinking heavily onto the divan.

But Adam and I had no intention of sitting down. Instead, knowing Georgina's old nemesis couldn't stop us if he wanted to keep up his threatening position, we both moved across to the window, desperate for a glimpse of Habiba. There was still a possibility she could raise the alarm before Max Savage got to her.

I expected to see her swimming around the front of the dahabeeyah. So it surprised me very much to observe her striking out across the lake. She'd removed her headscarf and also her clothes. As far as I could tell she had on a one-piece modesty-style swimsuit – the type Muslim women tend to wear in public. It was long-sleeved and reached down to her knees.

'What's she doing?' I whispered to Adam, frowning.

Once she was some distance from the dahabeeyah, Habiba stopped swimming. She turned back towards us, treading water.

'Creating a distraction, I imagine,' he whispered back. 'There was no need for that enormous splash. Her window is close enough to the water line that she could have slipped into the water unheard.'

We both cottoned on in the same heartbeat. Darting across the room, we held the muslin drapes aside at the opposite window. Just in time to see Mehmet swimming strongly along the jetty beyond the aft of the dahabeeyah. I nearly cheered. They'd hatched a plan between them, and it seemed to me to be working.

'What is it?' Philip Sinnerman demanded suspiciously. 'What are you whispering about?'

I glared at him. 'You may think you hold all the cards. But you're wrong.'

At the sound of Max Savage coming back along the corridor, Adam and I moved quickly away from the window.

'What does the damned woman think she's playing at?' Max barked out angrily, slamming into the room.

'I imagine she's playing you for a fool!' Georgina smirked up at him without getting up from the divan. She could see through the floor length window from where she was sitting as the muslin drapes were still pulled aside. 'She can shout to Ahmed from out there as easily as she can get to him dripping wet on the bank.'

His big black eyebrows swept downwards as he sent her a fulminating frown. 'Right! Let's get the photographer in here. We don't want anyone else slipping off. I want everyone where I can see them.'

Adam and I exchanged a glance. 'I'll go and get him,' I offered. We needed to stall for time to give Mehmet the best chance of getting onto dry land and intercepting Ahmed on his way back. Or else there was a very real chance we would indeed need Habiba to put her vocal chords to use from the lake.

'No, dear lady, you won't,' he said harshly. 'But you will come with me to his cabin, so I can be assured of him opening his door.'

'Meredith is not going anywhere alone with you.' Adam spoke with an air of finality. I knew exactly what he was doing. He was arguing to buy Mehmet a few more precious seconds.

'Well, you had better come along as well then,' Max invited pleasantly, holding the door open.

Perhaps Georgina sensed something in the electricity surging between Adam and me. She heaved herself to her feet. 'You are not leaving me here with this loathsome individual.' She indicated Philip Sinnerman with a disparaging gesture.

'Please, Georgina,' Adam entreated as another couple of seconds crept by. 'I want someone to stay with Rabiah and Khaled.'

'I suggest you stand by the window and keep an eye on Habiba,' I said just by way of keeping the conversation going.

'Nobody is going to hurt your crew,' Max growled impatiently. 'Come with us, or stay here. I really don't care!'

Georgina got up and trudged towards us, holding back the drapes at the window and peering out.

'Right,' Max said. 'Let's get the photographer.' He held the door wide for me to pass into the corridor ahead of him.

I joined him as slowly as I could, Adam coming with me.

Mehmet's cabin was in the middle of the row of three on the starboard side, moored alongside the jetty. I made a play of knocking rather theatrically on the door. 'Mehmet? False alarm! It's fine for you to come out now!'

Of course there was no response.

Max Savage rattled the door handle. It remained steadfastly closed.

'I told him to lock himself in,' I supplied with satisfaction.

'You don't have a spare key?'

'If I did, I wouldn't give it to you!' I declared boldly. 'Mehmet, like Rabiah and Khaled in there,' – jerking my thumb back towards the lounge bar – 'is an innocent caught up in all of this. He's simply here to do his job, as they are. Now, why don't we leave him alone, rather than give you one more blameless person to terrorize. Aren't Adam and I enough for you? Whatever's gone on between you and Georgina, it has nothing to do with us!'

Max looked thunderous. This was a quite literal description. Big, dark and glowering, he appeared very much like a storm cloud about to burst.

He banged on the door with his fist. 'Photographer! Are you in there?' Then he stood away from the door, braced himself, and smashed himself back at it, his shoulder taking the impact.

I watched aghast as the door flew off its hinges with a loud crack and crashed against the cabin wall.

'Hey!' Adam cried out with his fists clenched. But it was too late. The door was a goner. It wasn't the first time our cherished dahabeeyah had suffered wanton damage at the hands of a deranged criminal.

I glared at this ape of a man and at least had the satisfaction of seeing the expression on his face when he stepped into Mehmet's cabin and found it empty. The window was wide open. Furious wasn't the word for it. Max was apoplectic with sudden rage that brought livid colour to his dark cheeks.

'What was that you said about having the upper hand?' I murmured.

Adam hauled me away as Max spun towards me with his fist raised. 'You'd strike a woman?' he glared.

Max clamped down on his anger with a visible effort. 'I have never struck a woman in my life,' he snarled. 'But *you* are not a woman.'

Whether or not he'd have hit Adam to vent his fury, we were never to find out. At that moment a loud shriek rent the air.

'That was Georgina!' I gaped. 'Oh God! What's he doing to her?'

Max Savage shoved us both aside and stormed back towards the lounge bar. Adam and I followed close on his heels. Max might have realised his grip on the situation was slipping through his fingers, but if Philip Sinnerman had taken it into his head to attack Georgina, the tables could turn once again.

But Philip Sinnerman was nowhere near Georgina. He was still in his menacing pose with the knife held at poor Rabiah's jawline.

Georgina shrieked again, flung the window wide open and pointed urgently out at the stretching waters of Lake Nasser. 'Crocodile!' she screamed. 'Habiba! *Swim!* Swim for your life!'

Chapter 9

Gripped with fear, I darted across the room and joined Georgina at the window.

Crocodiles died out along the Nile after the building of the Aswan dams in the twentieth century. But there's a thriving population of the fearsome beasts in Lake Nasser. Nile crocodiles are among the largest in the world, with a ferocious reputation, and a track record of attacking fisherman. I had good reason to be terrified of them. Adam once had a close encounter with one, also on Lake Nasser. In truth, it's a miracle he survived.

The panic in Georgina's voice was enough to bring Philip Sinnerman running too. 'Where?' he demanded, thrusting her aside. 'Where's the crocodile?' The eagerness in his voice sent a spreading chill through me. That he relished the opportunity of witnessing it attack Habiba was sickening.

What happened next unfolded so quickly I almost didn't follow it. Adam, perhaps sensing something in Georgina's stance, saw his chance and took it. As Philip Sinnerman moved, with Max Savage approaching the adjacent window, he barged into the ex-journalist, sending him spinning. As Philip lost his balance, staggering backwards, Adam gave him another shove. It sent the journalist toppling across a coffee table, which splintered beneath him. As he fell, Adam stamped on his hand. Sinnerman yelled. The knife slipped from his grasp and Adam kicked it hard. It shot across the wooden floor, disappearing from sight beneath our Victorian dresser, out of reach.

Max reacted in a heartbeat, shoving past Georgina and me at the window. Drawing back his fist he landed a stunning blow on Adam's chin. Adam reeled backwards and crashed down onto one of our patterned sofas.

Philip regained his balance and, seeing that Max had Adam cornered, advanced on Georgina. 'You bitch!' he spat.

But there was no time to sag with the relief that swept over me as it finally struck me the crocodile about to attack Habiba was in actual fact a ploy Georgina had used to create a further distraction. Philip Sinnerman flung himself at Georgina and wrapped his hands around her neck.

Georgina choked. She was a lot bigger than him, but he was taller and had the strength of rage on his side. I guessed his hand must be painful where Adam stamped on it. But it didn't stop him using it. As Philip pressed both thumbs hard into her throat, I watched in horror as Georgina's eyes bulged and purple colour surged in her cheeks.

My eyes darted everywhere at once; looking for something I could grab to whack him over the head. But, yet again, Max Savage's reactions were swifter than mine. He spun back towards the window while Adam sprawled dazed and groggy across the settee. As Max reached with big hands to haul his accomplice off his ex-wife, Georgina's knee came up between her ex-colleague's legs and I lunged with a vase.

Missing my intended target, I caught Max Savage in a glancing blow to the side of his head. Flowers and water cascaded down his back and the vase smashed to smithereens on the floor. Max staggered sideways, losing his balance. But he didn't hit the floor, flinging out one big hand to prevent his fall. Georgina's aim was rather more successful than mine. As her knee connected exactly where it was supposed to, Philip Sinnerman let out a howl of pain and dropped to his knees. Georgina sagged weakly against the window frame as her cheeks turned from puce to white with two livid spots of bright pink at the centre.

As Max righted himself, Philip Sinnerman groped about on the floor and grabbed a shard of the broken vase. He slashed with it wildly. The jagged edge caught Georgina just above the ankle. She screamed and blood spurted across the wooden floorboards.

I could scarcely believe what happened next. I stood wide-eyed and incredulous as Max Savage let out a roar. He grabbed Philip Sinnerman by his shirt collar and physically hauled him to his feet. Philip was still slashing frenziedly with the broken shard, perhaps blinded by pain and anger. It cut Max across the bicep. A thin gash of blood oozed.

Max growled, brought back one fist and sent it slamming into his co-conspirator's face. Philip Sinnerman's neck snapped backwards. He fell heavily back against Georgina. I grabbed her arm and yanked her with all my strength. She fell into me with all the power of a freight train and we both toppled backwards. But not before I'd seen Philip Sinnerman slip on the wet bloodied floor and lose his footing. Yelling, he tumbled backwards out of the window. With nothing to break his fall, with the window wide open behind him, and with Max Savage still lunging at him, there was nowhere else for him to go. Even as I hit the deck, with Georgina pinning me to the floor, I heard the loud splash of him entering the water.

I shoved Georgina off me with an effort and scrambled to my feet, avoiding the sharp shards of shattered vase among the slippy wetness of spilled water and blood. Adam, winded by his fall, also pushed himself up from the sofa with a grunt. 'What the…?' Adam gaped, staring at Max's dripping back.

When Max ignored him, showing no sign of turning to fight, Adam edged forward to join me at the window, helping Georgina up from the floor. We were all trying to figure out exactly what had just happened. Whether Max Savage had indeed just turned on his partner in crime. We all backed away from him uncomprehending. Adam picked up one of the dining room chairs. It would make an effective weapon, or perhaps shield. Adam was younger than Max but Georgina's ex-husband was considerably bigger, with a solid and muscular physique.

But Max was staring out of the window. 'Oh my God!' he breathed, a fixed look of horror on his face.

Forgetting the danger he posed for a moment, we three all turned to stare out of the window adjacent to the one Max had just punched Philip Sinnerman through. His tone, threaded with panic issued a warning impossible to ignore.

'Habiba!' I cried out in terror, fearing the journalist had taken it upon himself to attack her in the water.

But even as the cry left me, I caught a movement outside towards the rear of the dahabeeyah. Habiba was hauling herself up from the water onto the narrow platform connecting the sail to the dahabeeyah. I sagged with relief. She was safe.

I tore my gaze back to see what Max was staring at so fixedly. Philip Sinnerman was splashing in the water below the window, shouting for help. But Max was looking past him, frozen in alarm. As I gaped, a long scaly form moved towards the flailing journalist. Its snaking sinewy movement caused barely a ripple. It sliced across the lake, long snout just breaking the surface of the water, evil eyes focused on target.

I stared in horror, breath stuck fast in my throat; then jolted to life on a surge of panic. 'Throw him a lifeline!' I yelled. I was already darting across the room to yank the rubber ring from the wall.

'Quick! We need to haul him out!' Adam shouted. He smashed the wooden dining room chair he was holding against the floor. It refused to break apart. 'We must have something!' he grunted, dropping it in frustration.

Max Savage snatched the lifeline from me and tossed it into the water. 'Philip! Grab the ring!' he yelled. 'We'll pull you in!'

Philip Sinnerman made one desperate attempt to lunge for the ring as Max threw it. But it was too late. I watched in sick horror as the prehistoric creature in the water surged alongside the dahabeeyah and clamped its mighty jaws around Philip's thrashing legs. I heard the stomach-turning sound of his bones crunching as the vicious-looking teeth sank into his flesh. Philip Sinnerman screamed. It was the last sound he made. I tried to tear my gaze away as blood spurted. But it was impossible. I found myself transfixed on the gruesome sight, powerless to help, trembling and traumatised by the savagery of the attack. I saw the agonised look on his face and knew it would haunt my nightmares. The crocodile snapped its huge jaws again, getting a better grip; rolled – and dived. Bubbles and a pool of bright red blood were all that was left on the surface.

'Oh my God,' I whispered, clutching my hand against my throat as my breathing stalled, staring at the spot where Philip Sinnerman had just disappeared in the jaws of the crocodile.

Georgina sagged weakly against the window frame with her hand clamped over her mouth as if to prevent herself being sick.

Max Savage swore roundly, still holding the rope with the life ring suspended from it, useless in the water.

Adam tried to pull me away. But I wouldn't let him. It was too late anyway. I'd already seen the full horror of the attack.

We waited for a long, tense, drawn out moment, eyes fixed and unblinking to see if the crocodile would reappear at the surface. Seconds dragged by, seeming weighed down with shocked inertia as none of us dared move or pull in the lifeline, just in case. I counted my own thudding heartbeats and listened to the rasping breathing of my companions.

The water stilled and the blood started to drift away.

'There was nothing any of us could do,' Adam murmured at last, pulling me against him. 'He didn't stand a chance.'

'I thought you were kidding about the crocodile!' Max accused harshly, turning on his ex-wife with a livid look.

'No, I...' But Georgina didn't get to finish the sentence.

A commotion at the door made me turn from Adam's arms. I gasped as Ahmed flung it wide and strode into the room. Mehmet followed closely, dripping wet.

I registered at once that Ahmed was not in possession of his gun. His arm was still in its sling. I watched him take in the scene at a glance: Rabiah and Khaled tied back-to-back on our dining chairs, staring and impotent; blood spattered across the floorboards among smashed fragments of vase, spilled water and strewn flowers; the broken coffee table; Georgina clutching at the bloodied wound on her ankle; and the shell-shocked expressions on Adam's face and mine by the open window. I saw him register our companion, and flick a quick glance around the room; no doubt looking for Habiba. I felt sure he couldn't have missed Mehmet's cabin door smashed and swinging off its hinges as he came along the corridor. It took a fragment of a second for these impressions to form. As I gaped, mouth open, at Ahmed and Mehmet, they were each thrust aside by the person coming into the room behind them. Unbelievably, Saleh el-Sayed pushed past them. My eyes nearly fell out of my head in shock as I realised he was holding Ahmed's gun!

And yet it wasn't aimed at either one of them.

As I gaped, incredulous and uncomprehending, Saleh stepped in front of Ahmed, lifted the weapon and pointed it directly at Max Savage. Ahmed made no attempt to stop him.

'Where is the other one?' Saleh demanded. He sounded nothing like himself. Wild eyed and fired up with a desperate sort of bravado as he held out the gun, he looked like a young vigilante.

I'm not sure Max – or indeed any of us – knew how to put into words what had just happened to Philip Sinnerman.

While I stood still sickened, shaking and unable to grapple with this latest turn of events, Max recovered his wits. 'What the bloody hell do you think you're playing at?' he bit out furiously.

'You thought you could buy me,' Saleh cried. 'You were wrong! You can't buy loyalty! You have to earn it. And, believe me, these people earned it!'

It was too much. Coming so fast on the heels of the horror of Philip Sinnerman's grisly death, I simply couldn't take it in. I felt my knees buckle and go weak. Next thing I knew I was sinking to the floor. Black splotches obscured the periphery of my vision.

It was all the distraction Max Savage needed. As Saleh's gaze darted to me, Georgina's ex-husband turned and performed a perfect swallow dive from the window into the bloodied waters of Lake Nasser.

* * *

Much later, we all sat around the lounge bar trying to work out where this left us. It had taken a long time for it to sink in that we were no longer under siege. I'm not sure any of us dared believe it was over; that we were all here and accounted for, even though not exactly unharmed.

We'd released Rabiah and Khaled from their bonds and told them to take the rest of the day off. I felt sure some time alone in their cabin below deck might be needed to restore them after their ordeal. They each refused. Rabiah fussed around making sandwiches and plying us with hot sweet mint-infused tea and bitter syrupy coffee. Khaled started up the engine and moved the *Queen Ahmes* several hundred metres from the shore, where he dropped anchor. He'd installed a power generator in preparedness for making this trip. So our electricity supply was not at risk. We no longer needed to be hooked up to the mainland, at the mercy of frequent power cuts. I have to say, it was a great relief to know nobody could now board the dahabeeyah unseen, not without taking a chance in what we now knew to be the crocodile-infested waters of the lake.

We'd cleared up and put things to rights as best we could. There was nothing to be done about the door of Mehmet's cabin. But we swept up the smashed vase and flowers, and cleared up the spilled water, wiping away the bloodstains. We cleaned and dressed the wound on Georgina's ankle using bandages from her own cherished medical kit. I stuck a big plaster over the knife wound below Adam's collarbone, throwing his bloodied shirt into the bin and persuading him to don a new one.

Habiba, wrapped in a fluffy bathrobe, was perched on Ahmed's knee; her short pixie cut drying naturally. He refused point blank to let her any more than an arm's length away. And she didn't seem inclined to move. She too had watched in horror, and at close quarters, as the crocodile attacked. From her position on the narrow landing platform she'd had what was effectively a front row seat. Had even been splattered in Philip Sinnerman's blood. No wonder she was pale and shaking and disinclined to talk.

As for the rest of us, shell-shocked by what we'd witnessed, I think we all felt the need to stay close. We knew as well as Habiba did it so easily could have been her in the jaws of that fearsome beast. Recognising what a lucky escape we'd all had – and not just from the crocodile – we needed time to take stock.

Mehmet donned cargo pants and a scruffy T-shirt in place of his swimming trunks, and re-joined us quickly. He didn't look anywhere near so traumatised as did Habiba. But he'd been in the water too. I think each of them was counting their lucky stars and perhaps wondering if they'd have been so courageous had they known what was lurking under the surface.

We'd thanked them both profusely for their daring rescue attempt. I'm not sure we could have pulled things off with anything like the same outcome without their swift and decisive action.

Adam retrieved the knife from underneath the Victorian dresser. And Ahmed relieved Saleh of the gun. We sat staring at these two weapons trying to figure out exactly what had happened. I forced myself to keep trying not to re-live the horrific moment of Philip Sinnerman's death. There was no solace in the knowledge that his final resting place, if there was anything left of him after the crocodile had sated its appetite, was in all probability the original site of the Abu Simbel temples below the waterline of Lake Nasser. He was a nasty piece of work. Even so, it was a particularly gruesome way to die.

Georgina, finally, was persuaded to come away from the window and sit down. 'I never saw Max re-emerge after he dived out of the window,' she said, accepting a strong coffee from Rabiah and pouring a glug of brandy into the cup.

Not knowing if this was an expression of relief or concern, I found it impossible to know how to respond. All I could think was, it took a brave man willingly to fling himself into the still-bloodied water where moments ago he'd watched his one-time friend and accomplice die a ghastly death; particularly so, since he, himself, had a bleeding gash on his upper arm. I shuddered. It was impossible to know if he'd met a similar fate. Other crocodiles were sure to have been drawn by the scent of blood.

'I'm not quite sure I followed exactly what happened back there,' Adam admitted. 'Did Max Savage and Philip Sinnerman turn on each other? Or did I imagine it?'

'It all happened so fast,' I frowned, equally unsure of what I'd witnessed. 'I think it was when Philip attacked Georgina when she pretended she'd seen a crocodile.'

'I *did* see a crocodile,' Georgina insisted.

'We realise that now,' Adam nodded. 'But I'll admit I thought you were bluffing at the time. I thought it a damned clever ruse.'

'Thinking you'd tricked him, Sinnerman launched himself at you and wrapped his hands around your throat,' I reminded her.

'Max snapped,' Adam said. 'And when Sinnerman slashed you with the broken shard from the vase, he let loose the blow that sent your ex-colleague flying out of the window.'

It was no great relief to know we had not been directly complicit in his death.

'Seems your ex-husband may still care for you,' I mused aloud.

'Preposterous!' she snapped. 'The man hates my guts!'

Adam frowned at her. 'I wouldn't be so sure. Philip Sinnerman seems to have been the one to follow us up onto the roof at Philae, and it was him holding the knife to Rabiah's throat.'

I cottoned on to what he was trying to say. 'Philip Sinnerman's motivation seems pretty clear. He lost his job and wanted to steal your scoop. What was in it for Max Savage is rather more opaque.'

'He'd just be happy to see me humiliated,' Georgina muttered.

'But not hurt,' Adam argued. 'I was watching his face when Philip Sinnerman talked about dropping the stone block from the temple roof. He was not at all happy. And he never answered my question when I asked him to explain his role in all of this.'

'He's a politician,' Georgina remarked cynically. 'He's well versed in how to dodge questions.'

'So, all in all, I'd say things are very far from clear,' Adam finished. 'Except that somehow they persuaded Saleh to team up with them.'

Perhaps inevitably, all eyes now turned to Saleh el-Sayed sitting straight-backed in one of our armchairs with his legs crossed. His foot jerking up and down betrayed he was nowhere near so relaxed as he may have wished to appear. 'You will want an explanation,' he said.

'If you please,' Georgina said with exaggerated politeness. 'At this point in time it's hard to believe anything but that you've deliberately played both ends to the middle.'

It was Ahmed, surprisingly, who interceded on his countryman's behalf. 'Saleh, he confessed all to me,' he said. 'He has been blacklisted by these bad men.'

'You mean blackmailed?' I questioned.

'They have threatened him,' Ahmed explained. 'But he telled all to me; even before Mehmet swimmed ashore and finded me.'

I didn't doubt it, since Ahmed is as straight as a die. Even so, I frowned at Saleh. 'They said you gave them a lift down from Aswan this morning.'

He shifted uncomfortably on his seat. 'This is true,' he admitted. 'I did not know exactly what they had in mind.'

'You didn't think to warn us?' Adam said in an uncompromising tone.

'I'm sorry,' Saleh hung his head. 'I should have spoken up after the incident at Philae. That's when I realised they were dangerous.'

'They?' I queried. 'You dealt with both of them?'

'Well – er – no,' Saleh admitted. 'Until that point, I'd only met the tall, thin one with the beard. But after I arranged to have the *Queen Ahmes* moved from the Nile to Lake Nasser, he came to find me. He had the other big dark man with him. They threatened me. I know I could have warned you then. But I figured nobody was seriously hurt. So I decided to play along. I actually thought I may be able to find a way to rescue you so you might think me a hero rather than a villain.'

I stared at him; not at all sure I was buying this. 'You took a very high stakes gamble,' I pointed out tersely. 'Habiba was in the water with a deadly crocodile. Philip Sinnerman did his best to throttle Georgina. And Rabiah and Khaled have been frightened half out of their wits. Not to mention Ahmed's lucky escape. That stone falling from the roof at Philae could have killed him!'

Saleh squirmed. 'Can you forgive me? I did not think things would take such a serious turn. I can see now I have misjudged matters very badly.'

'You said earlier they tried to buy you,' I reminded him. 'I imagine they offered you something alongside the threats you claim they made?'

Saleh met my gaze unhappily. 'I admit I have been torn,' he owned up. 'It is true; those men did offer me riches in return for my co-operation – alongside unspecified threats about my employment. I am not proud of my behaviour. The truth is, I still harboured resentment towards you. My employers overlooked my part in bringing those granite tablets to light, while still sponsoring your trip. It seemed unfair. What more can I say? I am a stupid, spineless man.'

Adam frowned. 'I can't help but think Georgina is right. You've played both ends to the middle. How do we know if things had worked out differently today you wouldn't have turned the gun on us? You talk about earning loyalty. All I can say is, I'm not sure I'll ever be able to trust you again!'

'I can see how it must look,' Saleh nodded, a desperate note of appeal in his voice. 'I have let you down very badly. I have been weak. I am ashamed, and truly sorry. I will do anything to prove myself to you.'

'We saved your life,' Georgina pointed out, lest he'd forgotten.

'I know, and in turn I have betrayed you,' he cried. 'I beg your forgiveness and ask for one last chance to prove myself. I was frightened by their threats and seduced by their promise of reward.'

'I'm not sure what riches or reward they thought they could offer you,' Georgina muttered with a raised eyebrow. 'Neither one of them was rich.'

'They talked only about a large sum of cash,' Saleh said.

Georgina rolled her eyes. 'But it's worthless,' she murmured.

I could only presume this cryptic statement didn't mean much to Saleh, who possibly didn't know to what she was referring. But Mehmet, sitting quietly and following the conversation intently, now spoke up. He looked from my face to Adam's and back. 'I would very much like to know what is going on here, and what you all seem to know that I do not.

Habiba said only that those men wanted to steal something, and were making their demands with menaces. You have talked about a scoop, and now you refer to cash that may be worthless. Although English is not my first language, I have understood enough to believe there is more to this trip to Abu Simbel than simply following in Giovanni Belzoni's footsteps. I believe I deserve an explanation. What exactly did those men hope to steal?'

It was the most I'd ever heard Mehmet say in one go. A modest chap with a ready – if gap-toothed – smile, he was slight and plain-featured with shaggy hair and dark, slightly pockmarked skin, the complete opposite of the usually smooth, sartorial Marketing Manager.

Adam and I exchanged a glance, and then turned our heads as one to look at Georgina. 'It's your story,' I said to her with a shrug.

She stared back, and snapped to a decision. 'He's right; he deserves to know,' she said. 'Sinnerman is dead and in no position to steal my scoop now. And it's quite possible, had Max not dived from the window when he did, that Saleh here would have shot him.'

Saleh nodded eagerly, invited back into the conversation and desperate to prove himself. 'I wanted to shoot them both!'

'Have you ever shot anyone before?' Adam asked mildly.

'No.'

'Then I'll take that as bravado speaking. I would not wish you to add murder to your CV, certainly not on our account. From now on, kindly leave the gun with Ahmed.'

Saleh gazed back at him. 'Does that mean I am forgiven?'

'I may be willing to forgive, but I certainly won't forget,' Adam said levelly. 'Assuming you are not actually needed in Cairo, then all the time you are here, you are not to leave my sight.'

'It strikes me he could be useful to us,' Georgina said. 'If I'm going to re-tell the story, Saleh may as well hear it.'

Saleh met her stare. 'I will do anything,' he repeated. 'I just want another chance.'

Georgina tilted her head to one side and regarded him speculatively. 'Can you arrange for us to have more than just a private viewing of The Great Temple? We need some serious time in there.'

Chapter 10

I felt quite queasy as Khaled deposited us at the shore. He raised the gangplank as soon as we had all stepped onto the quayside, and immediately moved the *Queen Ahmes* back to her position several hundred metres away from the bank, where he once again dropped anchor. This time we were taking no chances with uninvited visitors. We left him in possession of Philip Sinnerman's knife, just in case.

It was late afternoon. We were all present and correct. I hadn't been sure Habiba would be sufficiently recovered from her ordeal to join us. But she insisted she preferred to come along rather than stay on board the dahabeeyah with nothing to do while the rest of us sallied forth. In truth, I imagine it was the prospect of closing her eyes and re-living the whole blood curdling experience that was her real reason for refusing to be alone. I, too, preferred to keep busy rather than think about what had happened.

Saleh had been on the telephone to the powers-that-be and arranged for us to access the Great Temple of Ramses as soon as the last visitor had left, and before the sound and light show began after it was dark. The temple would be closed and guarded. We'd listened in on his call to ensure he wasn't playing both ends to the middle this time around. I'd been shocked and hurt by his duplicity. But he seemed genuine in his contrition. Ahmed championed his cause. And Ahmed was the one, after all, to whom Saleh had confessed his double-dealing before storming the dahabeeyah, apparently doing so even before Mehmet swam ashore to raise the alarm. So, all things considered, I was inclined to grant Saleh his second chance and give him the opportunity to prove himself deserving of our forgiveness.

Even so, as we walked around the headland towards the temple, I felt a growing sense of unease. Listening to Georgina re-tell the story of The Great Train Robbery to bring Mehmet and Saleh up to speed, it was hard to avoid the notion that John Daly's portion of the stolen money was cursed. I decided he'd had a lucky escape when he drove to Cornwall after his astonishing acquittal only to find his erstwhile friends had betrayed him and already dug it up. Turning over a new leaf, he'd lived the rest of his life on the straight and narrow. It seemed to me he'd escaped not only with his freedom but also with his life.

Not so anyone else who came into contact with his stash. The initial turncoats Bill Goodwin and Michael Black, who tricked him and stole the money, both died within six months – apparently of natural causes – but died nonetheless. Mickey Black, the jailbird son of his trickster father was killed in a road traffic accident on his way to Abu Simbel to retrieve the cash after his release from prison. A stone block slipped from the crane shifting it into position and crushed the Egyptian labourer who helped Mickey's father hide the stolen loot at Abu Simbel during the UNESCO project. And we all knew what had happened to Philip Sinnerman. My ears still echoed with the sound of his scream. And every time I so much as blinked I re-lived the horrific sight of the crocodile attack.

It's fair to say the excitement I'd felt earlier at the possibility of making such a headline-grabbing find was replaced with a stomach-churning trepidation. Part of me wished very much that Adam and I were simply on the innocent little trip our employers believed us to be. I felt I might give quite a lot right now to have nothing on my mind beyond the determination to bring Giovanni Belzoni's adventures to life for a modern audience. It would be quite wonderful to attend the sound and light show this evening as a member of the audience and simply enjoy the spectacle. I scarcely remembered what it was like to have no thought of subterfuge, no secret mission. In short, no plan.

I reminded myself that, unlike all the others, we were not here to steal the money – or, in Philip Sinnerman's case, the scoop. We merely wanted to bring it to light, and provide Georgina with a career-making story. But it still meant making a search of the temple under false pretences. And possibly breaking through the wall in the inner sanctuary. Despite some of my former wanderings from the path of the righteous, I wasn't at all sure this time around it felt right. I had no wish to call down a curse on our heads. Or indeed any other sort of trouble.

'You know, there is another way we could do this,' I said as we walked towards the temple complex. 'We could go to the authorities with the story and ask someone official to check out the inner sanctuary. Maybe use infra-red scanning or Muon technology or whatnot to see if there's anything hidden behind the walls. You'd still get the credit, Georgina.'

She stopped dead in her tracks and turned to look at me as if I'd gone stark staring mad. Her bosom heaved alarmingly. 'I have not come all this way only to hand over my scoop to some faceless bureaucrat right at the last minute!' she declared fiercely. 'If you're getting cold feet, you don't have to come along. You're perfectly welcome to return to the dahabeeyah.'

She stared me down and I caved in. 'No, I – It's just I – er –' I trailed off. I already knew Georgina's view on the veracity of curses and had no wish to invite her ridicule. So I clamped my jaws shut and stared at her mutely.

'Merry, this isn't like you,' Adam murmured at my side. 'You're usually Lara Croft personified at the chance of unlocking Egypt's secrets.'

'The trouble is, this isn't *Egypt's* secret,' I muttered in response. 'It's a stash of British stolen money that's left a trail of untold death and destruction in its wake.'

'True; but it's quite a story nonetheless.' I could see Georgina's re-telling of the tale had once again fired him up with the spirit of Boy's Own adventure.

I tilted my head and stared into his eyes. 'I just want us to emerge from this unscathed,' I said. 'We have other fish to fry, if you remember.' I accompanied this with a meaningful look.

Neither of us would mention the statuette of Helen of Troy in front of the others. Georgina knew of it of course, having been there at the fateful moment of discovery. Although, she appeared to have forgotten all about it in the drama of the last few days. But, beyond her, it was just Adam, Ahmed and myself, so far as I knew, who had the inside track on that particular discovery. If the others heard me, I could only hope they'd assume I was referring to our genuine purpose in being here.

I saw Adam cotton on. I guessed maybe Georgina did too. Her tone was certainly a good deal more conciliatory and her expression a whole lot less severe as she added: 'To my way of looking at it, Habiba and Saleh here *are* the authorities. Saleh even has the word in his job title. Marketing Manager with the Egyptian Tourism *Authority*.' She placed a heavy emphasis on the last word, eyes gleaming at me. 'And Habiba is an Inspector with the Ministry of State for Antiquities, is she not?'

'Er – yes,' I faltered.

Georgina rounded on our companions and skewered them with a look. 'Are you both willing to stand witness to the fact that I have hidden nothing from you about my reasons for being here? That I have been entirely open and transparent about wishing to recover money from The Great Train Robbery for journalistic reasons alone? That I have made it clear all along the money itself is, in fact, worthless?'

Georgina Savage was a very clever woman, I realised, not for the first time. A journalist by trade, she had quite a way with words. She was certainly skilled at putting them in other people's mouths. And had a knack of asking others to agree with closed questions, to which the answer could only ever be yes or no. Had she asked either of them openly whether either jointly or severally they had any qualms about what we were about to do, I daresay she may have elicited a different response. As it was, she'd cornered them neatly. And, glaring at them as she was, it would have taken a person braver than Habiba or Saleh to protest.

Given no choice but to agree with every point, since they were, in fact, true, they both nodded the affirmative. Which, to be fair, wasn't the same thing as giving the plan a ringing endorsement. I saw the flash of worry in Habiba's eyes and felt sure she was wondering how she might square things with Director Ismail as and when the day of reckoning arrived.

Georgina nodded her satisfaction. 'I am here in a crowd of you for the very purpose of ensuring I can be accused of nothing underhand,' she asserted. 'I might have stumbled onto this story through phone hacking – a part of my former life about which I am not proud. But from now on I do things above board.'

Her expression, chin jutting forward, challenged one of us to contradict her. Of course no one dared. Seeing her standing there as solid and immoveable as a huge granite building block, I was unusually cowed – a rare feeling for me. But Georgina was a force of nature. If she was resolved to be fully legit in her dealings from now on, I for one was not going to argue with her.

When none of us questioned her claim, she bared her teeth in a smile and layered on a bit more justification. 'Ahmed here is seconded to this trip from his substantive role as a police officer, I understand?' It was both a statement and a question. 'Yet another example of involving the authorities!' she finished triumphantly. 'Now, may we proceed?'

'I wasn't accusing her of anything underhanded,' I whispered to Adam as Georgina stomped away, having made her point and brazened things out very effectively. He took my hand as I went on, 'I just don't want any of us getting hurt. It seems to me that stolen money has played a part in more deaths than I care to count.'

He squeezed my hand and smiled at me as we rounded the headland and the magnificent façade of the Great Temple of Ramses came into view. 'Saleh has arranged for guards to be posted on the temple entrance while we're inside,' he said. 'What can possibly go wrong?'

* * *

An hour or so later it was all too plain what could go wrong.

'This is impossible!' Georgina huffed in exasperation. 'Between the six of us, we must have checked every inch of this sanctuary. It's not as if it's a particularly big space. Nothing! No sign of a false wall. No mysterious cracks or flaking reliefs. Just a big, fat nothing! It's hopeless!'

In truth, I shared her frustration. And she was right. Once Mehmet had joined us from taking his fill of photographs, each one of us had scoured the walls. Mehmet, being tall and gangly and Ahmed, being – well – big – were given the task of checking the upper reaches. The rest of us traded places every now and then and searched everything else.

Wearing lint-free gloves (provided by Habiba) to protect the wall reliefs, we'd carefully and minutely explored the inner sanctuary section by section. Sometimes on our hands and knees, sometimes on tiptoe, we'd spent our time feeling for gaps, knocking the stone for any sign of a hollow space behind, and shining torches across the surface to check for unexplained shadows.

The inner sanctuary was a small square space, the entire back wall taken up with the seated, slimline stone statues of Ramses among the gods. The reliefs above, behind and surrounding them were centuries-old images of the pharaoh and Egypt's deities interspersed with closely packed columns of hieroglyphics. Faded for sure; but intact.

Knowing the temple had been broken apart and reconstructed was one thing. Spotting any evidence of it was quite another. My admiration for the workers engaged on the 1960s UNESCO project escalated in direct proportion to the dawning futility of our search. It was quite clear there was nowhere a modern security box full of cash possibly could be hidden. 'Are you absolutely sure we're looking in the right place?' I asked.

'Oh, please,' Adam grunted. He was crouched on the floor, making a meticulous study of the spaces between the legs of the four seated statues of Ramses, Amun-Ra, Ptah and Ra-Harakhte. 'This temple is huge! There's no way we can search every inch of wall space. It would take us all year!'

'In every conversation I ever overheard between members of the Black family, they spoke about the inner sanctuary,' Georgina declared. Her chin jutted again, defensively this time. 'I don't think it likely they'd have got a detail like that wrong.'

Reaching the end of the wall, Adam gave up and got to his feet. 'We said all along the likelihood of finding anything here was slim to non-existent,' he reminded us. 'I mean, really; what were the chances?'

'It was always going to be a long shot,' I agreed, pulling off my gloves. Seeing the expression on Georgina's face I amended quickly: 'But we can check out a couple of the other smaller side chambers while we're here, if you want?' In truth, I couldn't help but think it would be a relief to get out of the cramped sanctuary, too small a space for the six of us to work comfortably. But my desire to leave was predominantly to get away from those four seated statues. It was impossible to rid myself of the notion they were watching us. Call me fanciful; but I kept imagining movement. Had lost count of the number of times I'd jumped, biting back a yelp. I schooled myself to get a grip; knowing it was just an illusion caused by the shifting shadows and our torchlight as we squeezed around each other in the confined space.

'You may be willing to admit defeat, but I am not,' Georgina announced stiffly. 'I know what I heard!'

'Is it possible the Egyptian labourer Michael Black employed to hide the box pulled a fast one?' Adam queried. 'Is there any proof that he followed through on his promise? He might have just taken his payment and either lost his nerve or decided simply to cut and run.'

'Or maybe he was crushed by that falling block before he had a chance to hide the box,' I suggested, warming to Adam's theme.

Georgina stared at us with her mouth working. But no sound came out.

'Your luck had to run out sometime,' Adam remarked, shrugging at her as if to say you win some, you lose some. 'You've already had the scoop of a lifetime finding Nefertari's stone tablets. To expect to come here and find the haul of Great Train Robbery money too was surely pushing it!'

Poor Georgina looked apoplectic, and found her voice at last. 'I don't know exactly how or why the Black family are so certain the money is hidden here,' she said snappishly. 'I just know they are!'

'It makes me wonder why they haven't sold the story to the Press,' I mused. 'Once they realised the money was worthless, you'd think they might look for another angle to make a fast buck or two off the back of it.'

'They could hardly go to the newspapers without admitting their own guilt,' Adam pointed out reasonably enough.

'Maybe so, but the actual theft took place a generation or two ago,' I frowned. 'It just strikes me they could have made some mileage out of it, that's all.' I turned to look at Georgina, starting to feel a bit sorry for her. 'You know, it's possible they could very well believe the money is here, even if it isn't. What's to say the labourer was trustworthy? Michael Black hired him, paid him handsomely, gave him the box and returned to England. As we know, he was dead within six months, and the labourer probably not long afterwards. The box could be sitting at the bottom of Lake Nasser for all we know.' As I said this, I had a horrible mental image of Philip Sinnerman's dead body coming to rest on it, and shuddered.

But Georgina was oblivious to my imaginings. 'We're going round in circles,' she snapped. 'The Black family wouldn't believe the stash was hidden behind a wall here in the inner sanctuary if the labourer hadn't confirmed it to be the case before Michael Black died. The money is here. It has to be. We just haven't looked hard enough!'

'But we've investigated every inch,' Habiba spoke up for the first time.

'Maybe it's time the gloves came off,' Georgina said. I was pretty sure she meant it literally rather than metaphorically.

'No.' Habiba said firmly. 'I cannot allow any damage to the reliefs.'

'There's a false wall here somewhere,' Georgina insisted. 'Perhaps a section of the paintings simply lift out, or are fitted to a sliding panel. It has to be something like that. I refuse absolutely to give up, and that's flat.' She glared mutinously around at us all.

'Georgina, Habiba is right,' Adam said gently. 'We're persuading ourselves that because the temple has been broken apart and put back together again, it's somehow alright to knock it about a bit. But it isn't. Alright, I mean. This sanctuary is thirty-three centuries old. We can't possibly start chipping away at the walls. I don't know what we were thinking!'

I couldn't let this pass, and looked at him accusingly. 'Adam! You were as eager as Georgina to find that box! Ever since she first told us the story you've been alight at the idea of discovering a stash of British money from one of the greatest heists of the twentieth century, here in one of the greatest temples to survive from antiquity.'

'This is true of me too,' Ahmed spoke up on Adam's behalf. 'The story of the removal of the temple in the 1960s has inflamed us all.'

'I admit I got a bit carried away,' Adam said. 'I guess I thought we'd spot a chink in the wall, or a button to press, or a lever to pull, or something like that. All that talk of a false wall made me think it must be a wooden panel that we could lift out easily enough. But, as Habiba says; I draw the line at tampering with three thousand year old wall reliefs.'

'So we've hit a dead end,' I brought us back to the essential point.

'I *cannot* give up!' To my horror I watched Georgina's chin – chins, I should say; because she had at least a double – wobble, and her face collapse in distress. 'I *have* to find it!' she cried. 'A man died today, believing he could wrest it from me! I may not have liked Philip Sinnerman. It's probably fair to say we were sworn enemies. But I didn't want him dead! Certainly not on my account! And God only knows what happened to Max…! I don't know if he's alive or dead! We may have destroyed our marriage between the pair of us. But I loved him once…!' She gulped out a choking sob. 'If I don't find the money then what was it all for? I'll have it on my conscience for the rest of my life!'

I stared at her, thoroughly discomfited. She was such a bulldozer of a woman; it came as something of a shock to discover she wasn't impervious to human emotion after all.

Saleh el-Sayed cleared his throat. 'Er – there is only one other thing I can think of,' he offered hesitantly. We all turned to look at him. I had to hand it to him; he'd searched the sanctuary as assiduously as the rest of us. Usually spotless, the knees of his smart linen trousers were caked in dust, his pale blue shirt creased and grimy where he'd been crawling on the floor shining his torch upwards to illuminate the walls. His handsome face was shiny with perspiration. We all stared at him, waiting for him to elucidate. 'I mentioned earlier that this temple was reconstructed within the skin of a manmade concrete dome, bigger than an aircraft hanger.'

'A concrete dome supported by steel girders,' I remembered. 'You said you might be able to arrange for us to have a little look behind the scenes.'

As he stared back into my eyes we all cottoned on as one. Even Georgina choked back a sob and sucked in a breath instead.

'You're suggesting the false wall may be *behind* the inner sanctuary,' Adam exclaimed. There was no mistaking the thread of excitement in his voice.

Saleh shrugged. 'It is just a thought.'

A certain stillness settled over Adam. I recognised that reaction. He often has one of these freeze frame moments when a new possibility takes hold. And it was clear this one wasn't letting go. Then he struck the heel of his hand against his forehead. 'Of course! We should have thought of it before!' he announced. 'We got so wrapped up in believing it had to be here *inside* the inner sanctuary. But of course that makes no sense. If *we're* baulking at the idea of tampering with the wall reliefs, you can bet your life an Egyptian labourer would have run a mile at the very thought. And how could he possibly have got in here unsupervised? We've managed it only because Saleh's pulled a few strings, and they think we're taking copious professional photographs, or making some sort of film to put on the website, or whatever cock and bull story he told them to justify the time we needed in here!'

'And if we need this long simply to find it,' I added, hearing my own voice rise with excitement, 'then he'd have needed even longer to find a way of hiding a great big metal security box!'

'But we're right at the back of the temple!' Adam went on. The inner sanctuary must have been reconstructed at the far end of the modern dome. I'll bet that was a far easier prospect for our Egyptian labourer – both in terms of getting inside unsupervised and constructing his hiding place for the box!'

Georgina had pulled herself back together by now. She and the others listened to this exchange wide-eyed and jaws hanging loose.

'You're saying that behind this wall,' Ahmed nodded at the back wall with the four seated stone statues lined along it, 'is the modern superstructure within which the temple was rebuilt.' He looked baffled, as if it took too great a leap of imagination to picture it. But I had to commend his use of language.

'Exactly that,' Adam said excitedly. 'If the box is anywhere, it has to be there!'

'Then we must go there at once!' our big police pal asserted.

I was only too pleased to leave the temple. If it had spooked me earlier in the day, in company of other tourists, it was a decidedly creepy place to be at dusk, and with only our own echoing footfalls. Some might say it's a privilege to have a place like this to oneself – well, to one's party. But, believe me, the Great Temple of Ramses is a place so laden with antiquity it positively weighs down the soul.

We trooped back through the huge pillared hall, past the standing statues of Ramses as Osiris, and out into the fading embers of sunset. Mehmet collected up his camera equipment and tripod on the way. As we emerged onto the forecourt between the four immense seated colossi of Ramses, we tried hard to act normal and look as if we'd been engaged in an innocent visit gathering impressions for the promotional activities we would undertake later for the Egyptian Tourism Authority. We'd taken time to brush the dust from our clothes and made good use of my supply of antiseptic wipes to clean ourselves up.

Saleh and Ahmed struck up a conversation with the two guards posted outside the doorway, looking spick and span in their smart tourist police uniforms. After a moment Saleh turned back to me. 'Only one of them may accompany us to open the back entrance,' he said. 'The sound and light show will be starting soon, and visitors are starting to arrive. The other will need to return to his usual duties.'

'One is all we'll need, providing he has a key and doesn't ask too many questions,' Adam remarked at my side.

I nodded, grateful we'd already had the foresight to think about how we might spirit a security box full of cash out from under their noses should we indeed be lucky enough to find it. Mehmet's camera equipment provided the solution. We'd found a packing case stored below deck on the *Queen Ahmes*. It had once contained a bedside cabinet I'd ordered for one of the cabins. We guessed it might be big enough to hide the security box inside. But in the meantime it was serving as a carry case for all of Mehmet's camera equipment. He'd brought everything he owned ashore with him. We'd figure out how to get it all back to the dahabeeyah as and when we found out if we would need to press the packing case into service as a decoy.

He and Adam now hoisted it between them, and we followed the single guard as he led us across the forecourt, up past the ticket office, tourist shop and café, and eventually around the back of the huge manmade cliff built to reposition the temple within. The general shape of it reminded me a bit of Ayers Rock rising up from the scrubby headland bordering Lake Nasser.

Other visitors were indeed arriving, coach loads of them. But they paid us scant heed as we trailed behind the guard. My heart was thudding against my breastbone. I don't suppose there can be many people granted permission effectively to go behind the scenes at Abu Simbel. I guess for most it would destroy the mystique. But Saleh had convinced the officials we were here on behalf of the Egyptian Tourism Authority to tell the full story of these temples' remarkable engineering – ancient and modern. Habiba had flashed her Ministry of Antiquities ID card; Adam his British Museum Egyptologists one, and Ahmed his police badge, which he still had since he was only on secondment as our security guard.

I imagine the combination of these sets of credentials was impressive enough to hold sway. Before we knew it, a big metal door was being swung open ahead of us. The guard switched on the lights and we crossed the threshold into a 1960s architectural wonder. What Saleh had described as bigger than an aircraft hanger was, in fact, not a very big space at all. I suppose this was only to be expected. It was filled front to back with an enormous ancient Egyptian temple after all. But the domed structure rose above our heads, and there was a walkway with a white metal railing leading inside. It was a bright, white space, lit with fluorescent strip lights; just about as far removed from the antiquity-laden atmosphere inside the temple as was possible.

'Right,' Adam said, as soon as the guard turned and left us, closing the door behind him to take up his position outside.

'By my reckoning the back wall of the inner sanctuary must be over there.'

He climbed over the metal railing and jumped down. One by one we followed. Mehmet pulled his little digital camera out of his pocket.

'If you want a breaking news story, I should capture the moment of discovery,' he said.

Funnily enough, I think not one of us doubted; now we were here, that we would find the metal security box. It took a few minutes of concerted searching as we felt along the inner walls – no need for our lint-free gloves this time. But finally Georgina let out a shriek and fell heavily sideways from her crouching position.

We all rushed to her side.

'I pressed against that section there, and it gave way!' she yelled, hefting herself up onto her knees.

The false wall turned out to be little more than a flap. But cunningly disguised to look solid.

Georgina reached forward, pushed it open and peered inside. We all pressed around her craning for a look. Mehmet raised his camera to his face.

A footfall behind me made me freeze.

I turned quickly, with the guilty expression and heart-stopping jolt of a little kid caught with its hand in the sweetie jar. It was no comfort to see that the guard had followed us inside. Impossible to explain what we were all doing on our hands and knees peering into a hole in the wall where it connected with the temple.

Then I looked more closely. There was no question the man was wearing the guard's uniform. But it wasn't the guard.

'Max Savage,' I said woodenly. 'You're alive.'

Chapter 11

'Did you think I wouldn't be?' Max said, coming forward. 'Let me guess, you thought – hoped, perhaps – the croc that got poor Philip was still hungry and came back for me? Or maybe invited one of his chums along to finish me off?'

'Any self-respecting crocodile would've taken one bite and spat you straight back out again!' Georgina said tartly. She slumped sideways onto her backside on the floor and stared up mutinously at her ex-husband.

'Come now; let's not fight,' he chided. 'Surely we've done enough of that over the years.'

'I always knew you were a risk-taker,' Georgina responded without changing her tone. 'But I never took you for a thug. Yet, here you are. And all within one day you've bound and gagged two innocent staff members on board the dahabeeyah – at knifepoint, I might add. Now I presume you have either killed or else somehow incapacitated the poor guard.' She raised an arch eyebrow at his stolen uniform.

'You do me a great injustice!' Max Savage pressed one hand theatrically against his breast with a heaving sigh. 'It was Philip, not I, who bound and gagged those people. As I am sure they will confirm if you ask them. I have neither killed nor incapacitated the guard. He is perfectly fit and well. But I admit I may have crossed his palm with silver. Alas, as you see, I am not in possession of his gun. To give him credit, the poor man baulked at handing that over. Still, I'll say one thing about these Egyptian fellows...' He managed to indicate Saleh, Ahmed and Mehmet in a single gesture. '...They are ridiculously easy to bribe.'

Saleh let out a muted roar. Adam shot out a hand and held him back when he would have charged at our unwelcome intruder.

'I blame the government,' Max went on conversationally, not seeming in the least perturbed. 'Keeps them employed but on what you or I might consider slave wages.' He addressed himself to Adam, perhaps because Adam had moved, or maybe because Adam was the only white male among us, so maybe he perceived him as an equal. 'And of course these Arabs thrive on baksheesh,' he added without breaking stride. 'Most of them would sell their grandmothers for a few shekels!'

'Are you being deliberately offensive?' Georgina heaved herself up off the floor and stood glaring at him, feet apart, hands on her hips.

'*Moi*?' His bushy black eyebrows rose in mock innocence. 'Now it is you who insults me! I am merely pointing out the ease with which I was able to follow you,' he added pleasantly.

'You're asking for it!' Saleh wrested himself from Adam's restraining hand and sprang forward.

'I wouldn't —' Georgina advised quickly, darting out an arm and pulling him back. 'Max packs a mean punch.'

I felt my eyes bulge at this, unsure if she was referring to the incident of sending Philip Sinnerman flying through the open window earlier, or if she had further independent evidence.

Ahmed unslung his gun. 'But he will not argue with this, I think,' he growled.

Max Savage smiled at him. 'My good man, I'm sorry if what I said affronted you. I didn't mean it personally. Besides which, I'd advise against use of the gun. The sound of a shot being fired would have the rest of those police chappies and guards out there on us in an instant.'

'The sound and light show, it will start soon,' Ahmed said. 'It is loud with booming music. It will drown out a gunshot.'

'But it would be a shame, don't you think, to foist yourselves with a dead body to dispose of, right at this critical moment of discovery? For, I presume, that flap is the hidden wall behind which the box with the cash is hidden. Am I right? You'd have no choice but to stuff my body into that packing case full of photographic equipment you've brought with you. And I imagine you were rather hoping to use that to secrete the loot and spirit it away.'

'Or we could leave you here to rot,' Ahmed ground out.

'But then your arrest and conviction would be assured,' Max pointed out, raising a single winged eyebrow as if to say he didn't think Ahmed a very good security guard. I supposed it was just as well he didn't know he was a police officer. 'The authorities are very well aware of who you all are. Indeed they've gone out of their way to grant you this usually unauthorised access. I imagine you've had to hand over all sorts of identity information to prove your credentials.'

'I've had enough of this!' I cried as my temper gave out. Max Savage spoke in an insufferable self-congratulatory tone that reminded me of someone. If only I could remember who...

Oh yes, it was Georgina! Maybe they'd learned it from each other during the years of their marriage. Whatever. It was starting to grate. It seemed to me the cat and mouse exchange we were engaged in might go on forever if I didn't put a stop to it.

'Ok Max Savage,' I said as everyone's eyes turned towards me. 'We can see you're unarmed. And you must see you're outnumbered. Surely even your punching ability can't hold out against six of us if we decide to make an attempt to overpower you. And the gun still remains an option should we fail. So why don't you just cut to the chase and tell us what you want?'

Max Savage let a long pause draw out. I wasn't sure he meant to answer me at all. I realised I'd asked a stupid question. Of course it was obvious what he wanted. He was here for the money, just as we were.

Slowly, almost deliberately, he moved his gaze so it came to rest on each of us in turn. Adam, myself, Saleh, Mehmet, Habiba and Ahmed each came under his scrutiny. It was Georgina his eyes settled on last. And there his gaze remained, seemingly locked on her fierce, accusatory expression. This time when he spoke the self-congratulatory tone was gone. But the candour and soft sincerity of his voice did little to mask the shock of what he actually said. 'I want my wife back,' he admitted.

The silence that greeted this announcement was so profound it seemed even the great domed space itself was holding its breath. All eyes swung inevitably now to Georgina. Hot colour surged in her cheeks. She opened and closed her mouth a couple of times in a fair imitation of a goldfish. Her throat convulsed and her chest expanded. I thought for one horrible moment she was about to spontaneously combust. Instead a bubble of hysterical laughter escaped her. 'Do me a favour!' she snorted rudely.

'I'm serious, Georgina.'

'Don't make me laugh!' she derided, doing just that. But it wasn't the joyous laughter of something funny, more a derisive guffaw of something preposterous.

'It's true.' Spoken in the same intent serious tone. 'I want us to give it another go.'

She stopped laughing on a loud gulp. Instead she stared at him with popping eyes and her jaw hanging slack for what seemed like an age. 'This is a joke, right?'

'No joke,' he said calmly, looking into her eyes. 'I want you back. Simple as that.'

Another weighty pause drew out while we all stared. 'You've got a damn funny way of going about it,' she said at last, big shoulders slumping. 'You team up with Philip Sinnerman, allow him to drop a bloody great hunk of masonry on me from a temple rooftop, you lay siege to the dahabeeyah I'm staying on; and then you have the brazen effrontery to steal a guard's uniform to muscle your way in here, and expect me to believe it's because you've suddenly decided you miss me!'

'I did NOT allow Philip to drop that stone on you!' he shot back. 'That was the point at which I realised I had to intercede. I had no idea he was dangerous until then.'

She blinked at him. 'Nice try, Max! But I'm not buying it! Not for one second. You're here to steal the money!'

'What the hell would I want with the money?' he enquired, eyebrows sweeping down. 'It's completely bloody worthless!'

'Not to me, it's not!' she shot back, puce in the cheeks. 'How typical of you to attempt to steal my thunder!'

'I'm not here to steal anything!' he ground out, losing patience. 'The guard's uniform was simply to get myself inside here. I knew you'd refuse to see me otherwise.'

'Damn right!'

He sighed heavily. 'Damned pig-headed woman!'

'Oh, so we're back to trading insults!' she glowered.

'I am not here to insult you, Georgina. Your companions here can bear witness to my intentions.' He indicated us all in an expansive gesture. In truth, I don't think any one of us knew what to think or say. Or where to look. A villain wielding a weapon was one thing. We had enough experience of that by now to know how to respond. But it was a different thing altogether to be caught up in the theatrics of someone else's personal relationship playing out for an audience. Quite honestly, I'd have felt far more comfortable with a knife. Max Savage snapped his attention back to his ex-wife. 'I will say it once again,' he started, 'since you clearly need telling twice. I did NOT team up with Philip Sinnerman to muscle in on your discovery. I joined him for the sole purpose of putting a stop to him.'

'I can't possibly believe that,' she retorted. 'All of the evidence points to the exact opposite.'

'Will you please just LISTEN to me!' he thundered.

Georgina clamped her jaws shut with an audible snap.

'I knew he was planning on attempting to steal your scoop, or the money, or perhaps both,' he said in more normal tones. 'But his attempt on your life took things too far. I had no idea he was dangerous. That's when I decided my only option to keep you safe was to pretend to want the same thing he did.'

'You see? I told you he still cared for her!' Adam murmured at my side.

Max didn't hear him. 'Things got out of hand this morning,' he admitted. 'I thought I could play along and then turn him in. That maybe you'd see it as some grand romantic gesture. That's what you always wanted, wasn't it?'

She stared at him open-mouthed.

'But I didn't reckon with this lot being quite so enterprising.' He jerked a thumb at us, all standing agog and disbelieving. 'Or on Philip attacking you right in front of me.' He cleared his throat. 'Anyway Philip is out of the picture now. I have his blood on my hands. Quite literally. I'm sorry for that. But I can't have you persisting in the belief that he and I were on the same side. It's you and me I want to be a team again. We were a great one once, remember?'

I found myself looking from one to the other, trying to picture them in wedded harmony. Georgina was an attractive enough woman; shapelier than the tent-dresses she favoured suggested. She could be witty and entertaining when she chose. Max was a beefy chap with the physique and musculature of a rugby player, also attractive enough in his own way. I guessed I could see how the first spark had flared between them.

Georgina snapped her mouth closed again. Her chest heaved. 'I can't possibly believe you want me back,' she remarked acidly. 'You were keen enough to go through with the divorce! The ink dried on the papers less than six months ago!'

'You left me no choice,' he replied bitterly. 'And let's not forget you're the one who filed the dratted papers! You knew it wasn't what I wanted. But after what you did, I could see no way back.'

'After what *I* did?' she gaped.

'You're the one who wrote the damn exposé that destroyed my career!'

'You're the one who stooped low enough to give me something to write about!' she shot back.

I stared. If this was an insight into how they dealt with each other, it was no real surprise their relationship hadn't lasted. I shifted awkwardly; torn between wanting to hear more, yet feeling I was listening in on something private and deeply personal not meant for my ears. Still, they each seemed happy enough with the audience. It wasn't for me to intervene.

'Things move on,' Max said with a shrug. 'I can forgive you.'

'So what changed?'

I was surprised by his reply. So it seemed was she. 'My mother died,' he said simply.

It took the wind from her sails. She stared at him for a long moment. Her expression changed from one of open cynicism and hostility to something that may have passed for sympathy. 'I'm sorry,' she said at last.

He shrugged again. 'With my mother gone, I thought you might see things differently. That we could perhaps talk civilly about the whole thing and maybe try again.' There was a note of appeal in his voice.

But Georgina still looked suspicious. 'When did she die?'

'October,' he said.

'So, what took you so long? That was months ago.'

'I wasn't sure where you were. I'd thought maybe you'd come haring out here to Egypt. You couldn't get away fast enough! But I couldn't track you down at any of your usual haunts in Cairo or Luxor. It was only when I saw all that stuff in the Press at Christmas that I realised you'd hooked up with these people. I imagine you've painted me as some Big Bad Wolf.' He broke off and unexpectedly turned to look at me, addressing his next words to me. 'But actually, you know, I'm not that bad if you take the trouble to get to know me.'

I didn't really know where to look. Actually the Big Bad Wolf persona seemed very apt. Dark and swarthy with big limbs and those fierce eyebrows, it was not a million miles from the mark.

'Er – she's said very little about you,' I faltered. 'Your relationship is no business of ours.' Marriage guidance has never appealed to me as a profession. And I certainly didn't want to get hooked up in it now. What I really wanted was to get on with checking out what was behind that flap in the wall. 'And this hardly seems the time or the place to discuss it,' I added for good measure.

'You're right,' he said. 'But you've all been caught up, inadvertently or otherwise,' – eyes shifting to Saleh's face and away again – 'in events as they've unfolded. It seemed only fair to offer you an explanation. You don't have to believe me. But every word is true. I'm sorry for the damage to your boat.'

'Dahabeeyah,' I corrected.

'Er – yes,' he said. 'And the manner of Philip's death is something I imagine none of us will forget in a hurry. Now, you've all heard me say my piece. I will leave you to proceed with your discovery. Georgina, you and I have unfinished business. But perhaps now is not the time to discuss it.'

And he turned his back on us and strode towards the door.

'That's it?' Georgina shouted after him as the rest of us gaped.

'You can find me at The Old Cataract Hotel in Aswan,' he called back over his shoulder. 'I might stay to watch the sound and light show. But then I really must be heading back. I'll hire a taxi, since it seems unlikely Saleh here will be moved to offer me a lift back in his hire car.'

And then he was gone. The metal door banged closed behind him.

We stared at each other in a protracted silence.

'I've met that man twice,' Adam said at last. 'And on neither occasion has he done what I expected him to do.'

'Try being married to him,' Georgina muttered sardonically. But she seemed as bewildered as the rest of us.

'So that is it?' Ahmed frowned scratching his head. 'He is not here to steal the money?'

'Apparently not,' I said, bemused. 'He didn't even stick around long enough to be sure there's any money to steal. What a thoroughly perplexing man!'

'Could it be a trick of some sort?' Adam frowned. 'I mean; why would he bribe the guard for his uniform – a damned strange thing to do – if he had no intention of escorting us out of here with the money and then making off with it?'

I shrugged, searching my brain but finding no answer. 'He's alerted us to his presence; which seems a bit odd if his intention is to play games. Ahmed still has his gun. And Max was patently unarmed.' I shook my head. 'I'm as mystified as you are.'

'Is it possible he was telling the truth?' Habiba suggested softly.

All eyes turned once more to fix on Georgina.

'What are you looking at *me* for?' she demanded hotly. 'Max Savage's motivations and behaviour are as much a mystery to me as they are to you! In truth I never could work him out. There was a time I might have found his unpredictability attractive, exciting even. But the novelty soon wore off; I assure you.'

That Georgina Savage was thoroughly rattled was plain for all to see.

'Now that he's decided to push off, I don't want to think about him,' she declared, standing with her hands on her hips, feet planted apart. 'And I most certainly don't want to talk about him! It seems to me he's disrupted things quite enough today already. Now, what do you say? Shall we carry on as we were before we were so rudely interrupted? I, for one, want to see what's hidden behind this giant cat flap!'

I had to admire her. She was pulling herself together with a visible effort, perhaps using bravado to mask the shock of her ex-husband's revelations. Whether or not these would turn out to be wholly unwelcome remained to be seen. That they were unexpected was beyond doubt.

'Well? What are you waiting for?' she demanded when none of us moved. 'Have you all turned to stone? For God's sake, let's get on with it!'

We didn't need any further invitation. Willing to forget temporarily about Max Savage and his bizarre behaviour, we crowded around once again. Although I admit I kept shooting glances over my shoulder to ensure Max had actually left.

'It's here!' Georgina shouted a moment later. 'The box! I can see it! I just can't reach it!'

That was the trouble with being a rather buxom individual. Her girth was too wide to enable her to squeeze enough of herself through the cavity.

'Please; allow me,' Adam moved forward.

My husband is fit and lithe. He had no problem ducking down, leaning forward and shunting through the gap. 'It's a metal security box!' he announced a moment later. No mistaking the elation in his voice. Grunting, he hefted it backwards and pulled it out through the flap.

Black, metal, with a combination lock; it was the approximate size of a carry-on-board flight suitcase. But without the convenience of wheels or a pull-out handle.

'Congratulations Georgina,' I breathed in wonder. 'You've found your stash of hidden treasure!'

Mehmet clicked away on his camera a few times. 'Wow!' he said between shots. 'This is exciting!'

'What do we do now?' Habiba asked, not sounding anywhere near so thrilled.

'Surely we must open it!' Ahmed, on his knees, leaned forward eagerly.

I glanced at my watch. 'Do you think that's sensible? Wouldn't it be better to get it back to the *Queen Ahmes*?'

A burst of music made me jump out of my skin.

'The sound and light show, it starts,' Ahmed said.

'Saleh, please go and stand guard by the door,' Georgina said. 'We don't want any more unexpected visitors.'

When Saleh looked as if he might argue, Georgina frowned at him. 'You are still serving your penance,' she advised him. 'I suggest you do as you're told.'

With no further demur, Saleh got up and moved towards the door Max Savage had not long since departed through.

'If Max is to be believed, the guard he bribed has taken his money and scarpered,' Georgina said. 'It strikes me the others are unlikely to interrupt us during the sound and light show. They will assume the original guard is still here keeping watch. So it seems to me we're at liberty to have a little look. If we're caught, we can simply tell the truth. My whole point in being here is to bring this money to light. No, it's Max, not the guards, I'm keen to keep at bay.'

I saw some logic in this and subsided.

'How do we know how many numbers the combination lock has?' Adam asked.

Georgina brushed dust from the box with one hand and squinted at the dials. 'I'd say it's eight,' she announced, straightening to look at him.

'Wouldn't it be easier to jimmy it open?' I frowned. 'We'll be here all night trying to work out the combination.'

'Jimmy?' Ahmed asked, uncomprehending. 'Who is this Jimmy?'

'It's a type of crowbar,' Adam explained. 'But since we haven't got one, let's try a few number sequences first.

'For an eight digit code, the most obvious sequence has to be a date,' I offered. 'I'm guessing you didn't happen to overhear the combination in any of your hacked telephone calls?' I raised an eyebrow at Georgina.

'Nothing quite so helpful,' she admitted with a small shrug. 'But I agree with you. A date makes most sense. It's more memorable than a random set of numbers. Since Michael Black is the one who stashed the cash inside, a date of significance to him would seem the most likely.'

'Do you happen to know his date of birth?' Adam questioned. 'That would seem to be the obvious bet.'

'As it happens, I do. I got it from the police reports of his obituary.' As she spoke her fingers started to work the dials of the combination lock. 'They are unsurprisingly stiff,' she grunted after a moment. 'Assuming this box has been here for upwards of fifty years, it's only to be expected, I suppose.'

We watched her forcing the stiff dials into motion for a long tensely drawn out moment. The booming music and narration of the sound and light show kept up a background accompaniment to her efforts.

'Any luck?' I said at last.

She sat back on her haunches and rubbed her fingers together, looking disappointed. 'Nope. It's not his birth date.'

'It was too much to expect it to be the very first number we thought of,' Adam remarked.

'What about wedding anniversary?' I suggested. 'That's another key date for most of us.' I glanced at Adam with a smile. We always used our wedding date for safety deposit boxes.

Georgina glared at me. 'Not everyone is quite so sentimental nor quite so loved up as the pair of you!' she remarked tartly. 'Besides which, beyond knowing that Michael Black was married, I have absolutely no idea how we'd find out the date. We don't have a handy Internet connection here you know!'

I realised I'd been a tad insensitive in view of her recent experience with her ex-husband. 'Sorry,' I said. 'It was just a thought.'

'What about the date of The Great Train Robbery itself?' Adam hazarded. 'That surely seems an obvious choice, and an easy date for Mickey Black, the son, to check; considering he knew where the stolen money came from.'

'That was 8 August 1963,' Georgina said. 'So... 08... 08... 1963...' Again as she spoke her fingers worked the dial. Once more she gave up in defeat. 'It's hopeless,' she announced, sitting back again. 'Maybe we'll have to resort to a crowbar once back on the dahabeeyah. You do have one, I suppose?' She addressed herself to Adam.

'I think Khaled may have a claw hammer, or maybe a drill,' he suggested with a shrug. 'Just tools to keep up routine maintenance on the *Queen Ahmes*. Remember, when we set out on this trip we had no idea we'd be needing to break into a metal security box.'

'So near and yet so far,' I murmured, staring at the box. Then an idea struck me. 'If not the date of The Great Train Robbery itself,' I ventured. 'What about the date of John Daly's arrest? Surely that was the more pertinent date to Michael Black, since he was one of the so-called "friends" who shopped him to the police. I know it's a long shot, but do you happen to know the date the police stormed the flat he was using as a hidey hole in Belgravia?'

'There are some advantages to being an investigative journalist,' Georgina announced with a self-satisfied smirk. 'I have a very good memory for detail, and for dates. John Daly was arrested on 3 December 1963.'

Once again we watched as her fingers worked the dials. The outcome was becoming increasingly inevitable.

'Oh well, it was worth a try,' I said as her shoulders slumped.

'Assuming it's a date rather than a random assortment of numbers,' Adam started, 'the only other suggestion I can think of is the date of John Daly's acquittal. Surely that's the date Michael Black and his partner-in-crime went haring down to Cornwall to dig up the buried loot before John Daly made a beeline there.'

'You said John Daly's first action on his release from custody was to throw a huge party,' I reminded Georgina. 'That gave Michael Black and the other guy...'

'Bill Goodwin,' she supplied.

'...Yes, that gave them their opportunity to get to the money. Suddenly they were on a deadline.'

'John Daly was acquitted on 14 February 1964,' Georgina said.

'Valentine's Day,' I remarked.

'And just as the UNESCO project to re-site the Abu Simbel temples was hitting the headlines,' Adam added.

It was our final roll of the dice, and we all knew it. Music and narration from the sound and light show echoed through the domed chamber. To my fanciful imagination it was a movie score playing a soaring accompaniment to our endeavours. All of us, except poor Saleh by the door, craned forward and held a collective breath. I felt goose bumps rise on the skin of my forearms and the little hairs lifted across the nape of my neck.

Georgina spoke the numbers aloud as her fingers worked the stiff dials. '14... 02... 1964.' There was an audible click. 'Oh my God!' Georgina slumped backwards looking dazed. Her features flooded with hot colour.

Adam and I fell to our knees alongside her.

'Did it open?' Ahmed yelled in my ear. No mistaking his exhilaration.

Habiba and Mehmet moved closer.

'Ok, Georgina; here's your moment. Time to lift the lid.' Adam invited.

Outside, the music swelled again.

Georgina sucked in a deep breath, reached forward with both hands and prised it upwards. Stiff with age and unaccustomed use, it took a moment to budge. 'Ahmed, I might need your help,' she grunted.

Ahmed's enthusiasm is greater than his finesse. He's also a big man and stronger than he thinks he is. He reached forward giving the lid a hefty tug. The lid flew open. The box toppled sideways. Banknotes spilled across the floor.

We all gaped. Never had I seen such riches. Wealth beyond my wildest dreams. Money. Everywhere. Ok, so none of it was legal tender anymore. But it was a heart-stopping sight all the same. A slice of British criminal history literally fallen into our laps.

'Congratulations, Georgina; you've got your scoop.' Adam said after a moment. Then he let out a whoop. 'And all without laying a finger on Ramses' Great Temple.'

'I think we should go,' Habiba said edgily. 'I'm pleased for you, Georgina. I know how much this means to you. Like Adam, I'm relieved we have not had to tamper with the temple itself. But still, I remain anxious about how my superiors at the Ministry of Antiquities will react.'

'Let's get back to the dahabeeyah and work out a plan of action,' I suggested. 'Remember, we're not supposed officially to arrive here at Abu Simbel until tomorrow. I'm sure we can think of a way for Georgina to claim her scoop without the rest of us getting into trouble if we put our thinking caps on. I believe we have some champagne on board. It seems to me a small celebration is in order.'

It was a strange feeling actually handling money I knew to be part of the stolen heist from The Great Train Robbery. Different from the shivery sensations I'd experienced in the past, handling relics from Egypt's ancient past. Now I felt more as if I were playing a role in a movie, especially with the music still booming away outside. The Great Train Robbery was an iconic chapter in British twentieth century history. And here was I, actually handling some of the stolen cash. The banknotes were not our more familiar modern ones, for sure.

But the Queen was still there in profile. The green one pound notes and the blue five pound notes would have been currency used by my parents and grandparents.

We shoved the money back into the box. I'd thought it might be neatly stacked in piles secured by elastic bands. But no; it seemed Michael Black had simply stuffed as much of it into the box as it was capable of holding. We did the same, re-closing the lid and turning the dials to lock it.

As planned, we emptied the packing case we'd brought with us of Mehmet's photographic equipment. The security box fitted easily inside.

'Ok, time to go,' Adam said as he and Mehmet hoisted the case between them.

Saleh came forward to help as the rest of us distributed Mehmet's lenses, tripods and cases between us, as unobtrusively as we could. Ahmed even managed to secrete a couple of filters inside his sling. Climbing back across the metal rail, we trooped towards the door.

I stepped forward to open it so I could hold it for the others to come through. As I pushed the door open, the sight of a gun cocked and ready to fire stopped me in my tracks.

'Max Savage!' I choked in fright.

He was standing there still dressed in the guard's uniform. Except Max wasn't the one holding the gun.

Even without his uniform, I recognised the guard who'd accompanied us here earlier. Dressed now in a vest and boxer shorts, he held the gun aimed squarely at the chest of Georgina's ex-husband.

Chapter 12

'It seems I misjudged this fellow's susceptibility to bribery after all,' Max said with an ironic tilt to one winged eyebrow. 'He doesn't speak good English, so perhaps something of my intention was lost in translation.'

By now, the others had all joined me, piling out through the open door. We stood frozen in a tableau of shock. I noticed Ahmed unsling his own gun. But it was Habiba who stepped forward, addressing the guard in a rush of soft-toned Arabic. Saleh el-Sayed also stepped forward, although there was no mistaking the expression of smug satisfaction on his face seeing Max Savage with a gun pointed at his heart.

With the music and voiceover from the sound and light show still booming out on the other side of the temple mound – louder now we were outside in the cool night air – things took on a rather surreal perspective. As if nothing else about the day so far had been in any way surreal! I caught myself in the thought and wondered just how much more surreal things could possibly get. First the ambush on board the dahabeeyah. Then the crocodile attack. There was Saleh's duplicity and prompt about-turn. The fruitless search of the creepy inner sanctuary was something I felt I might not forget in a hurry. All topped off of course by our discovery of the haul from The Great British Train Robbery – not in the Temple of Ramses but in the modern dome that housed it. Add the bizarre and contradictory behaviour of Max Savage into the mix and it amounted to a very strange sort of a day indeed.

And now a guard dressed in only his underwear, shoes and socks was holding that self-same unpredictable and capricious character at gunpoint. It was all a bit much to take in to be honest.

Habiba and Saleh took turns to jabber away at the guard in Arabic. It was impossible for me to follow what they were saying or interpret their many hand gestures. Mehmet, perhaps sensibly, held back. Maybe he was happy to leave it to the others. They were the ones who'd flashed their professional ID to grant us our special admission after all. I wondered if he, like me, was thinking he would soon be kissing goodbye to this wonderful venture we were engaged on, commissioned by the Egyptian Tourism Authority. It was surely too much to hope for that we could emerge from all this with our employment intact.

At some point I had no doubt we would have to report Philip Sinnerman as dead. And right now it looked as if Max Savage was on a sticky wicket. It was impossible not to wonder how the day might have played out had Georgina's two exes (colleague and husband) not decided to show up and throw a spanner in the works.

I watched indecision flicker across the guard's stony features in response to what he was being told. Max Savage stood with the too-small uniform straining at the seams on his apelike body and a wolfish expression on his face. There really was something quite animalistic about him, now I looked at him properly. I think it had to do with raw energy. Even standing still and watchful, he seemed vigorous. I could see more and more why Georgina had once found him attractive. Vitality is a strangely captivating quality. A woman as large and forthright as Georgina would need a man with some strength of character to match her.

The Arabic stopped. Without lowering the gun, the guard turned his head to look at Georgina. 'Dis is true?' he said in thickly accented English. 'You are marriage to dis man?'

I watched Georgina look from the guard to Max and back again. 'I was once,' she said heavily. 'But it was a while ago. You may shoot him if you wish.'

I was sure Georgina had understood the frantic conversation between our Egyptian companions and the guard. She spoke Arabic well enough. I realised Habiba must have stuck to Max's own story about why he was here. As implausible as it sounded, she and Saleh seemed to be spinning the yarn Max himself had started. Perhaps they too saw it as the only way of hanging onto their jobs.

'Georgina!' I exclaimed, shocked.

Max, unbelievably, let out a bark of laughter. 'Still determined to hold onto that grudge, eh Georgie?'

'I haven't forgotten that you said if I made another go of my career it would be over your dead body,' she muttered.

'I didn't mean it literally!'

'Yes, well; you got yourself into this. You can damn well get yourself out! Why should my friends and I suffer the consequences of your decision to strip this poor chap down to his underwear? You could at least let him have his clothes back!' Then she turned her head and addressed herself to the guard. 'I am sorry to say that, yes; this man was once my husband. And now he is here with the intention of harassing me. If you're not going to shoot him, then you would be doing me a very great service if you could please take him into custody.'

I gaped at her. 'Georgina, are you quite sure that's what you want?'

'He's playing both ends to the middle!' she declared. 'I'm convinced of it! You know, it wouldn't surprise me to learn this charade is all part of the act. It's quite possible his bribing of the guard here is all part of an elaborate hoax!'

'You think I've bribed him to point a gun at me?' Max roared.

'You're capable of just about anything,' she accused. 'Now, for God's sake, give the poor man back his uniform!'

I stared long and hard at Max Savage as he started to unbutton the guard's shirt. And no, it wasn't the musculature of his broad hairy chest I was interested in, impressive though that was. It struck me suddenly that Max was telling the truth when he said he wanted to make a go of things with Georgina. Why else wasn't he directing the guard to investigate what was inside the packing case Adam and Mehmet had lowered to the ground on seeing the gun? And I suddenly realised what Georgina needed to do.

'If you want your career back, I should think you might want to own up to what we've just found,' I prompted, looking at Georgina meaningfully. 'Adam, tell her,' I instructed, knowing he would cotton on in a heartbeat.

Of course he didn't fail me. 'The guard is a pretty good eye witness,' Adam nodded emphatically. 'You know, it strikes me you could turn this to your advantage.'

'The only way to stop Max stealing your scoop, or the money – or both – is surely to announce it now, before he can.' I urged in an undertone. 'If you come clean right now, there's even a possibility we might avoid arrest.'

I saw the speculative light come into Georgina's eyes. 'You're right,' she said, and seemed to snap to a decision. 'Saleh,' she instructed. 'Please go and find another guard. Make sure he's armed and bring him back here. If you really want to be the hero of the day and prove whose side you're on – ours, I trust – your testimony will be necessary to get my dear ex-husband banged to rights.'

Saleh el Sayed seemed more than motivated to do as he was bid. He stood to attention and nodded briskly. I thought he might even click his heels and salute.

'Don't be a fool, woman!' Max Savage paused in the action of shrugging out of the guard's shirt and glared at her. 'If Saleh makes a police statement about me he'll lose his job!'

'Don't pretend you have any scruples on that score!' Georgina shot back. 'Perhaps you should have thought of the possible impact on his livelihood before you ensnared him in your web.'

I watched Saleh hesitate and saw the dawning comprehension on his face. He was by no means innocent of the circumstances that had brought Max Savage and Philip Sinnerman into our lives. But he'd got in way over his head. The consequences of admitting it could be career limiting to say the least.

'Bribing and threatening your young colleague here was Philip's idea; not mine,' Max reminded her. 'My role all along has been one of attempted damage limitation.'

'Easy for you to say! But they're just words, Max.'

'It's the truth.'

'We need someone else with a gun out here!' Georgina maintained, looking at me. 'The guard will have to put his down to get back into his uniform. And the minute he does, Max will jump him. Just you mark my words!'

'You really don't trust me at all, do you?' Max enquired with a dark look. He unbuttoned and unzipped the guard's trousers and, kicking off his trainers, stepped out of them.

I scarcely knew where to look. The scrawny guard in his vest and pants with his knobbly knees exposed above his shoes and long socks was one thing. Max Savage, swarthy, thickset and hairy – oh, so hairy – and standing there in just a set of black jersey briefs, was quite another. I never knew near-nakedness could be quite so intimidating.

'I know what you're capable of,' Georgina accused. 'Of course I don't trust you.'

'No, you don't – know what I'm capable of; I mean,' he responded sourly. 'You have chosen wilfully to believe the worst about me at every possible turn.'

'You made it so easy,' she muttered.

He fixed her with a ferocious stare. 'For an investigative journalist, I always found it particularly ironic that you didn't want to know the truth. You were perfectly happy to condemn me and throw me to the wolves without a backward glance!'

'Er – I really don't think –' I started, hoping to avert the insight into the disintegration of their marriage I could see coming. Georgina's next words cut me off before I could finish.

'YOU were the one consorting with prostitutes!' she flung at him.

I broke off what I'd been about to say and stared. An accusation like that hurled at a semi-naked man brought all sorts of images flashing before my eyes.

'But you never bothered to find out why, did you?' Fury brought his bushy black eyebrows sweeping downwards.

'Why does any man visit prostitutes?' she remarked bitterly.

'Shame you didn't ask me that question at the time,' he ground out. 'It might have given me the chance to tell you.

Instead, you packed up your stuff and moved out. The next thing I knew, you'd written that piece about me, and my name was plastered all over the media. You knew my career couldn't take a hit like that!'

'Yet you seemed to think our marriage could take a hit like that!'

They squared off against each other; a big woman with her chest heaving, eyes flashing fire, and a solid gorilla of a man showing not one jot of embarrassment or self-consciousness at his state of undress.

'For God's sake, Max; what did you do with your own clothes?' Georgina muttered, while he continued to brazen it out, confronting us all aggressively with his near-nudity. 'I really can't have this conversation with you standing there in your underpants!'

'They're behind that rock over there.' He jerked his thumb.

I looked at the guard. To what extent he'd followed the conversation I had no idea. That he wanted nothing more than to get back into the uniform Max Savage had tossed at his feet was obvious. But it left him with the dilemma of his gun. It was clear he didn't dare put it down. And he could hardly get dressed still holding it aimed at Max Savages's bare chest.

'We need another guard,' Georgina repeated. 'Honestly! Is this sound and light show going to go on all night?'

I'd scarcely paid any attention to the background musical score, so caught up was I in the drama unfolding around me. It was with some surprise that I remembered on the other side of the artificial cliff were rows of tourists enjoying the show.

'I have a gun,' Ahmed said, stepping forward. 'It will be my pleasure to keep it trained on your divorce.' By which he meant her ex-husband of course. He fitted the action to the words, disregarding his sling and lifting the nozzle to point it at Max Savage.

The guard hesitated. But whatever else he'd discerned, it was evidently clear to him that the man who'd crossed his palm with silver fell a long way short of being our bosom buddy. That Georgina was spitting fire at him was plain with or without the language barrier. He put his gun down and rested one foot on it, possibly just in case any of us should take it into our heads to try something funny. He couldn't scramble into his clothes fast enough. I've never seen a man do up shirt buttons so quickly.

Mehmet jogged over to the rock Max had indicated and returned with the pair of jeans and polo shirt Max had been wearing earlier. They showed some evidence of his swim in the lake, being stiff and creased as he tugged them on.

With Max and the guard both once more dressed in their own clothes and with Max staring down the barrel of not just one gun, but two, things returned to whatever passed for some semblance of normality around here.

Max wasted no time in wresting back control. As the man with two loaded firearms trained on him, this seemed his prerogative, and nobody argued. 'Now, I'm going to tell the story, and you're going to listen.' He glowered at his ex-wife. 'And when you've heard me out, you can decide what you want to do about announcing your scoop, and whether you want to have me arrested.'

'This should be interesting,' Adam muttered softly at my side.

Max Savage assumed the pose of a rugby player about to enter a scrum. Unexpectedly, he addressed himself to Adam and me. 'I think we have established my career was as a politician and Member of Parliament,' he said.

'Yes,' I acknowledged.

'My dear ex-wife has just flung a nasty accusation at me,' he remarked. 'Taken at face value, I'm sure it paints a rather ugly picture. So, let me say this: a couple of years ago the Home Affairs Select Committee began an inquiry into prostitution legislation in the UK. As you may or may not be aware, prostitution itself is not illegal, but running a brothel is.'

I darted a lightning glance at Georgina, standing stiff and tight-featured alongside the guard. He, poor man, didn't seem to know quite what to make of things. I'm sure when he set out for duty earlier, he expected a nice normal shift. Certainly not to be treated to an insight into prostitution law in the United Kingdom after the rest of the evening's shenanigans. In truth, it was just about the last thing I could have predicted too. Still, Max seemed determined to say his piece, and it seemed the rest of us – including the guard – had little choice but to let him.

I saw Max Savage's gaze also flicker to his ex-wife. She seemed determined not to be drawn, so after a pause he went on: 'Debate about the possible reform of prostitution laws in the UK centres around the question of whether new legislation is necessary or even desirable. It set out to assess whether the balance in the burden of criminality should shift to those who pay for sex rather than those who sell it.'

This was more information than I wanted or needed. The rights and wrongs of those who traded in personal services weren't something I'd ever particularly considered. And I wasn't at all sure I especially wanted to consider them right now. Adam, perhaps thinking the same, decided to bring us to the crux of the matter. 'You're saying any involvement you had with prostitutes was purely professional,' he said.

'Of course that's what I'm saying,' Max said impatiently. 'It's an important debate. At its heart are allegations of human trafficking and exploitation. Given the current absence of robust data on the subject, I recommended the Home Office should commission a research study to inform future legislation. But of course it all came crashing down around my ears when my darling wife wrote her exposé. She accused me of visiting prostitutes for my own pleasure. Worse, her piece claimed I couldn't be objective because I was covering up my own past.'

'Your past?' I asked in spite of myself.

'Tell them, Georgina,' Max demanded.

'His mother ran a brothel back in the early sixties,' Georgina said woodenly.

I felt my jaw drop.

'Max spent his entire life protecting her!'

'She did not run a brothel,' Max remonstrated. 'She ran a cabaret club.'

'It amounts to the same thing,' Georgina muttered. 'What kind of woman employs showgirls to dance topless in a Soho club visited by aristocrats seeking a thrill?'

I saw the flash of anger. 'A poor one!' he bit out.

Georgina raised an arch eyebrow but didn't comment.

'You still refuse to show a jot of empathy!' he accused. 'I'd have thought in these enlightened times you might have some understanding of the victimhood of the women so many powerful men profited from!'

'Your mother was anything BUT a victim!' Georgina shot back. 'She was a very clever manipulator of men! She manipulated *you* your whole life!'

'She married a man she did not love – a man who was not my father – because he threatened to turn her in if she did not,' Max shouted, losing his temper. 'It was the only way to protect herself from the media intrusion when the story broke.'

'Yes! And what a story! Wouldn't we all love to know who your father was!'

He bit down hard on his anger. 'That information died with my mother. And since Christine Keeler is also now dead I don't think I am ever likely to find out. In truth, I don't think I want to know.'

I blinked, recognising the name.

'Christine Keeler?' Adam choked. 'But she was at the heart of the –'

'– Yes, the Profumo Affair.' Max supplied. The anger left him on a great rush of air as if someone had stuck a pin in it.

'The Profumo Affair?' I parroted weakly. Honestly! This conversation was becoming more bizarre by the second. 'That was the story that broke?'

'There were those who wanted my mother arrested for running the club where Christine Keeler first met Stephen Ward,' Max Savage nodded. Then, perhaps feeling the need to explain, added, 'Ward was the *"man about town"* who introduced Christine Keeler into the aristocratic social set that included Profumo, then Secretary of State for War, and the Russian military attaché Yevgeny Ivanov. She went on to have affairs with both men. When the relationships came to light in 1963, amid fears of a cold war security leak, it rocked the Harold Macmillan government.'

Adam and I exchanged an incredulous glance. But Max hadn't finished, and went on:

'Even now the tentacles of that scandal reach into the heart of modern politics. Once Georgina's article started to raise questions about what my mother may or may not have known, the Select Committee couldn't get me off the case fast enough! Georgina managed to make it sound as if I might have an axe to grind, and as if my mother still harboured secrets. And all because she got it into her head that I was paying lady escorts for sex!' He turned his head to look at his ex-wife. 'Honestly Georgina, it's laughable!'

'You never denied it!' she accused.

'You never gave me the chance!' he shot back. 'You simply plastered my illegitimacy all over the papers. Thank God, my mother was too ill by then to know what was going on. Alzheimer's is a cruel disease but it has its blessings. It was an unkind thing that you did, Georgina.'

'You always did side with your mother against the world,' she said bitterly. 'Maybe I just wanted you to notice me and put me first for once.'

'Dragging my mother's name through the gutter press more than fifty years after the original scandal got my attention alright,' he parried. 'And for all the wrong reasons. If that was your idea of throwing down a gauntlet, you miscalculated badly.' He sounded more weary than angry now.

'What was I supposed to think when night after night you were out all hours, and came home smelling of cheap perfume?'

'You could have tried asking me rather than staking me out and drawing your own misguided conclusions.'

'I would think it's a pretty strange wife, seeing her husband leave a known "massage club" –' she put inverted commas around the word to lace it with the intended innuendo ' – not to make the same assumption I did,' she said acidly.

'But, really,' he said. 'Raking up the whole Profumo Affair. Was that really necessary?'

I sent a hard look at Georgina. I saw a woman whose first line of defence was attack and realised suddenly this was the weapon she used to mask insecurity. My instincts told me that under the surface she was nowhere near so bombastic as she appeared. Her next words seemed to confirm it.

'I was hurt and wanted to lash out,' she admitted. 'It just seemed particularly ironic to me that a man born in the shadow of the shady affair that shook British politics in the 1960s should risk his own political career – and our marriage – consorting with prostitutes!'

'Ironic is hardly the word!' he thundered, temper flaring again. 'It was absurd!'

'Yes, well I didn't know that then, did I?' she pointed out defensively. 'I just thought you'd decided I wasn't enough for you.'

Max looked at her in surprise. 'Georgina, you were *more* than enough for me. You were enough for me with bells on! You were, are, and always will be, my sparring partner of choice.'

Unexpectedly my throat clogged, and I choked. As declarations of love went, that one sounded pretty grand and romantic to me.

Sadly my little coughing fit rather ruined the moment. Georgina gathered her armour once more. 'You know, I always believed your mother knew a whole lot more about what went on in the early sixties than she let on.'

The fight seemed to go out of Max and his shoulders slumped. 'Yes, well, whatever my mother may or may not have known died when she did. It's not relevant anymore. But sadly your scurrilous little article put paid to my career.'

'And yet you're here claiming to want me back!' she declared. 'Unlikely is hardly the word for it!'

A speculative light came into his eyes as he looked at her. For the first time, I saw him dart a glance at the packing case still sitting on the dusty ground where Adam and Mehmet had put it. A small smile played about his mouth. And then he looked back at her. 'You're very quick to condemn my mother,' he said. 'But let's not forget where you got your first whiff of the story about what might have happened to part of the haul from a certain robbery…'

He allowed a long pause to draw out.

Georgina regarded him watchfully.

Max turned his head and glanced at Adam and then me. 'She's no doubt told you it was a prime piece of investigative journalism.'

'She's admitted she was guilty of phone hacking,' Adam said levelly, invited into the conversation. 'And, to be fair to her, she confessed it long before you and Philip Sinnerman turned up.'

'Hmm, yes,' Max said thoughtfully. 'But I wonder if she thought to enlighten you about how she knew whose phone to hack.'

Georgina was breathing heavily, glaring at her ex-husband with open hostility. I glanced from his face to hers and back again. I couldn't help but think they deserved each other, and were quite possibly as bad as one another. She accused him of undermining his own career – and their marriage – consorting with prostitutes. But she was the one guilty of criminality and had been thrown out on her ear by her employers as a result.

I glanced around to see what the others were making of things. Our Egyptian companions – not forgetting the guard – were each observing the spat between Georgina and Max Savage as if watching a tennis match: eyes shifting and heads turning to look from one to the other as the conversation batted back and forth. I had no idea whether they'd understood any of what was said about the Profumo Affair. The reality was, I knew very little about it myself; although I'd read some News reports that Christine Keeler had died before Christmas, and the articles had re-hashed the essence of her story.

We all looked at Max Savage expectantly. He bared his teeth in a wolfish smile and continued in the same conversational tone as before. 'Politicians and aristocrats weren't the only ones to frequent my mother's Soho cabaret club in the early sixties,' he said. 'Petty criminals and antiquities dealers did, too. And in 1963 when the Profumo scandal came to light there was another story also grabbing headlines.'

'The Great Train Robbery,' I breathed.

Max Savage bared his teeth again. 'Yes! And the salvage of the Abu Simbel temples began the following year. The beginning of the swinging sixties – it was quite a time! And it's fair to say my mother knew many of the key protagonists!'

Georgina cast him an evil glance. 'You're every bit as bad as Philip Sinnerman,' she spat. 'Everything you said earlier is just a cock and bull story! You're here to steal my scoop! Either that or claim it as your own!'

His bushy eyebrows lifted and swept down again. 'No, Georgina; I am here to help you.'

'I fail to see how!' she retorted.

This time, he spoke in the slightly condescending tones of one pointing out something rather obvious to somebody particularly dim-witted. 'I imagine you will have concocted a plausible story to tell the Black family when the story breaks about how you came to learn the location of the money hidden by their grandfather?'

Georgina opened her mouth once or twice. But when she didn't speak, Max pressed home his advantage. 'I'm assuming you'd rather not pay further damages for phone hacking. After all, you don't have the shield of a major News corporation to protect you now, even if you did hack the phones while still technically employed by them. If you seek to profit from what you learned now, I would think they'll leave you to face the music on your own.'

Max turned his head to look at Adam and me. Then he turned triumphantly to his ex-wife. 'Team up with me on the other hand,' he invited, and I can testify that my mother told the story of a stash of train robbery cash being hidden away here during the re-siting of the Great Temple of Ramses from gossip she overheard at her cabaret club.'

'Pillow talk, more like,' Georgina muttered.

'Whatever,' Max said benignly. 'I can legitimise your search here, and perhaps you can let these good people get away without being arrested!'

He spoke into a sudden silence as the background accompaniment of the sound and light show stopped abruptly. It had been so much a feature of this strange unfolding drama I'd forgotten to notice it – just taken the swelling music and spoken narration booming from the other side of the manmade rock as part and parcel of this whole bizarre circumstance. But the precipitate cessation of sound left a void. It seemed an unnatural ending, as if it had broken off in mid flow. I started to discern the reality of this when I heard a shriek and then another.

'What the…?' Adam exclaimed, and not for the first time today.

We all cast somewhat blank and panicked glances at each other. Not one of us could have imagined what was causing such alarm among the gathered tourists. But it didn't take long to find out, since we were the quarry.

I recognised the approaching guard as the second of the original pair who'd kept watch outside the temple while we conducted our abortive search of the inner sanctuary earlier. He'd returned to duties as the sound and light show got underway leaving us in the care of his poor beleaguered colleague.

With a sickened jolt of shock and horror I also recognised the man two further guards were hoisting along between them. A man bleeding copiously from two mangled stumps that had once been his legs.

'Philip Sinnerman!' I gasped.

No longer dripping wet, he must have hauled himself from the water some hours ago. Grey-featured, with crippling injuries, I could only imagine he'd somehow dragged himself to the temple forecourt to bring the sound and light show to its abrupt ending. He was caked in grime and barely conscious.

But he remained sufficiently in possession of his critical faculties to raise a condemnatory finger, pointing towards us as crowds converged behind him and mobile phones were raised to record the macabre scene.

'There...' he accused in a voice loaded with pain. 'There are the people who as good as murdered me!' And, just for the avoidance of doubt about identity he added, 'Max and Georgina Savage!'

My gasp of shock became an indignant choke.

Pain-crazed and clinging to life by a fraying thread as he clearly was, I saw Philip Sinnerman's failing eyes alight on the packing case. 'Ask them what they have hidden in that box!' he wheezed. 'Michael Black always said he'd send his son to retrieve it. And there he is!'

And then, as if the fight to point the finger of blame had robbed him of every last scrap of determination – indeed of life – he slipped from the grasp of the two guards holding him up, slumping in a pool of his own blood on the rocky terrain in front of them, us, and assorted witnesses.

Chapter 13

After an accusation of murder, the guards had no choice but to detain us *en masse*.

This time around Philip Sinnerman was very clearly dead. It was quite possibly a blessing. Half eaten by a crocodile, and with such devastating injuries, he was beyond all hope of recovery.

The poor traumatised guards worked hard to disperse the crowds. To be fair, a number of the staring onlookers appeared equally shaken by what they'd witnessed. I don't imagine seeing a critically injured man haul himself in front of an assemblage gathered to enjoy a sound and light show can be high on many people's holiday itineraries. In truth, I felt stunned and sickened too. Try as I might to tell myself he'd been the architect of his own demise – no matter how unwitting – it was still horrific to have seen the crocodile attack and then been forced to observe its gruesome outcome.

An ambulance was called to remove Philip Sinnerman's body. With loaded firearms trained on us we had no choice but to sit on the ground in the dark outside and wait to see how the authorities planned on dealing with us.

One thing was for sure: we'd lost the opportunity to initiate the big reveal. The guard who'd accepted the bribe Max offered him for his uniform was tasked with investigating the contents of the packing case. The metal security box inside was removed, and we each gave up the various bits and pieces of Mehmet's camera equipment it had replaced inside.

The guard regarded the security box – and each of us – suspiciously, and with undisguised foreboding.

Max Savage took pity on him. 'Don't worry,' he cajoled. 'I won't tell them you loaned me your uniform if you don't. It can be our secret.'

Ahmed translated into Arabic. The look of relief that swept over the poor chap's features was almost pathetic to observe. I felt quite sorry for him. The reaction of the crowds, and indeed our own, to the sight of Philip's half-eaten body was one thing. But the guards had to keep up a semblance of control, despite whatever they may be thinking or feeling. I could well imagine that for this poor chap, being forced to admit he'd earlier accepted a bribe from someone now accused of sending a man into the jaws of a deadly crocodile might be a somewhat terrifying prospect under the circumstances. I'm sure none of this was at all what he'd expected when he reported for duty this evening.

I was glad we'd had the foresight to re-lock the security box before leaving the temple dome. Opening it now to reveal the cash when there were still a number of straggler tourists loitering around, and with an accusation of murder hanging in the air, seemed unwise.

But the accusation of murder and the direction to investigate the box weren't the only of Philip Sinnerman's dying words echoing on the airwaves.

As the ambulance departed with its grisly cargo, the guards led the last onlookers away. I gathered my composure. Trying not to look at the pool of drying blood where Philip Sinnerman's body had lain, nor the stained trail in the dust leading up to it, I captured the drifting words and translated them into a question. 'What was all that about Michael Black?' I asked, frowning.

'It's obvious, isn't it?' Georgina piped up. She was slumped on the floor with her knees drawn up to her chin and the skirt of her ubiquitous tent dress wrapped around her calves. She turned her head to look at her ex-husband, sitting in a more casual pose on the dusty ground with his legs crossed at the ankle, and leaning back on the palms of his hands behind him. 'You've always suspected your mother had an affair and was made pregnant by someone caught up in the Profumo Affair. I think that's partly why you went into politics. But it seems quite clear to me her lover was none other than Michael Black! A petty criminal, Max – you must be so proud! How inconsiderate of him to die so soon – and apparently of natural causes – having just laid claim to his share of John Daly's stash. I imagine he and your mother must have dreamt of running away together. Instead she was left no choice but to marry the man who brought you up. He gave her a veneer of respectability at least.'

Max Savage tilted his head on one side and regarded her with glittering eyes. 'You don't have to sound quite so gleeful about it. That man was not kind to my mother. Or me. It was a relief when he had his heart attack a few years ago. At least my mother was able to live the last few years of her life without him and his mean spiritedness.'

Georgina observed him steadily. 'You don't seem particularly shocked by the revelation. You claim your mother took secrets to the grave. But it strikes me you must have known all along you're Michael Black's son. Why else would you be here? You've come to claim the money as your own! That's been your motivation all along. Like father like son!'

'I did NOT know,' he said emphatically. Then shrugged and added, 'Although, I'll admit it occurred to me as a possibility. My mother always seemed to get a bit misty-eyed talking about The Great Train Robbery.'

Georgina grunted but refrained from further comment.

I looked from one to the other, wondering distantly what the others were making of all this. It may have come as no particular shock to Max to have his paternity confirmed, but I'll admit I was taking a little while to have it sink in. But then, everything I'd heard tonight was news to me. Being fathered by someone on the edges of the Profumo scandal, or operating on the borders of The Great Train Robbery, seemed to me equally disturbing. But, as Georgina had once said: we all have to be descended from someone! Poor old Max! Either way, it was some dodgy ancestry he'd inherited.

He was still regarding his ex-wife steadily, having only paused for breath, and now went on, 'As for my reasons for being here, please don't make me repeat them. I'm sure these people have no desire to be bored by my soul baring all over again.'

She stared at him. And I stared at her, wondering if finally she might give him a break and accept what he was saying. 'I wish I could believe you,' she said at last, shoulders slumping. 'But all I can see is that you and Philip Sinnerman were here together, very probably in possession of the facts of your paternity in the wake of your mother's death, and almost certainly on a mission to cut me out of the discovery.'

Max was silent for a long moment. When he spoke it was obvious he'd decided not to rise to the bait. 'I don't mind admitting I'm intrigued to know how Philip Sinnerman came by the knowledge of my probable parenting,' he confessed. Then shrugged. 'Although, I suppose I shouldn't be surprised. He liked to have a portfolio of dirt on just about everyone he knew. So he'll have raked it up from somewhere or other, thinking it may serve him well. As maybe it just has.'

'What do you mean?' she addressed him sharply.

He looked at her and sighed. 'Only that it seems very likely I'm about to be arrested for Philip's murder.' He spoke in that deep gravelly voice of his. 'As you've just pointed out so eloquently, my likely paternity would seem to give me a motive for wanting to get to the money before both you and Philip. You accused me earlier of standing by when he dropped that hunk of masonry from the roof of the Philae temple that could have killed you. And I was the one who landed the blow on Philip that sent him tumbling into the crocodile infested waters of Lake Nasser. So, congratulations, Georgina. As a witness for the prosecution I'm sure you'll have a field day! You can lay sole claim to your discovery and take all the plaudits while I rot in jail.'

She stared at him with her mouth opening and closing. When no sound emerged, he smiled at her and drove home his point. 'So, Georgie, my love; whether or not my real reasons for being here are genuine is all academic.' He sounded jaded but resigned, and his smile was definitely sad around the edges. 'Shame really. It's been good seeing you again. I've missed the simple joy of our bickering! Ah well, I remember reading somewhere that marriage is a stalemate between two equal adversaries. In our case, let's call it checkmate, with you the winner.'

'But we're no longer married,' she whispered as the sound of a police siren cut through the still night air.

Max stood up as the police car came to a stop at the top of the slope. He marched towards the vehicle with his arms outstretched. 'Don't bother reading me my rights,' he announced as uniformed officers jumped out of the car and slapped a pair of handcuffs onto his wrists. 'I'm not sure I necessarily have any here in Egypt anyway. And I don't speak Arabic. But it doesn't matter. I am perfectly prepared to confess. Philip Sinnerman is dead. And I'm the one responsible. Nobody else.'

Georgina Savage jumped up as quickly as her size and the folds of her skirt tucked around her legs would let her. 'Max! No!' she cried out. ' You don't have to do this!'

* * *

We were all arrested and taken into police custody of course. It's not an experience I'll be in any hurry to repeat.

The small town of Abu Simbel is compact and run down with just a few basic hotels and restaurants to cater for those travellers who may wish to stay overnight to visit the twin temples before or after the tour parties from Aswan have made their day trips.

The police station is equally small and basic. Its officers were quite clearly unused to dealing with the arrest of four UK foreign nationals, an inspector from the Ministry of State for Antiquities, an Egyptian Tourism Authority Marketing Manager, and a big, beefy Egyptian security guard. Ahmed of course confused matters greatly by casting aside his sling and waving his Luxor Tourist and Antiquities police ID card energetically in everyone's faces. That he was doing his utmost to intervene on behalf of Adam, myself, Habiba and Mehmet was touching for sure. But it didn't really help when he seemed to find it impossible to make his own status as our security guard and seconded policeman understood.

It took some considerable time for the ill-equipped officers to take the testimony of the temple guards and get to grips with our assorted professional credentials. The language barrier didn't help. Though many of the Egyptians in our party spoke English with a high degree of fluency, and were able to translate for us the various questions and then provide our answers; and even allowing for Adam and Georgina's reasonable command of Arabic, getting to the crux of things still seemed to demand communication skills beyond our collective abilities.

Max Savage had been taken into a cell. Having confessed to his part in Philip Sinnerman's gruesome demise, he seemed determined to face the music. The temple guards had borne witness to Philip's shocking interruption of the sound and light show, and their English was good enough that they were able to repeat his accusation word-for-word. Of course, he'd cited Max *and* Georgina as the ones who'd "as good as" murdered him. But we'd all had to confess to being on the scene during the fateful exchange of blows that had sent him hurtling through an open window into the lake.

It meant there was no need for any tourists to add their testimony; although I felt sure it was already going viral on social media. But there was no way of avoiding telling the story of how Max and Philip came to be on board our dahabeeyah. Attempting to put that into a few explanatory sentences was proving impossible.

Naturally neither the Abu Simbel police nor their counterparts the Abu Simbel guards had ever heard of The Great British Train Robbery. Our attempts to explain were laughable and absurd. In the end it became clear we were getting nowhere.

With a man in custody, the officers concluded they could let the rest of us go. An officer returned with us to collect our passports, and we were under strict instructions to remain moored at the lakeside. An Inspector would be called from Aswan. He would arrive with an interpreter tomorrow.

Sadly for us, these weren't the only visitations we could expect. Calls were made to the British Embassy in Cairo, as well as the Egyptian Tourism Authority and the Ministry of State for Antiquities.

It felt like a very long time later that we convened in the lounge bar onboard the *Queen Ahmes*. Rabiah's delight at having us safely back was touching. We'd managed a short telephone call from the police station, just to explain that we'd been detained, but were alive and as well as could be expected. It was clear our tiny crew had been worried sick about us, wondering if there was anything they could do to spring us from custody. Khaled moored, lowered the gangplank for us, and was only prevailed upon not to sail away and drop anchor off shore again when it was made clear we'd be guarded around the clock. Sadly, I doubt this was for our protection. To ensure we stayed put was more like it.

'Georgina is not with you?' Khaled asked in his broad Scottish brogue.

Adam and I exchanged a glance. 'She decided to stay behind with her ex-husband,' I said. The truth was, far from fulfilling Max Savage's expectation as prime witness for the prosecution, Georgina seemed determined to prove herself his staunchest defender! No amount of cajoling had persuaded her to leave. Offering himself up for arrest seemed the grandest romantic gesture Max could have made. I guessed there was hope for the pair of them yet. Either that or they could stew in their own juices as far as I was concerned. I'd grown to quite like Georgina during the time she'd foisted herself upon us. And Max seemed as though he might become an acquired taste. But the simple truth was this trip would have been a whole lot simpler, and certainly less dangerous, without them.

The fact was; no amount of joy at being safely home again could dissipate the trepidation of what lay ahead tomorrow, or the knowledge of who had embroiled us in it.

Adam summed it up. 'I was thrilled to bits when we found that money. But now I wish Georgina had kept the whole damn story to herself. Facing a delegation from Cairo was not what I had in mind when we set out on this adventure!'

* * *

Luckily for us, it was only Director Feisal Ismail of the Ministry of State for Antiquities and Zahed Mansour of the Egyptian Tourism Authority who strode up the gangplank and onto the *Queen Ahmes* the following morning under the watchful eye of the guards posted to keep us under surveillance. The Police Inspector summoned from Aswan, plus interpreter; and the British Embassy official both went directly to the Abu Simbel police station where Max and Georgina Savage remained ensconced.

I say lucky for us. But in truth, luck had very little to do with it. Strictly speaking, Zahed Mansour was my boss – every bit as much as he was Saleh's and Mehmet's. He had a direct say over my continued employment here in Egypt, and theirs on this project. Habiba was the only one to report directly to Director Ismail. Even so, there could be no doubt about who was in charge. The Ministry of Antiquities Director outranked the junior Tourism Minister, and would be the one to call the shots. I hadn't forgotten that Director Ismail had invited Adam and me to leave his country once before – not quite revoking our visas, but making it very clear we had little choice but to comply. No doubt he could do so again. So while there was a measure of relief in not having to face the Police Inspector or British Embassy official, it was with a heavy heart that I stood in our little panelled reception area with Adam at my side to welcome them on board.

Ahmed, Habiba, Mehmet and Saleh were all waiting in the lounge bar where Rabiah had set out coffee and homemade pastries, perhaps hoping quite literally to butter up our guests.

We all knew we were in trouble. When I'd negotiated for Adam to join me on this trip, for Ahmed to be seconded from his tourist police duties in Luxor to become our security guard, and for us to live aboard the *Queen Ahmes* with Khaled's services as our salaried skipper thrown in for good measure, it was because I'd known how badly these two bigwigs wanted me to come back to Egypt. They'd had high hopes for my ability to jumpstart the ailing tourist industry. It had gone into free-fall during the almost three years Adam and I spent back home in the UK. Political unrest and terrorist incidents, not to mention the rise of Islamic State all played their part in the meltdown. In the meantime of course, Adam and I had helped stage the British Museum's most successful exhibition, bringing Giovanni Belzoni's story back from oblivion to capture the international imagination. Their eagerness to secure my return had given me the confidence to be bold in my demands. But everything was different now.

Our discovery of Queen Nefertari's granite tablets last year precipitated a media storm. That was all well and good. There were close enough ties between the ancient Egyptian queen and Belzoni, arguably the first Egyptologist, for the Tourism Authority in particular to make much of the discovery. Nefertari's tomb in the Valley of the Queens had just been re-opened after decades off-limits, and for the Belzonis *Reis* to have been the one to secure and then re-hide the tablets made a nice circular story lapped up by the Press. Georgina was able to say how she'd learned about the tablets in papers handed down from her forebear, the British Consul General Henry Salt. That he was Belzoni's bitter enemy added a certain *frisson* to the story. Director Ismail and Zahed Mansour had both been of a mind to consider the discovery a bonus that put Egypt firmly back on the world stage.

But this was different. I doubted Media interest in the Great – British – Train Robbery – even allowing for the discovery of the stash in the Great Temple of Ramses at Abu Simbel – would be enough to betoken a resurging tourist trade. It was a bizarre story for sure. But hardly one to get potential holidaymakers rushing to pack their bags, desperate to see the spot where the fateful discovery was made. And, lest we forget, a man was dead.

I swallowed hard as Director Ismail stepped off the gangplank and preceded his compatriot over the threshold.

The Director's opening words were encouraging. 'Meredith, my dear, what have you got yourself mixed up in this time?' The fact that he took both my hands in his as he made this enquiry was further inducement to relax. The trouble was, the paternalistic tone was deceptive. Director Ismail was so sharp you could cut yourself on him. To say I had a healthy respect for him is wildly to understate it. The fact is I was terrified of him. An urbane man with hair greying at the temples, suit trousers ironed to razor-sharp precision and a single golden molar that gleamed when he smiled; he had a leashed-in quality about him that made him unpredictable and more than a little intimidating. Put it thus way: I wasn't fooled for a moment by the bonhomie. This was a man who refused to suffer fools and meant business.

I don't like to think of myself as a fool. But I'd admit to a nagging doubt about whether I'd allowed myself to be reeled in on this latest escapade, and was now about to suffer the consequences.

Adam stepped forward before I could respond. 'Sir, I'm sorry it's been necessary to drag you all the way from Cairo.' He thrust out his hand, giving the Director no choice but to drop mine, take Adam's and shake it. He did the same with Zahed Mansour, including him in the apology. 'Please, come in and make yourselves comfortable. We will of course tell you the whole story.'

We stood back so the two bigwigs could precede us along the short corridor and into the lounge bar, where the others rose to greet them.

I saw the Director's gaze travel around the room, resting in turn on each of our companions. He observed also the broken coffee table and the splintered door of Mehmet's cabin, which was propped against the wall, awaiting repair.

Saleh el-Sayed leapt across the space as Zahed Mansour entered the room, and offered him the seat he'd just vacated. 'I want you to know the blame is mine,' he announced, speaking rapidly and looking rather wildly from one gentleman to the other and back. 'I have been very stupid. And I must bear the consequences. I will ask you please to accept my resignation so that Meredith and Adam can continue their trip without my further interference!'

'Saleh, we've forgiven you,' Adam said firmly. 'There's no need for this.'

'But I led those two men to your door!' the Marketing Manager cried. 'Everything that happened yesterday was my fault! If I had not been so easily bribed they would not have been able to take your people hostage yesterday! And maybe that man would still be alive!'

Zahed Mansour's hand came up and he slapped his Marketing Manager stingingly across the face. 'Saleh, you are hysterical! Control yourself!' he commanded sharply.

Saleh stopped speaking abruptly and stared at his boss, sudden tears springing into his eyes.

'There will be no talk of resignation until I understand exactly what has gone on here.' Zahed Mansour seated himself and looked around at us expectantly. A balding man with a deep crease across his forehead in the shape of a smiley-faced emoji, it was impossible to square his air of authority with his rather comedic appearance. Director Ismail also sat, accepting the cup of coffee Rabiah handed him before she withdrew from the room in a swish of black robes.

Adam cleared his throat. But Saleh seemed determined to be the one to tell the story and fall on his sword. Composing himself, he confessed in far less emotional terms to his involvement with Philip Sinnerman and Max Savage.

'So, you see, I betrayed Meredith and Adam, even after they had saved my life last year,' he admitted. 'Those men had persuaded me that it was only Georgina Savage they wanted to intercept. But I should have known I was putting everyone here at risk, while also jeopardising this whole Belzoni enterprise.' He hung his head. 'I am truly sorry.'

Thanks to our discovery of Nefertari's granite tablets there was no need to explain who Georgina was. Zahed Mansour and Feisal Ismail were already acquainted with our ballsy houseguest and her profession. Her relationship to the two exes in her life was swiftly told. Georgina's reasons for wanting to come to Abu Simbel with us, and the supposed motivation of her ex-husband and ex-colleague for aiming to steal her scoop took rather longer to set out.

Director Ismail quietly sipped his coffee while all this was explained. When everyone had finished speaking, he looked across at me and met my nervous glance with a narrowed gaze. 'So, Meredith, my dear, I feel I have to ask … When you sailed south from Luxor with Ms Savage on board, did you do so in the knowledge that you were coming here to the Great Temple of Ramses in search of the money from a famous train robbery that took place in England more than fifty years ago?'

As ever, it was mildly asked. But I knew better than to dissimulate. His unfailing politeness masked the savage instincts of a Rottweiler. He was not a man to cross. I also knew that Zahed Mansour would take his lead from the

Ministry Director. I felt sure our continued employment in Egypt might depend on how I answered his question. 'Er – Georgina had alluded to a stash of treasure,' I faltered. 'I should add we had no idea what it actually was.'

Adam spoke up in my support. 'We were humouring her,' he said. 'Knowing the temple had been broken apart and re-sited, we considered there was no chance of actually finding anything that might date back to Pharaonic times.'

Looking at the Director's unchanging expression, I wondered if he might accept this as justification for not making a clean fist of it at the time.

'We only found out the "treasure" was in fact a stash of money stolen from The Great Train Robbery – and was hidden here during the re-siting of the temples – when Philip Sinnerman decided to play nasty at Philae,' I added.

'Hmm,' he said non-commitally. 'And where is the stolen money now?'

'At the police station in Abu Simbel town with Georgina and Max Savage,' I said.

Adam nodded, 'I imagine the British Ambassador will determine what happens to it. And whether Georgina can have the scoop that will make her journalistic career.'

I looked at the Ministry Director, sensing what he really wanted to know, and determining to answer it without him needing to put it into words. 'I admit I was excited to see if we could find the cash,' I owned up. 'But I quite honestly couldn't care less if I never see it again. I imagine it will make quite a

News story back at home. But I very much hope my name, and Adam's, can be kept out of it. Of course, it's dreadful that a man died.' I shuddered, looking across the lounge bar at the window and picturing Philip Sinnerman plunging out through it as Max punched him. 'And that Georgina's ex-husband may have to take the rap for killing him, even though we all know it was unintentional. But, speaking for myself – and the rest of us I think,' – glancing around at my companions – 'I can say for sure I won't be sorry if we can get back to the original purpose of our trip.'

Aware of the others nodding, I looked at the Director hopefully.

He allowed a long pause to draw out. I wasn't sure he was going to speak at all. Perhaps he didn't feel it necessary. After all I hadn't asked him anything directly. But surely the implicit question in what I'd said must be obvious. Eventually he let out a sigh. 'It seems to me Philip Sinnerman got what was coming to him. And perhaps Georgina and Max Savage may each get what they deserve...' He rather left this hanging, making me wonder what it was he considered they might each deserve, if not the obvious or perhaps each other. 'In truth, my dear, what becomes of them is a matter of supreme indifference to me. You, on the other hand...'

He let it trail off again. I caught and held my breath. In that moment I knew exactly what it must feel like to lay one's head on Madame Guillotine and wait for the blade to fall. I looked into his eyes and sensed exactly what he was thinking.

Adam, Ahmed, Habiba and I shared a deep and closely guarded secret with the Director of the Ministry of State for Antiquities. He was wondering, as I was, whether our shared knowledge of that "undiscovered" tomb lying hidden behind Hatshepsut's Temple on the west bank near Luxor might unite or divide us. He'd relieved us of responsibility for it when he exiled us from Egypt nearly four years ago. We'd sworn a solemn oath never to speak of it. Director Ismail had been the man to oust us from his country. He'd also been instrumental in inviting us back. He'd known then the risk he was running. Although in our continued silence I like to think we'd proved ourselves worthy of his trust. That, despite the confession we'd just had to make of our most recent activities.

His thoughts were running along rails with mine. 'Meredith ... Adam ... It does seem to me that you find it almost impossible to spend time under the Egyptian sun without getting mixed up in some misadventure or other. And you are rather too good at rushing into things head first without paying any heed to the possible consequences and without the transparency I think I may consider myself entitled to expect.'

I bit my lip on hearing this and found it impossible to maintain eye contact. Despite the pleasant tone, I recognised a ticking off when I was on the receiving end of one. But the Director wasn't finished and drew my gaze back to his with his next words.

'So, tell me … just for the avoidance of doubt, you understand … are there any other matters you are withholding from me? Any other little discoveries you might want to reveal while we're on the subject?'

I stared back at him in an agony of indecision. With his eyes raking mine like that, I rather felt he might be capable of taking a brain scan with just his unremitting gaze.

It was Ahmed, who'd sat solid and silent throughout the confession and interrogation, who now leaned forward. 'Hurrumph,' he started, drawing everyone's attention. 'Merry, there is no need to protect me. I think you may want to tell to him about Helen of Troy.'

Chapter 14

There were many possible reactions I might have expected to my halting confession that we were in possession of a solid gold statuette purporting to be of Helen of Troy and apparently found at Abu Simbel by Giovanni Belzoni's one-time *Reis*. The one I got never would have occurred to me. Indeed was beyond my wildest imaginings.

Director Ismail stared at me as if I'd handed him the pot of gold at the end of the rainbow. From stunned and frozen disbelief, a look of pure wonder swept over his features. Gone was the severe, daunting, endlessly self-controlled Ministry of Antiquities Director. In his place was an altogether different person. It was as if he'd shed twenty years while I'd been talking. With shining eyes and an open, eager expression, he reminded me of nothing so much as an excited boy. Looking at his joyous countenance I started to dare think we might not be about to be flung out of Egypt on our ear for a second time after all. And it was looking possible that Ahmed might avoid a lengthy spell in jail, his police badge confiscated.

I heard Adam suck in a breath, sitting alongside me on the divan. None of us dared speak, too terrified of misinterpreting the incredulous look on Director Ismail's face and ending up with egg all over ours. I risked a glance at Zahed Mansour sitting alert and attentive but otherwise unreadable in the armchair Saleh had vacated. Saleh himself was perched on the floor by the broken coffee table listening no less intently. This was breaking news to him too. Neither he nor Habiba had been there for the fateful discovery. Although, catching sight of Habiba's watchful expression, I wondered if Ahmed might have let something slip. Mehmet certainly was learning of it for the first time. His gaze darted between the Director's and my own as if he didn't know where to let it settle.

'You have proof?' the Director managed at last, on a croaking whisper.

'Er – proof?' I hesitated, nonplussed by the question.

He cleared his throat, and succeeded in getting his voice back. 'That Helen sat out the duration of the Trojan War here in Egypt?' He gazed at me eagerly and with undisguised impatience, as if he could drag her story from me with that look alone.

I looked at him blankly. 'Er – Helen was *here*? In *Egypt*? During the *Trojan War*?' I'm sure I sounded perfectly ridiculous parroting his words like this. But repeating what he'd said back to him seemed my only hope of making sense of his surprising statement.

He cleared his throat yet again, apparently feeling the need to unblock his re-clogged larynx. 'It is what some scholars have hypothesised,' he croaked. 'I always longed to find out it was true. Ever since studying the ancient Greek civilisation in Athens before graduating. I read Homer as a boy. I've had an enduring fascination with Helen ever since.'

I stared at him with no less fascination of my own, permitted this glimpse of the private man behind the formidable Ministry Director for the first time. Even so, I felt the need to check my hearing. 'Forgive my ignorance, but I always assumed Helen of Troy was a fictional character, more myth and legend than flesh and blood. Of course, finding the statuette made us wonder … But I'm not sure we've dared to take it as concrete evidence of a real historical woman.'

Unexpectedly, Adam interjected at this point. 'I've been doing some research,' he announced. 'From what I've read on the Internet it seems Helen's tale may well be rooted in late Bronze Age reality. That being the case, there's a chance it could be closer to history than to myth. I'm not saying Homer was a historian. But I think we can discern some kernels of historical truth in his writing. If scholars look at moments where archaeology and the stories overlap, it's possible to edge Helen further from fiction and closer to fact.'

Director Ismail looked impressed. 'I was forgetting I am dealing with serious students of history,' he murmured.

'I'm an Egyptologist, sir,' Adam qualified respectfully, 'not a fully-fledged historian. But I'll admit to being intrigued enough by what we found to investigate and see what I might learn. Helen of Troy is an enigma. It seems to me that from the first moment she entered the written record in Homer's Iliad, for the next 2700 years she has never once left the human radar. If she existed, I think it's fair to say she was far more than just a pretty face.'

I stared at my husband agog. But of course he'd been doing his own homework. I don't know what I was so surprised about. Adam is first and foremost a student of ancient Egypt. When I first met him, he introduced himself as a "thwarted Egyptologist", forced to give up his formal studies and university place when his parents died tragically in a car crash. But his obsession with ancient civilisations never left him and he pursued part-time online studies throughout what he now describes as his tortuous career in banking. He finally qualified three years ago, having called time on his banking career just as his first marriage broke down. Second of all, Adam is a man whose brain is set alight by a mystery. Egyptological by preference. Archaeological as the next best thing. The golden statuette had lit the usual fire. That the discovery clearly posited a link between Helen of Troy and ancient Egypt at the time of Ramses II was the best of both worlds.

If all the drama over The Great Train Robbery hadn't been such a distraction, I don't doubt we'd have shared many happy hours of online investigation. That he'd somehow found the time to surf the worldwide web without me was certainly pause for thought. But then I remembered the hours I devoted to my blog and the articles I was contracted to submit for my Belzoni opus. In all fairness, Adam was left to his own devices rather more than either one of us may desire.

This evidence that he used his time productively was further reminder – as if I needed it – of what a lucky woman I am. Sure, he likes a spy novel or a thriller as much as the next man. But given a chance to research a historical mystery, the competition's over before it's begun.

Congratulating myself silently on having found such a man, I cast my husband a loving look and counted my blessings. That I could now anticipate learning the fruits of his online labours being high among them.

While I was looking at Adam with doe eyes, Director Ismail was observing him with a renewed respect. 'It is certainly true that from ancient Greece to Hollywood, Helen – the myth – endures. Most women are written out of history. Helen is written in. She is the inspiration for the earliest masterpieces of literature, Homer's Iliad and Odyssey. She's been called the most beautiful woman on earth. She became the face that launched a thousand ships; blamed for starting the Trojan War, a war that brought death and destruction to thousands. She's a reminder of the terrible power that beauty can wield. A muse for writers, artists, poets and movie-makers alike.' Starry-eyed wasn't the word for it. Director Ismail spoke as a man in love. His voice was deep and intense, filled with passion. It was impossible not to be swept along. 'And now, if I may, I would very much like to see the statuette you found.'

We dispatched Ahmed to retrieve it from the metal safe in our reception area. It had been his discovery, after all, hidden inside a secret compartment in the lid of the casket in which the *Reis* Abdullah Soliman secreted Nefertari's tablets when he recovered them from her temple here at Abu Simbel almost two hundred years ago. I'd thought the Director might succumb to a coronary on first hearing this, and seeing the way the breath left his body. Lucky for us this turned out to be breathless delight. I was starting to dare hope Helen's statuette might just represent our get-out-of- jail-free card.

'What is the story of this Helen?' Ahmed asked, returning and handing over the heavy statue – approximately the size of a modern Oscar – to the Director. He stood back deferentially as Feisal Ismail took it lovingly into both hands, turning it and holding it aloft, his throat working convulsively as he struggled to keep his emotions in check.

'Exquisite,' he whispered.

Poor old Ahmed. He didn't seem to know where to look seeing such unabashed passion. After an uncertain pause, he retreated back to the sofa where he'd been seated alongside Habiba. It was perfectly clear the Director wasn't going to relinquish the precious statuette any time soon.

Glancing around the room, I registered the reactions of our companions, from Zahed Mansour's eye-popping stare to Mehmet's gasp of pure wonder. I doubted he'd ever seen a precious objet d'art up close like this before. Saleh and Habiba each sat silent and staring. Habiba was pressing her lips together as if holding back some utterance or other. Ahmed, looking at me rather than at the golden statuette or his fiancée, was clearly waiting for his question to be answered.

I took pity on our erstwhile police pal. Until now, he hadn't shown much interest in the tale of Helen of Troy. Ahmed is a man who likes to propound the great queens of his own country's ancient civilisation. Little though he knows personally of the likes of Nefertari, Hatshepsut, Nefertiti and Cleopatra – Ahmed is no Egyptologist – he is staunchly patriotic. Helen of Troy was new to him. Until now I might have said it was the gleam of gold that seduced him. There was undoubtedly something irresistibly alluring about it. The statuette was of a woman in flowing Grecian robes caught in at the waist, with sandals on her feet and flowers in her long hair. I'd have said Ahmed was delighted to have found the statuette for its own sake, but with no real interest in learning about the individual whose likeness was captured in solid gold. But perhaps I did him a disservice. Helen's epic tale was hardly one to diminish the lustre of her glittering image.

Besides which, I was pretty keen to be reminded of it for myself. 'Tell him, Adam,' I invited. 'I'll ask Rabiah to refresh the coffee.'

As I rang the little bell Rabiah had given me to alert her whenever we required her services, Adam tore his gaze from Director Ismail's adoring worship of the statuette, and smiled at me. 'It's one of the greatest narratives of all time,' he said. Then he grinned at Ahmed. 'Prepare yourself my friend. It's a story of lust and adultery, and of how men will find any excuse to go to war and really enjoy battling over a woman. In many ways Helen is the perfect male fantasy. She is exquisitely beautiful, and becomes an agent of male destruction. She represents a heady combination of pleasure and pain, sex and violence, love and hate.' As he said this, his gaze travelled back to the golden statuette cradled in Director Ismail's long-fingered brown hands. 'But also it is not just a story,' he went on. 'Helen and the Trojan War have become epic and iconic. But if you look closely it's a very human tale. The drama starts with a messy love affair and ends up in a bloody and disastrous conflict.'

He broke off as Rabiah came into the room. Anticipating our every need as usual, she carried a tray laden with clean cups and a plate of my peanut crunch cookies. Khaled followed her with a tall stainless steel pot of fresh coffee.

'Rabiah, Khaled; you are a godsend,' I smiled at them as Rabiah busied herself pouring coffee while Khaled passed around the plate of biscuits. I saw them each glance at the Director, their gazes snagged by the glittering object he was holding. But they knew better than to enquire. A quick look at me, and a raised eyebrow were all the reaction either one allowed themselves. As unobtrusively as they'd arrived, they made their departure again. Adam was free to get on with his retelling of Helen's tale, while I sent up a silent prayer of thanks for such a wonderfully discreet crew, and promised myself to let them in on the secret later.

'Homer's poems tell the story of how Trojans and Greeks fought a long and bloody battle over Helen, all stirred up by the gods on Mount Olympus,' Adam said. 'Written down in approximately 700 BC, they're based on much older events, actual conflicts that took place at least 500 years earlier, in the 13th century BC. It's what has come to be known at "The Age of Heroes".' He put quotation marks around this with his fingers. 'The fall of Troy came to represent a fall from an illustrious heroic age, remembered for centuries in oral tradition before being written down.'

I glanced across at Ahmed, knowing how much he loves a good story. That he was already engrossed was evidenced in his unblinking expression, gazing back at Adam as he prepared to be entertained.

'Helen's drama starts in the Peloponnese,' Adam went on. 'Three-and-a-half thousand years ago this peninsula of southern Greece was home to the powerful Mycenaean civilisation: enjoying a golden age at its peak in circa 1300 BC. Historians agree this was the century most likely to have witnessed the Trojan War and therefore the birth of Helen. Of course, it also sets Helen's drama in the same period as the 19th Dynasty of Pharaonic Egypt, at around the time of Ramses the Great.'

I sat up straighter hearing this. I'd had no idea the two dated from the same period of ancient history. Maybe the discovery of Helen's statuette in the Great Temple of Ramses might come to make sense after all.

'Myths say Helen was born in Sparta, south of Mycenae,' Adam continued. 'Her intimate association with violence went right back to her conception. Zeus, king of the Gods, in the guise of a swan, attacked and raped her mortal mother Leda on the riverbank as she went to bathe. There are also tales of Helen herself being abducted and raped as a girl dancing on the banks of the river with her girlfriends. According to the mythology the perpetrator was Theseus, King of Athens. Helen was barely more than a child. He was seventy. Legend has it that he said that, despite all his blessings, life wasn't worth living unless he could enjoy her. The allure of Helen was too strong to resist,'

He broke off as Ahmed choked in outrage. Ahmed is a man who wears his heart on his sleeve. Violence against women is anathema to him. His reaction to the story so far was plain for all to see.

Adam looked across into his eyes and smiled grimly at him. 'You see, Helen's terrible tragedy is to make men yearn and long for her. From this point onwards Helen is always linked with passion and pain. She has begun her career as an irresistible prize and a creator of conflict.'

Director Ismail set the statuette carefully on the occasional table alongside him and re-joined the conversation. 'An irresistible prize indeed,' he said, staring at the beautiful statue for a long moment. Then he looked up and addressed us all. 'Helen's era – the late Bronze Age – was a time of aggressive male culture. Men would find any excuse to go to war. It was the time in ancient Greece that gave us names such as Achilles, Hercules, and Odysseus; and the Trojan soldier Hector. Here in Egypt, the great men were warrior Pharaohs such as Seti and Ramses. In Mycenaean civilisation – and particularly relevant to Helen – women owned huge swathes of land, had independent wealth and could speak out confidently to the world around them. A highborn woman like Helen would have been part of the Mycenaean elite. This was an age, not just of heroes but of heroines too.'

Adam leaned forward. 'And this is where mythology and legend trade places with history and archaeology,' he said. 'Homer's epics tell us Helen was prized for her beauty and a contest was fought for her hand. More likely is that as a real Spartan princess she was seen as a great catch, principally as a marriage prospect with a kingdom to give away.'

Director Ismail nodded. 'To this day the plains around ancient Sparta are some of the most fertile land in the whole of Greece. It's easy to see why suitors may have come from far and wide to compete for the chance of winning her. Marrying for love was a low priority for these men. They came to Sparta for the chance to improve their lot and display their physical prowess. Surviving records tell us these marriage contests were grand events comprising a range of competitive sports including boxing and wrestling. We call it the "Age of Heroes". But in actual fact, this was not in your English romantic sense of the word. The origin of the word "hero" in ancient Greek actually means "he who is worthy". The marriage contest was one way of finding out.'

Adam looked from the Director to the golden statuette of the Grecian princess on the low table alongside him. 'The myths describe how the most powerful princes of the day gathered to compete for the hand of the beautiful Spartan princess. But in Helen's marriage games the men wrestled and boxed in vain. In the end it came down to spending power. Agamemnon, the great King of Mycenae impressed with the most amount of treasure and won Helen for his brother Menelaus.'

Ahmed snorted. 'He did not even buy her for himself?'

Director Ismail smiled grimly. 'According to legend Helen became Menelaus's trophy wife without him lifting a finger. In reality of course, it's more likely the marriage brought together two of the strongest dynasties in the region. Menelaus and Helen ruled the rich lands of the Spartan kingdom together. Little remains of it now, but archaeologists have found the remnants of a palace complex on the hills around Sparta.'

Adam nodded. 'Yes, I was reading up on it. The first archaeologist at the site was the flamboyant Heinrich Schliemann. He described an archaeology of military might and bejewelled heroines.'

'But what happened next?' Ahmed was eager to return to the story, without getting side-tracked onto the archaeology.

'Ah, this is where the story really gets going,' Adam smiled, 'Helen – the queen of Sparta – is about to be stolen away to Troy by the dashing eastern prince, Paris.'

'A prince came and *stole* her?' Ahmed gaped wide-eyed.

Adam grinned. 'Well, according to the mythology, it was all predestined by the gods on Mount Olympus. Paris, a Trojan prince, came to Sparta to claim Helen, in the guise of a supposed diplomatic mission. But before his journey Paris had been appointed by Zeus to judge a beauty contest among the goddesses Hera, Athena and Aphrodite. In order to win his favour, Aphrodite promised Paris the most beautiful woman in the world as his prize. Swayed by her offer, Paris chose Aphrodite. From that point onwards Helen's fate was sealed.'

'I remember this part,' I piped up eagerly. 'When Paris arrives in Sparta, Helen falls in love with him and sails away with him to Troy.'

Adam smiled at me. 'Trust you to prefer the romantic version.' He favoured me with a lingering look that assured me he saw nothing to criticise in this preference, and then went on: 'Although Helen is sometimes depicted as being seduced by Paris, ancient Greek sources are often elliptical and contradictory. Some suggest he raped and abducted her. Others say she did indeed go willingly, leaving a loveless marriage and abandoning her small daughter Hermione. Homer is vague on the subject, although he does not imply she left by force. I imagine the fortifications around a late

Bronze Age palace would have made such a thing nigh on impossible. Whatever; I think this opaqueness is part of Helen's enduring fascination. Whether she left by choice or was kidnapped, whether she was a victim, a harlot or a woman following her heart. Or whether she was simply a puppet of the gods. One thing is clear. From this point forward, Helen and Paris are on the run: hurtling their way into history.'

Unaccountably, I felt goose bumps rise on my flesh.

Director Ismail was still gazing at the golden statuette, almost as if he were seeing the real woman depicted in the precious metal. 'Homer gives Helen and Paris prophetic lines in his poem,' he said, and then quoted, '"*On us the gods have visited an evil destiny. We shall be a singer's theme for generations to come.*"'

'And here we are, more than three thousand years later, still making films about them,' I murmured, pulling myself together.

'So it was this abduction or seduction of Helen by Paris that sparked the Trojan War?' This time it was Habiba who spoke. Sitting quietly alongside Ahmed, it was clear she'd been following the story intently.

Adam nodded. 'Yes, a war that dragged on for ten long years. Menelaus, discovering his wife gone, called together the Greek fleet. Troy was situated on the coast of modern day Turkey, probably several days' sailing across the Eastern Mediterranean from mainland Greece. In antiquity the seas around Greece were the great highways and byways. Homer calls them "*the sea's foaming lanes*"'

I sat smugly delighted while my husband proved he could quote from the Classics every bit as eloquently as the Ministry Director. I've always been in thrall to his ability to memorise and recite ancient texts. That in all probability he'd found this one on an Internet search engine bothered me not one jot. Or maybe he too had read the Iliad and the Odyssey. Adam is a well-educated man, and ancient history is his specialist subject.

'But the ships could not set sail as there was no wind,' he finished.

'We're supposed to believe that Agamemnon sacrificed his own daughter to appease the gods,' Director Ismail remarked, looking up. 'Of a far-fetched story, this seems to me to be the most improbable part of all. It's impossible for me to believe that a man would kill his own daughter for the chance to go to war over the supposed abduction of his brother's trophy wife and seek to reclaim her.'

Adam smiled at him. 'I think we can safely assume all the parts of the story directed by the gods are there for literary and dramatic effect,' he said. 'In reality, I suspect Troy itself was the prize, and Helen just an excuse to lay siege to it. We can imagine the huge Greek fleet setting sail across the Aegean Sea to bring Helen back to Sparta. These were rich trade routes. Historically, trade and aggression have always run hand in hand. There were rich pickings at stake. Even today the Dardanelles are one of the busiest shipping lanes in the world, the route from the Mediterranean to the Black Sea. I would think the twenty-first century equivalent to Troy must surely be Istanbul. A cosmopolitan trading post and cultural melting pot where east meets west. Some Classical writers say Helen was lured away not just by Paris, but by the wealth and luxury of Troy and the east.'

Director Ismail looked across at Adam with open admiration. 'If Rashid Soliman does not require you back at The British Museum at the end of your year's sabbatical, let me know and I will offer you a position myself. You are a fine researcher. I am sure I could put you to good use in the Ministry of Antiquities archives.'

Adam coughed modestly and looked at his feet. 'Thank you, sir; but all I've done is look beyond the story of a woman's beauty and a husband's betrayal for a more believable reason why two powers might fight a bloody and protracted war.'

'Troy was uniquely located,' Feisal Ismail agreed. 'Sandwiched between the mighty Hittite empire to the east and the great Mycenaean culture to the west. The Hittites, as you will all be aware, were a superpower reaching all the way to the borders with the ancient Egyptian empire. They were also great record keepers. Not only do they tell us their own version of the battle of Kadesh against Ramses II, stone tablets also preserve a pact of non-aggression between the Hittites and the Trojans, a personal treaty between the king of the Hittites and the king of Troy. Although it is not clear whether this king of Troy was King Priam, against whom the Greeks waged war when Paris supposedly returned to his big citadel city with Helen. What we *can* say is the battle of Kadesh was definitely contemporaneous with the era of the Trojan War.'

I looked around the room and realised how much I was enjoying myself. My companions were sitting quiet and attentive while Adam and Director Ismail told the story of the woman rendered in solid gold whose statuette kept drawing our gazes as her legend unfolded. As for myself, after the unlooked-for violence and trauma of the last twenty-four hours, this felt like exactly the tonic I needed. I thrived on this sort of thing. Keeping company with clever people who could somehow bring ancient history to life such that I felt I was seeing it enacted before my eyes.

The Director looked around at us and went on: 'As more Hittite texts are translated it becomes clear there were historic conflicts over Troy. It seems Homer may have woven a number of tales together into a single story, which he embellished with the interference of the gods for dramatic effect, as you say Adam. I think it is perfectly possible that the behaviour of a highborn woman like Helen in the late Bronze Age could spark a serious diplomatic incident. But I agree a ten-year war is unlikely in defence of her husband's honour.'

'Homer was writing several centuries after the event,' Adam said. 'And pulling on traditions handed down verbally.

He saw an intimate connection between war and lust, sex and violence. As if, being primordial urges, they were two sides of the same coin. It's probably why his epic poems have endured over millennia. He saw no dividing line between lust for love and lust for blood. You have to admire his ability to capture the imagination. But historically accurate? No. For one thing, Homer was writing in the Iron Age when hand-to-hand combat with swords was the style of warfare. And this is what he describes in his epics. But, as we know from the battle of Kadesh, the elite weapon of the late Bronze Age was the chariot, with skilled archers waging war on their opponents.'

Director Ismail nodded. 'In much the same way as the puppetry of the gods, I imagine the Trojan horse was another literary device to bring about the fall of Troy and allow the Greeks to emerge victorious.'

'Please, do not abdicate the story,' Ahmed interrupted crossly, clearly bored with all this talk of geography and ancient warfare. I felt sure he must mean abbreviate, but didn't have the heart to correct him. His meaning was clear enough. 'I want to know what happened after Helen and Paris returned to this so-wonderful city.'

'I think it's fair to say Homer is more interested in writing his battle scenes than he is in recounting the domestic side of Helen's time in Troy,' Adam said wryly. 'Helen has rather served her purpose by being the catalyst for the war. Homer latched onto an oral tradition where heroes fought and made their name. His famous single combat scenes provide some of the most dramatic – and gory – episodes in the epics. Achilles, the great Greek warrior finally kills the Trojan hero Hector. In another famous scene, Paris and Menelaus fight in single combat with spears and shields, only for the goddess Aphrodite to intervene on Paris's behalf, casting a mist over the plain. Aphrodite transports Paris back to Helen and Troy.'

I decided Adam must have read – or maybe re-read – Homer's great poems. As ever, my husband's encyclopaedic knowledge wowed me while reminding me in the starkest terms why I fell in love with him. That he could give Director Ismail a run for his money made me glow with pride.

'Paris is represented as a less than heroic warrior,' the Director remarked. 'His single act of bravery seems to be shooting a poisoned arrow at Achilles, which strikes him in the heel. Paris himself soon afterwards receives a fatal wound from an arrow shot by a rival archer. Even with the main Trojan warriors dead, the fighting rages on. That is, until the Greek army conceives of the idea of the Trojan horse.'

'Horse?' Ahmed asked inevitably.

Adam smiled at him. 'The Trojan horse was the subterfuge – cunning plan, if you prefer – the Greeks used to gain entry to Troy and finally win the war. After their fruitless ten-year siege of the walled citadel, the Greeks constructed a huge wooden horse and hid a select force of men inside. It would serve as a lesson in the superiority of Greek brain over Trojan brawn. The Greeks pretended to sail away, and the naïve and unsuspecting Trojans pulled the horse inside the gates of their city as a victory trophy. That night the Greek force crept out of the horse and opened the gates for the rest of the Greek army, which had sailed back under cover of night. The Greeks entered and destroyed the city of Troy, ending the war. As the Director says, it's likely a dramatic device. But metaphorically speaking a "Trojan Horse" has come down in history as a stratagem or trick to attack an enemy behind secure lines.'

Ahmed stared back wide-eyed before his gaze was drawn to the golden statuette once more. 'So what happened to Helen?'

Director Ismail also gazed at the statue of the beautiful Spartan queen. 'Homer paints a poignant, lonely picture of Helen in Troy,' he said. 'She is filled with self-loathing and regret for what she has caused. By the end of the war, the Trojans have come to hate her. We're told that Menelaus hunts the burning city for Helen, blinded by blood lust and wanting to kill her. But when he sees her, his hatred turns to physical lust. Legend says Menelaus carries her home to Sparta in triumph, taking back glittering treasures from Troy for their palace.'

'And in the most unlikely part of the epic tales of all,' Adam interjected, 'we're supposed to believe that there were hardly any recriminations between the two. As depicted in The Odyssey, she and Menelaus are completely reconciled and live a harmonious married life; he holding no grudge at her having run away with a lover and she feeling no restraint in telling anecdotes of her life inside besieged Troy.'

'It's a tall tale indeed,' Director Ismail said, smiling at Ahmed's doubtful expression. 'Remember, it's a great epic of historical literature, woven from threads of an oral tradition. We're not meant to take it literally. But I think there are enough kernels of historical and archaeological evidence for us now to accept the probability that Helen herself did actually exist.'

Adam stared at the statuette. 'You know, as the siege of Troy dragged on and the Trojan heroes were killed, I've always wondered why King Priam didn't simply hand Helen back to the Greeks.'

Director Ismail looked back at him with glittering eyes. 'He did not hand her back, my friend, because she was never there. Helen spent the duration of the Trojan War here in Egypt!'

Even though this was the second time the Director had made this surprising statement, I still found it impossible to take it in. What he said next astonished me even more.

'The evidence you found in Amarna suggested a link with Sparta. This statuette seems to set the seal on it.'

Chapter 15

Frustratingly, it proved impossible to pursue this tantalising comment, for the time being at least. Voices from our reception area alerted us that we had company.

Khaled and Rabiah had seen our visitors approach the *Queen Ahmes* from their position at the back of the dahabeeyah, and now came through the lounge bar to inform us and greet the new arrivals.

Adam and I got up to join them, unsurprised when the introductions were performed to find we were welcoming the British Ambassador to Cairo, and a Police Inspector from Aswan on board. I felt my heart go into my mouth, wondering if this was to be the point I stopped living the dream. Maybe it was all about to come crashing down around my ears. It was enough to have me looking into their eyes and shaking hands with perhaps less than my usual verve.

Evidently, they'd come directly from the police station in Abu Simbel. Unexpectedly, Georgina Savage came with them, plodding up the gangplank with a heavy step. She looked tired and dishevelled; as well she might after the whole night spent in custody, even though by her own choice. At least the rest of us had managed to grab a few hours sleep in the comfort of our own cabins before the delegation from Cairo turned up this morning. I imagine she'd spent an uncomfortable night on the wooden bench we'd left her sitting on when she refused to accompany us back to the dahabeeyah in the early hours.

Max Savage was not with her.

Having dispensed with the pleasantries of welcome, I looked at her enquiringly as she slumped heavily into her favourite armchair in the lounge bar.

'Any chance of a gin and tonic?' she asked as Rabiah went to pour coffee. 'It's after eleven, after all.' This was Georgina's personal watershed hour of the day: the point in the morning when a pre-prandial aperitif became allowable as the hours of breakfast made the transition to those of lunchtime. 'The Inspector here wants to interview you to confirm the story Max has given him,' she answered my unspoken question as Rabiah busied herself at the bar. 'It seems they're willing to let him go if you can corroborate what happened yesterday.'

'Is Max ok?' Adam asked. Perhaps he, too, was hoping to put off the moment things got official. Our two 'guests' were taking seats, accepting the coffee Khaled was now pouring since his wife had been dispatched to mix Georgina's tipple of choice.

'He's surprisingly chipper,' she said. 'Now he's had time to think about it, he seems perfectly delighted by the idea that his mother had an affair with one of the villains who spirited away a share of the Great Train Robbery money. I have a feeling he'll dine out on the story for years to come.'

'And you?' I asked.

Her eyes slid sideways to meet those of the British Ambassador. A square cut, straight-backed and cleanly shaven man in a smart linen suit and floral patterned tie; he'd introduced himself as Christopher Higgins. My gaze followed hers and I caught the look on the Ambassador's face. Suffice it to say, it was not what I expected. I couldn't claim to know what 'officious' was meant to look like as an expression. All I could say for sure was this wasn't it. But I recognised barely concealed excitement when I saw it.

'I'm daring to hope I may get my scoop,' Georgina announced, baring her big teeth in a smile.

'I have been fortunate enough to see the contents of the metal security box you all found yesterday evening,' Mr Higgins spoke up, looking across the room at me. His eyes were bright and shining. I wondered how old he was. Around fiftyish at a guess. It was easy to see how he felt at the discovery. I found myself breathing a sigh of relief. He didn't seem nearly so scary as his job title suggested. 'What a story!' he exclaimed. 'The heist of the twentieth century hidden behind the Great Temple of Ramses at Abu Simbel!'

At a grunt from the Police Inspector, his expression sobered. He instantly appeared to age ten years. 'But a man has died, so we must not get carried away.'

What a shame, I thought. I'd dared to think we might be getting off to a good start. But the expression on the Police Inspector's face warned me not to count my chickens. He was older, perhaps knocking sixty. And, looking at him, I suddenly knew exactly what 'officious' looked like as an expression. He was tight-lipped, humourless and surveyed us all with an air of barely concealed disapproval. Here we go, I thought. It's not going to be plain sailing from here. In fact, the waters looked as if they might be about to get very choppy indeed.

But before the Police Inspector could open his mouth to speak, Director Ismail cleared his throat. It drew everyone's attention to him. Having seen how carried away he'd got over learning of our golden statuette, I'd rather forgotten what a forbidding character he could be. Always urbane and polite, he nevertheless wore an effortless air of authority. He was one of those men who could make the airwaves crackle. I should know. I'd rubbed up against his serrated edge in the past.

I expected him to say something in English. Instead he issued a deep-voiced command in Arabic. At least, it sounded like a command; short and barked out like a military tattoo. Whatever, it had the Police Inspector sitting up straighter and putting down his coffee on the side table alongside him.

I watched in open fascination while Director Feisal Ismail and the Egyptian Police Inspector spent a few moments locked in a rapid exchange of short-burst Arabic. The Director could pull rank on everybody in the room. But a police investigation was a police investigation after all. The Inspector responded to whatever the Director was saying with no less energy of his own. So I held my breath and waited to see what happened. Not for the first time, I found myself wishing I'd been more diligent in my attempts to learn the language.

After a while the back-and-forth exchange stopped. The Inspector nodded respectfully when the Director stopped speaking. He turned his head and addressed me in careful and faultless though heavily accented English, 'I understand you are on an important azzignment on behalf of ze Ministry of State for Antiquities,' he said.

Zahed Mansour – who was actually my boss – coughed meaningfully, but I intercepted the warning glance Feisal Ismail sent him. The Junior Tourism Minister clamped his jaws shut on whatever he may have been about to say.

'Mr and Mrs Tennyson were caught up in the alarming events of yesterday entirely innocently,' Director Ismail announced firmly, switching to his perfect English. 'If you wish to interview anybody to ascertain what happened and how it came about, you may interview this young man, Saleh el-Sayed. He apparently played an unfortunate part in the matter. He will, I feel sure, answer your questions fully and factually.' He smiled pleasantly at Saleh as if to say *you wanted a chance to fall on your sword, so here it is.* I saw poor Saleh's expression and knew what a lamb to the slaughter looked like. But, to be fair, it was probably no more than he deserved for playing both ends to the middle. Not quite done, the Director finished: 'As I understand it, Ms Savage here also was present throughout the hostage incident which took place in this very room twenty-four hours ago. I don't imagine there is anything else Mr and Mrs Tennyson can add to what she has already told you, since I feel sure you have interviewed her already.'

Of course I realised what he was doing. The Director was extricating Adam and me from this whole scenario. Whether this was for our own sake, and to preserve our anonymity and ability to continue our Belzoni assignment unhindered; or whether to speed up the chances of getting rid of the Police Inspector and with him the British Ambassador, I couldn't say.

I was pretty sure Director Ismail had no particular interest in the Train Robbery – despite the hiding place for the money being here at Abu Simbel. But by his own admission he was in the grip of a lifelong fascination – obsession might be more like it from what I'd seen – with Helen of Troy. My guess was he was itching to get back to finding out how her statuette came also to be here at Abu Simbel. In truth, so was I.

Thankfully we'd had the foresight to whisk the statuette out of sight into the cupboard at the base of our Victorian dresser when it became clear we had company. I didn't know what the British Ambassador or indeed the Police Inspector from Aswan might make of our solid gold treasure. Or of the knowledge there was a second story unfolding. Happily we need never find out.

Whatever Director Ismail's motivation, it had the desired effect. The Police Inspector – whose name spoken rapidly in Arabic when he'd introduced himself – I'd failed to catch, acquiesced to an interview with Saleh alone. Perhaps relieved that this could take place in his native tongue, relieving him of the need to practise his English, he allowed Ahmed to show him to the cabin I'd converted into an office where the necessary interrogation could take place.

Ahmed was slow to return. When he did, it was with a broad grin. 'I have told to that man about the bravery of my own Habiba,' he announced proudly. 'Mehmet, you also I have commended for your actions,' he added solemnly. 'I spoke as one police officer to another, and I am sure my testosterone has convinced him of the truth of this matter.'

'Testimony,' Adam murmured, smiling, while I rolled my eyes heavenward at Ahmed's usual struggle with the more advanced aspects of our language.

With the Police Inspector and poor Saleh el-Sayed out of the room, Georgina wasted no time in squaring up to Ambassador Christopher Higgins. 'Can you get me on a flight back with you to Cairo?' she demanded. 'I need to break the story while Max is still in custody.'

'Georgina!' I exclaimed, shocked.

'What?' she glared at me, unrepentant.

'You *still* think he'll attempt to steal a march on you?' I gaped. 'Even after everything he said? And after you spent a whole night at the police station with him when he voluntarily gave himself up for arrest?'

'I'm not talking any chances,' she muttered darkly. 'Maybe I stayed simply to ensure he remained safely under lock and key. We'll see if he still wants me back once I've broken the story. Until then, all bets are off!'

'You're a hard woman,' Adam said, but it was with a smile.

'No, just one who doesn't believe in the triumph of hope over experience,' she corrected. 'I'll think about giving Max his second chance once I've got my scoop in the bag.'

'She said, "hope",' I murmured to Adam in an undertone. 'Maybe she secretly does want to believe Max meant what he said.' Looking at her closely, I could see a new brightness in her eyes. I had a suspicion Georgina was secretly thrilled to have Max back in her life and declaring everlasting love. But her history with him had taught her to be wary and perhaps her instinct for self-preservation had kicked in. Well, if so, I couldn't blame her. But I don't mind admitting I was privately rooting for a happy ending for Georgina and her ex-husband.

Adam raised an eyebrow at me but didn't comment. To be fair, he didn't really get a chance. Georgina had only paused for breath. She finished by saying, 'Until then, if he can stay safely in police custody; that will be just fine by me!'

But it wasn't to be. The Police Inspector and Saleh el-Sayed re-joined the rest of us after a while.

'I can see nothing to charge ze British national wiz,' the Police Inspector said carefully. 'Zere was a fight, for sure. But zere is no evidence zat Mr Max Savage pushed ze ozzer British man into ze lake wiz the intention of him being attacked by ze crocodile.'

As for Saleh el-Sayed, the upshot appeared to be that, while he'd been stupid, gullible and duplicitous, he hadn't actually committed a crime. The Inspector released him back into the care of his employer Zahed Mansour. The Junior Tourism Minister looked as if he might very much like to box the Marketing Manager's ears. He restrained himself with an effort, saying instead: 'There is an early afternoon flight back to Cairo. Saleh, you will accompany me on it. I am relieved there will be no criminal investigation. Nevertheless, a man has been mauled to death by a crocodile within a stone's throw of the Abu Simbel temples. Many travellers here for the sound and light show witnessed his sad demise. This is not good news for our tourism industry. While not quite as serious as the shark attacks in the Red Sea a few years ago, as Lake Nasser is not a destination for swimmers, we will still need to focus our efforts on damage limitation. We will talk further about whether your resignation is necessary after we have done all we can to reassure holidaymakers that this was a freak accident.'

'Please,' Adam interjected. 'Saleh has said how sorry he is. I really don't think he should lose his job over it.'

Saleh sent him a grateful glance.

Zahed Mansour allowed a long pause to draw out. 'That is as may be,' he said slowly. 'But I will defer my decision on the matter until I have assessed the fallout.' Ignoring Saleh's crestfallen expression, he looked at Georgina Savage. 'Let us hope and pray your News story about finding the stolen money at the Temple can keep the other unfortunate incident off the front pages. This foolish young man's career may depend upon it.'

Then I found myself the subject of the Junior Tourism Minister's scrutiny. 'Meredith,' he looked at me with a frown, obliterating the smiley-faced crease in his forehead. 'No matter what other distractions you may encounter,' – I caught the meaningful glance he shot Director Ismail – 'I will expect a dazzling article ready for publication on how Giovanni Belzoni dug The Great Temple from the sand. You may also write, of course, about how Belzoni's *Reis* found the granite tablets in Nefertari's temple. As for the story of the money…'

'That's *my* story,' Georgina burst out.

'Quite,' Zahed Mansour allowed. 'All things considered I think I would prefer for Meredith to remain silent on that particular subject.'

'Fine by me,' I agreed, relieved.

'Right! I'll pack my bags.' Georgina heaved herself out of the armchair and put her empty glass on the bar. 'Thank you Merry and Adam for your hospitality. I've had a blast. But I think it's time now for me to take my leave of you.' She rounded on the Police Inspector, standing quietly in the background now he'd completed his investigation. 'If you can please take your time over my ex-husband's release, I'll consider it a personal favour.'

'Don't worry, Ms Savage,' Christopher Higgins spoke up. 'You have your scoop. I will happily vouch for you.'

Georgina went to clear her cabin, and everyone else trooped up on deck to enjoy the sunshine while waiting for her. I turned to Adam in relief. 'How nice that it will just be you, me, Ahmed and Habiba on board with Rabiah and Khaled looking after us. Oh, and Mehmet of course.'

I spoke too soon. I'd thought Director Ismail might want to hang around for the evening flight rather than travel back to Cairo with the others (the Police Inspector had already taken his leave to return to the station in Abu Simbel to secure Max's release before making his way back to Aswan). I was perfectly happy for this, eager to understand his oblique reference to what we'd found at Armana and its possible link to Helen of Troy's apparent sojourn in Egypt.

But the Director rather pulled the rug from under me. Following Adam and me up the spiral staircase onto the sundeck, he put a hand on my elbow at the top, gesturing me into the shade of the canvas awning. 'Now you have a spare cabin,' he started, 'I believe I will take some of the leave that is owing to me. We have much to discuss. And, Meredith dear, I am coming to realise it is perhaps best for me to not let you out of my sight for too long.'

I knew way better than to argue, and could only hope the dismay I was feeling wasn't telegraphed in mile-high letters from my face.

*　*　*

So, we'd lost our hefty houseguest Georgina Savage, only to have her unexpectedly replaced by the Director of Antiquities. To add insult to injury, I didn't have the guts to negotiate with Director Ismail for payment of his board and lodging. So it looked very likely we'd be losing out on Georgina's generous remittance as well. It was all decidedly abrupt and discomfiting.

I resigned myself as nobly as I could to being foisted with yet another self-invited 'guest'. In this regard, the Director and Georgina shared an unwelcome characteristic. In fairness though, it was impossible to imagine how differently our adventures since arriving back in Egypt might have turned out had Georgina not muscled her way on board. And so, while the indispensible Rabiah performed a lightning makeover of the spare cabin, I was able to muster enough willpower to wave Georgina off with genuine good wishes, even while I wondered if the stern Ministry Director might yet prove to have an adventuresome streak of his own.

It occurred to me I ought perhaps to be a bit more hospitable. Director Ismail could so easily have thrown us to the wolves. Instead he'd got us off the hook with the Police

Inspector rather neatly. Added to which, he could have taken a decidedly dim view of our discovery of Helen's golden statuette and failure to disclose it. It was a disciplinary matter at the very least, quite possibly a criminal one. Instead he'd reacted like an excited schoolboy. I decided it would serve me to be gracious and endeavour to make the best of things. After all, with Saleh el-Sayed, Zahed Mansour, Ambassador Higgins and the Police Inspector all now departed, there was nothing to stop us returning to the topic of the moment.

Rabiah served a light lunch of pitta bread with homemade tahini, hummus and aubergine dips up on deck, and we got straight down to business.

'You said Helen spent the entire duration of the Trojan War here in Egypt,' I prompted the Director. 'And that the evidence we found in Amarna suggested some link to Troy.'

'To Sparta,' he corrected, dipping a hunk of pitta into olive oil then spreading it thickly with hummus. 'The evidence you found in Amarna suggests a link to Sparta. Remember, Helen was Queen of Sparta before Paris spirited her away. But of course she is remembered as Helen of Troy; always to be associated with the blood shed there in her name.' He popped the hummus-laden pitta in his mouth and chewed with appreciation. 'Mmm, this is good.'

I tried not to let my impatience show at the evident relish with which he was tucking into Rabiah's simple feast. I wanted to get to the point. 'And what of the "evidence" we found?' I pressed.

He forced me to wait while he chewed and swallowed. I knew the evidence to which he was referring of course. A few years ago, Adam and I rather thrillingly stumbled across an ancient cellar in the abandoned city of Akhet-Aten, modern day Amarna. Inside, we found clay wine jars dating back to the time shortly after Akhenaten's reign.

They'd never contained wine. Instead, each was packed with tightly wrapped parchment scrolls. These – unbelievable though it may sound – turned out to be letters giving the inside track of The Greatest Story Ever Told … the Exodus! … written by a man serving under the High Priest at Akhenaten's great temple, who helped lead the Hebrews out of Egypt. This High Priest, Meryre, was none other than Moses of the Bible! Incredible, I know. But true. The letters told the whole story. No wonder the world Media had gone nuts when Director Ismail broke the story last autumn, shortly after the granite tablets containing Nefertari's Narrative came to light.

Between the parchment scrolls and the granite tablets the truth about Ramses II came out. He was not the pharaoh of the Oppression or of the Exodus as popular culture cast him. Those characters were Horemheb and Ramses I respectively. Ramses the Great, as he turned out, was in fact the infant son of Biblical Moses, stolen away from his people when Seti I pursued the fleeing Israelites into the Sinai. He was also descended from the great Thutmoside pharaohs of the 18th Dynasty, his mother being Setepenre, one of the younger daughters of Akhenaten and Nefertiti.

Ramses swore always to keep Seti's secret. He ascended to the throne of Egypt as third in a line of commoner Military pharaohs. Perhaps he had no wish to undermine the legitimacy of his father's and grandfather's rule. Or perhaps he feared tainting himself with Akhenaten's heresy. Whatever; he took the secret to his grave.

It was staggering enough, even without a link to Troy – or Sparta as Director Ismail had pointed out. I looked at the Director expectantly, aware of Adam, Ahmed and Habiba also waiting to be enlightened.

Director Ismail put down his knife and regarded us for a long moment. His gaze came to rest on Mehmet, dipping pitta into the tahini. Mehmet was now one of us. Since his daring rescue mission yesterday, we wouldn't dream of excluding him. But of course Mehmet didn't know about our earlier discovery of the wine jars. So perhaps he was waiting with rather less impatience than the rest of us.

'I'll come to the evidence you found in a moment,' Director Ismail said. 'First, I should probably start by saying there has long been a school of thought among certain historians that Helen was never in Troy. At least three ancient Greek authors suggested she stayed in Egypt during the duration of the Trojan War. Those three authors are Euripides, Stesichorus, and Herodotus.'

'I've heard of Herodotus,' I said.

'Often referred to as "The Father of History",' Adam remarked.

'That's correct,' Director Ismail nodded. 'He was the first historian known to have broken from the Homeric tradition of historic story telling. Herodotus treated historical subjects as a method of investigation — specifically, by collecting his materials systematically and critically, and then arranging them into a histographic narrative. He wrote a rationalising account of the Helen myth, adding weight to the "Egyptian" version of events by putting forward his own evidence — he travelled to Egypt and interviewed the priests of the temple at Memphis. According to these priests, Helen arrived in Egypt shortly after leaving Sparta, because strong winds blew Paris's ship off course. The Egyptian Pharaoh, appalled that Paris had seduced his host's wife and plundered his host's home in Sparta, refused to allow Paris to take Helen to Troy. Paris returned home without a new bride. But the Greeks wouldn't believe Helen was not within Troy's walls. Thus, Helen waited in Memphis for ten years, while the Greeks and the Trojans fought. Following the conclusion of the Trojan War, Menelaus sailed to Memphis, where the pharaoh reunited him with Helen.'

We greeted this with a moment of profound silence.

'Well, that would certainly support the hypothesis that a runaway bride – even if she was the most beautiful woman in the world – was a rather feeble reason to fight a bloody and protracted war,' Adam said at last.

'It would also explain why King Priam didn't hand Helen back to the Greeks when they lay siege to his walled city,' I said, remembering Adam's earlier comment. 'He could hardly hand her back if she was never there.'

'It might also make sense of the lack of recrimination once Helen and Menelaus finally got back together,' Habiba added thoughtfully.

'I said all along the Trojan War was far more likely to be about trade routes, or to lay claim to Troy itself since it was so strategically located,' Adam said sagely.

Mehmet simply stared. And a quick glance at Ahmed told me he was once more engrossed in the story, perhaps wondering if there was a way to get his name up in lights as the one who'd found the statuette.

I tilted my head to one side, scratched my left ear and looked back at Director Ismail. 'Still, it sounds as if Helen really did leave Sparta with Paris, which sparked the whole thing off,' I conjectured. 'But the story of strong winds sounds a bit unlikely. Egypt is a long way from Greece, and in the completely opposite direction from Troy. Maybe she had second thoughts. Or perhaps Paris did kidnap her against her will, and she somehow managed to throw herself on the mercy of the Egyptian Pharaoh – Ramses II as it turns out. I wonder what made Ramses decide to give her refuge here in Egypt for such a long time. You'd think – if the Greeks discovered the pharaoh was harbouring her, they might decide to launch a hostile attack on Egypt.'

'The Greek army against the military might of the Egyptian Empire...' Adam commented. 'Hmm, somehow I don't think so.'

'I think the reason Ramses II was of a mind to shelter Helen is hinted at in the parchment scrolls you found in those wine jars,' Director Ismail said.

I looked at him eagerly. Finally we were getting to the point.

'There are a few passages in those letters that even your esteemed Professor Edward Kincaid struggled to decipher,' he started. 'I've had a team of philologists working on a translation. The writings seem to reflect that a group of Hebrews left Egypt at the time of the Exodus and, rather than preceding east into the Sinai Peninsular with the largest group of escaping Atenists, they sailed to Mycenae for refuge.'

I saw Adam sit up straighter. 'But that would have split the Hebrew camp,' he frowned.

'Apparently this was not without precedent,' Director Ismail said. 'I have been researching the number of Hebrews who left Egypt with the High Priest of the Aten, Meryre; and also the possible movement by some of the peoples of the Exodus to Greece. Remember, these were descendants of the twelve sons of Jacob. My team has analysed the ancient census numbers. We've noted that over half the tribe of Simeon inexplicably "disappears" from the totals between the first and second census counts.'

Now it was my turn to frown. 'So what happened?'

'Well, the wine jar letters are not very clear, as I have explained,' Director Ismail said. 'But they seem to mention some great dissention took place in the camp of Israel. We know from the Torah that the Israelites were very prone to revolting against Moses over various provocations. And civil war among the tribes was not improbable. The Bible's Book of Numbers tells us that a Levite executed a prince of a chief house among the Simeonites. The letters seem to suggest that most of the tribe of Simeon literally 'walked out' of the camp and left the main body of Israelites and Atenists to strike out on their own. The letters definitely make mention of Mycenae.'

'Mycenae,' Adam repeated. 'Not specifically Sparta?'

Director Ismail favoured him with a long look. 'There is a group – famous in the ancient world – which acknowledged a tribal tie to the Israelites. That group was the Spartans of ancient Greece. The Spartans were known to be descended from a people non-native to Greece. They had a vigorous, martial community, very different from the rest of the Greek city states.'

'That's hardly proof,' Adam said warily.

'I have studied the book 'Sparta' by A.H.M Jones, a Professor of Ancient History at Cambridge University,' Director Ismail said. 'In it, he notes several things about Sparta. He states the Spartans worshipped a 'great law-giver' who had given them their laws in the 'dim past'. This 'law-giver' may have been Moses, or Meryre as we should perhaps call him.

Interestingly, the Spartans were themselves divided into several 'tribes', which constituted distinct military formations within the Spartan army. If the Spartans were descended from Simeonites, as one of the twelve tribes of Israel, it would make sense that they would be allied together as distinct tribes even in a new homeland like Sparta.'

He looked around at our faces to ensure he had our full attention. I'm sure our avid expressions were assurance enough, and he went on:

'I have saved the greatest proof to the last. The Spartans themselves declared that they were a fellow tribe of the Jews and corresponded with an ancient Jewish High Priest about their relationship. The Book of I Maccabees records this correspondence. It includes reference to a copy of a letter in which the Spartans send greeting to the elders, the priests and the rest of the Jewish people, *"our kinsmen"*!' He made quotation marks with his fingers around this last statement.

We continued to stare at him, bug-eyed, letting it sink in. We'd all stopped eating, too wrapped up in the unfolding story to do justice to Rabiah's lunch.

'Notice, the Spartans called the Jews "our kinsmen",' he repeated, just in case we weren't getting it. 'The Spartans did not proclaim themselves to be Jews, but rather that they were 'kinsmen' to the Jews. That surely means members of one of the other tribes of Israel.'

'You're saying that the Spartans acknowledged a common ancestry with the Jews of the tribe of Judah, which gives powerful weight to the assertion that they were Israelites who migrated to Greece instead of the Promised Land.' Adam said; spelling it out to ensure he – and perhaps the rest of us – had it straight.

'More than that, my friend,' Director Ismail said, his voice deepening at the import of what he was about to say. 'If Helen, a Spartan, was descended from the Simeonite tribe of Israel, who left Egypt with the Atenist priests at the time of the Exodus, then her links to Egypt were more than just happenstance. Ramses II also had Hebrew blood in his veins, inherited from his great-grandmother Queen Tiye, who was also born into the tribes of Israel.' He let a long pause draw out, looking at each of us in turn. Finally he delivered his denouement. 'I'm saying Helen of Troy and Ramses II were related.'

Chapter 16

Ahmed leapt up. His glass of iced water went flying. It smashed onto the varnished wooden deck, spilling water and ice cubes in all directions and shattering into pieces. He ignored it, dark eyes flashing. 'Helen was an Egyptian queen!' he yelled. 'I have finded de statue of an unknown Egyptian queen!' His forgetfulness to pronounce his t-h's said it all.

I jumped up and so did Adam. But not quite with Ahmed's excitement. We started carefully collecting up the shards of broken glass, mindful of our propensity to walk about the dahabeeyah in bare feet. The ice from Ahmed's glass melted away in moments in the fierce glare of the sun. Rabiah appeared from nowhere with a mop and a dustpan and brush. I'd swear that woman has a sixth sense where the upkeep of our beloved *Queen Ahmes* is concerned.

As Rabiah smilingly took over the clearing up operation, releasing Adam and me to resume our seats, Director Ismail leaned back in his chair and regarded our police pal quizzically. 'I wouldn't go that far,' he said mildly. 'I don't think Helen can claim any royal Egyptian blood. The most we can say, in my view, is that she was descended, as was Ramses, from the twelve tribes of Israel. Probably, in her case, a direct line of descent from Simeon. Hence her status as a Spartan princess. Whereas Ramses had the blood of Joseph in his veins. He of the Biblical coat of many colours. I think we have previously established that Queen Tiye and Vizier Ay were Joseph's children. Tiye was Akhenaten's mother, married to the pharaoh Amenhotep III. And Ay was Nefertiti's father. So Ramses, child of Akhenaten and Nefertiti's younger daughter, had a double dose – both royal and Hebrew blood. Not so Helen. I contend she and Ramses were distant cousins through their Hebrew forebears. Nothing more.'

Ahmed subsided heavily back onto his chair. 'Oh,' he said flatly.

Seeing his disappointment, Director Ismail took pity on him. 'But still, the statuette is a remarkable discovery,' he mollified. Then he bit his bottom lip. 'I am starting to think the world Media will not know what to make of all the revelations coming out of Egypt right now. First there were Nefertari's granite tablets, which forced me to publish the contents of the Amarna wine jar letters. Your – er – friend, Georgina Savage will no doubt break the story about the money from The Great Train Robbery being hidden here at Abu Simbel the moment her feet touch the ground in Cairo. And I can have little hope of keeping Helen of Troy's apparent sojourn here in Egypt a secret, since Zahed Mansour and Saleh el-Sayed have both been treated to the vision that is her statuette.'

He met my troubled gaze and, when I remained silent, went on:

'Ah well; I suppose these things are a test of how well equipped we are to manage such remarkable discoveries.'

This time it was Adam's gaze he met in meaningful communion. I knew he was thinking about our tomb, still hidden away from the world behind Hatshepsut's mortuary temple on the west bank near Luxor. I decided it was time to steer the conversation away from these troubled waters.

'We don't actually have any concrete evidence that Helen was in Egypt for the duration of the Trojan War,' I said dampeningly. 'I know the statuette is suggestive, particularly being found here in the Great Temple of Ramses. And what you've just told us of her probable antecedence is mind-boggling. But none of it constitutes irrefutable proof.'

The Director watched Rabiah as she retreated with the dustpan and brush. She negotiated her way down the spiral staircase below deck, disappearing from sight in her usual swish of black robes. Rabiah had perfected the art of apparent deafness when we were talking about anything Egyptological. I had no qualms at all about speaking openly in front of her. I knew I could trust her and Khaled implicitly. Director Ismail, perhaps understandably, was more inclined to be circumspect. 'Tell me again, slowly this time, how the statuette came to be found here at Abu Simbel,' he said.

Adam told the story. It took a bit of telling. This time he didn't attempt to compress it into a few explanatory sentences. He simply started at the beginning and went from there.

I could repeat every word to you. Instead I'll flesh out the essentials, as I have a feeling you've heard it all before.

It all linked back to the British Consul General Henry Salt's theft of Sarah Belzoni's diary of her travels in Egypt and Nubia alongside her husband. In it, she described her first visit to Abu Simbel with Giovanni in 1816. This pre-dated Salt's bitter falling-out with Belzoni over the sale to the British Museum of the antiquities he discovered. Salt learnt of Sarah's journal – and of the tablets she'd spotted in the smaller temple of Nefertari – when Sarah wrote an appeal to the Trustees of the British Museum after her husband's tragic and untimely death. Sarah wanted sponsorship to mount an expedition of her own back to Egypt to retrieve the tablets. The Trustees were having none of it, and stonewalled her. And Salt, in England at the time, got wind of the tablets.

The story of ancient Egypt was emerging from the sands thanks to Champollion's recent decipherment of the hieroglyphics. No doubt Salt thought he could steal a march on the widow, claim the find for himself, and bring to life another chapter of Egypt's ancient past. He returned to Egypt and employed Abdullah Soliman as his *ghaffir*. Abdullah had served Giovanni and Sarah Belzoni as *Reis* during the four years of their excavations in Egypt. He knew where his loyalties lay. Spotting Sarah's journal – into which he himself had sketched drawings of the ancient monuments – among Salt's possessions, he promptly stole it back.

As things turned out, Sarah Belzoni did indeed return to Egypt and Abu Simbel. But it was incognito and in disguise. She joined the Robert Hay expedition in 1825, masquerading as a young male epigrapher. But by the time she returned, Nefertari's granite tablets had vanished.

If only Sarah could have known it was the ever-faithful Abdullah who'd retrieved them. He'd made it his mission, when Henry Salt succumbed to ill health, to ensure his new employer would not get his hands on them.

Sadly for Abdullah, one of the Abd el-Rassul brothers (Ahmed's ancestors and as criminally-inclined a gang of thieves as ever lived) learned of the tablets when Abdullah returned home with them to Luxor. Abdullah hid them in the tomb of Seti I; discovered by Belzoni, and over which he still stood guard. Hakim Abd el-Rassul followed Abdullah there one night. A fight broke out. Hakim murdered Abdullah. Whether by accident or on the orders of Henry Salt was unclear.

Luckily, it seemed Abdullah, perhaps fearing for his life, had already taken the precaution of moving the tablets to a cave behind Seti's tomb and putting a curse on the place. There they remained for nearly two hundred years until last autumn. That's when we found them.

Thus bringing Nefertari's Narrative to the world.

The Ottoman-styled casket in which Abdullah had transported the granite tablets also contained the statuette of Helen of Troy in a hidden compartment in its lid. This no doubt accounted for its astonishing weight. Wrapped around the statuette was a page torn from Sarah Belzoni's diary. On it, Abdullah had sketched a drawing of the statuette emerging from the Great Temple of Abu Simbel. There was only one way to interpret this. Abdullah had found it there.

I said now what I'd first said on thrilling to the discovery. 'How everyone else missed it is a mystery to me. Early nineteenth century explorers crawled all over the place in the years after Belzoni first dug an entrance through the sand.'

This was too much for Ahmed. He leapt up again, thankfully with nothing to spill this time. 'Abdullah's notebook!' he yelled. 'I tried to tell to you yesterday!'

I looked up at him in shock as the memory clicked. My God, was it only yesterday? It felt like much longer ago that we'd stood inside Nefertari's temple staring at the spot where she'd first spied the tablets. I'd forgotten all about Ahmed's mysterious pronouncement in the melodrama of everything that had happened since. But now his words flooded back, and I felt my blood start to fizz in my veins. 'You said you'd made a study of it,' I breathed on a note of discovery. 'You suggested it contains a clue about the location where Abdullah found the solid gold statuette!'

'That's right!' Ahmed shouted, his black eyes snapping with excitement, his voice booming out across the open deck. 'The moment, it has not been right since yesterday to return to the subject.'

'Er – notebook?' Director Ismail said sharply, eyes narrowing on Ahmed's face.

'We were given it legitimately,' I said quickly. 'Ibrahim Mohassib, when he was still curator of the Luxor Museum found it in the storerooms.' I had no need to explain who Ibrahim Mohassib was. The Director had been the one to cart him off to Cairo and butter him up with a dazzling promotion, cataloguing antiquities ready for the move to the new Grand Egyptian Museum. You see, Ibrahim Mohassib, as I may have mentioned, knew – or *thought* he knew – a little too much about our secret tomb. And a little information, as we've had cause to remark before, can be a dangerous thing.

'We'd asked if he had anything he could date confidently to the early 1820s,' Adam added, rushing into speech the way I had. 'Abdullah's notebook had somehow made its way into the museum archive, perhaps because it named him as both Giovanni Belzoni's *Reis* and Henry Salt's *ghaffir*.' He looked at the Director's raised eyebrow and went on, 'We didn't take much notice of it last year because, of course, it's written all in Arabic …'

'…And we didn't actually need it to help us find the cave where the casket was hidden,' I finished. 'As you know, Ahmed's sister spilled the beans on the secret location.' This was another strange twist in the story. Ahmed's sister Atiyah was descended from another Atiyah Abd el-Rassul. This lady had been Abdullah Soliman's sweetheart, and had known about the secret cave. She'd also known of the curse. Her fear of this had been enough to secure her silence. But she'd handed down the secret through generations of female Abd el-Rassul. Perhaps she viewed this as atonement for her brother being the one to leave his knife sticking out of the dead body of her boyfriend!

The Director's head was moving as he looked from one of us to the other in apparent bewilderment. Finally he turned it to narrow his gaze once again on Ahmed. 'You are still in possession of this notebook?' he asked.

* * *

Finally, it seemed there might be some chance of shedding light on how Abdullah Soliman had found the statuette of Helen of Troy here at Abu Simbel. I felt the buzz of excitement in the pit of my stomach.

'Remember, Merry;' Adam tugged at my sleeve as Ahmed was dispatched to fetch the notebook. His darkly lashed blue eyes were softly serious as they looked into mine. 'The Abu Simbel temples have been broken apart and pieced back together again during the latter part of the two centuries since Abdullah Soliman was here. Don't get your hopes up. There's almost no chance of anything being as it was when he visited in the early 1820s.'

I recalled this was exactly what I had planned on telling Ahmed had Georgina not interrupted us yesterday. I cautioned myself to calm down. Even so, it was hard to control the quickening of my breath as Ahmed came bounding up the spiral staircase – no easy feat for a man of his size, (which said much for his eagerness to share his discovery) –

and I spied the small leather bound notebook he was gripping in one big brown hand.

He handed it respectfully to the Director. I noticed he was marking a page with his finger. Before subsiding back into his chair he addressed Director Ismail with a touch of puffed up pride, standing straight with his chest out and his chin up. 'You will see on this page here, sir, a reference to how Abdullah Soliman made the discovery.'

Director Ismail accepted the notebook, putting one of his own fingers between the pages so he didn't lose the marker Ahmed had made. He crossed his long legs, pulled a pair of reading glasses from his trousers pocket, slowly put them on, and started to read.

I watched him closely as he frowned over the tightly packed Arabic hand-written scrawl from two centuries ago. Director Ismail is a tall, formal man; always elegantly and impeccably dressed in a suit, pressed shirt and tie. It said much, I felt, that in the short time he'd been with us since coming on board this morning planning who-knows-what, he'd dispensed with his jacket and tie, and opened the top button of his pale grey shirt. It exposed a tanned throat with a little tuft of greying chest hair peeking above the vent.

He took his time. Even though Ahmed had passed him the small leather notebook open at the relevant passage, he nevertheless turned back a few pages, and read forward, eyes scanning the writing several pages beyond Ahmed's marker.

The rest of us remained absolutely still and silent, observing him. We didn't move even when Rabiah came unobtrusively to clear away the remnants of the lunch she'd prepared us.

The Director's concentration was absolute. Almost as if he'd forgotten we were there. I could well imagine his difficulty in reading the text, in faded ink and written in a tiny script as it was. At least it was in his native Arabic. So he didn't need to perform a translation.

I watched his foot jerk up and down a couple of times, clad in a brown, polished leather lace-up shoe. The sun had moved across the sky. Its rays reached under the canvas awning and glowed on his close-cropped black hair, turning the greying sideburns silver, and glinting off his reading glasses. And still he kept on turning the pages with long manicured fingers, silently absorbing the contents, utterly focused in studied concentration.

When I was starting to think I couldn't bear the suspense a moment longer, and might have to snatch the little notebook from his hands and demand a translation, he uncrossed his legs. He looked first at Ahmed, lifting his gaze from the notebook, which he set carefully on the table, to meet our police pal's darkly flashing eyes. 'Not much of a writer, was he? That's as impenetrable a jumble of words as I've encountered. Almost as if he was transcribing a kind of code. The thing's not written in sentences. Just abbreviated notes. I certainly wouldn't call it a journal. Although it does certainly record his journey from Luxor here to Abu Simbel to retrieve something. Nothing is referred to directly. Not the granite tablets. And certainly not the golden statuette of Helen. Although he does mention the casket he apparently stored them in.'

Ahmed nodded. 'A man of mystery,' he said solemnly. 'He was better at drawing than writing. But sadly for us he did not draw any pictures into this notebook.'

I tried hard to bite down on my impatience. 'So, what's the bit you think gives a clue to how and where he found the statuette?' I asked as mildly as I could.

Now Director Ismail's steely gaze came to meet mine. 'The passage Ahmed refers to is rather bizarre,' he started. 'From what I can gather, Abdullah was inside the Great Temple in one of the antechambers and tripped on an uneven surface. He talks about stones coming loose at his feet. I get the impression he fell flat on his face. There's a whole paragraph about the benefits of wearing a turban. As if this might have cushioned his fall and prevented a nasty injury.'

'Tell to them about the submarine bit,' Ahmed said excitedly. His eager expression told me everything I needed to know about his determination not to be left out. After all he'd read it first.

'Er – submarine?' the Director enquired confusedly, a deep frown creasing his brow.

'Yes! You know! The underground bit!'

'Ah,' Director Ismail said after a lengthy pause. 'You mean the – er – *subterranean* chamber.' Clearly the Ministry Director was not au fait with Ahmed's' mangled attempts at certain English words. He shook his head as if clearing it of cobwebs. Then his expression cleared and he looked at me with an expression suggesting it was a relief to communicate with someone for whom English was their first language. This said much, I thought, for his own command of our foreign tongue. 'Abdullah seems to be referring to a chamber carved deep into the bedrock underneath the temple.' he said.

I stared back bug-eyed. 'Does he say any more about it?'

'He mentions wall reliefs. But – remember – this was before the hieroglyphs had been deciphered. Abdullah had no idea what he was looking at. But I'm guessing this is where he found the Helen statuette. Because his notebook talks of riches and gold.'

'Riches in the temple of Ramses,' I breathed.

Adam was frowning. 'I'm not aware of any underground chambers being found in the Great Temple of Ramses. It was carved backwards from the cliff face into the rock. But I've never heard of anything subterranean in this particular temple. It sounds a bit like a crypt.'

Director Ismail met his gaze. 'Hidden crypts, niches and small, mysterious chambers built into walls or beneath the floors are not uncommon in ancient Egyptian monuments. We find them in temples from the 18th Dynasty through to the Roman period. Their purpose is unclear.'

Adam was nodding, pulling on his own Egyptological knowledge. 'Sometimes they've been referred to as priest holes. Many Egyptologists believe priests used them to remain hidden while providing oracles in the name of the gods.'

'That's certainly a popular school of thought,' the Director confirmed. 'But some of these crypts or niches may have had some unknown symbolic purpose. There's even a suggestion they were intended to be tombs of the gods, in the same way the pharaohs carved underground tombs in the Valley of the Kings.'

I frowned at them, not really in the mood for a masterclass about temple design or theological hypothesis. 'Isn't it more likely they were used to hide away particularly valuable treasures of the temple?' I wasn't giving up on the idea of Ramses' riches just yet.

All eyes swung towards me.

'That is certainly a possibility,' Director Ismail allowed cautiously. 'Many beautiful stone statues were found hidden beneath the Open Court in Luxor Temple as recently as the 1980s. They're now on display in Luxor Museum.'

I stared back at him, trying not to let my impatience show. 'So, isn't it possible that Ramses had a secret subterranean chamber built beneath his temple here at Abu Simbel to hide away certain things he might not have wanted others to see – something that revealed his kinship to Helen of Troy for example…?'

I swear I observed Director Ismail's brain catch on fire as the full import of this suggestion struck him. He'd already said the subterranean chamber was where Abdullah appeared to have found the statuette, but he apparently hadn't made the mental leap that it may have been constructed specifically for that purpose.

'I repeat…' Adam said slowly. '…To the best of my knowledge no underground hidden chamber has ever been found in The Great Temple of Ramses at Abu Simbel.' But his eyes were shining, deepening from dark blue to an intense violet, which gave him away.

We all spoke at once, six voices overlapping. Whilst we didn't all use the same words, the sentiment was exactly the same. Ahmed was loudest, 'There's a chance it's still there!'

The realisation that the secret underground chamber may still be hidden underground was so profound we all stared at each other in silence for a long moment. The echo of our joint proclamation drifted across the stretching waters of Lake Nasser.

Adam met my gaze. He was frowning. 'You realise, if the secret chamber was far enough underground not to have been found by Giovanni Belzoni or successive early nineteenth century explorers – or more particularly during the 1960s re-siting of the entire temple complex by UNESCO – then there's only one place it can be.'

I blinked a couple of times as the import of what he was saying dawned on me. 'It's under water,' I said flatly. 'At the bottom of Lake Nasser to be precise.'

* * *

We checked and double-checked our facts of course.

Adam brought his iPad up from our cabin and trawled minutely through every website he could find that even remotely referred to the re-siting of the Abu Simbel monuments.

Director Ismail put calls through to his team at the Ministry of State for Antiquities. He asked for all archive documents to be searched for any reference to the temple plans, and the records chronicling the UNESCO project to be similarly scrutinised. Luckily these had been scanned into computer files a number of years ago. So the search was not impossible. He was senior ranking enough not to need to offer an explanation, but to expect his instructions to be obeyed without question. Even so, I imagined there might be a few raised eyebrows in Cairo right now.

Mehmet returned to his cabin and scoured his digital photographs searching for any clue at all for which antechamber Abdullah might have been inside when he apparently tripped and made his fateful discovery.

Ahmed, Habiba and I went one step further. Taking Abdullah's notebook with us – they could both read the Arabic script after all – we retraced our steps around the rocky headland where the *Queen Ahmes* was moored to pay another visit to The Great Temple of Ramses.

The place didn't spook me quite so much this time. As the gigantic colossi sitting recessed against the temple façade hove into view as we neared the temple forecourt, I found myself gazing at a pharaoh with secrets. He'd kept his true lineage hidden his whole life. And it was a supremely long life. The man had died in his nineties, looking nothing like the vigorous, youthful and mighty ruler depicted here so grand and grandiose in sandstone.

I wondered if he was harbouring secrets still. What riches – even beyond the haul of Great Train Robbery money – might remain hidden after all this time? I asked myself.

I thought of Giovanni Belzoni. His bitter disappointment at finding no treasure inside the temple when he dug its entrance from beneath metres of drifting sand. It seemed he never thought to excavate down under the stone floor.

There was poetic justice at least in Abdullah Soliman – Belzoni's trusted *Reis* – being the one to make the discovery.

I stopped my musings as we stepped through the tall doorway and walked into the temple itself between the legs of the two immense seated colossi either side of the entranceway.

We weren't the only visitors. But since most of the tour parties arrive in the morning, we had the place pretty much to ourselves. It seemed impossible that it was less than twenty-four hours since we'd been here to make our surreptitious search of the inner sanctuary.

Thankfully, on this occasion, we had no need to check out that particular chamber. In all honesty, the four seated statues of Ramses among the gods still gave me the chills in a way the colossi outside did not.

Abdullah's notebook spoke of an antechamber. We were here to investigate. So we moved through the large rock-cut hall with its eight massive pillars fronted with statues of Ramses posing as Osiris, ignoring the wall reliefs of the battle of Kadesh. We had no need to enter the second hall, constructed with four pillars and decorated with religious and offering scenes. It led to the vestibule and inner sanctuary.

There were six rooms that might qualify as antechambers. Four led off the right hand side towards the back of the first hall, and two branched out from a diagonal corridor on the left. Adam had said these were most probably storerooms when we'd made a study of the floorplan on the Internet before setting out this afternoon. Each was decorated with faded, three-and-a-bit-thousand-year-old wall reliefs showing Ramses making offerings before various gods.

It wasn't possible to check the floor for missing or uneven stones. The entire interior of the temple was decked out with wooden floorboards. I guess these served the dual purpose of protecting the actual stone floor, while also being health and safety conscious and providing a less hazardous flooring for visitors.

Instead Ahmed and I scanned the walls while Habiba read Abdullah's notebook and attempted to provide a translation into English of his rather opaque writings.

'Director Ismail is quite correct,' she said, adjusting her headscarf around her face. 'It is almost impossible to make sense of some of these notes. But he does seem to have a strange fixation with lotus flowers.'

'Lotus flowers!' I exclaimed. 'There! Look!'

We were in the first of the two chambers off the diagonal corridor on the left of the temple behind the great pillared entrance hall. The wall in front of me was decorated with scenes of Ramses offering lotus flowers to the goddess Hathor. Behind me an almost mirror image showed him making the same offering to Isis.

'This has to be it! I cried out, elated. 'I didn't see any lotus flower offerings in the other chambers.'

Ahmed came forward excitedly. He'd brought one of Mehmet's small digital cameras with him. He started snapping away with enthusiasm.

Habiba tilted her head to one side, watching him with a fond, indulgent smile. 'It would make sense,' she said thoughtfully. 'The Lotus was one of the most important religious symbols in the mythology of ancient Egypt. It was used in art to represent creation, rebirth and regeneration. As a symbol of re-birth, the lotus was closely related to the imagery of funerary and Osirian cults. If Ramses wanted to create a hidden sub-chamber almost as a sort of tomb to his secret heredity and to hide treasures that might relate to his kinship with the Spartan queen, these female gods – look there are Nephthys and Nekhbet too –' she pointed upwards at the opposite wall – 'would be the obvious choice for guardians of his secret.'

My brain burst alight with the possibilities.

Ahmed seemed similarly fired up. 'Habiba, please stand by the door and ensure no one comes,' he instructed. Then he dropped to his knees.

'Ahmed! What are you doing?' I gaped.

But it was all too obvious. He was pulling up a section of the floorboards. He'd dispensed with his sling last night. The vigour with which he applied himself – and his undoubted strength – to the task reassured me he no longer needed it. But this thought didn't distract me for long.

'Ahmed! Stop! You can't do that! We'll face charges of criminal damage!'

But it was too late. Ahmed had prised up several interconnected planks of the wooden flooring.

I couldn't help myself. While Habiba kept watch, I dropped to my knees alongside him. I'd brought my iPhone, which has a handy torch built in. I shone it into the gap he'd created, angling its beam to illuminate the space beneath the floorboards.

'Concrete!' I spat out, thoroughly put out and discouraged at the sight that greeted my eyes.

'Concrete?' Habiba repeated from the doorway as I got disconsolately to my feet. 'But that means this is not the original floor of the temple!'

I caught her drift, feeling my spirits surge again. 'Which means …'

'Yes!' Ahmed yelled, leaping up. 'They did not rebuild the original floor. At least not in these outer chambers. But put these floorings over the new concrete base of the manmade dome!'

'Which means…' I said again.

'It's possible the UNESCO team never discovered the underground chamber,' Habiba said, her bronze-flecked eyes shining.

'Which means…' I said for a third time.

'It's still there!' Ahmed exclaimed.

Funnily enough, Adam and Director Ismail had reached the same conclusion.

'Listen to this…' Adam said as we re-joined them on the upper deck of the *Queen Ahmes* and Rabiah served pre-dinner drinks. We'd told them all about our discovery. Not forgetting Ahmed's magnificent achievement at putting the floorboards back pretty much as we'd found them. I prayed, at least, no one would suspect our "excavation".

Adam pulled his iPad onto his lap and quoted from the website he'd called up about the re-siting of the Abu Simbel temples. It's fair to say he had a captive audience as he read aloud, 'Between 1964 and 1968 a workforce and an international team of engineers and scientists, supported by funds from more than fifty countries, dug away the top of the cliff and completely disassembled both temples, reconstructing them on high ground more than sixty metres above their previous site. In all, some sixteen thousand blocks were moved.'

He stopped reading and looked around at us. 'Now, what about that description is suggestive?'

I cottoned on immediately. His eyes fixed on mine might have had something to do with it. I'd swear Adam and I are learning the art of telepathic communication. 'It's the bit about digging away the top of the cliff!' I said excitedly. 'They started from the top and worked down!' I exclaimed. 'By the time they hit what they thought was the bedrock, I guess they had no need to search further for hidden subterranean chambers. Why would they?'

'Exactly!' Adam grinned. 'I think we can safely say that underground chamber is still there, carved into the bedrock of what is now the bottom of Lake Nasser!'

My excitement crumpled in a sudden burst of deflation, as if someone had stuck a pin in a balloon. 'But you've just said, that's under nearly sixty metres of water,' I pointed out dejectedly. Unbidden, the horrific image of Philip Sinnerman's half-eaten body flashed across my mind's eye. 'And, Adam! That water – Lake Nasser – is absolutely infested with deadly, man-eating crocodiles!'

Chapter 17

It's amazing how the lure of gold and the chance to unlock secrets from Egypt's ancient past can separate a man from all reason. Two men, in fact. Both Adam Tennyson, my adored husband, and Feisal Ismail, fearsome Director for the Ministry of State for Antiquities, seemed to me to have taken leave of their senses.

Even Ahmed – usually first in line for anything hazardous or potentially career-limiting – baulked at what they had in mind.

This, of course, was a scuba-diving excursion to check out the underwater terrain and see if they could locate the subterranean chamber.

'I took a scuba diving course in the Red Sea many years ago,' Adam enlightened me. 'I'm fully qualified.'

I can assure you, it heartened me not one jot to have this little insight into his life before the advent of me in it.

'I also have the necessary qualifications,' Director Ismail assured us self-importantly. 'I learnt to dive in order to explore the underwater remains of Cleopatra's palace, offshore from Alexandria. I can arrange to have all the equipment we need sent here.'

You see; that's the trouble with having a man at the top of the Egyptian hierarchy as houseguest. Director Ismail can snap his fingers and expect everyone to jump to his command.

So, true to form, a special courier delivered everything needed for an aquatic surveillance of the underwater site of the original Abu Simbel temples the following day.

Everything, that is, except specialist underwater camera equipment. This, Mehmet informed us, was his domain. And, of course, he had exactly what we needed! He professed his willingness to join in the underwater exploration once he knew if there was anything worth photographing down there. It turned out he'd also put his skills to use photographing Cleopatra's sunken palace.

So, make that three men who'd abandoned all critical faculties!

Ahmed had mentioned a submarine – not familiar with the English word *subterranean*. I couldn't help but think a submarine would be a safer way of checking out the landscape beneath the floodwaters of Lake Nasser. But of course my tentative suggestion was thoroughly pooh-poohed when I made it.

I'd earlier wondered idly if Director Ismail might have an adventuresome streak. Little could I have guessed at his hidden tendency towards juvenile delinquency! A suitcase arrived along with the scuba diving paraphernalia. Somebody evidently had been given the task of packing his casual clothes for the little "holiday" he was treating himself to.

My eyes widened when I saw his hat. Adam has one just like it. Deep down, it seems all men – or these two, at least – must carry around some fantasy alter ego of themselves as Indiana Jones personified!

'So, you really *are* going to dive to the bottom of Lake Nasser to see if you can find the hidden underground chamber,' I said to Adam in the privacy of our cabin in the early afternoon. He was easing himself into a wetsuit even as we spoke, tugging it up over the Lycra undergarment he was wearing, so I scarcely needed to ask the question.

'It would be too dangerous to allow Feisal to go on his own,' he responded. This progression to using the Director's first name had coincided with his change of clothes. It seemed ridiculous to go on calling the man 'Director Ismail' when he was wearing shorts, flip-flops, a tee shirt, and that beaten-up and dusty-looking Indiana Jones-style hat. This get-up exposed long taut-and-tanned limbs, and took years off him. 'Scuba dives in unfamiliar waters should always be done in pairs,' Adam went on, pulling the wetsuit up over his chest. 'It's a health and safety thing, Merry.'

'Liar!' I accused rudely. 'You're acting like a little boy on a treasure hunt!'

He paused in the action of pushing his arms into the wetsuit's tight sleeves, and looked at me levelly. 'Isn't that exactly what this might be?' he asked guilelessly. 'In fact, hasn't our entire time together in Egypt been one long treasure hunt?'

'Well, yes,' I acknowledged, thinking back over some of our escapades. 'But…'

He finished pulling the sleeves up over his arms and smiled with understanding. 'But before it's always been you and me,' he finished for me. I swear he knows what I'm going to say before I say it half the time. 'Believe me, Merry; you and me is how I like it best.'

'I'm not lowering myself into any water that's got huge bloody great crocodiles in it! ' I shuddered. 'I might like a treasure hunt. But I don't have a death wish!'

He smiled at me. 'We'll have gas tanks on. It's open circuit scuba kit. The bubbles should be enough to keep the crocs away.'

'Should be,' I repeated, not in the least reassured. 'You're stark staring mad, Adam!'

He smiled at me again, saying gently, 'No; I am doing what we came here to do. I am following in Giovanni Belzonis footsteps.'

I gaped at him. 'How do you figure that one out?'

Fully in his wetsuit now, he turned around, inviting me to fasten the zipper. I moved across to him and yanked it up his back. 'Giovanni Belzoni came here to dig the temple out of the sand,' he said as I zipped him in. 'In that pursuit he was remarkably successful, as we know. But he missed a bit. I want to finish the job.'

I reached up to secure the clip at the nape of his neck, ensuring the wetsuit was fully done up. I wondered about

322

throttling him while I was at it. 'If you're justifying yourself by thinking it's alright to leave me behind on the *Queen Ahmes* because Giovanni Belzoni left Sarah behind on the roof of Philae Temple, then I'm not impressed!'

He turned around and grinned at me. 'I want you to hero-worship me, Merry! I want you to think me brave, and daring and adventurous.'

'Crazy, reckless and foolhardy is more like it,' I muttered. 'But you do look awfully sexy in that wetsuit.'

He stopped grinning. His eyes flared signals. And his lips descended on mine. It was a long, lingering, deeply satisfying kiss. I felt myself responding as I always do, all molten heat and softening limbs.

He laughed against my lips. 'I think we might have to hold this thought for later,' he murmured. 'It's just taken me ten minutes to get into this wetsuit. Believe me, Merry; there's not room in here for what I feel happening right now! And there's not time to unpeel it and struggle back into it again.'

I let him go with a small puff. But it was amazing how much better I was feeling. 'I'll hold you to the "later",' I said.

'I'm counting on it,' he grinned.

I picked up his flippers and mask, and followed him into the corridor, through the lounge bar, out through the French doors and down a couple of steps into our gleaming stainless steel kitchen. Rabiah was there, wiping down the already spotless surfaces with a cloth soaked in anti-bacterial spray. She smiled nervously, seeing Adam clad ready for his potentially suicidal spot of underwater exploration, but, meeting my eyes, pressed her lips together and didn't comment.

Adam led the way out the back door of the kitchen and down onto the landing platform at the rear of the dahabeeyah. Director – sorry – Feisal – was already there and waiting, similarly decked out in a form-fitting black wetsuit. It clung to his long limbs like a second skin.

'Well, I suppose at least it's an *official* treasure hunt this time,' I muttered. It was hard to think of a bigger stamp of officialdom than to have the Director of the Ministry of State for Antiquities in charge of proceedings.

Mehmet wasn't joining them on this first dive. Adam and Feisal had decided to do an exploratory underwater recce first, just to see what there was to see.

Ahmed and Mehmet helped Adam and Feisal on with their twin gas cylinders and checked the air supply. Mehmet handed Adam a small specialist underwater camera.

'Just in case there is anything worth seeing down there,' he said.

Khaled started up the engines, broke the moorings and moved the *Queen Ahmes* around the headland. When we were in open water in front of the awe-inspiring Great Temple of Ramses he dropped anchor.

Director Ismail – er – Feisal, I mean – had had the foresight to get the area along the shoreline cordoned off.

Any tourists visiting the twin temples wouldn't be able to get close enough to observe our activities. But the four – three, I should say, since one of them was broken off at the hip – seated colossi of Ramses were different. They towered above the cordon staring out mute and impassive across Lake Nasser as they had once stared across the Nile. The eyes of those immense statues were blank, unseeing stone. Even so, I fancifully imagined them watching us closely as Adam and Feisal undertook this mission to see if Ramses had any last secrets – or maybe riches as described by Abdullah – to reveal. I turned my back on the temple so I didn't have to look at them.

Habiba joined us, squeezing onto the lower platform where the day before yesterday she'd hauled herself out of the water just as the ferocious crocodile attacked poor Philip Sinnerman. The four of us stood back as Adam and Feisal fitted their flippers and masks, made one final check of their breathing apparatus, then gave each other the thumbs up and stepped one-by-one from the safety of the dahabeeyah into the water.

I was pleased to see Ahmed had his gun. Khaled was also on stand-by with rocket flares hoping to frighten off any crocodiles that may be lurking in the shallows. Between us, we'd kept a close eye out all day, and seen no sign whatsoever of these fearsome beasts. But it didn't mean they weren't there.

I was pleased to see the promised bubbles jetting up from the gas cylinders as the compressed air started flowing under water. Even so, I had a serious case of the jitters. It was impossible not to keep re-living the awful moment of the crocodile attack on Philip Sinnerman. How he'd managed to get away and live long enough to haul himself in front of the audience watching the sound and light show two evenings ago would forever remain a mystery. I knew one thing, and one thing only. It was an experience I dreaded Adam sharing in. Adam, or Feisal Ismail, come to that; but most particularly, Adam. He'd had a close encounter with a crocodile once before. And once was enough. He still wore the crocodile tooth charm on a bootlace around his neck as a lucky talisman.

I prayed it would cast its magic protection over him now.

'We'd have a better view from the upper deck,' Habiba said as the bubbles moved further away. Adam and Feisal were swimming down the underwater cliff face to the original site of the rock cut temple. It was submerged some sixty metres below us.

They were each diving with two air tanks. Adam had explained that the deeper you dive, the faster you consume air from your scuba tanks, no matter how much air they hold to start with. This, I supposed, was so much common sense. I'd asked how long a scuba tank might last. He'd said an average open-water certified diver using a standard aluminium eighty-cubic-foot tank on a forty-metre dive would be able to stay down for about forty-five to sixty minutes before surfacing with a safe reserve of air still in the tank. As he and Feisal were diving deeper, he'd reckoned at forty-five minutes tops, even with the double tanks. I'd absorbed the timescale only among all the other scuba jargon.

As the bubbles reaching the surface drifted away, I followed the others up on deck, resigning myself to a lengthy, impatient wait. I consoled myself with Adam's undoubted – if hitherto unknown to me – experience. The memory of our kiss and promise of the thought we were holding also sustained me. It gave him a reason to want to hurry back, after all.

It was a strain to keep scanning the brightly glinting surface of the water. Sunlight danced across the rippling waves, diamond bright and painful to look at for any length of time. The seated stone colossi of Ramses kept drawing my gaze, despite my determination not to look at them. There was something magnetising about them.

The goddesses Isis, Hathor, Nephthys and Nekhbet no longer guarded the entrance to Ramses' secret underground chamber. I tried to imagine this subterranean crypt, undoubtedly filled now with water. After more than fifty years submerged it was almost certainly too much to hope for that the wall reliefs Abdullah had observed still remained. That was even supposing Adam and Feisal could find where it was located and figure out a way of reaching it. Let's face it; this couldn't be obvious. Explorers, archaeologists, Egyptologists and *engineers*, for heaven's sake, had missed it! But, what a discovery, if they could only find it! Something to prove an irrefutable link between Ramses and Helen of Troy! It was a movie-maker's dream. And it would be a fantastic way to round off my mission to follow the trail Belzoni blazed through Egypt, bringing his story to life for a modern audience. To know there were still discoveries here to be made in the temple he first started digging from the sand two-hundred-and-one years ago!

In such happy musings, forty-five minutes passed readily enough.

And then I started to get anxious.

'Shouldn't we start to see some sign of the bubbles coming back towards the surface?' I asked, scanning the gentle waves again.

Ahmed and Mehmet both glanced at their watches. There had been nothing to disturb the tranquillity or cause so much as a ripple on the surface of the lake in the time the men had been underwater. No bubbles and, thankfully, no long, scaly, prehistoric-looking snouts breaking through the waves to reveal the presence of what I feared to see the most.

Habiba leaned forward over the handrail, as if it might allow her gaze to penetrate beneath the water lapping gently against the side of the dahabeeyah. 'Yes, they should be coming up by now,' she said.

Anxiety started to turn to panic as another five minutes crawled by. Then ten.

'Is there any chance a crocodile could have attacked them underwater without us realising it?' I asked worriedly.

'Highly unlikely,' Mehmet said. 'Crocodiles have to come up for air too. We'd surely have spotted some sign.'

Blood, I thought. He meant blood. And there was assuredly no blood on the surface of the lake. I tried my best to view this positively. But it was hard when minute-by-minute the time slipped by.

Forty-five minutes had seemed an age when I thought it was how long I'd have to wait. Time can crawl ever so slowly when you're counting the seconds. But now, knowing their air supply must surely be diminishing, each passing minute seemed to zip by faster than the last.

'Do you think they have finded something?' Ahmed asked, not quite keeping the excitement from his expression, despite his concern.

'Surely they wouldn't be stupid enough to investigate on the first dive,' I frowned. 'All they were planning to do was to search out the location of where the antechamber with the lotus flower wall reliefs once stood.' They'd taken measuring equipment for this purpose, having made meticulous calculations of the floor plan of the original temple this morning. 'Oh God, what's keeping them...?' I wailed when another minute sped by.

'Bubbles!' Ahmed yelled a moment later. 'I see bubbles!'

Mehmet ran across the deck and swung himself down the spiral staircase while I was still sagging with relief. Ahmed followed at a statelier pace. Habiba whooped with delight. A radiant smile lit up her face.

But the joy was short lived. It soon became horribly clear it was only one jet of bubbles, not two. I craned over the side of the dahabeeyah, unable to move from the spot or tear my gaze from the streaming bubbles until I could see whose they were.

The trouble with wetsuits and facemasks is it makes it almost impossible to tell who is inside them. Adam is dark haired. Admittedly not the jet black with silvery streaks of Feisal Ismail. And not cropped as closely against his head. But with hair soaking wet and plastered against his scalp it was impossible to tell which of the men was swimming up from the depths, even when he broke the surface.

All I could see was that, whoever he was, he was gesturing frantically.

'What? What is it?' I cried out desperately, feeling fear and dread creep up my windpipe.

The black wetsuit-clad figure splashed closer. Reaching up, he ripped off his facemask. I nearly passed out with relief when I saw Adam's face. But, once more, it was short-lived. Although, thank God, not because of any scaly monsters in the water. None that I could see at any rate.

'Mehmet!' Adam yelled, still several metres away from the dahabeeyah. 'Get into a wetsuit, grab another oxygen tank and get the hell down here! Feisal is trapped!'

I took a moment to grasp what he was saying. I'd been so fixated on crocodiles; sure one must have attacked them underwater; my brain didn't seem capable of assimilating anything else.

And then the true horror of what he'd said sank in. 'How can he be trapped?' I shouted. 'What happened?'

I don't suppose he heard me. But he was intent on giving us as much information as possible. 'We found the spot surprisingly quickly,' he yelled from the water. It was clear he had no intention of coming back on board. He was treading water, waiting for Mehmet to tug on his wetsuit and join him. 'Our measurements were bang on! We started feeling about for loose stones, and got lucky at the first attempt! Guys, there's a stairway down there! Don't ask me how the UNESCO gang missed it!

'You knew what you were looking for,' I murmured under my breath. 'They had no idea there was anything underground to find.'

It was strange, the sudden juxtaposition of my feelings. I knew Feisal Ismail to be somehow trapped down there under sixty odd metres of water, and with his air supply running out. Even so, I thrilled to the knowledge that they'd hit the jackpot and discovered the stairway that apparently led to the subterranean chamber. Still, I wanted Adam out of the lake. I wasn't quite sure which of these accounted for my suddenly weak and wobbly knees.

I knew only that all of these conflicting feelings surged through me while Mehmet struggled into his wetsuit below us on the landing platform. Ahmed too, I noticed, had stripped off his galabeya and was attempting to force his big frame into another way-too-small wetsuit. Director Ismail had thought to have a number sent.

'Ahmed! You can't...!" I shouted. 'You're not trained, and you're not a strong enough swimmer!' He'd only learnt to swim a few years ago, for heaven's sake! And he certainly didn't have the scuba diving credentials the others had boasted.

'But I am strong physically!' he shouted back. 'And the Director, he is trapped!'

'OhmyGod,' I wailed. 'Habiba, stop him!'

I watched indecision raging on her beautiful face. 'Ahmed is a brave man,' she said quietly at last. 'It's why I have agreed to be his wife.'

I stared at her in open disbelief. 'You might very well be a widow before you're a wife,' I pointed out harshly, uncaring of how this might sound. 'There's bravery, and there's downright stupidity. If Ahmed gets into trouble under the water, he'll get in the way of Adam and Mehmet rescuing Feisal. See sense, Habiba! Please! Besides, we might still need him up here with his gun. Everyone else may have forgotten about crocodiles. But I most certainly have not!'

If what I'd said before hadn't got through to her, the mention of crocodiles did the trick. She, after all, had been the one spattered with Philip Sinnerman's blood.

'Ahmed! No!' she cried out. 'You'll slow them down! We need you up here with your gun!'

'Mehmet! Quickly!' Adam shouted from the lake. 'We're running out of time!'

''What happened?' I called out to him, cupping my hands around my mouth to make my voice travel.

'Feisal started to investigate the descending stairway while I took photos with Mehmet's camera,' he yelled back. 'His foot got caught between two chunks of rock. He couldn't pull it free. Neither could I. We couldn't even get his flipper off! We've got to get back down there to him! He's running out of air! We knew, even with twin tanks, at that depth we couldn't last much more than an hour!'

'Adam! For God's sake, come and get another tank for yourself!' I cried.

Thankfully, he saw the sense in this. So, rather than Ahmed don a wetsuit of his own, he helped Adam replace his air supply as my husband swam up to the landing platform.

Moments later Mehmet was ready. He joined Adam in the water, and they both bent their bodies to make the dive underwater. I watched them go in a twin surge of bubbles, praying it wasn't too late.

I tried not to imagine what it must be like for Feisal Ismail, with his foot trapped in the ancient stonework of the original temple floor, beneath sixty-odd feet of the waters of Lake Nasser. The Director may have dedicated his life to the pursuit of Egyptology. But this was no way to die. I remembered my heebie-jeebies about the trail of destruction the Great Train Robbery money seemed to have left in its wake. I could only hope Ramses hadn't laid a curse on anyone who dared enter his hidden subterranean chamber. The remembrance of Abdullah Soliman's murder so soon after getting back home to Luxor did little to quell my spiralling fears.

It was another long and anxious wait up on deck. This time, I didn't dare lift my eyes from the rippling surface. Ramses might well be watching. This time, I refused to give way to such fanciful imaginings as curses and deadly spells. It was an accident of the natural world that had trapped the Director's – Feisal's – foot, flipper and all, in the ancient stonework. Or so I kept telling myself.

Another forty-five minutes dragged by. And still I didn't lift my eyes from the water, notwithstanding the eyesight-ruining glare of the sun on the lake. Ahmed had re-joined Habiba and me on the sundeck. He held his gun unslung and pointed at the water the whole time. A crocodile attack now would be catastrophic.

Despite all my earlier protestations to the contrary, I now wished I too had taken a course in scuba diving so I could join the men underwater. Of course I wanted to be part of the rescue mission to save Feisal Ismail. But, even allowing for crocodiles, I'll admit, too, to a sneaking desire to clap eyes on that staircase. It was impossible not to think of Howard Carter and his discovery of the fabled sixteen stone steps leading down to the undiscovered tomb of Tutankhamun.

And, of course, that's how my adventures in Egypt had started. Following the trail of clues Carter laid and uncovering secrets: both his and those of ancient Egypt. Impossible not to dare to imagine what this new staircase might lead to.

I counted my own heartbeats while Adam and Mehmet were under water. For Egypt to have offered up her secrets to me only to snatch away those I held most dear now seemed an unfair price to pay. I couldn't believe it had come to this. That Adam – my soulmate and the love of my life, – Mehmet – that unassuming and friendly photographer, – and Director Feisal Ismail – feared but respected head honcho at the Ministry of State for Antiquities – might not emerge from the depths of Lake Nasser alive, meant none of the rest of it was worth toffee.

So I had to place my faith in Egypt loving me as much as I loved her.

I dared believe this dream might be coming true when I saw three jets of bubbles surging up from the depths.

But there was one thing – or person – I should say, I'd failed to account for.

'Hey!' a male voice called from the bank, within what was supposed to be the cordoned-off area.

I turned in dismay to behold none other than Max Savage standing at the lakeside. This sight alone may not have perturbed me. The fact he was holding a gun did. Very much.

Chapter 18

All my worst fears about Max Savage and his dubious motivation crowded in on me at once. Even as it occurred to me Georgina had been successful in her bid not to have him released until she was well on her way to Cairo, my heart sank at seeing him standing there. My misgivings came especially to the fore when I saw the gun.

All the more so when I saw one of our brave scuba divers – impossible to tell which one – break the surface holding aloft a bright, glistening object. The sunlight glinting off it spoke volumes. It was solid gold.

I'd wanted to believe Max was genuine in his declaration about making another go of things with Georgina. They were a strange pairing, for sure. But they'd certainly seemed to set sparks flying off each other. I could well imagine their relationship might be a love-hate one, but it would certainly never be dull.

Now I realised his arrival, at what looked to be the critical moment of discovery, could only mean one thing. If he couldn't lay any sort of claim to the Great Train Robbery money, or, perhaps, to Georgina, it struck me he must have decided to hang around to see what we were up to, and now wanted to muscle in on our find. In shock, all I could do was stare at him.

With horror, I saw him aim his gun at the water. With a loaded firearm pointed at them, our brave men would have little choice but to hand over whatever that intriguing golden object was.

At the precise moment Max Savage raised his weapon, so did Ahmed. At first I thought it was at Georgina's ex-husband, as Max's shout had called all our attention to him. My God! He's going to shoot him! I thought.

The deafening twin explosions of two guns being fired simultaneously, and at very close range to one another, sent fireworks exploding inside my head, and had me leaping out of my skin in fright. My feet lifted off the deck as if they had rocket launchers attached to their soles.

Unbelievably, Max was still standing. And then I saw he wasn't the only man at the shore with a gun in his hand. One of the Abu Simbel guards came running. He, too, had his gun pointing at the water.

Even as I screamed out a warning, the guard fired a third shot into the water.

I couldn't believe they could shoot our three men in cold blood, exposed and defenceless in the lake.

And then I saw the great surge in the water as something reared up alongside the dahabeeyah. It drenched me, as if a bucketful of water had been hurled at the open deck.

'Crocodiles!' Habiba yelled. 'Four of them!'

Snapping back to the water, my gaze fell on this gut-wrenching sight. I couldn't believe how quickly they'd come, and from nowhere. The first had been hit, by whose bullet I had no idea. It threshed about in the water in its death throes, its huge tail flailing, and tossing its gigantic head from side to side. Spray splashed in all directions.

The jet of water that soaked my clothes seemed to freeze on my body.

'Get out of the water!' I screamed. I couldn't believe that in the single heartbeat I'd spotted Max, these grisly creatures had converged on the spot, seemingly from nowhere.

Habiba clutched at my arm, even as Ahmed aimed and fired again. 'If Feisal was injured and trailing blood, it will have drawn them,' she stated in strangled tones what I now saw was the blindingly obvious.

I couldn't breathe. I could see all three men – thank God – swimming towards the landing platform at the rear of the dahabeeyah.

A second crocodile was hit. I saw it rear up and crash back into the water, sinking beneath the waves. A direct hit this time, square between its eyes. The first stopped threshing and also drifted underwater, leaving just two beasts circling the swimmers. But I dreaded to see more, drawn now by the scent of the blood of their own kind, not just of one injured man.

As I watched in an agony of dread, Khaled let off a rocket flare. It screamed up into the sky, exploding with a loud crack. The crocodiles zigzagged away, moving with a sickening sinewy speed, but soon circled back.

'*Move!* ' I screamed again.

The explosion of gunfire didn't let up. Two guards now stood with Max Savage on the shoreline, raining bullets into the water. But it was a risky business, needing a precision aim and steady-handed fire. The swimmers and the crocodiles were moving targets. Their scuba kit hampered our men. And the crocodiles weren't giving up.

I stood, frozen in horror – rooted to the spot, unable to tear my eyes away – knowing I'd have no choice but to watch if the awful moment came that one of the crocodiles launched its attack.

Even as I watched, one of the beasts surged forward. My knees buckled as I saw its jaws open. One of the swimmers was just slightly behind the other two. He was an easy target. I wanted to close my eyes. But it was impossible not to watch. My heart seemed to jump from my chest to my throat. It thumped there painfully, almost choking me. But I couldn't swallow, could hardly breathe. Desperate prayers to Sobek tumbled through my mind. We'd all witnessed the vicious attack on Philip Sinnerman, all seen its grisly outcome. To be re-living it was terrifying. That was one of our men down there. My God! It could be Adam!

I scarcely heard the bullet-fire now. I thought my lungs would explode with the breath I was holding. The crocodile snapped its mighty jaws and connected with the diver. I screamed.

The gas canister exploded, hurling the deadly crocodile up into the air, and flinging the diver forward in the water. I felt the thud as he smashed into the side of the dahabeeyah. The crocodile crashed back into the water with its head hanging off. It was a gruesome sight for sure. I could hardly bear to watch but was equally powerless to look away as it drifted in a spreading pool of dark blood. The once blue and sparking lake was awash with crimson and patterned with chunks of flesh. Just one crocodile remained now, circling our men. It seemed more maddened by blood lust than frightened of the onslaught of bullets.

Khaled shouted from below. He'd run from the engine room to the landing platform ready to help haul the swimmers on board. I could well imagine the explosion of that gas canister and being flung against the hulk of the *Queen Ahmes* had knocked the diver out cold.

Ahmed didn't dare move from the spot. I had no idea how much ammunition his gun could hold, but he was still taking careful aim and firing with steady precision. It wasn't easy, given how quickly the crocodiles were capable of moving in the water. I stood, tense, rigid and terrified, the breath rasping in my throat as my lungs forced it up through my strangled windpipe. But I knew I had to get down to the landing platform and help Khaled haul our swimmers in.

I moved away from the handrail on jerking limbs that didn't seem connected to my body. How I managed to descend the spiral staircase, don't ask me.

Rabiah's terrified gaze met mine as I tore through the kitchen. She was standing at the window. The glass was smeared with blood.

Somehow I made it out onto the landing platform.

Khaled was already hauling the unconscious man onboard. Ripping off his facemask, this turned out to be Mehmet. Between us, Rabiah, who'd followed me, and I, dragged him through the door into the kitchen so there was room outside to help Adam and Feisal out of the water. I knew she could be relied upon to give him whatever medical attention she could. He was still breathing, and didn't appear to have any physical injuries that I could see. The gas canister exploding into the mouth of the crocodile had clearly done damage to the animal, but it seemed the wetsuit and his propulsion forward might have protected the photographer. Unbelievably, one hand still gripped a golden object. The twin of the Helen of Troy statuette, I saw at a single dazed glance.

Curiously numb now, I turned back to the landing platform. 'Adam?' I yelled out. I could hear splashing, but couldn't see the divers or the crocodile from this angle.

'Here!' he shouted. I almost fainted with relief on the spot at the sound of his voice. With my breath stuck in my throat, I watched him swim around the side of the dahabeeyah. He had one arm under Feisal's shoulders, steering him towards the platform.

The gunmen on the shore were beyond range now. There was no way they could get a clear line of sight with the dahabeeyah anchored with its landing platform pointing towards the stretching waters of Lake Nasser.

I sensed Ahmed moving on deck above us, keeping his sights trained on the swimmers and the ever-circling crocodile. I couldn't see the beast. But just knowing it was there was terrifying. It had the advantage. The water was its natural domain. It could dive and surge upwards again from underwater, using its huge tail to propel it forward.

Khaled reached forward with strong arms and took hold of Feisal's reaching arms. Feisal was conscious, but white-lipped, his face creased with pain beneath the mask. Or, perhaps it was fear.

I stood back to allow as much space as possible for Khaled to haul him from the bloodied water. Adam pushed him from behind, and the Director sprawled forward onto the platform. He was safe.

But I saw movement in the water. Beyond my husband, the water was broken by a triangular wake with a long scaly snout at its tip.

'Adam! Get out of there!' I screamed.

He put both elbows up on the platform in readiness to pull himself up. I heard Ahmed's gun go off above us. Saw the bullet hit the water just behind Adam's left shoulder. But it missed the crocodile.

As I watched in swamping terror, Adam was jerked physically backwards and lost his grip on the platform.

I screamed. Khaled flung out one arm, and caught Adam's flailing hand, gripping it tight.

I moved then without thinking. Spinning backwards to the kitchen, grabbing a long carving knife from the butcher's block, I was back almost before I'd gone.

Everything slowed down to super-slow-motion. All the noise of everyone shouting faded to a low buzz. I could see the strain on Khaled's face as he exerted all his effort to keeping hold of Adam's hand.

The crocodile didn't seem to have got a proper hold of Adam. It circled away again, in a tight arc, coming back to get a better grip. As it reared up from the water, jaws open, ready to strike, I lunged forward with the knife.

The blade embedded itself into one of the crocodile's eyes. I felt it squelch as the sharp edge plunged into the soft cartilage.

The beast let out a dreadful sort of bellow and jerked its mighty head away, nearly pulling me into the water with it. I let the knife slip from my nerveless grasp.

Dropping to my knees on the wet platform, awash with stinking bloodied water, I joined Khaled in desperately reaching forward for Adam. I grabbed his other hand, yanking him forward with every ounce of strength I possessed. Adam slammed into the side of the dahabeeyah and we hauled him upwards.

The crocodile, frenziedly thrashing in an agony of pain, with the knife sticking up out of its eye, reared up behind him, ready to make one last attempt – or perhaps to land on the platform and knock all three of us into the water.

I watched its long razor-toothed snout explode. Blood and torn flesh rained all over us. Ahmed had scored a direct hit on top of its head.

As the dying crocodile crashed back into the water, sending a sheet of bloodied spray in all directions, we yanked Adam fully onto the platform and safety.

'Are you hurt?' I yelled, as he lay sprawled there on his stomach with the air cylinders on his back. 'Did the crocodile bite you?'

He reached up to tug off his facemask, and pushed himself slowly up onto his knees, turning over so he could sit and examine his lower leg. My gaze followed the direction of his stare and I saw the shredded neoprene of his wetsuit.

'These bodysuits do more than just keep the water out!' he said. And then, uncaring of the blood and guts we were covered in, he pulled me towards him and held me tight. 'Bloody Hell, Merry! That was a close call! I think you just saved my life!'

'Ahmed shot the crocodile,' I managed. And then, just as I had once before when Adam miraculously survived a close encounter with a crocodile, I pulled away, leaned over the side and was comprehensively sick.

* * *

Quite a crowd of onlookers had gathered at the shore. The cordon wasn't much of a barrier when people could hear gunfire, shouting, and see rocket flares being set off. They'd crowded onto the foreshore, irrespective of the barrier, to gape at the scene, iPhones, camcorders and cameras held up to record the spectacle.

So, twice, in nearly as many days, Abu Simbel became the scene of a major incident. Although thankfully, this time, not resulting in anyone's death. The four crocodiles were casualties enough. Truthfully, I was sickened by their slaughter, even allowing for one of them being the beast that attacked and mortally wounded Philip Sinnerman. They were God's creatures after all, acting on a natural killer instinct. And I don't condone animal cruelty. But, when it boiled right down to it, it was a simple choice: their lives or ours. So I could be regretful, but not truly sorry.

Feisal Ismail did the only thing he could do in the circumstances. He called a Press Conference.

'Yes, I can confirm we have discovered a hidden subterranean chamber,' he announced sensationally, as television cameras rolled and journalists held out microphones. The assemblage of film crews and reporters had gathered with lightning speed. They crowded around the Ministry Director in the hastily prepared – and, again, cordoned-off – area on the forecourt in front of Ramses' Great Temple. As ever, the three stone statues still in possession of their upper bodies stared on, mute and impassive as history unfolded at their feet.

The Director was speaking in English to ensure his words could be understood by all. 'The contents of this chamber do seem to suggest a link between Ramses II and the fabled Queen of Homer's great epics: Helen of Troy,' he went on thrillingly. The statuette, the twin of the one safely locked away on board the dahabeeyah, shone brightly in the sunshine, drawing all eyes to the little plinth on which it stood, with an armed Abu Simbel guard at its side. 'But we will need to undertake significant further investigation before we can say with any confidence what that link might be.'

Director Ismail, once more impeccably clad in a crisp grey suit, with a pressed shirt and tie, sat with one foot propped up on a stool. It was bandaged, and plastered, encasing his broken ankle and covering the badly scraped skin of his lower leg.

This injury had prevented us doing anything more than carting him off in an ambulance to hospital in the immediate aftermath of the crocodile attack. Mehmet, too, had been thoroughly checked over, and pronounced to have had a miraculous escape. It wasn't hard to imagine how much worse the injuries of an exploding gas canister might have been. Indeed, I had no need to imagine. I'd seen with my own eyes what it had done to the crocodile that dared clamp its jaws around it! Adam had been treated for shock. But of the three of them, he appeared to have come off most lightly. I didn't fail to see the tell-tale white lines around his mouth though. Adam was traumatised, as was I. If I'd thought crocodiles might haunt my nightmares after witnessing the attack on Philip Sinnerman, I was damn sure they would now, having been up close and personal with one as it latched on to my husband! Although my memory now of using the knife on it was a blur, with no detail attached. This might prove to be a blessing, I realised – especially if I ever wanted a good night's sleep again.

'It is also true that a stash of money was found hidden in the modern dome encasing the temple a couple of nights ago,' Director Ismail confirmed crisply. 'This is unrelated to what we have discovered today. As your colleagues in Cairo may well have told you by now, this appears to have been hidden here during the re-siting of the temple in the mid 1960s. I gather it was loot taken during a train robbery, which took place in Britain at that time. I am sure the whole story will come out in due course. It is coincidence that these two discoveries have been made within a couple of days of each other.'

'Ramses had plenty of riches to reveal, after all,' I whispered to Adam.

'And, yes, tragically, a man did die here a couple of days ago, on the same day the hidden box of cash was found,' the

Director responded calmly to this next question from the battery being fired at him. 'But, no, he was not murdered, as speculation has suggested. A full police investigation has been carried out. I was on the scene to ensure its probity. In a freak accident, the man fell into Lake Nasser and a crocodile attacked him. I am not able to comment on why the man was here at Abu Simbel. His family have been informed, and any further conjecture is beyond my remit.'

I looked at my feet. I was sorry for Philip's death; well, certainly for the manner of it. But it was impossible not to be thankful for it in a sense, when the alternative, had he lived, might have been so much worse – for us clearly; perhaps not so for him.

The questions turned to the crocodile problem around Abu Simbel, and whether tourists were safe from attack. The Director fielded these as patiently as he could, reminding the assembled Media that the twin temples were on dry land, several metres away from the water, and giving assurances that full checks would be made of the surrounding area to assess the risk. Swift action would be taken, he promised, if there was any possibility of crocodiles getting anywhere close to the vicinity.

'No more questions for now,' Director Ismail said with an authoritative air of finality. 'As we learn more, I will, of course, keep you apprised of developments. Er – yes,' he said as a female journalist fired one further question at him. 'Our underwater discovery is exciting. And – er – no – I do not believe we have a tomb of any sort on our hands. This is NOT Tutankhamun all over again.'

* * *

'Not Tutankhamun,' I said later as we congregated in the lounge bar for our first proper opportunity to discuss what we'd actually found beneath the waves of Lake Nasser. 'Maybe not, because, in truth almost nobody had even *heard* of Tutankhamun before Howard Carter made his fateful discovery. In contrast, surely almost everybody in the civilised world has heard of Helen of Troy! This is going to send a buzz across the planet to rival anything ever found in Egypt to date!'

Max Savage had joined us, but not for long. 'I've come to bid my farewells,' he'd said. 'I'm booked on the early evening flight from Abu Simbel to Cairo. I'll be squeezed in alongside a lot of the Press contingent. So I should get to hear what they're making of the stories.'

'Is Georgina meeting you off the flight?' I asked brazenly.

'I'm daring to hope,' he smiled wolfishly. 'She's had her precious scoop. I gather she's been queening it over her own Press Conferences for the last twenty-four hours. Now she's got her name all over it, I daresay she thinks she can throw me a peanut or two. But I'm not under any illusions about a nice romantic tryst in Cairo. Georgina will want to get back to the UK. That's where the best story is to be had about The

Great Train Robbery. The Press coverage will be...' He'd broken off and paused, searching for the right word.

'Epic,' I said. 'It will be epic.' It was a favourite word of Georgina's. And I couldn't help but think it was exactly what she was longing for: the scoop of her lifetime. Well, I wished her well with it – and them their chance at finding love again.

Max had already explained his part in shooting at the crocodiles to save our scuba divers from attack. On his release from custody, he'd come to say goodbye, and perhaps to ask after Georgina. Seeing the dahabeeyah had broken her original moorings, he'd gone to enquire of the guards what had happened. At that point, he was still fearful we might be under serious police investigation. He well knew the Police Inspector and British Ambassador had paid us a visit. The guard had indicated the cordon, but Max, being, well – Max, I suppose – had ignored it and marched across to the shore, with the guard in pursuit, to call across to us and find out what was going on.

His call of 'hey' coincided with Adam, Feisal and Mehmet breaking the surface of the waves. At the precise moment I'd spied him and given way to my suspicions, he'd spotted the crocodiles. He'd grabbed the gun from the dithering guard – I hadn't even noticed the guard, so focused had I been on Max, his sudden appearance, and my own dark forebodings – and fired into the water. So, yet again, he'd proved himself unpredictable and not the villain I'd first assumed him to be.

Whether he was the right man for Georgina a second time around was a matter for her own judgement. It was none of my business, I decided.

He declared himself 'intrigued' by our discovery, but regretfully lacking the time ahead of his flight to stay and find out more. So we'd waved him off, somewhat less regretful than he was, I'll admit.

Rabiah served brandy all round, and then unobtrusively took her seat alongside her husband Khaled on the two-seater divan in the corner. After their involvement in getting the men out of the water earlier, there was no way we'd refuse to allow them to join in the conversation. They'd proved themselves our loyal and trust-worthy comrades once again. I noticed Rabiah even poured a tiny thimbleful of brandy herself after passing a full measure to her half-Scottish husband. Even Ahmed, Habiba and Mehmet were partaking. After an encounter like the one we'd shared this afternoon, the ruinous effects of alcohol and strict religious adherence seemed less imperative than its calming and bonding properties.

Feisal sipped from his glass and glanced at us each in turn with a magnetic gaze. 'Helen of Troy, or, to give her her proper name – Helen of Sparta – was distant cousin to Ramses the Great, and never set foot inside Troy. Of that much, I am now certain.'

'You descended the underwater staircase?' Ahmed asked, leaning forward, dark eyes dancing with excitement.

'We did,' Feisal said thrillingly. 'Once these boys set me free and rigged up my new air supply, we just had to explore!'

'But your broken ankle...' I protested.

He met my gaze across the room. 'It's amazing, my dear, how Egyptological fervour can overcome physical discomfort.'

In fairness, there have been occasions I've had cause to note this for myself. So I subsided, giving a small understanding nod.

'A very dangerous decision as it turned out,' Habiba addressed her boss sternly. 'The blood from your scraped legs attracted the crocodiles.'

'Yes, of course I realise that now,' he admitted. 'At the time, we allowed excitement to drive every other – sensible – thought from our heads.'

'Men!' I said. But I said it mildly, and with more affection than disdain.

'So, you descended the underwater staircase,' Ahmed said again, bringing us back to the point. 'And finded – what...?'

'It's a single room chamber, buried deep underground, as far as we could work out,' Adam supplied. 'Of course, it's filled with water.'

Mehmet leapt up, went a bit dizzy, and abruptly sat down again. I took it this was from the after effects of being catapulted against the hulk of the dahabeeyah rather than the unaccustomed alcohol hitting his bloodstream. 'The wall reliefs are still there!' he exclaimed, steadying himself. 'I was able to take a number of images in the short time we had.'

'Short to you, maybe,' I muttered. 'To me, it seemed the three of you were down there an age.'

Ahmed tut-tutted to convey that I was at risk of dragging us away from the point again. 'You have these pictures?' he demanded.

'Well, I haven't had time to upload them to my computer. Everything's in my cabin, where Rabiah put it when we were all carted off to hospital.' He sent Rabiah a grateful look, and she dimpled shyly at him.

'I will fetch them,' Ahmed said, getting up. 'Your laptop, it will work equally well?'

Mehmet eased himself back to his feet and went with him. Between them, they wheeled his computer, on its portable stand, through the still-splintered door of his cabin and back into the lounge bar. We crowded around while he fiddled with the SD card taken from his specialist underwater camera.

Before long, we were all staring entranced at the photographs appearing on the screen. But it wasn't the wall reliefs that caught my attention first.

'My God! Is that *gold*?' I rasped, as the breath caught in my windpipe and I nearly choked.

'It's gold alright,' Adam nodded, staring intently at the images. 'The place is positively stuffed to the gunnels with it! When Abdullah spoke of gold and riches, he wasn't fooling around. Perhaps the Helen statuette was all he could carry away with him. He had the granite tablets to transport, after all.'

I gaped at the pictures. Golden statues there seemed to be aplenty. And golden bars, golden images of various gods and goddesses, among golden objects too numerous to name, piled high, and stacked against the walls. 'Well, it may not be Tutankhamun's tomb, but there can be no doubting that lot's priceless! Heavens! When Georgina said there was a stash of treasure buried at Abu Simbel, she had no idea how close to the mark she was! The Great Train Robbery money pales into insignificance alongside *this*!'

'But what's it doing there?' Habiba asked, a dazzled expression on her face. 'Why did Ramses amass a treasure trove like this here at Abu Simbel? I'd always thought his Treasury was at the new capital city he built in the Delta, Pi-Ramesse! Sir, do you have any theories?' she respectfully addressed the Director.

Feisal sat up straight, adjusted his plastered foot on the footstall, and looked around at us with dark, gleaming eyes. 'I have more than a theory,' he said. 'I believe I know the answer. The clue is in the wall reliefs.'

I lifted my gaze from the gold to study the reliefs, somewhat blurry though they were in Mehmet's underwater images. He'd been right: they were in a quite remarkable state of preservation, given the immense passage of time and more than fifty years spent submerged under the floodwaters of Lake Nasser.

When the Director didn't immediately go on, I dragged my gaze from the computer screen to his face. It seemed he was waiting to speak until he had our full attention.

'The gold is tribute to the Pharaoh,' he said baldly.

'Tribute?' I repeated stupidly. Not grasping his meaning, I rushed on, 'But, like Habiba said, why would Ramses store tribute from Egypt's vassal states all the way down here in Nubia – and in secret...? Surely he'd have kept it in the Treasury...?'

'Who said anything about Egypt's vassal states?' Feisal enquired mildly.

I stared at him, uncomprehending. 'But... if not Egypt's vassal states, then who...?'

He smiled at me. 'I think it's safe to say Mycenae was never considered a vassal territory of Egypt's.'

'Greece?' I gasped. 'This gold is tribute to Ramses from ancient *Greece*?'

'Precisely, my dear,' he nodded, smiling at my stunned expression. 'You see this column of hieroglyphics here...?' he pointed one long finger at the screen. As I nodded dumbly, he went on, 'It identifies ancient Greece... Mycenae... Sparta, to be exact.'

My eyes nearly tumbled out of my head. 'Then, that means...?'

'Yes!' he exclaimed in triumph. 'The Greeks knew Helen was here in Egypt throughout the duration of the Trojan War. In fact, they paid Ramses to have her! It is my belief we'll find, once a full transcription of the wall reliefs has been made and translated, that Helen colluded in the Greek plan to lay siege to the city of Troy and seek to claim it for themselves!'

I gaped openly at him, and sensed the others reacting similarly around me.

Feisal Ismail smiled, a man content in his newfound knowledge if ever I saw one. 'She may well be the face that launched a thousand ships. But I think this proves she was neither a victim, stolen away by Paris against her will, nor his star-crossed lover. Even less was she a puppet of the Greek gods on Mount Olympus. It is my contention that Helen set sail knowingly, willingly complicit in a plot by the Spartans to wage war on Troy!'

I opened my mouth once or twice, but found it impossible to find my voice. So, after a pause, Feisal Ismail went on, warming to his theme.

'Helen knew Ramses would support her as she could claim distant kinship to him. And Greece ensured his cooperation by paying him handsomely for having her to stay.'

Still, we stared at him, taking it in. So he pressed home his ultimate deduction.

'To my reading of it, Helen was the one to seduce Paris,' he said. 'How could he resist her? She was the most beautiful woman in the world, after all! As the catalyst for the

Trojan War, she gave the Greeks the excuse they needed to send their fleet, apparently giving chase, to Troy.'

'I always said Troy itself was the prize,' Adam murmured, looking a bit spellbound, but finding his voice before any of the rest of us.

'Perhaps she didn't know she was hurtling her way into myth and legend, a poet's muse,' Feisal said with a lift of one eyebrow. 'I daresay Homer's version of the story is more thrilling than the truth: that she sat out the entire ten-year duration of the Trojan War here in Egypt as the guest of her cousin, the Pharaoh. It's what I always dared to believe. And now I know it to be true. Merry…? Adam…? I'll admit I have had cause to question it in the past, but I am so very glad for your unerring talent at sniffing out the truth behind ancient Egyptian mysteries!'

'Er – hum!' Ahmed coughed loudly. 'Excuse me, but it was I who finded the statuette! Please, sir, be so kind as to reserve your gratitude for me!'

Epilogue

The invitation to the wedding celebrating the re-marriage of Georgina and Max Savage arrived a month or so later. So, Adam and I were headed back to England.

This was probably just as well. If I didn't enjoy the Media circus over the discovery of Nefertari's granite tablets last year, then this one over the sojourn of Helen of Troy – or Helen of Sparta, as I supposed we must all now get used to calling her – in Egypt, I liked even less.

Nefertari's is a name known to those with a love of Egyptian history. But most of the general public confuse her with her more famous forebear, Nefertiti. Helen suffers no such identity crisis. The mythology surrounding her as the most beautiful woman in the world ensured attention-grabbing headlines everywhere after Feisal Ismail called that first Press Conference. The first of many, as it turned out.

As I may have mentioned before, I love my adventures in Egypt. But I'd rather have them in private. Feisal – another name I was still getting used to using in place of the more formal manner of address I was more familiar with and, in all honesty, preferred – did his best to shield us from the Press scrum. But it proved sadly impossible to stay wholly on the periphery of things.

Once Feisal's team arrived in Abu Simbel and lowered their big industrial nets into the water, the excavation of the underwater chamber could get underway properly. The nets kept the crocodiles at a safe distance and, slowly but surely, specialist archaeological divers brought the Greek gold – Greek *tribute*, or blood money, as it was in fact – to the surface. And the whole story came out to thrill the world.

If Georgina's hastily scrawled note, included alongside the wedding invitation, was anything to go by, the headlines in Britain, re-hashing the story of The Great Train Robbery, were also making waves – enough even to knock Brexit off the front pages! Nearing the end of March, and still the UK government was struggling to agree the terms of its exit from the European Union! I could only guess at the delight with which the newspaper-reading public devoured the story of the daring heist, embellished now with the knowledge that so much of the money that had been hidden and believed lost forever had now been found – and where!

There was one good thing that could be said about all the astonishing News coming out of Egypt right now: that tourists were starting to flood back.

'You know, I might have to have a rather difficult conversation with Rashid when we get back to the UK,' Adam said, straightening up after booking our flights. Rashid Soliman was Senior Egyptologist, and Adam's boss at the British Museum. He'd gallantly granted Adam a year-long sabbatical to undertake our mission retracing Giovanni Belzoni's travels through Egypt and ancient Nubia. But even he couldn't possibly have foreseen what discoveries Sarah

Belzoni's journal – treasured and passed down through generations of the Soliman family – would lead us to.

'Oh?' I raised an eyebrow.

'Well, you know; it strikes me we could get our fledgling business up and running again. Feisal has got our measure now. He knows we're on the level. Zahed Mansour and Saleh have got their hands full up in Cairo making hay while the sun shines ...' (I'm pleased to report Saleh kept his job, perhaps realising he didn't need to fall on his sword after all.) '...We've said about all there is to say about Giovanni Belzoni ...'

'Hardly!' I interrupted. 'I haven't even got started on his mission into the desert in search of the ruined city of Berenice on the Red Sea!'

Adam raised one eloquent eyebrow. 'Forgive me, but, set against his other towering achievements, I hardly think your readers will thrill at his search for a lost city most people have never heard of, and of which next to nothing survives!'

I grunted, reluctantly having to accept the truth in this. Belzoni had scaled and penetrated pyramids, discovered Pharaonic tombs, and famously excavated The Great Temple of Ramses from the millennia-worth of sand blocking the entrance. I'd written blogs and articles on them all. Adam was right. Alongside them, everything else paled into insignificance. So it seemed our mission retracing his steps was really at an end.

So, the choice was a simple one, and also stark. Either we could return to England, Adam to the British Museum and me to, well, to who knows what...? Or we could pick up the threads of the old life we'd been building ourselves here in Egypt, return to Luxor and offer tailored Nile cruises aboard the *Queen Ahmes* to discerning travellers wanting to explore this antique land in the lap of luxury, sailing a genuine and beautifully restored Victorian dahabeeyah. I even dared hope our newfound – and unlooked-for – fame might prove to be a further inducement, giving us an edge over the competition.

There was also the small but not insignificant matter of the wedding of Ahmed Abd el-Rassul to Habiba Garai coming up in the not too distant future. It seemed to me this gave us another very good reason not to be away from Egypt for too long.

In the meantime, though, Ahmed and Habiba would also make the trip to England for the wedding of Max and Georgina Savage. I was pleased Georgina had seen fit to include Ahmed in the invitations to her nuptials. He had saved her life, after all, when Philip Sinnerman hurled the hunk of stone from the roof of the Temple of Isis at Philae. I hoped Georgina might also see fit to providing an excellent wedding gift to Ahmed when his own happy day arrived. It seemed to me, it was the very least she could do.

Although, I have to say that Ahmed, despite the injuries he had once more sustained in the line of duty, was having the time of his life right now: letting anyone and everyone know that it was he who had "finded" the original statue of Helen of Troy! His name would now enter the annals of history alongside those of his notorious ancestors – although, thankfully, with some licence around how long he'd kept hold of the golden statuette before coming clean to the Director.

So, all things considered, I was looking forward to our return to Egypt after the wedding with some considerable anticipation.

But it was Feisal Ismail who had the last word on the subject. 'You know, once all the dust has settled, and we've had a little while to assess the fallout from all the discoveries here in Egypt during this last year, I wonder if we might have a little discussion about when you think the time might be right to announce our secret tomb to the world...?'

The End

Author's Note

I took a decision, writing this book, that some of Merry and Adam's discoveries needed to be brought into the open. Their adventures in Egypt span five years now, from 2012-17. If you've followed the series, you'll know they've turned up more artefacts, treasures and knowledge from Egypt's ancient past than you can shake a stick at. To keep every one of these their closely guarded secret was starting to stretch credulity, and my writing ability, beyond all limits.

I always receive it as a great compliment when any of my reviewers describe my books as believable, considering how far-fetched they are.

You'll know, I'm sure, that there's not a shred of evidence to suggest Ramses II was in any way descended – legitimately or otherwise – from the mighty pharaohs of the once-glorious 18th Dynasty of the New Kingdom, or indeed from the Hebrews. This is a fiction of my own making. Having started out on the conjecture I have run with it. Although I have to say I find some of the possibilities explored in this book intriguing.

His Great Royal Wife Nefertari is, possibly, a different matter. This is thanks to Ernest Schiaparelli's discovery in her tomb of a knob bearing the cartouche of Pharaoh Ay. Ay succeeded Tutankhamun to the throne, and is posited by many to have been the Amarnan Queen Nefertiti's father.

Others better qualified than me have explored possible links between the Amarnan royal family, most notably Queen Tiye and her son Akhenaten, and the Exodus story. Most noteworthy among them is Ahmed Osman, whose theories I have enjoyed reading immensely.

As for Helen of Troy, I consider it perfectly possible that her ancient Greek civilisation was contemporaneous with the late Bronze Age of Ramses the Great. Sheldon Lebold in his book *The Legacy of Moses and Akhenaten: A Jewish Perspective* posited that the Spartans might have been a breakaway group descended from the Hebrew Exodus. That was simply too tantalising a conjecture for me not to wish to explore it.

But ultimately I am writing fiction. One of the challenges I didn't realise I was creating for myself when I started out on my Egyptian mystery adventure series was setting the stories in the present day. I have tried to stick closely to the real life contemporary events that have unfolded in Egypt and around the world since 2012. These have provided a backdrop for my stories and sometimes forced the action; in particular when I felt I had no choice but to bring Merry and Adam home to England following the toppling of the Morsi administration. But I'm sure my readers will understand I'm treading a fine line between fact and fiction, occasionally blurring the two. The search for hidden chambers behind Tutankhamun's tomb, and the 'ScanPyramid' project at Giza are examples of genuine media coverage over the last couple of years. But of course there were no world headlines in 2016-17 about the origins of Ramses the Great or revelations about the Exodus. Nor indeed about a hidden subterranean chamber beneath Lake Nasser at Abu Simbel.

The story Georgina tells in chapter 4 about The Great Train Robbery is absolutely true up to and including Michael Black's death from natural causes within 6 months of stealing a half share of John Daly's haul. It was at that point I allowed my imagination to take over. It was just too tempting to be able to link the two great 1960s stories: The Great Train Robbery, and the rescue of Abu Simbel, which started the following year. When I saw the headlines about the death of Christine Keeler, it threw another tantalising idea into the mix, and I let my imagination run with it.

So, what of Helen of Troy and her chances of being more flesh-and-blood than myth-and-legend? Well, we know she was a literary figure in Homer's epic, and she certainly crops up in purportedly historical works from the ancient world, just as Feisal Ismail describes in the book. But no physical proof of Helen as a late Bronze Age princess exists. Even so, she has come to embody and represent the Classical Age of Heroes.

But, like a flame burning brightly before it gutters, Helen and her golden age were about to be extinguished. Shortly after the period about which Homer was writing, earthquakes and fires devastated Mycenae and Troy, and the cities were abandoned. The dark ages had come to the Greek empire.

Helen now enters mythology as a goddess-like creature. If indeed she ever lived, it is now that she moves from real woman to sublime beauty. As the fatal seductress at the heart of Homer's epic, she will always be remembered as a brilliant and beautiful queen in a brutal age. Ah, the stuff of legend, and a fiction-writer's muse.

Egypt, of course, endured. And Ramses II ruled on into his nineties.

I should point of that there are, of course, crocodiles in Lake Nasser and, quite possibly, in the waters around Abu Simbel. To my knowledge, no attack on a human has ever taken place in the area, although crocodiles have been known to attack fishermen on the shores of the lake. I'm quite sure that anyone taking a cruise across the lake will be perfectly safe unless he or she should decide to indulge in a spot of swimming. I've used the crocodiles for the purpose of my story, which is, of course, fiction. My firm belief has always been that human swimmers are best advised to use swimming pools, and to leave the sea, lakes and rivers to fish, and the other creatures that inhabit them.

I hope you've been able to suspend your disbelief sufficiently to enjoy this book, and will take my liberties with both modern and historical events as the fictional devices they are to keep my stories moving forward.

On a final positive note: tourists do seem to be returning to Egypt. Perhaps it's more of a trickle than the flood I've portrayed in this book, but the signs are good. I can only be delighted for all those employed in the tourist-related trades in Egypt, whose livelihoods depend on foreign visitors. And, of course, it means I have high hopes that more adventures await Merry and Adam in the future.

Those of you interested in the New Kingdom of ancient Egypt, may wish to check out the chronology on the next page.

Please do leave me a comment on my website www.fionadeal.com. I also read and appreciate all reviews on Amazon.

Fiona Deal
June 2018.

Chronology of New Kingdom Pharaohs

A number of my readers have asked me to include a chronology of the pharaohs of the 18th and 19th Dynasties and their links to my books, so here goes …

Pharaoh	Comment	Approximate Dates
18th Dynasty		
Ahmose	Expelled the Hyksos, the hated foreign invaders of Egypt, who'd presided over a time of chaos and conflict. United Egypt	1557 – 1541 BC
Amenhotep I	Son of Ahmose. Little is known about him.	1541 – 1520 BC
Thutmosis I	A warrior who expanded Egypt's territories. Married to Queen Ahmes. Parents to Thutmosis II and Hatshepsut. First pharaoh to have a tomb in the Valley of the Kings	1520 – 1492 BC
Thutmosis II	Married to his half-sister Hatshepsut. Also had a son by a royal concubine (Thutmosis III)	1492 – 1479 BC
Hatshepsut	Declared herself pharaoh after the death of her brother-husband Thutmosis II. Ruled jointly with her infant nephew-stepson Thutmosis III. *Carter's Conundrums* *Hatshepsut's Hideaway*	1479 – 1458 BC
Thutmosis III	Warrior pharaoh famous for his expansion of territories into Levant and Nubia. Under his rule the Egyptian Empire was at its greatest extent. Late in his reign he obliterated Hatshepsut's name from temples and monuments.	1458 – 1425 BC

	Some posit Thutmosis III as King David of the Bible. *Hatshepsut's Hideaway* *Farouk's Fancies*	
Amenhotep II	Son of Thutmosis III. Ruled at the height of Egypt's power.	1425 – 1400 BC
Thutmosis IV	Son of Amenhotep II. Famous for his "Dream Stele" at the foot of the Sphinx. May have been the Pharaoh in the Bible story of Joseph and the Coat of Many Colours – the interpreter of dreams. *Farouk's Fancies*	1400 – 1390 BC
Amenhotep III – The Magnificent	Father of Akhenaten and grandfather of Tutankhamun. Ruled at the height of Egypt's power. A great builder, who had a long and peaceful reign. Some posit Amenhotep III as King Solomon of the Bible. *Farouk's Fancies*	1390 – 1352 BC
Amenhotep IV / Akhenaten	The second son of Amenhotep III. Founder of the Amarna Period in which he changed the state religion from the polytheistic worship of animal-headed gods and goddesses to the monotheistic worship of the sun god, the Aten. He built a new capital city, Akhet-Aten. He changed his name to Akhenaten to reflect his religious belief. Married to Nefertiti. Had 6 daughters. Some posit Akhenaten as Biblical Moses. Some believe he was Tutankhamun's father. *Tutankhamun's Triumph* *Akhenaten's Alibi* *Seti's Secret*	1352 – 1336 BC
Smenkhkare	Shadowy figure about whom very little is known. May have had a co-regency with Akhenaten who may have been his father or brother. Some believe he was another son of Amenhotep III (or possibly Akhenaten), and may have	1336 – 1332 BC

	been Tutankhamun's father. *Tutankhamun's Triumph*	
Tutankhamun	Thought to have come to the throne as a boy of 8 or 9 and died at 18 or 19 – hence the term "the boy king". Howard Carter famously discovered his intact tomb in 1922. He reverted to the old polytheistic religion of ancient Egypt and changed his name from Tunankh-Aten to Tutankh-Amun. Debate rages about whether he was the son of Akhenaten or Smenkhkare. *Carter's Conundrums* *Tutankhamun's Triumph*	1332 – 1324 BC
Ay	Grand Vizier to Tutankhamun and an important official in the reigns of Akhenaten and Smenkhkare. Possibly the brother of Queen Tiye, wife of Amenhotep III, and possibly father of Nefertiti, Akhenaten's Great Royal Wife. Succeeded Tutankhamun due to his lack of an heir, possibly enforcing his claim to the throne by marrying his granddaughter and Tutankhamun's widow, Ankhesenamun. Some posit Ay was son of Biblical Joseph. *Tutankhamun's Triumph* *Farouk's Fancies* *Akhenaten's Alibi*	1324 – 1320 BC
Horemheb	Born a commoner. Was a Military General during the Amarna Period. Seized the throne on Ay's death, possibly enforcing his claim by marrying Ay's younger daughter Mutnodjmet. Obliterated images of the Amarna pharaohs and vandalised and destroyed monuments associated with them. Some posit he was the Biblical Pharaoh of the Oppression.	1320 – 1292 BC

	Tutankhamun's Triumph *Akhenaten's Alibi* *Seti's Secret*	
	**19th Dynasty**	
Ramses I	Of non-royal birth. Served alongside Horemheb in the army. Succeeded Horemheb due to his lack of an heir. Some posit he was the Biblical Pharaoh of the Exodus. *Seti's Secret*	1292 – 1290 BC
Seti I	Son of Ramses I. Regained much of the territory lost under Akhenaten. *Seti's Secret*	1290 – 1279 BC
Ramses II The Great	Ruled for upwards of 60 years, coming to the throne at 25 and dying in his 90s. A prolific builder who usurped many previous temples and monuments. He is credited for finishing the hypostyle hall at Karnak and for building the Great Temple of Abu Simbel. He also built a new capital city, Pi-Ramesse in the Nile Delta. He continued expanding Egypt's territories until he hit a stalemate with the Hittite Empire, at the Battle of Kadesh in 1275 BC, after which the famous Egyptian-Hittite Peace Treaty was signed. His Great Royal Wife was Nefertari. He had a huge harem and was said to have fathered well over 100 children. *Belzoni's Bequest* *Nefertari's Narrative* *Ramses' Riches*	1279 – 1213 BC
Merenptah	13th son of Ramses II, as the elder sons all pre-deceased their father.	1213 – 1203 BC

After Merenptah the 19th Dynasty entered a confused period, only lasting approximately 12 further years, and with 3-4 rulers. It appears to have been characterised by civil war, possibly because Ramses II lived so long and had so many children born of different wives, many of them perhaps staking a claim to the throne.

About the Author

Fiona Deal fell in love with Egypt as a teenager, and has travelled extensively up and down the Nile, spending time in both Cairo and Luxor in particular. She lives in Kent, England with her two Burmese cats. Her professional life has been spent in human resources and organisational development for various companies. Writing is her passion and an absorbing hobby. Other books in the series following Meredith Pink's adventures in Egypt are available, with more planned. You can find out more about Fiona, the books and her love of Egypt by checking out her website and following her blog at www.fionadeal.com
.

Other books by this author

Please visit Amazon to discover other books by Fiona Deal. The author reads and appreciates all reviews.

Meredith Pink's Adventures in Egypt

Carter's Conundrums – Book 1
Tutankhamun's Triumph – Book 2
Hatshepsut's Hideaway – Book 3
Farouk's Fancies – Book 4
Akhenaten's Alibi – Book 5
Seti's Secret – Book 6
Belzoni's Bequest – Book 7
Nefertari's Narrative – Book 8
Ramses' Riches – Book 9

More in the series planned in 2019.

Also available: Shades of Gray, a romantic family saga, written under the name Fiona Wilson.

Connect with me

Thank you for reading my book. Here are my social media coordinates:

Subscribe to my blog: http://www.fionadeal.com
Visit my website: http://www.fionadeal.com
Friend me on Facebook: http://facebook.com/fjdeal
Follow me on Twitter: http://twitter.com/dealfiona

Printed in Great Britain
by Amazon